Praise for Julia Crouch:

'Very enjoyable; expertly paced and cleverly ambiguous' *Daily Telegraph*

'An entertaining rollercoaster of a read . . . I devoured it in hours' *Stylist*

'A tale of slow-burning suspense, but Crouch, whose debut novel this is, deftly avoids the obvious and builds up a very convincing air of menace in her extremely well-described portrait of family life becoming frayed at the edges with fatal results' *Daily Mail*

'Hot on Sophie Hannah's heels' *Daily Mirror*

'Dangerously addictive' Erin Kelly, author of *The Poison Tree*

'A gripping and thrilling debut – you really don't want it to end' *Sun*

'Locked-door-checkingly scary' Julie Burchill

'Crouch's first novel is a gripping read. Fluently written with mounting suspense and foreboding' Cath Staincliffe, author of the Sal Kilkenny mysteries

'This luscious and sinister British psychological drama is a chilling read. A fluid, tension-filled and gripping debut novel. Deliciously creepy' *Marie Claire Australia*

'From the very first page, this novel had me entranced . . . an amalgam of brilliant writing and heart-stopping tension!' Sam Hayes, author of *Tell Tale*

'An utterly gripping read' *Sydney Morning Herald*

After a drama degree at Bristol University, Julia Crouch spent ten years devising, directing and writing for the theatre. During this time she had twelve plays produced and co-founded Bristol's Public Parts Theatre Company. She lives in Brighton with her hushand, the actor and playwright Tim Crouch, and their three children.

Also by Julia Crouch and available from Headline

Cuckoo

EVERY VOW YOU BREAK

JULIA CROUCH

headline

First published in Great Britain in 2012 by
HEADLINE PUBLISHING GROUP

First published in paperback in 2012 by
HEADLINE PUBLISHING GROUP

2

Cataloguing in Publication Data is available from the British Library

B format ISBN 978 0 7553 7802 9

Typeset in Sabon by Avon DataSet Ltd,
Bidford-on-Avon, Warwickshire

Printed and bound in Great Britain by
Clays Ltd, St Ives plc

Headline's policy is to use papers that are natural, renewable and
recyclable products and made from wood grown in sustainable forests.
The logging and manufacturing processes are expected to conform to the
environmental regulations of the country of origin.

HEADLINE PUBLISHING GROUP
An Hachette UK Company
338 Euston Road
London NW1 3BH

www.headline.co.uk
www.hachette.co.uk

Thanks to Carmela Marner, Gene Marner, Carole Lucia Satrina, Ed Vassallo and everyone at Franklin Stage Company for many glorious theatre summers in a truly inspirational environment; Felix Marner Bridel (aged 11) for his knowledgeable wildlife consultancy; John Vassallo and Howard H Weiswasser for invaluable and generous NY legal advice; Chloe Ronaldson for sharing her midwifery wisdom.

Thanks to all my Franklin friends for their generosity and all the good times – especially Xina Sheehan and Tim, Cedric, Stella and Reggie Duerden; Anne, Dave, Jake and Sam Ohman; Pam Peters and Walter, Lizzie and Evan Putrycz.

Thanks for the inspiration to The Police; to NoFit State Circus for their great show *Tabu* (which provided the model for the circus show); to Alice Neel, whose Whitechapel show kicked off a lot of ideas, and, as ever, to Mr Morrissey.

Thank you to my agent, Simon Trewin and assistant Ariella Feiner; to Jessica Craig and all at United Agents; to my wonderful editor Leah Woodburn and assistant Emily Kitchin; to publicist extraordinaire Sam Eades and everyone at Headline.

Finally, thanks as ever to Nel, Owen, Joey and Tim Crouch.

The Unknown

SHE LIES IN THE SAND, A FULL FIVE FEET UNDERNEATH THE scrubby, wind-blown surface. Her eyes, once so keen, so well used, are now nothing, staring into nothingness, jammed up against the tiny pebbles and grains which are the last things they would have seen, had there been light.

So much of her is gone that of course she doesn't know it when the digger lifts the final gritty covering from her skull and the construction worker shouts 'Stop!'

She is not aware, later, of her desiccated remains being lifted and bagged and transported to be stored in a different, chillier place. Nor does she feel the scrape and cut of samples being taken – parts of her to be dissolved and bottled in the coroner's labs in an effort to find out the facts of identity, date, time and crime.

She would have been amused, though, by the label attached to her toe and the name of the file opened on Detective O'Halloran's computer. She had always liked to go incognito.

Detective O'Halloran is dogged. He won't be letting the case of Jane Doe go.

One

FROM THE AIR, NEW YORK LOOKED TO LARA LIKE A catering-sized Croydon. As they circled over Newark, the out-of-town Ikea confirmed the illusion. On the ground, as they rolled along the steamy New Jersey Turnpike in their massive hired Chevrolet, the Manhattan skyline exposed its more classic aspect. So grand did it appear in the distance that the entire Wayland family – little Jack apart, of course – joined together for a brief mouth-trumpet version of *Rhapsody in Blue*, an outcome of the pre-trip Woody Allen research.

Lara had to ask Marcus to stop before they got out of the built-up tangle of roads heading north, because she felt sick. She was also bleeding pretty heavily. After she had thrown up her Virgin Atlantic pre-landing ice-cream snack, she sat in the service station cubicle and pressed her brow against the steel coldness of the toilet-paper dispenser.

For the thousandth time, she asked herself what on earth she had been thinking. Marcus had said they should look on it as a miscarriage of sorts. Every part of her body wanted to believe it had been like that.

She looked down and watched the drops of potential leach away from between her legs into the pan, and she prayed for redemption – or at least a stilling of the hurt that had, for the past five weeks, silently twisted her gut. Yet again, she castigated herself for not listening to her own voice more fully, for being a coward and going along with Marcus.

Eventually she rose, cleaned herself up and flushed the toilet. Outside the cubicle, she splashed her face with cold water. After checking in the mirror that she could still muster a smile, she went to rejoin her family. The summer ahead was going to be an awfully big adventure, and she really needed to kick herself into gear for it to do the healing she hoped it would.

She crossed the heat-hazed tarmac of the service station car park and flopped into the passenger seat, glad Marcus had kept the engine and the air conditioning going in her absence.

'Everything OK?' he asked.

She turned and gave him the smile she had practised in the mirror.

He shifted the car into drive and they set off north, away from the city. They were completely new to this USA game. When they reached a toll plaza near the New York State line, Marcus had to ask which coin was in fact the requested dime.

'You're kidding me, right?' drawled the attendant, a sweating, toxic-looking woman who seemed to be chemically sealed into her booth.

As the road unravelled before them, the long, long day prepared to put itself to bed, and the fourteen hours they had already journeyed began to make their mark on the family.

Lara turned to look at her three other children. Jack, of course, had slept almost from the moment he had climbed into his car seat, snuggling his sweaty little copper head into Cyril, his constant teddy companion. His big sister Bella cuddled around him as if she were his mother.

Lara could see a long-abandoned version of herself in her daughter. Just sixteen, her smooth black-brown bob greasy from the journey, Bella still held on to the doll-like demeanour that had seen her through childhood. This neatness was in direct contrast to her twin brother Olly, who, tall, gangly and dark-eyed, already had a touch of the wild man about him. He lolled back against the window, possibly asleep too, unfazed by the pounding beats of his iPod earphones, which Lara could hear even across the vast distance between the front and rear seats.

Cocooned amid his two dark siblings, four-year-old Jack looked like a gingery foundling cherub. But that he was the spit of his father, it would be hard to believe he came from the same gene pool as the others. Due to the twelve-year gap between the two births, Marcus's recent joke was that Jack was the mistake they *had* permitted existence to: their *happy* accident.

Lara turned back to face the road and tried to enjoy the comfort of the car. A whole world stood between its immaculately valeted interior and their beaten, be-littered Volvo back home. She thought perhaps this must be how it felt to be American. Or at least how it might feel to have Arrived. It was enormous, top of the range – an unexpected free upgrade, dropped on them at the Avis depot at Newark. The vehicle she had originally chosen had cost as much as Marcus was willing to spend, and God knew they had to watch their pennies. But even so it would have been really cramped for the five of them, with their suitcases, cabin baggage, Jack's old buggy – which she thought she had better take in case of extreme heat and long walks – and Olly's guitar. She had argued for something bigger when she was making the online booking, but Marcus had held fast, even though they both knew he had a lot of conceding to do in the great Reckoning Up that stood between them. She was glad that some unseen hand had intervened to make her wishes come true with this massive Chevrolet.

She wasn't going to get attached, though. Marcus's plan was that any hire car would be returned to the nearest depot after a week. The beneficence of the upgrade didn't change his stance in any way.

'Something will come up. We'll bag ourselves a cheap means of transport somehow,' he said, giving his best, actor-charm wink.

But for the meantime this big, pearl-grey monster was her treat: a pretence at luxury, paid for by plastic.

Lara stretched her legs into the vast, dark space in front of her and tried to keep herself from nodding off. Marcus turned off the Palisades Parkway and they moved further north, past a series of giant billboards boasting in English, and what Lara supposed must be Hebrew, of 'Your Complete Vacation Playground in the Catskills'. And then all around them were darkening woodlands.

After another hour, Lara, who was reading James's directions by the light of the glove compartment, directed Marcus to turn off the main highway. On they went, climbing up into the night, occasionally passing through a dimly lit settlement, slipping along silent streets lined with clapboard houses. They crept over traffic-free crossroads guarded by mysterious, blinking orange lights, which, after some discussion, Lara and Marcus decided must mean 'watch out'.

The children were all asleep now. Olly's gentle snoring and the low amber glow from the dashboard made Lara feel like curling up and nodding off herself. Her ears popped with the increasing altitude.

Marcus yawned.

'Are you OK with driving?' Lara asked across the chasm between the two front seats.

'I'll live,' he said. 'Find me a true American radio station, keep me awake.'

She reached forward and, after pressing a number of buttons on the large audio console, landed on an Evangelical Christian station. They listened, amused for a while as a deranged-sounding preacher expounded his views on neighbourliness and how the curse of sodomy could be overcome. He diverted Lara until his sermon took a pro-life theme, at which point she changed the channel to something called W-ZEETEE 101, which took them through some country greats, with mercifully minimal country chat. Marcus sang along loudly and badly, and Lara finally gave herself over to sleep.

A strange feeling of stillness interrupted her dreams of rushing through space and time. She opened her eyes to find they were stationary in amongst some tall trees – moonlit outlines stirring in the sky above them. Marcus's head was thrown back at an alarming angle and he was completely motionless. For a chilling second Lara felt a prickle of adrenaline across her cheeks, but then he let out a sigh and a snore that drilled through the leather upholstery and into her sinuses. He had simply pulled off the road to take a nap. She tried to push her annoyance aside with the thought that at least he hadn't fallen asleep at the wheel and finished them all off.

She turned round to check on the children, looking at them one by one to reassure herself they were still breathing. This was, after all, the land of roadside serial killers, Freddie Krueger and gruesome urban myths. Satisfied they were alive, she leaned over and, not as gently as she could have, shook Marcus awake.

'How far have we got to go?' she asked.

He rubbed his eyes and instinctively checked his reflection in the rear-view mirror, rearranging his thatch of red curly hair. 'I'm sorry. I just couldn't stay awake . . .' he said.

'How far?' she said again.

'About fifty miles? I'm not sure, I—'

'Oh, I'll drive,' Lara said. She got out to walk around to the driver's side, slamming the door rather too noisily. Bella sat up, blinked, asked if they were nearly there, then turned and closed her eyes again. Lara pulled the car out into the dark, tree-lined road. She noted that Marcus, having manoeuvred himself over to the passenger seat, had also gone straight back to sleep.

It took a few minutes to get used to everything being on the wrong side of everything else, but Lara quickly began to enjoy herself. Sitting up in the lorry-height driving seat of the Chevy, she experienced an almost-forgotten sense of power and possibility.

She clicked the car into cruise control and set off, down the northern slopes of the Catskills towards Trout Island. Six weeks, they were going to have here. Six weeks, removed from all contexts. Clarity and determination were not Lara's default mode, but, as she sat there at the helm, this much she knew: anything was possible, and she was going to do everything in her power to get her feelings, and her family, back on track.

Two

'WE'RE THERE!' LARA SAID AS SHE FINALLY TURNED ON TO Main Street, Trout Island, upstate New York.

It had been a long fifty miles since she had taken over the wheel, supplemented by a full circle around a reservoir thanks to a missing signpost. James's emailed instructions had been precise in all the wrong places and vague where it most mattered. It hadn't helped that, although it was only about nine in the evening, Lara's brain told her it was two in the morning.

The family stirred. Bella prodded Jack awake. Disoriented, he started to grizzle, but she found his dummy and he calmed down.

'Can you get me to the theatre?' Lara asked Marcus, shoving the sheets of barely useful directions into his lap.

'OK, OK, so it says here . . .' Marcus fumbled in his jacket pocket for his reading glasses. ' "After the turn, drive straight down Main and take a left at the crossroads. You can't miss us." '

A few minutes later, they turned on to a quiet, moonlit street. To their right stood a building so tall as to appear cartoonish. Square white columns, as high as Lara imagined redwoods must be, soared up from a hundred-foot-long veranda to a pointed, pedimented gable. It looked like a clapboard Parthenon.

'I guess that's the theatre, then,' Olly said, peering out of the car window, up through the curtain of his fringe.

Lara pulled the Chevy in and they got out, surprised by the sticky warmth of the night after the icy air conditioning inside the car. The street was deserted except for a couple of parked cars, but the air clattered with the sound of crickets, underscored by an electric buzzing. In the distance, several dogs barked. A heavy, musky scent hung in the night, a little like fox, Lara thought, but more burned. Like the inside of a new rubber glove.

'What do we do now?' Bella said. Having unstrapped Jack, she had him leaning against her, clinging on, a sweaty, sleepy limpet.

As if to answer her question, the door to the tall building opened with a clatter and a large man ran down the steps from the veranda, arms flung wide, white cotton shirt flowing behind him like a flag of surrender.

'You got here!' he cried as he streamed across the lawn and threw himself at Marcus.

'James!' Marcus said, returning the giant bear-hug. 'How the devil are you?'

'Rehearsed near to death, but all the better for seeing you, my love,' said James, stepping back and taking them in. 'And here's all the little family! Delightful. Welcome all.' He sweatily pumped their hands, then planted a wet kiss on Lara's cheek. 'Lara, darling. It's been ages. Not since this one –' he bent to flash his blinding white teeth at Jack – 'was barely toddling. Aren't we a bit old now for a binky?' He raised a mock-stern eyebrow at the little boy. Jack folded himself further into his sister's leg, the playfulness of the reprimand lost on him.

'Come on in!' James straightened, swept his arm around Marcus and steered him up the steps to the building. 'Your journey was OK, I take it. You need something to eat. A beer.'

The others made to follow, but Jack, put out by all this late-night ebullience and strangeness, hung back, pulling on Bella.

'Come on, Jacko,' Lara said, plucking him away from his sister. Hoisting him up on to her hip, she noted the incriminating squelch and stench of a pull-up in need of a change. Marcus accused her of babying Jack, but her youngest son still hadn't quite got the hang of bladder control while sleeping, and she hadn't wanted to take any risks on the long journey.

'Hand me the Jack bag,' she asked Olly, who, sighing, reached back into the car to rummage around the footwell beneath Jack's seat. He lifted out the blue holdall and swung it over to Lara.

The two men, oblivious to the delay, went on ahead, Marcus talking animatedly, James listening intently.

Pretty much par for the course, thought Lara.

By the time she and the children got to the high-ceilinged, wooden foyer, James had laid out drinks and snacks.

'Welcome all,' he said, handing round beers. 'Welcome to Trout Island Theatre Company. I thought we'd have chips and dips here before I took you to your digs. Tuck in, Waylands!'

He was fiftyish, handsome in an overgroomed, pudgy way, and he dressed like someone you might come across on a beach in Goa – Thai fisherman's trousers, open cotton shirt, Birkenstocks. It was an unsettling look, as if an overfed otter had paid a visit to a beauty parlour.

'Jack needs a change,' Lara said to Marcus.

'Can't it wait?'

'No it can't.'

James pointed across the foyer. 'Use the bathroom, if you will.'

Lara lifted Jack on to the fold-down changing table inside the ladies'. As she rooted around in his bag for a clean pair of pull-ups and wipes, she heard Olly and Bella outside the toilet door. Like ducklings they had followed their mother across the foyer.

'I'd forgotten what a tosser he was,' Olly whispered to his sister.

'Shhh!' Bella said.

'Fat old poof.'

'Shut up, Olly.'

'Look at him hanging on Dad's every word. It's pathetic.'

Lara sighed. Olly was like that. Over the years he had fought so hard for his father's attention that he found it galling when someone simply swept Marcus away. The last time James had visited them in Brighton, he and Marcus had sat up drinking whisky and chewing the cud after dinner while Olly hung around trying in vain to get a word in edgeways. Defeated, he had sloped off up to his bedroom and plugged in his bass guitar, thumping through the floorboards so fiercely that Marcus stormed up and yelled at him to turn the damn thing off. Once Olly had a grudge, it was hard to dislodge it.

'You've got a rude, moody brother,' she said to Jack, tickling his ribs so he giggled with pleasure.

She had a pee herself and noticed that the gush of blood from a couple of hours ago seemed to have stilled. She hoped it was nearly all over. As if, now done, it could ever be fully over. Once again, she pushed the hollow feeling aside, stood up and steeled herself.

'I heard that,' she whispered to Olly as she came out, Jack beside her, holding on to her index finger.

'He's such a twat though, Mum,' Olly said.

'Give him a chance, love. He's just excited to see your dad. We'll get him back in a bit.'

Olly made a face.

They headed back across the wide, wooden expanse of the hall. James was laughing heartily at something Marcus had said, throwing back his tanned head, his eyes fixed sideways on his ageing protégé.

'Ah. Refreshed,' he said, turning to them. 'You two look so gorgeous.' He beamed at Lara and Bella. 'So alike, like a couple of matrioshka dolls.'

'That's what you said last time,' Olly said. Lara leaned on his foot.

'And you've *certainly* grown up, young man.' James turned his attention to Olly, raising his manicured eyebrows. 'How old are you now? Fourteen?'

Olly bristled.

'Sixteen. We're sixteen,' Bella said.

'It's wonderful to see you again, James,' Lara said quickly. 'How's Betty?'

'Oh, she's back up at the farm doing a couple of last-minute rewrites. She sends apols, but things arc going a bit tits up with the musical at the moment. We're having artistic differences with the leads, who have *also* decided to start fucking each other, excuse me children.' He rolled his eyes. His years away from Britain had given his accent a slightly Australian twang. 'Super poster though, look.'

He gestured at the lime-green playbills dotted around the foyer. Standing between a bright red, italicised script proclaiming *Trout Island Theatre Presents the World Premiere of a*

Major New Musical, stood a highly saturated photograph of a group of uniformed firemen bearing aloft a plumpish besequinned woman. Two of the men, positioned on the far edges, held hoses that gushed at an unfortunate angle. The words SET ME ON FIRE! blazed across the poster in flame-serifed capitals and James and Betty's names featured prominently over the remaining space.

'Lovely,' chorused Marcus and Lara.

'It's by a very gifted kid at the local high school.' James sighed. 'There's such a lot of talent in this community, just waiting to be unlocked,' he added, popping a blue corn tortilla chip into his mouth. 'It's part of our mission here.'

Bella pulled on Lara's skirt. 'Mum, I'm really tired.'

'And our Scottish Play is gonna rock the world, now we've got our main man.' James winked at Marcus. 'I always said we'd do it again one day, didn't I?'

'James directed me in the Scottish Play back at drama school,' Marcus turned to explain to his family, who knew this already.

'And the beard's coming on nicely,' James said, running his hand along Marcus's bristled cheek. 'What does it feel like, having such a *man* for a father, kids?'

Lara leaned her weight once more on to Olly's foot as she heard him shudder.

'Where's Cyril Bear, Mummy?' Jack said, tugging her finger.

'He's in the car.'

'I want him . . .' he whined.

Lara was dizzy with fatigue. She wanted the day over and done with so she could get on with starting afresh in the morning.

'So!' James said, picking up on their mood, clapping his hands in the air. 'Wayland family. You look pooped. Let me take you to your quarters.'

Taking Marcus by the hand, he led them out of the building, towards his little sports car, dwarfed in front of their own monolithic vehicle.

'I don't think I'm going to be able to stick him for six weeks,' Olly grumbled to Lara. She turned and saw that, from the look on his face, he was serious.

And Olly, she knew, was not to be messed with.

Three

JACK'S DESPERATE FIGHT FOR BREATH PULLED LARA FROM the sleep that had, until that point, totally claimed her. She found him struggling next to her on the double bed trying to get air into his lungs and coughing with a noise like an extended death rattle, louder even than Marcus's snoring on the other side of her.

Jumping out of bed, she scooped Jack up while at the same time struggling with the odd twisty knob on the bedside light. She rushed him over to where his bag was on the floor and rummaged in it for his inhaler.

'What the hell's going on?' Marcus heaved himself to a sitting position on the creaky bed.

'Must be the dust,' Lara said as she gave Jack five blasts of Ventolin. While Marcus watched, she rubbed the little boy's back until his breathing had calmed to normal, then she fed him an antihistamine pill and bundled him into the bed.

'Are you all right now, Jacky?' she asked, leaning over him.

'He's fine,' Marcus said. 'What he needs is sleep.'

You mean what *you* need is sleep, Lara thought as she settled back down to the useless remainder of the night, where instead of sleeping she would be listening out for every change in Jack's breathing.

All too soon, a stifling morning light filled the room. Lara couldn't lie there any longer. She checked Jack's chest before extricating herself from the tangle of his sticky limbs and leaving him in a sweaty, sheety heap next to Marcus. She fumbled on the floor for her clothes from the day before, then tiptoed down the dusty wooden staircase, across a hallway with an unspeakably filthy carpet to the large living space below they had only glimpsed the night before.

So, she thought, looking around her, this was to be their home for the summer. James had told them the night before that it was an unoccupied house, newly donated by its well-wishing owner, for the theatre company to house actors in lieu of anything approaching pay. He had made it abundantly clear that the Waylands, being a whole family attached to just one actor, were getting special treatment in having the place to themselves.

A far cry from the gleaming American domestic interiors she knew from TV, the sparsely furnished house was devoid of any of the overstuffed comfort she had been expecting, and a layer of grime covered everything.

Something British in her was pleased by this.

Walking through a vast living room with the same footprint of her entire house back in Brighton, Lara realised what she had assumed to be a rug on the floor was in fact a painted, faux-Persian floorcloth. The antique bookcase leaning against the sloping wood-panelled wall was actually made from MDF, broken down to appear aged. Around the edges of the room stood an assortment of sofas and easy chairs running the historical style gamut from Shakespeare to Ibsen, with a Tennessee Williams side table thrown in for a twentieth-century touch. And wasn't that sixties circular bamboo chair slightly Pinteresque? Lara smiled. James and Betty had furnished the house with spare set dressings.

Three large windows looked out over a shabby but bucolic scene of green meadows, large, leafy trees and peeling Greek Revival houses. The house smelled of damp and something else, almost like nutmeg – sweet but faintly rotten. Lara tried to open one of the windows to let fresh air into the dusty fug, but, probably during the cold winter months, some idiot had applied thick paint around the sashes, gluing them tightly shut.

She moved on straight through an arch to the large, linoleum-floored kitchen.

What she noticed first was the blue vase holding the two dozen red roses. Their scent leached into the hot room. A nice touch, Lara thought.

Tea was what she craved, but she couldn't see a pot or kettle, nor anything in the cupboards beyond some evidence of insect activity. The giant, genuinely retro fridge that stood humming and whirring in the corner was empty too, except for a light furring of mould. She tried to get the six-ringed enamel stove to work, but there didn't appear to be any gas connected to it.

At the far end of the kitchen, at the very back of the house, a glassed-in porch baked in the morning sun. Again, there seemed no way of getting any air in. Dead flies littered the sealed window frames and the once-white woodwork was covered with a greasy layer of dust. As she gazed at the empty, potholed car park at the back of the building, Lara tried to breathe, but her lungs felt furred up.

Despite the heat of the room, a coldness began to percolate into her bones. What had she done, insisting they all tagged along behind Marcus to come *here*? Dragging her three children halfway around the world to *this*? She tried to take herself back to the excitement they had all felt when Marcus had got James's email begging him to do the job. It had been Lara, in fact, who had driven forward James's suggestion that the whole family could accompany him. She had found the money, located and booked the cheapest flights, let out their own house for the summer, sorted out the car hire. She had also worked insane hours at her local government graphic design job, combining her inflated time-off-in-lieu allowance with her entire annual leave so she could come away for six weeks and still be paid. This had been a necessary step, since, aside from the accommodation, the theatre was only paying Marcus one hundred dollars and five diner lunches a week.

She returned to the kitchen and opened the back door, letting in air washed by the mist hanging over the grass beyond the car park. Again she caught that musky rubber-glove scent from the night before, though the damp morning diluted it. Pushing her way through the fly-screen door, she crossed a small deck and sat down, her bare legs dangling over the edge, her ankles brushing the dewy grass beneath. A light breeze filtered over her face, and she breathed in. Her eye was drawn to a shed that stood less than twenty feet from where she sat. Dangling from the eaves on the corner closest to her was a long, transparent tube full of a clear liquid, and buzzing around it were what looked like a couple of large moths. Lara hated moths, but her curiosity got the better of her and, jumping down off the deck, she padded over the hot tarmac to take a closer look.

'Little birds,' she said with delight. 'Little tiny birds.'

Two hummingbirds fluttered around what she saw now was a feeder full of something delicious to them. Their wings an iridescent blur, their long beaks held still among all the motion, they sipped at the liquid. Lara stood and watched, enchanted by their exoticism.

And *that* was why she had brought everyone here. To see the new and, furthermore, to entertain the opportunity for change. Marcus, she hoped, was going to have his long-awaited moment of success – the first time since drama school he had played an eponymous lead. In doing so, she hoped he would rediscover a part of himself that he seemed to have discarded too many years ago. The part, she feared, she had once loved.

She hoped it would work out for him. At first sight, the theatre didn't seem to be quite the cultural powerhouse James had painted in the long Skype calls he and Marcus had shared in the weeks leading up to their arrival. But then she had only just glimpsed it the night before. And perhaps they did things another way over here. Perhaps different things carried different weight in America.

No, she thought, this was going to be a brilliant summer. People would come up from New York City to see Marcus and he would land a Manhattan agent – it was much easier, he said, for an English actor to make his mark in the States. And she would leave her soul-sucking job at the council to start her own business.

And then they would be happier than they had been for a long, long time.

Lara looked at the little birds, busy at their nectar, and allowed herself to enjoy the anticipation.

The slam of the fly-screen door brought her back with a start. She turned to see Jack, in his long T-shirt nightie, his eyes puffed up and pink.

'My chest is all stuffy, Mummy.'

'I know. Poor baby.' She went to him and held him close. He felt hot, but then again, he had just got out of bed.

'Here, do this,' she said, standing up, holding her arms out and letting the breeze stroke her limbs. Jack did as he was bid, and they both stood for a while, smiling, enjoying the brush of the air.

'I'll get you another pill, then let's find something to eat,' Lara said. She tiptoed upstairs and felt around their bedroom to pick up Jack's clothes, pills and inhaler without waking Marcus. Then the two of them crept out of the slumbering house to look for a shop. Jack insisted on sitting in his buggy, flopping in the heat in a cheap baseball cap that had come free in a rucksack supplied 'For Kidz' by the airline.

They turned right and trundled along the uneven pavement away from the house. The road they were on was long and straight – called, she remembered from the directions the night before, Main Street. To her left was a grid of side streets named Third Street, Fourth Street and so on. When they got to Sixth Street, just before a vast, lawned cemetery, she realised they had reached the end of Trout Island, so they took the turning on to Sixth until they came to a junction to their left with a smaller road called Back Street.

'Inventive road naming,' Lara said to Jack, who nodded though he didn't have the slightest idea what she was going on about.

The houses lining the roads were mostly large, detached wooden buildings, set back on open lawns. Hills thick with trees rose almost vertically from behind the gardens of Back and Main. So far, so small-town movie set. But there was an emptiness, an eerie unkemptness to all but a few of the houses. The lawns weren't neatly mown, and the paint on the shingles was far from fresh. Old icicle fairy lights hung from porches, abandoned toys lay in the front yards, and faded flags drooped from chipped poles on every other lawn.

Where was everyone?

They reached the end of Back Street and pushed on along First, past the theatre, and found themselves back on Main. They passed a couple of chapels, a closed 'free' library, a deserted fire station, a locked-up diner and a row of silent antique shops. Lara's hopes rose when they got to a wooden building with a lit neon window sign declaring it to be a deli, but she tried the door and it was locked tight shut. They were nearly back at the house, and they hadn't found a single open shop.

'What will we do for breakfast, Jacky?' Lara said. Jack shrugged. Then, just as she was about to give in, she spotted a petrol station, almost diagonally across the road from the house.

Behind the empty forecourt was a sort of shack. As Lara and Jack crossed the gasoline-scented tarmac, she realised what she thought was a jet-lag-induced hallucination was in fact canned music wafting out of speakers beside each petrol pump.

'Whatever will they think of next?' she said to Jack, as she pushed open the door to the shack. The minute she smelled the bad vanilla-scented coffee and saw the riot of goods inside, she knew she had found her shop.

'How ya *doin*'?' a voice drawled from somewhere behind the counter. Lara peered and finally made out, camouflaged among the visual riot of doughnuts, cigarettes, coffee machines and point-of-sale displays, an overweight, middle-aged woman with multiple ear piercings, blond hair and dark black roots. Squeezed into her red uniform, she chewed her gum with an open mouth and peered into a too-small hand mirror, attempting to clean a smear of mascara from under her eye.

'Um, hello,' Lara said. 'Do you have stuff like milk and cereals for breakfast?'

'Hey, cute accent,' the woman said. 'Where you from?'

'England.'

'No way.'

'We're here for the theatre.'

'The what?'

'The theatre. Trout Island Theatre?'

'Oh. OK.' Either she couldn't fathom Lara's accent, or she didn't know what she was talking about. 'Milk's round the back. You got all you need for breakfast over there.' She pointed a fat finger at the middle aisle.

Lara also picked up some cleaning stuff to tackle the mouldy fridge, a carton of orange juice and a packet of cookies, which she opened immediately, handing one to Jack. Finding no tea on offer, she consoled herself with a cup of scalding hot coffee, which, despite its plastic lid, took some carrying back to the house while pushing the buggy.

'Anyone awake?' she called once they were back inside, but there was no response. Lara was jealous of Marcus and the teenagers' sleeping abilities. She was still firmly on British time; her body was telling her it was the middle of the afternoon, even though the clock in the shop had said it wasn't yet nine.

The phone, sitting on an Arthur Miller side table, suddenly rang, breaking the silence. Lara ran to get it before it woke everyone up.

'Hi hon.' It was James, who offered no apology for calling so early. 'Just checking on my star, his dame and the pretty chickens. Everything OK? Isn't the house divine? Do you have all you need?'

'More or less,' Lara said, wishing she had the guts to tell him what she really thought. But she did manage to mention the windows and the gas, and James promised to get someone round to sort it out 'A-sap'. She also got directions to the nearest town, where, he told her, she would find a marvellous independent supermarket called Green's.

'And hey, hon, Betty's breaking out the fire pit for the first-night party tomorrow. You have to come. It's compulsory. We've got a little surprise for you, too.'

'Really?'

'Can't tell you though. My lips are sealed.'

'I'm intrigued.'

'Oh, you should be, darling. You should be. Now then,' he said, changing the subject. 'You're all set?'

'Well, I was just wondering if you'd managed to get the internet access sorted?'

This was the one thing she had asked to be in place for their arrival – she had a couple of small jobs to do for the council while she was here, and Olly and Bella would die without Facebook. She also didn't know how she and Jack would get through the days without any CBeebies. He had always gone to her workplace nursery and being together all day every day was going to be a test for both of them.

'Well, is the router there yet?'

'The what?'

'The router. You know, the box thing.' He pronounced it 'rowter'.

'I don't think so.'

'Damn them. They said it'd be there for you. I'll chase it up,' he said, in a way that managed to convey he had quite enough on his plate with the musical opening the following night without having to worry about the concerns of actors' wives.

24

'Oh, and thank you for the roses,' Lara said, not wishing to appear ungrateful.

'Roses?'

'The roses in the kitchen?'

'Oh. Oh, Not me, I'm afraid. That sounds like a Betty touch. She does love her blooms,' James said.

Lara hung up and looked at her watch. She wondered how she was going to last the day.

'Let's go to the shops, Mummy!'

Smeared and temporarily enlivened by his chocolate chip cookie, Jack had jumped out of his buggy, grabbed Lara's bag and was holding it up for her to take. He had heard Lara mention a supermarket during the phone call, and he was one of those rare small boys who viewed a shopping trip as an outing to get excited about.

Lara smiled at him. She loved the way children could help you find your momentum when everything ground to a halt. She scribbled a quick note to the others, and picked up the car keys from where she had left them the night before. She folded the buggy and checked her purse for her credit card. Then she and Jack set off in the giant car, following the directions she had taken down from James, over Trout Mountain to the nearest town, 'just' twelve miles away.

Four

THE SIREN BUILT AND BUILT UNTIL BELLA THOUGHT SHE couldn't bear it any longer. Then, as slowly as it had started, it faded down and away, and she was sitting bolt upright in her soft, sweaty bed, hyperventilating.

What the fuck was that?

She rubbed her eyes. Overnight, the dust in her room had crept all over her face and up into her nose. Her body, unwashed since England, gave off a sour smell.

She jumped out of bed and, grabbing her camera from her hand luggage, darted towards the window, scuffing her feet along the worn linoleum floor. Drawing back the sheet tacked on to the frame as a sort of curtain, she peered outside. What was that siren about?

The street outside was deserted. No one was running for shelter, or shouting for help. The only movement was the leaves of the big trees that lined the road dancing in the breeze, the only sound that of insects, chattering and buzzing from somewhere unseen. In the distance, a dog's bark echoed against the hills. Then, from further along the road than she could see, she heard the rumble of a truck. Her heart picked up its beat.

This is an invasion, she thought. The Axis of Evil – a phrase she had heard on the TV throughout her childhood, without ever fully understanding it – has finally invaded the USA. And it had to happen on her first morning here. She unhooked the fly screen, leaned out of the window and focused her lens on the vanishing point of the long, straight road. The rumble grew louder and a large truck finally hove into view. Slowly, it transformed from a shimmering pinprick in the hazy tarmac to a full dusty red presence. Bella clicked the shutter as the vehicle thundered towards the house, revealing itself to be a great tanker with GOT MILK? written on its side in fading letters. Far from being an invading menace, the driver didn't seem to be concerned with anything other than the sandwich he was cramming into his mouth. Bella zoomed in and caught him, open-mouthed, in the act of biting.

So perhaps it was nothing, then. Perhaps she had dreamed it in amongst her habitual nightmares.

She collapsed back on her bed, setting off a squeaking of bedsprings that could have come straight from the soundtrack of a dirty movie. Somewhere up the hill behind the house, a horse whinnied.

'New York, New York. It's a helluva town,' she sang.

She hadn't really believed her mother when she had said they wouldn't be within sight of skyscrapers. For some reason – probably connected to her recently completed GCSEs and subsequent celebrations – she hadn't bothered to look at a map, to see what she realised now must be the immense size and rural expanse of New York State.

Feeling the itch to explore her new surroundings, she got up again and found her washbag in her suitcase. As she crossed the room she made resolutions. Here, away from her peers, away from what everyone knew about her, she would begin to be the reborn Bella, the real Bella. She would put the past behind her, cross the line from teenager to adult and return happier, wiser and ready for a new start at college in the autumn. And she was going to put together a great portfolio of photographs of her time here.

She found the bathroom across the landing from her own room, and once inside was annoyed to find it had two doors: the one she had just come through and another opening on to her parents' bedroom. Neither had a lock. As the only young woman in the family, she supposed she would have to devise and announce a system to make sure no one burst in on her. She peered through to her parents' bedroom and saw her father, splayed out on his back, snoring, the tangle of greying red hair on his chest like some sort of crouching cat. She was grateful the sole sheet on his bed covered his middle section, because underneath he was clearly naked. Her mum wasn't there, nor was Jack. She pulled the door tight shut then wedged an old chair from beside the bath up against the door to the hallway.

The bath looked filthy. It was old, roll-topped and small, with a rusty water-ring. The taps had dripped brown trails down the greying enamel. She would use the chipped shower-head for now, but she was going to have a word with her mum about the bath – no way was she forgoing her daily soak for a whole summer. But equally she was not going to lie down in that tub in its current state.

As she used the feeble shower, soaping herself with the special tea tree gel she had packed for her own personal use, she tried not to meet her reflection in the warped mirror propped on the wall opposite her.

The handle of the hallway door rattled.

'Bella, you in there?'

It was bloody Olly.

'What?' she asked, eyes closed, shower overhead, shampoo
– matching tea tree also – streaming down her face.

'I need a crap.'

'I'll be ten minutes.'

'Can't wait.'

'Shit.' Bella quickly rinsed off and threw a towel around
herself.

She barged out of the door, knocking into her brother.

'Sor-ry,' he sang as he rushed in.

She pulled on shorts and a vest – her specially purchased
smart New York wardrobe wasn't going to get much of a
showing in Trout Island, she feared – combed her hair out,
slipped on her silver flip-flops and went downstairs to see if
she could find her mother. Instead she found the note on the
kitchen table.

Great, Bella thought. Abandoned.

Seeing the cereals and milk on the worktop, she remembered
she felt hungry, so she helped herself to breakfast. Shortly, she
heard the toilet flush and Olly loped down the stairs to join her.
He stuck his hand into the cereal packet.

'Whoah, peanut butter cereals!' he said, through a mouthful
of Reese's Puffs. 'Wanna go out and explore?'

'All right,' she said. 'What do we do about keys?'

'There aren't any. Mum asked last night. Jimmy boy said no
one locks their doors around here.'

'But this is America. Isn't it meant to be dangerous?'

'I know.' Olly shrugged.

They wandered along Main Street, in the direction of the
theatre. It was gone midday and the heat seeped through their

bodies, slowing them down. They stuck to the shade of the large trees on either side of the road.

'Man, it's so old school here,' Olly said, as Bella took a photograph of him in front of a tree bound by a faded yellow ribbon. 'Not like I imagined.'

'And where are all the people?' Bella said, screwing her lens cap back on. Then she remembered. 'Did you hear that air-raid alarm?'

'Yeah. Woke me up.'

'What's that about?'

'I reckon it's just a practice. I read about it somewhere. All towns have them since nine eleven. In case of a terrorist attack.'

'For real?' Bella was never sure if Olly was bullshitting her or not.

'Sure,' Olly said, looking around.

'So paranoid.'

They went past what they supposed was the village school, a wide, porticoed building opposite the theatre building. The grass at the front was overlong and in need of a mow. A forlorn collection of graffitied twisted slides and rubber swings stood to the side of the school, as deserted as the rest of the place. Bella wheeled around, taking pictures: click, click, click.

They sat on a couple of swings and dangled their feet, squeaking backwards and forwards in the heat.

'And are they really suggesting we stay the whole fucking summer here?' Olly said after a while.

'I think it's gone beyond a suggestion,' Bella said.

'And where are all the kids?' He gestured at the deserted playground.

'Away, I suppose,' Bella said. 'Or all slaughtered in some Satanic ritual. Oh my God, what's that?' She jumped off her swing and moved over to the edge of the playground, where dark oaks loomed up into the hazy sky, and thick, rank under-growth crowded out the dusty earth. Olly came up behind her.

'Yerk,' he said as Bella leaned forward and pulled aside some foliage to reveal a gravestone.

'There's loads, look,' she said, pointing out a second and a third,

'A graveyard. By the playground,' Olly said. 'That's not right.'

'They're really old, look.' Bella read out the dates that hadn't worn right away: '1876, 1899, 1840.'

They traced the graveyard round to their left until they reached a steep ridge overlooking a vast playing field. The dusty tracks worn into the baseball pitch made the place look even more forlorn.

'Perhaps it'll get better when the theatre starts up,' Bella murmured, shielding her eyes from the glaring sun.

'From what I've seen, I don't think so,' Olly said.

'Or perhaps we'll meet some people, make some American friends. There's got to be some kids who live around here.'

'That's our only hope,' Olly said. 'Shall we move on? This place creeps me out.'

They wandered along Back Street, taking a turning along a street called River Road. Soon they found they were on a dirt track.

'Ah, look, sweet,' Olly said as they passed a dilapidated building whose front lawn was almost entirely covered in sunbathing kittens. Bella squatted to take a photograph as he went over to them.

'Careful. That's someone's house,' Bella said.

'Nah, no one lives here. Look at it.' Olly gestured at the broken fly screens, the litter on the porch and the general air of abandonment.

'What's that about, then?' Bella said, pointing to a washing line full of grey vests and nappies. 'I'll bet they have a gun in there, too.'

Olly hopped back on to the path and they kept going. The houses petered out and they found themselves on a small sandy beach by a fast-flowing river.

'Fancy a dip?' Bella said.

'Don't they have alligators and water snakes here?' Olly said.

'I don't think so.'

'And they have catfish, and they bite really badly.'

'Oh.'

They sat on the bank and looked at the river, inspecting it for critters. The movement of the light on the water and the sun beating down on her bare head sent Bella into a daze. She reached up and stretched like a cat, trying to work herself back to earth. Olly shifted and she stopped in mid-reach, feeling his gaze on her.

'What?' she said, turning to meet his look. 'What?'

'Jonny gave me this to give to you.' He fished in his jeans pocket and brought out a crumpled, sealed envelope.

She sighed, and left the letter in his hand. 'Don't even try, Olly. It doesn't do you any favours.'

'What do you mean?' He narrowed his eyes at her.

'Stop it,' she said. 'Just fucking stop it. It's over. I've finished with him. I know and you know he's just your little puppet.'

'That's not true,' Olly said, his cheeks flushing.

'It is. He'd do anything for you. It's *you* he wants, you know. Not me.'

'That's fucking disgusting.'

'And you trying to control me through your gay little "best mate" isn't?' Bella was on her feet now, slapping the dust from her bare legs. 'If there was ever anything between me and Jonny – and there wasn't, not really – it's over, Olly. And you've just got to get used to it.'

'Bella.' Olly grasped at her leg.

'Don't you fucking touch me!' she shouted, jerking away from him. Then she ripped the letter from his hand, tore it unopened into two pieces and flung it into the river, which carried it away like the paper boats the two of them had made as children.

Olly jumped to his feet and grabbed her by the arms. 'What did you do that for?'

'Leave me,' she said, fighting her way free from him. 'You can't do this, not any more. I'm my own person now.'

'You think so?' he said. 'You think so? Well let me tell you, Bella. I've got my eye on you.'

'And what's that supposed to mean? You're not my keeper.'

'Just watch me.' He took a deep breath, lowered his shoulders and said it again. 'Just watch me.'

'For fucksake.' Bella had had enough. She snatched up her camera and headed off up the lane towards the village. But she knew he was behind her, and she could feel those eyes boring into her, all the way back to the house.

Five

JAMES'S DIRECTIONS HAD ONCE AGAIN PROVED TO BE completely useless. In the end, Lara had to stop and ask the way of a Goth kid leaning against a buckled crash barrier on a bend in the middle of nowhere. By the time she got over the mountain to town, it was early afternoon.

Once she hit the town, Lara found Green's pretty quickly. It was a massive structure with its name spelled loud and proud on its roof in Hollywood-style letters. Lara swung into a parking place near the front of the building. Like Trout Island and the road she had just travelled, the vast car park seemed to be practically empty. For a second she entertained a fantasy that the end of the world had arrived and she and Jack were the only survivors.

She opened the car door, almost having to push against the heat waves coming from the baking tarmac. Not only was it hot outside the chilled car, but the clouds had come down on this side of the mountain and the air hung damp and steamy as a Turkish bath.

'Phew,' Jack said, as she got him out.

She found a trolley and put him in the child seat. As they went through the automatic glass doors into the building, a blast of icy air struck them and Lara shivered with relief. Inside, the shop was vaster even than the colossal exterior suggested. But Lara was pleased to see actual people. Mothers with small children glided up and down acres of brightly lit aisles, filling their trolleys with packets and boxes and loud foil sacks. Muffled muzak added a surreal, trance-like quality to the place, reminding her of the gas station back in Trout Island. She steered her trolley into the first aisle and began to work methodically up and down to get her bearings, so she knew what lived where and how much things cost.

Her little boy was in Jack heaven, reaching out with want whenever he saw something that took his fancy: a shiny advertising balloon, a brightly coloured packet of biscuits. There was so much stuff in this store – so many different varieties of coffee and breakfast cereals, so many different types of juice. Lara's brain tried to take in a whole hundred-yard wall of various blends: from sugar-free and made-from-concentrate, to not-made-from-concentrate, protein added, fibre added, organic, gluten free . . .

In the end, she settled for the things that looked familiar. She had enough on her plate without having to worry about her children turning their noses up at the unusual. So she piled the trolley with pasta, tinned tomatoes, dried beans and a delicious-looking Italian sausage that could pass for a luxury British banger. She was pleased to find organic milk, having read horror stories about the amount of hormones forced down the throats of intensively farmed American cows. She didn't want her boys growing breasts.

She put two six-packs of beer into the trolley. But when she asked one of the many uniformed employees on the shop floor where they kept the wine, he told her they didn't sell it in supermarkets and she would have to visit the liquor store at the far end of the plaza. Her informant spoke slowly, as if she were somehow backward for not knowing this.

She stood for a while debating with herself whether she should buy a small but hideously expensive jar of Marmite. In the end she slid it into the trolley. Marcus wouldn't last the summer without it.

Six weeks was a long, long time. A long time for making things right, and a long time to keep a young boy amused. She cruised the toy aisle and grabbed a sketchbook and a colouring book, cheap watercolour paints, felt-tip pens and child-friendly scissors and glue. She didn't want Jack getting bored, because that led to guilt on her part, and they had only been allowed one suitcase each on the flight, so she had brought just a couple of his essential toys with them. She also added a ball, a hoop and something called a 'whiffle ball set' to the trolley.

Jack reached for the ball. She let him hold it.

'Excuse me.' A small, dark-haired woman with a tiny baby in a wire cage on the top of her trolley needed to reach the shelf behind Lara.

Lara moved along a little way and the woman reached up a toned, freckled arm to lift down a plastic tub of formula milk.

The baby slept, its wrinkled face closed like that of a dead little old man. Lara's knees gave way slightly; she wavered as her insides contracted.

The mother looked over at Lara and caught her in the act of gazing at her baby. Her questioning mascaraed eyes flicked up to meet Lara's.

'What a lovely baby,' Lara blustered.

'Why, thank you so much,' the mother said.

'How old is he?'

'Three days.'

'Gosh. Well then. Good for you. He's gorgeous.' Lara smiled, then turned and swept Jack and her own trolley away as quickly as possible.

That woman and her baby appeared every time they rounded a corner. They were there, choosing bagels from the bewildering array shielded from germs in giant perspex bins. They were there sliding past the automatic misting at the green vegetable display, and they were there when Lara looked up from a swimming-pool-sized freezer full of lobster and giant shell-on prawns. It was as if the woman were following her around expressly to rub the baby in her face. It was as if she were some sort of physical manifestation of Lara's own guilt – *look what you went and didn't do*, she was saying.

And then, when Lara had just about emptied the entire contents of her trolley on to the checkout conveyor belt so there was no turning back, she looked up and there they were, standing directly behind her in the queue.

Lara tried to look away, to concentrate on setting the last bits of her shopping on their passage to the till.

'Hey, how ya doin'?' The rotund checkout girl smiled up at her.

'Oh, um fine, thank you,' Lara mumbled.

'Say, I love your accent!'

'Thank you.'

Jack dropped his ball.

'Get it for me, Mummy,' he said.

' "Mummy". Say, ain't that just the cutest?' the checkout girl chuckled, as Lara bent to retrieve the ball.

'Oh shoot,' the new mother gasped behind her. She was struggling to get her shopping on to the conveyor but her baby was now awake and demanding attention with its newborn mewl. 'Oh shoot.' She looked flustered, unable to deal with the competing demands of her baby and her shopper's duty to keep the checkout machine running smoothly.

Three days was too soon to bring a baby to a supermarket, Lara thought. For the first time, she noticed the spotlessness of the woman's appearance. Her face immaculately made up, she wore a silk shift of lime green and fuchsia swirls on a black background.

'Can I help?' Lara said, gesturing at the woman's trolley.

'Oh, thank you so much,' the woman said, lifting the baby out of its cage and placing him into Lara's startled hands. Then she turned back to her trolley and started unloading formula milk, nappies, packets of cake, a gallon of grape juice . . .

That wasn't what Lara had meant.

She stood there, her lips opening and closing like a carp as she stared down at this unwelcome burden. The baby strained, his eyes tight shut, his mouth a gaping hole in his red little face. His body contracted with each sob, as he alternately arched his back and drew his knees up to his stomach.

He was so alive, yet so vulnerable. She could just throw him down on the ground and . . .

'Ahhh. Baby,' Jack said, reaching out his hand.

'Yes. Baby,' Lara managed to say. She put the baby up on her shoulder and did the little dance every mother knows, jiggling him and patting his back, helping him with whatever his problem might be. She made sure she breathed through her mouth, so she couldn't smell his delicious head.

That really would have been too much.

While Lara stood holding the baby, her own shopping made its passage through the checkout. At the other side, a spotty, low-browed boy of about Olly's age packed her purchases, putting one or two items into each of the thin plastic bags positioned on a metal carousel. If Lara hadn't been lumbered with the baby, she would have been worrying about whether or not she should be helping. She certainly thought he was using too many bags. And was she supposed to tip him?

'You're all set!' he said, looking up with a gormless smile that revealed crooked yellow teeth. Lara was surprised. She thought all Americans were dragged off to the orthodontist as soon as their last adult molar came through.

'Oh, um . . .' Lara tried to fumble in her bag for her purse, the baby still in her arms.

'I'll take him back now. Thank you so much.' The smart young mother reached over for her baby.

Lara paid with her credit card.

'Have a nice day!' the checkout girl beamed.

'Have a nice day!' the bag-packer gurned.

'Thank you,' Lara muttered. Then she wheeled her trolley out into the steaming car park, relieved to be leaving that baby far behind her.

She found the liquor store, where she bought a dozen assorted bottles of Californian reds and whites under the disapproving eye of the bearded proprietor, who asked her for age ID. At thirty-six, she chose to view this as something of a compliment. She pushed the trolley back across the baking mall car park, bottles clanking in their box next to the plastic bags of her shopping. But when she got to the front of the super-market, the car wasn't where she thought she'd left it.

'Shit,' she said to Jack.

She felt a surge of panic. If the car had been stolen, they would have to pay the swingeing thousand-dollar insurance excess. Her mind went back to the hissed argument she and Marcus had had in the car rental depot at Newark. She had suggested that, in view of the free upgrade, paying an extra seventy dollars to waive the excess in case of an accident would be a sensible move because they were driving an expensive vehicle on the wrong side of the road. Marcus had countered that they were just going to have to drive carefully, because the bloody car and child seat were costing them a fortune as it stood, upgrade or no upgrade. Lara was concerned now that this economy, like so many chosen by Marcus, might prove to be very false indeed.

'Where's the car, Jack?' Lara said. Jack turned around in his trolley seat. The sun baked down on them both, burning through the haze, and Lara realised she should have put sunblock on him – little lines of red had started to track between his freckles, matching the colour of his eyes, which were puffing up again. She pulled his baseball cap down so it shielded his face more effectively. For her own part, she could feel the beginnings of a headache setting in.

'There, Mummy, look.' Jack pointed a little finger at the other side of the shimmering expanse of tarmac. If you drew a line down the centre of the symmetrical supermarket building and its car park, the Chevy was standing in the mirror image place to where Lara thought she had left it.

'That's odd,' she said, shaking her head. 'I'm sure I parked over there.'

'Silly Mummy,' Jack said, giggling.

'Yes, silly Mummy. Must be more bonkers than I thought.'

She trundled the trolley across the car park, by now more concerned for the fate of the ice cream she had bought than about having got confused as to where she had left the car. It was hardly unprecedented – she was always forgetting where she had parked the Volvo – and in this case she could add jet lag to her list of excuses.

'Oh, no,' she said as they neared the car.

'Bum,' Jack said.

One of the front tyres, the one closest to her, was completely flat.

'I don't believe it.'

She lifted Jack out of the trolley and they bent to look at the tyre.

'What do I do?' Lara said.

Jack shrugged.

'Can I help you, ma'am?' A tall security guard, uniformed all in khaki, appeared behind her.

'I've got a puncture,' Lara said, straightening up and lifting a strand of hair out of her eye.

The security guard squatted down to take a closer look, and Lara wondered where she had seen him before. Something about the set of his shoulders reminded her of someone. Then she smiled to herself. She was going quite mad, first forgetting where she left the car, then thinking she knew a security guard in a supermarket car park in upstate New York.

'It's a nail,' the guard said, standing up with the culprit held between his long fingers.

Lara looked up at her reflection in his mirrored aviator sunglasses. She was wrong, of course. She had never seen this man before in her life. The nose, the shape of the face, the dark skin. Nothing was familiar.

'I can get a guy out to see to it for you,' he said.

'That's very kind of you,' Lara said. As the guard pulled his phone from his jacket pocket, she realised who he reminded her of. There was something about the form of him, the way he moved, that brought Olly to mind. That was all.

The guard walked round the car as he made the call.

'You got another flat here, ma'am,' he said, pointing to the tyre Lara couldn't see.

'My God,' Lara said. 'I must have driven through a nail spill.'

'He'll be here in an hour,' he said, pocketing his phone.

'An hour? I don't think my shopping's going to last that long in the heat,' Lara said.

'If I'm not mistaken, you'll have a factory-installed refrigerator on this model,' the guard said, leaning an arm on the top of the Chevy. Lara could see a dark patch of sweat on the underarm of his khaki uniform.

'Really?' Lara said. 'I wouldn't know. It's a hire car.'

'Gimme the key,' he said, and without really thinking, Lara did as she was told. 'There you are.' He summoned her round to see a black box inside the boot. He opened it and, holding her wrist, put her hand right in so she could feel the cold. 'Hear that hum? Stays on for an hour after you stop the engine.'

'Thank you,' Lara said, drawing her arm back. She made to get her trolley, but he beat her to it. 'It's fine,' she said, as he started to unload her shopping, opening each bag to inspect its contents and putting the cold stuff in the fridge. 'I can manage by myself now.'

'You like your wine, ma'am,' he said, ignoring her and heaving the box of bottles from the trolley.

Lara began to feel uneasy. Was this man overstepping the boundary of helpfulness into some other sort of territory? Or was he, like the bag-packer and the checkout girl, just showing that American knack of casual courtesy? She went to scoop up Jack, who was busy kicking his new ball around on a patch of scrubby grass to the side of the car park.

'Thank you,' she said as the guard loaded the last piece of shopping into the boot. 'I think we'll sit in the car now, with the air conditioning on.' She held her hand out for the key.

'Good idea, ma'am.' He handed it over, and she felt relieved. 'Be sure to keep an eye out for the tyre guy, though. I told him to look out for a pretty little lady with a handsome young man. He won't see you if you're hiding inside.'

'I'll be sure.' Lara put Jack into the passenger seat then went round to the driver side. 'Thanks once again,' she said, getting in.

'My pleasure. Part of the service.'

Relieved, Lara shut the car door behind her, pressed the *Lock All Doors* button and got the engine running so she and Jack could start to cool down. She watched through the wing mirror as the guard wheeled her empty trolley towards the store. Just before he went inside, he turned and gave her a salute, as if he knew she was watching him.

Cocky twat, she thought. But something troubled her. It had been over two hours since she had parked the car. But the fridge, which he said kept going for an hour, had still been on.

Six

THE NEW TYRES COST HER NEARLY SIX HUNDRED DOLLARS, because she had to replace exactly the model used on the car, which was, of course, of a top specification. This also meant that the mechanic had to go back to his depot to pick them up, so the operation took up most of the afternoon. She called Marcus on the house number and told him what had happened.

'Shit,' he said.

'I'm not sure when I'll be back,' she said. 'It seems to be taking an inordinately long time. And there's no food in the house.'

'Don't you worry about a thing. I've got everything under control here. There'll be a lovely meal waiting for you when you get back.'

Wow, she thought. That's a turn-up for the books.

It took her quite a while to navigate out of town. By the time she found herself out on unfamiliar, deserted country roads, Jack had fallen asleep and it was the tail end of the day.

She was never much good at being alone with nature, even within the fortification of the big car. Her imagination had an annoying tendency to bloom. Turning a bend, she would half expect to discover a ghastly old crone cursing her from the side of the road. Glancing in the rear-view mirror, she would be afraid of encountering mad, glinting eyes and the outline of a figure in the back seat, breathing down her neck, meaning her harm.

A little way out of town, a greyish-brown car roared right up behind her, tailgating her along a particularly twisty stretch. By the time the driver overtook her, flashing his lights, blaring his horn and going to the extent of winding down his window to flip her the bird – at which point she realised he was in fact a she – Lara was in full fight-or-flight mode, palms sweating, heart pumping.

'Wanker,' she said to the other driver, just to steel herself.

As she forced her breathing back to normal, she tried not to think about what might be going on up in the densely wooded hills all around her. That car could have forced her off the road and no one would have known until she was found years later, a desiccated skeleton, the rusting Chevy obscured by creepers.

As she finally rolled into Trout Island, past the graveyard, Lara decided not to mention the tyre bill to Marcus. If he asked, she would say it was a hundred dollars. He would think that sufficiently outrageous, but nowhere near as bad as the real amount, which would trigger a whole week of silent brooding. Thankfully, his squeamishness about money stretched to him not even being able to open the envelopes containing their bank and credit card statements. Financial management was entirely her realm, and she saw it as her duty to protect him from some of the harsher realities by occasionally scaling down the truth.

She turned into their driveway. If she looked through half-closed eyes, the house still hinted at what must have been a former glory. But the overgrown front garden and the loveless

45

tarmac at the rear were stark reminders that those days were long gone.

She lifted Jack out of the car seat and carried him up the rickety back porch steps. The kitchen door had a note pinned to it informing her – in handwriting so florid it had to be James's – that the gas was now fixed.

The house was completely silent. 'Hello?' she called, taking Jack through to the living room and laying him down on the sofa.

There was no reply.

'"Got everything under control",' Lara muttered as she went back out to bring in the shopping. '"Lovely meal waiting for you". My arse.'

Marcus could be so irritating.

And she felt so tired she could barely move.

It took her five trips to get everything into the house. She put things that needed to stay cold in their bags in the fridge, which she decided she would clean in the morning. The cupboards were filthy too, so she left the other groceries unpacked on the counter. She was just opening a bottle of red and biting into an Everything Bagel when she heard footsteps on the front porch and the swing of the fly screen.

'Hello? Weary travellers?' Marcus bellowed. 'We bring provender.'

Then he, Olly and Bella appeared in the kitchen, each of them bearing a pizza box almost as wide as Bella was tall.

'And we have wine too!' Marcus boomed, spotting the bottle at Lara's side. 'And our car is reinflated. Life is good!'

They ate so much pizza they could scarcely move, then they watched a DVD of *Schenectady, New York* on Lara's laptop. No one quite understood it except Olly, who was pitiless in his scorn at his family's lack of comprehension. Jack curled up against Lara and slept.

'Time for bed now, everyone,' Lara said, as Marcus lugged Jack upstairs. Olly sighed and pulled himself to his feet, but Bella hung back.

'Mum,' she said, once Olly's heavy tread had journeyed its way to the top of the stairs. 'Olly's being a total pain in the arse.'

'Not still?' Lara said, as she folded up the empty pizza boxes, taking care not to spill too many greasy crumbs on the floor. 'Pass me that glass, will you?'

'He's still going on about Jonny. It's just . . .' Bella stood on the threshold of the living room, twisting her knuckles, a bloom of red rising in her cheeks.

'Well, it meant a lot to him, you going out with his best mate,' Lara said, busy tidying up the room after the slobbish feast. 'He'll get over it soon enough, though. Come on; don't just stand there like a lemon, Bella. Pick up those plates, will you?'

Sighing, Bella clattered the plates into a pile, carried them through to the kitchen and dumped them on the draining board.

'I know Olly can be a bit of a headache,' Lara said, taking her by the hands. 'But it's only because he loves you.'

'Oh what's the use? You don't understand,' Bella said, breaking away. 'I'm going to bed.' She stomped into the living room, and, shoving the door as if she had a personal grudge against it, flew into the hall and noisily up the stairs.

Teenagers, Lara thought in the silence of Bella's wake. Who'd have them?

Then she turned to get on with the washing-up.

When she got back downstairs from kissing the children goodnight – a ritual she adhered to, no matter how much the older ones insisted it was no longer necessary or desired by them – Lara found Marcus sitting on the porch swing seat having a cigarette. Beside him stood another bottle of wine and two glasses. She sat down next to him.

'This is the life,' Marcus said. 'I think for once we have made completely the right decision.'

She searched his face for meaning. Was this a sort of apology for the baby? She thought perhaps it was. That was what she needed to believe, anyway. He put his arm around her and leaned forward to kiss her.

'I l-l-l-love you L-L-L-Lara.' It was how he always said it.

'Me too you,' she said. Her habitual response.

'I suppose a shag's out of the question?'

Lara broke away. 'I'm not ready yet.'

'Yes. Yes. Of course. Sorry.'

An army of biting insects had begun to gather around the light on the porch. Marcus slapped a mosquito on his neck. 'We'd better go in or we're going to be eaten alive,' he said. 'Always a serpent in paradise.'

'I'm pooped,' Lara said. She picked up the bottle and glasses and headed back indoors. Marcus switched out the light and followed her.

'What did the tyres cost?' he asked as they went upstairs.

'A hundred dollars,' she turned and told him.

'Jesus Christ.'

Seven

LARA STOOD ON THE PORCH IN HER RUNNING GEAR, drinking a pint of water to replace the fluid she had perspired over a muggy, sleepless night. Dawn cast a spidery light across the sky and a green freshness tempered the rubbery stink of Trout Island.

She put down her glass, plugged in her earphones, set Morrissey playing on her iPod, and moved off on a brisk, warm-up walk along Main Street. When she turned down Sixth, she started to run.

Since she had used it to lose the weight gained while pregnant with Jack, Lara and running had been an item. Her favourite route was along the seafront back home – all flat concrete to keep her ankles safe, with the ever-changing sideshow of the English Channel to her side.

The early sweat prickled on her. She crossed a bridge over a fast-flowing river and headed out of town, welcoming the tall trees that lined the road, enjoying the extra oxygen that seemed to pool underneath them. She powered on up a slight slope and took a turn along an unmetalled track running parallel to the river. Mist spilled out of the wild flowers that formed a hedge-row before the forest proper began. Her footsteps echoed in the empty countryside, and she settled into her rhythmic running breathing. She rounded a bend and came upon a large white bungalow set on a massive lawn manicured to within an inch of its life. Two four-wheel-drive vehicles sat on the driveway and, like everywhere else, the place appeared to be deserted.

'Ugh,' Lara said. It looked like the kind of place you suffocated in. She carried on, but a fearsome barking from behind the bungalow made her stop in her tracks and pause her iPod. A large black dog rocketed across the grass, straight towards her. Standing still and keeping her eyes on it, Lara bent and picked up two stones. She had read somewhere this was the thing to do. If an animal came at you, you chucked the first like a ball and shouted 'Fetch!' hoping your attacker would be fooled into playing with you. If that failed, you kept the second to use as a weapon.

Lara threw the first stone. It had no effect on the dog, which she could see now was at least half Rottweiler, red-eyed and foam-jawed. She braced herself with the second, ready to kill the beast if necessary. It continued to bound towards her, its legs pelting so quickly they blurred into one. But, as she raised the stone above her head, the creature seemed to hit an invisible brick wall, jolting backwards with a yelp. Lara noticed a line of metal poles, each about the size of a fairy wand, stuck into the lawn at regularly spaced intervals. That was what was stopping it.

Regaining its composure instantly, the animal continued to bark, snarling and baring its teeth, but unable to get at her. Other distant dogs took up its noise, echoing around the surrounding hills.

'Extraordinary,' she said, sticking her tongue out at it. She dropped the stone and picked up her pace.

She had only run a couple of hundred yards when another large dog came loping along the road towards her. Like its predecessor, it clearly had her in its sights; but it had a different air to it. Lara looked around for stones, but there were none close to hand. She froze, hoping by doing so she would show the creature she was no threat.

A few paces away from Lara, the dog stopped and stared at her with round, yellow eyes. It was enormous, bigger even than the previous animal, like a black Great Dane. It hunkered down and she got herself ready, her fists clenched, to deliver a punch to the heart as it launched itself at her. But, to her astonishment, it settled on the ground and gazed up at her, whimpering.

'Hello, boy,' Lara offered, and held out a hand. Better to make a friend than an enemy.

Keeping himself low, the dog crawled along the dirt road towards her, until his muzzle was close to her fingers. As Lara held her breath, he touched his nose to her palm. She reached forward to stroke him and he leaned into her, rubbing himself around her like a cat. Then he sat and held a front leg out.

'Pleased to meet you,' Lara said, shaking his paw. She felt round his neck for a collar so she could address him by name, but there wasn't one. 'What shall I call you? How about Dog? Better be getting on my way, Dog.'

She started to walk away from the animal, then stopped and looked back. He sat there, watching her leave, seeming as if he would wave at her if he could.

She ran on with no further incident – except nearly running into a bright blue bird with a reversed quiff jutting from the back of its head – until she reached a bridge that took her back over the river without having to return past the hellhound.

It was nearly too hot to run by the time she arrived at the house. But the hour of exercise had flushed her brain with endorphins and she felt almost reborn. She used the handrail on the back porch to bend forward and stretch out her thighs, breathing deeply to bring her heartbeat down.

The house was quiet inside – no one else was up. Again, she marvelled at the ability of her family to sleep through jet lag. As she crossed the kitchen to fetch herself a glass of water, she heard a scratching at the front of the house. She went through to the nasty hallway and pulled the door open to find Dog standing there, looking at her, his paw held up again.

'Hello,' she said, scratching him behind the ears. 'I'd invite you in, but I'm afraid I can't because of Mr and young Master Wayland's allergies to fellows like you. Wait there, though, boy.'

Seeming to understand what she was saying, the dog made no attempt to cross the threshold. Lara went back into the kitchen, found a plastic bowl, filled it with water and carried it through to the front deck. Dog, clearly thirsty, lapped it up.

Lara spent the next two hours using her post-exercise energy to scrub out the mouldy fridge and the kitchen cupboards, with their greasy fifties plastic lining and litter of dead flies.

She was on her hands and knees reaching into the last cupboard when she felt a presence behind her.

'Nice arse,' Marcus said.

She ducked up and looked at him, brushing her hair back with her forearm.

'Is Jack all right?'

'Fine. Sleeping like a baby. What are you doing?' he said, looking down at her. He was wearing his T-shirt and underwear from the day before.

'What does it look like?' she said. 'It's going to take quite a bit of work to make this place bearable.'

'It's fine,' Marcus said. 'Relax.'

'That's easy for you to say.'

'Did you get any coffee?' He rummaged in the grocery bags still waiting to be unpacked on the table. 'Ooh, fancy,' he said, finding the brown bag Lara and Jack had filled fresh from the supermarket grinder.

'It's not all that expensive,' she said.

'Did you get milk?'

Lara pointed to the carrier bag she had lifted out of the fridge in order to clean it.

'Shouldn't that be in the fridge?' Marcus said.

He set about making coffee in the ancient percolator and Lara went back to scrubbing the cupboard.

'You haven't been out for a run, have you?' he said.

'I couldn't sleep, so I thought I'd go out before it got too hot.'

'You should be taking it easy.'

'I can't. You know that.'

'What are these?' Marcus said, peering in another shopping bag and pulling out the toys she had bought in the supermarket.

'I've got to have something to keep him busy.'

'Of course. Just remember we're on a tight budget here.'

Lara turned and concentrated hard on cleaning her cupboard. She could feel the last endorphin leave her brain.

'Coffee?' Marcus said.

'Yes please.'

'It's on the side,' he said, placing a steaming mug just out of her reach. 'I'm going back to bed to look at my lines.' And he wandered off towards the hallway.

Unbelievable, Lara thought. Just unbelievable.

A little while later, Jack appeared. He held Cyril Bear close and was scratching his sweat-slicked hair, but his eyes seemed to have settled down from the day before.

'Morning.' Lara gave him a kiss.

'I'm hungry,' he said.

She poured him a bowl of Reese's Puffs and sat him down with his new colouring book and paints while she finished putting away the shopping. Then, checking he was still busy, she took a glass of water out on to the front deck, to sit in the shade and cool down in the mild breeze filtering down the street.

But for the orange rubbish bags and wheelie bins put out since she set off for her run, she would barely have believed anyone lived here. She held her breath and listened. Beyond the hiss and click of cicadas and other, louder insects, she could hear the buzz of a TV – a distant canned laughter, carried on the warm breeze. Despite the emptiness of the place, sitting framed by the porch she had a peculiar sensation of being observed. She scanned the fly-screened windows of the houses around her, but they remained inscrutable. The gauze masked whatever was behind it. It was a peeping Tom's paradise.

She became aware of the growl of a distant engine. It was so far away, and the road so empty, she didn't know what direction it was coming from.

The vehicle finally rumbled into view and Lara saw it was a UPS van. It pulled up in front of her, and a tall, brown-uniformed man leaped out of the driver's seat. He stretched his legs, looked up at the house and whistled to himself, shaking his head.

He disappeared inside the back of the van and a few moments later emerged with a package about the size of four bricks. Slamming the doors shut, he bounded up the steps to the front porch. Lara stood up and the man jumped.

'Jeez, lady. I didn't see you there in the shadows.'

'Sorry,' Lara said.

'Trout Island Theatre Co?'

'Um, yes.'

'Sign here, please.' He jabbed an electronic gizmo under her nose, his hand grazing hers as she took it from him.

When she handed it back she saw he was craning his head around her, trying to catch a glimpse into the house.

'I could open the fly screen so you get a better look,' Lara said.

'Sorry, ma'am. It's just—'

'Yes?'

'Is this—' the delivery guy blushed – not a good look in his sweat-soaked brown uniform. 'Is this the Larssen place?' He wrinkled his nose as he said the name.

'Larssen? I have no idea. We've just moved in.'

'Oh. OK, then. Me and my big mouth. Gotta split. You have a nice day, now.'

He handed her the package and turned to go, hurrying down the steps and across the front lawn. Like the supermarket security guard, he had something of Olly about him. Perhaps it was a generic American look – tall and gangly with a slightly swaggering walk. Before he got into his van he turned, took one last glance at the house, and grimaced.

Lara watched the vehicle disappear into the distance. Strange, she thought. Larssen place?

The parcel was addressed to James, but she was pretty sure it was the 'rowter', so she took it indoors and ripped it open anyway.

She was annoyed to find the packaging had been opened; they had sent one that someone had used and returned or something. But, after half an hour of fiddling around, she managed to get online and had a fruitful session catching up on emails and Facebook, connecting with work and friends back home in a world that seemed, even after only two days, another lifetime away.

Eight

'SO YOU'VE HAD A BIT OF A GANDER, THEN?' MARCUS SAID, helping himself to another plate of pasta. Lunch was early, because everyone gathering downstairs to pick at the Reese's Puffs like scavenging animals had prompted Lara to prepare some proper food.

'It's *so* dead here,' Olly said.

'There'll be loads going on. You've just got to hunt it out,' Marcus said, chewing. Lara wished he wouldn't eat so noisily, but he always maintained that table manners were for the bourgeoisie.

'You reckon?' Olly picked up his plate and licked it, something Lara had also given up complaining about.

'And once you get to know the actors and theatre people, well, that'll be fun.'

'There's James and Betty's party tonight for starters,' Lara said.

'What party?' They all turned to look at her.

She slapped her forehead. 'I completely forgot to tell you, didn't I? It's tonight at seven thirty. After the show. "Meet the guys", James said.'

'Do we *have* to go?' Olly said.

'Of course you have to go,' Marcus said. 'You were complaining how there's nothing to do, and now you don't want to go to a party.'

'Chill pill.'

'I hate it when you say that.' Marcus glared at his sullen son.

'That's why he says it, Father,' Bella said.

'Where is it?' Marcus asked Lara.

'Out in the sticks somewhere. I've got the address, and, now the internet's working, we can Google Map it,' Lara said.

'We're online?' Marcus said. 'Well done, you clever little geek.'

'And James said something about there being a big surprise for us,' Lara added.

'Ooh, a surprise from James. Can't wait,' Olly said, waving his hands in the air.

'You watch your step, young man,' Marcus said.

'Chill pill.'

Marcus's riposte was swallowed by the slow crescendo of a siren somewhere close by. It grew until Lara had to put her hands over Jack's tender ears, for fear of them being hurt. Then, as slowly as it started, the noise faded, leaving a dense silence in its wake.

'What was that?' Lara said. She felt as terrified as Jack looked.

'It was the same yesterday,' Bella said. 'When you were in town.'

'It's cool.' Olly shrugged. 'It's some practice for terrorist raids. I read about it.'

'Oh did you?' Lara said, raising an eyebrow.

'Actually,' Marcus said, through a mouthful of the pasta he

had continued to eat throughout the siren, 'it's a test for the fire brigade. They do it every day at noon during the summer. James told me when it went off once when we were Skypeing. So,' he said, shovelling the last forkful into his mouth, 'chill pill, Olly.'

'Right,' Lara said when they had finished their meal. 'You lot are going to clear up and I need a couple of Jack-free hours this afternoon to get this place together.'

'I've got lines to do,' Marcus said, shrugging.

'Bella? Olly? Can you look after your brother for a bit?' She would have liked Marcus to take responsibility just for once, though. Rehearsals started in two days, and he would be completely out of the picture. She resented having to use up her twin babysitting hours too soon.

Olly groaned.

'I suppose we can take him to the playground,' Bella said after a pause.

'There's a playground? Fantastic!' Lara said to Jack, whose ears had pricked up.

'I'd hardly call it that,' Olly said. 'Crap would be a better word.'

'Well, whatever, you'll help your mother out,' Marcus said, standing up. 'Now. Washing-up. I'll wash and you two dry and put away.'

'And don't forget Jack's sunblock,' Lara said. 'His skin's not like yours, remember?'

'I think we know that by now, Smother,' Bella said.

Lara gave her daughter a look. Then, without warning, her insides cramped. She gasped and grabbed the back of a chair.

'Everything all right?' Marcus said.

'Yes,' Lara said. She didn't want to tell him. She wanted to look forward rather than back.

'You sure?'

'I'm fine, really.'

As the others carried the plates into the kitchen, Lara headed off upstairs to unpack, picking up her laptop on the way to provide her with a bit of music while she worked. She paused at the bottom of the stairs and wondered what it was about that part of the house that made her want to run through as fast as she could. In the centre of the pale brown hall carpet a large dark purple blotch stared up at her. It could possibly be, she thought, an Agatha Christie set dressing. She knelt and sniffed at the stain. It smelled faintly metallic and rancid, like a rusty saucepan containing some old dishwater, and it was slightly rough to the touch.

She sat back on her knees and surveyed the hallway. The carpet was fitted to the room, so was no theatre prop; it must have been here for many, many years. She would ask James if she could pull it up.

Up in the bedroom, she set The Smiths' *The Queen is Dead* going on iTunes, using the drum break of the first track to give the energy to haul the suitcases on to the bed.

Lifting Jack's clothes out of the case she had shared with him, she placed them in neatly folded piles on the wooden shelving in the eaves room at the side of the bedroom.

She liked unpacking. Even if they were only going away for a night or two, she would find a home for everything. To an outsider, it might look like a housewifely habit, but it was only partly that for Lara. If things were organised, lined up in piles, serried in their ranks, then she could cope. The same love of order had drawn her to graphic design as a career. It was also why she found Marcus and his slobbish chaos so infuriating. If it weren't for her, the children wouldn't ever have clean clothes, food in their bellies, dentist appointments . . .

She stopped that train of thought and instead applied her mind to getting the individual pills and creams out of the first-aid kit and lining them up on the shelf.

Circumstances had forced domesticity on to Lara at an early age. When she was nineteen, her plan had been to go to drama school, to train to be an actress. But during her year off, when she was working as a barmaid at the Dirty Duck – the Royal Shakespeare Company actors' watering hole in Stratford-upon-Avon – she met Marcus. Thirty-one years old, a proper actor, he seemed impossibly glamorous to her. He asked her out and in six months' time they were married – a royal one in the eye for Lara's staid parents, who had found her theatrical plans hard enough to stomach, let alone an older man taking her, their only offspring, for his child bride.

Morrissey's vocals and Johnny Marr's jangly guitar pulled her back, as they always did, through the fabric of her past.

She tried, as she placed the box of plasters next to the antiseptic lotion on the shelf, to recall the feeling of excitement she had experienced whenever Marcus came into her bar.

It was hard to remember. A short while after their wedding – a while Lara tended to gloss over – they moved to Brighton and the twins were born. Marcus had to be available to go off to, say, Pitlochry, for, say, five weeks, at the drop of an agent's phone call, and it would have been unthinkable for Lara to get a job when the twins were tiny. With no qualifications beyond her A levels in Art and Drama, she would never earn enough to cover two lots of childcare. So that was when the pattern was set: he went off and she found herself stuck at home with not enough pairs of hands to care for her two voracious infants. That was the end of any acting thoughts for Lara. She stepped off the ladder before she had even found the first rung.

She wondered if that was the root of her current disgruntlement. Thwarted ambition. It was, she thought, like a maggot boring into an apple. Just one small hole, but the entire fruit ruined. Looking back over the first three years of the twins' lives, she couldn't recall any sort of interaction with Marcus. He was there sometimes, though. He must have been there.

Perhaps that was when she began to shut down. But she knew it wasn't. She could pinpoint *that* moment exactly, and it was even earlier. But she refused to let herself think about it any further.

She lined Jack's few toys up on a low, reachable shelf: Floppy Dog, Woody, Power Rangers, some Star Wars junk.

In the end it was the Art A level that took her out of the house. When the twins hit three, they qualified for free day-care while Lara did a part-time Visual Communication course at the local college. Initially she had signed up as a way to regain her sanity after spending her early twenties up to her neck in baby paraphernalia. By the second year, she began to see its potential. She even managed to acquire real-world clients for some of her final-year projects. After she graduated with a distinction, she won a grant to buy an Apple Mac, scanner and printer, and set herself up in a corner of their front room.

She didn't earn much, but felt good bringing at least some pennies in. And she could fit around Marcus's work, which was brilliant in theory, except he was going for months at a stretch without so much as an audition. This was useful for Lara, because she had become quite busy and she welcomed the free childcare. But he hated it.

'It's just that the right job hasn't come along yet,' she would say, trying to cheer him up. 'It will, soon.' But it didn't, or it didn't very often. And if it did, it would be Equity minimum wage for some small part in a tiny regional theatre hundreds of miles away. He got these jobs through old friends putting in a good word for him. Not once after Bella and Olly were born did he find employment by stunning a director with a blinding audition.

Lara dutifully dragged the twins up and down the country so some wardrobe assistant could mind them for a tenner while she watched her husband perform. She remembered the moment – during an Agatha Christie as it happened, in a theatre somewhere up North – that the penny dropped for her. It had always been a given that acting was the only thing Marcus knew how to do. In the long, penniless stretches between jobs he refused to do anything else to earn money. While he never exactly said it was beneath him, he maintained it would be a diversion from the main project. He had to be ready to act, he said.

But that day, sitting in the dark of the auditorium watching him mark his way through the play, Lara realised his main project was missing something. His neck and shoulders had tightened up; his voice was slightly strangled. What had once looked as natural as breathing for him now appeared false and strained. He was committing that most awful of actorly sins: he was being unbelievable.

The lacklustre production – a stilted postmodern rendering that failed to be sufficiently ironic – didn't help; but, the truth was, Marcus stank.

Of course, as she went backstage afterwards she couldn't tell him. No one would tell him, she thought as she kissed him and said how marvellous he was. The work would just trickle away slowly as the same realisation struck the people he relied on for employment. Back then, when the children were tiny, she hated herself for disrespecting him. She had made her choices and she worked hard at keeping to them. Knowing he was a bad actor was very difficult for her.

She sighed at the memory and studied the two suitcases side by side on the creaky bed. Her own clothes were rolled into cigar shapes as her house-perfect mother had taught her to do when they went on their package holidays to Corfu or Majorca. 'You get more in,' she had said. 'And the creasing is minimal.' This habit her mother had of talking like a walking advertisement had always irritated Lara. It was one of the many things she now checked in herself – little genetic or habitual tics that parents, willing or not, hand down to fuck you up.

The random scramble of mostly chinos, baggy shorts and T-shirts in Marcus's case showed he was not what you would call a natty dresser, and he didn't exactly take care of his clothes.

It was this chaotic side of Marcus that finally got in the way of her working at home. He didn't respect her time or her space, interrupting her to ask her where the toilet paper was, filling the house with fellow unemployed actors who would sit around all day, drinking endless cups of tea – graduating in the afternoon to wine – and bitching in well-modulated tones about *this* director or *that* agent.

Lara sat at her desk in the corner of the living room, trying to concentrate on her Quark layouts. Her job was to bring order and form to the bare text she received from clients, and the noise and desperation around her made her wince.

She thought about renting an office, but it seemed like such an enormous leap. At twenty-four she had been too young, too green. She hadn't had a head for business – for example, her prices were far too low – and besides, she was too tied up at home to take any big risks.

So when Lara heard about the council job, she jumped at it. The pay, while not riches, covered the bills, and the hours were perfect: nine thirty until three, five days a week. She could leave the house to Marcus, and nothing would fall apart if he had to go away for work. She applied for the job and got it, despite feeling she was somehow bluffing her way in.

And, she wondered as she arranged Marcus's clothes on the shelf above Jack's things, where had that got her? Not very far.

She hung up his one good shirt, a Paul Smith number she had bought him the previous Christmas. It was beautiful: blue with tiny pink flowers on it. But she couldn't look at it without remembering how annoyed he had been at how much he thought she had spent on it. His estimate, as it happened, was well below the mark.

It had taken her one week to realise that in working for the council she had dug herself into a graveyard of ambition. Her office was full of people who liked an easy life: any display of spark was met with mistrust. And she had no respect whatsoever for her team leader, a vacillating man in his early forties who didn't have it in him to make a single decision.

But she stuck with it because it fitted her life. And when Jack – as Marcus said, her *happy* accident – came along, the council's maternity policies proved to be munificent. When he was six months old, she secured a place in the subsidised workplace nursery and returned to work. It all seemed so effortless that her new plan of giving up her tenured, risen-through-the-pay scales status and going back to freelancing looked bonkers.

But something had to change. She was bored. So bored she sometimes felt like screaming. When she first married Marcus, she had imagined she would lead a life of bohemian glamour.

Now she found herself a local government employee with a pension plan and a weekly time sheet.

She knew that, older and wiser, she could now make a business work. In a few years' time she would have her own office – a modern affair, she imagined, of taut steel wire banisters and pale oak – and two or three employees working on contracts with those mysterious blue chip companies that paid so well.

The deal she had struck with herself after the abortion was that if there were not going to be any more babies, there would be a career. If her marriage was going to survive after all these years, she had to make herself happy again.

She sat down on the squeaky bed and finally got her own few things out of the suitcase. What had she been thinking when she packed? Besides her running gear and the clothes she had worn on the journey, she had one pair of olive linen trousers, a green sleeveless top, two T-shirts, an inky tunic, a black jersey Boden thing and a pink floral dress she had bought years ago in a slim phase and hoped still fitted her. There were not enough clothes there, not really for a whole summer.

Wondering what she was going to wear to the barbecue, she eyed the pink dress. Before she let herself have a chance to think about it, she had peeled off her clothes and slipped it over her head. It was low cut, with a slightly structured front section that laced up like a corset. Smoothing down the front, she looked at herself in the worn, full-length mirror someone had propped up against the wall thinking, no doubt, that no actor's bedroom is complete without one.

She was pleased to see that the dress fitted. Her breasts were still quite large from her recent pregnancy, giving her something of a cleavage. She turned for a side view, breathing in as much as she thought she could manage for the whole evening. It wasn't too bad. She decided that this dress would be her outfit for the night, worn with her denim jacket and her black pashmina.

She was still looking at herself when she heard the staircase rumble under Marcus's heavy step.

'So the big 'uns have taken the little 'un off to the playground, or something,' he said.

'Great.'

'Can we get the suitcases off the bed?' he said. 'I've got my lines to do and there's nowhere else for me to go.'

Lara thought of the big, empty house, about how many perfect line-learning nooks and crannies there were.

'Don't you want to wait until you've done the read-through before you learn them?' she said. 'You've always said that's the best way.'

'Best way unless you've got the fuck-off lead part,' Marcus said, smiling and pushing the suitcases on to the floor. Then he stopped and looked at Lara. 'What's that you've got on? Did you buy it?'

'It's ancient. What do you think?' She breathed in and held her arms out.

Marcus looked her up and down.

'Yes,' he said in his slightly strangled acting voice.

'You don't like it, do you?'

'I do,' he said.

'What's the matter with it?' She wished he was a better actor.

'Don't be angry with me.'

'I won't be angry with you if you tell me the truth,' she said.

'OK. Well, you look a little, well, bulgy in it.'

'Bulgy?'

'Um yes.'

Lara paused for a second and took a sideways glance in the mirror, catching herself unawares, not pulling in.

It's true, she thought, her spirits plummeting.

'Thank you for your honesty.'

'No look. It's lovely. It really is.'

Lara pulled the pink floral dress off and hung it up at the far end of a rail running down one side of the eaves room, where it would stay all summer. She walked naked back into the bedroom holding the black jersey thing Johnnie Boden promised would flatter any shape. Marcus was already lying on the bed, studying his script. He didn't look up at her.

She slipped the jersey thing on.

'How about this?' she said. 'With my amber beads?'

Marcus sighed and raised his eyes. 'What? Oh yes, that's a lot better,' he said. Then, pointedly, he returned to his script.

'Right,' Lara said, taking off the dress and hanging it up again. 'Well. I'm going to have a shower, then I'm going to get on for a bit.'

'Great,' he said.

'We'll leave for the show at about four thirty, then?'

'OK, babe. Could I just get on with this?' He gestured to his script.

'Fine,' she said. And, picking up her laptop, she went out of the door, pulling it tight shut behind her.

Nine

'THIS HEAT IS DISGUSTING,' BELLA SAID, AS SHE, OLLY AND Jack dangled on the school playground swings.

The wooded hills beyond the perimeter of the playground made Bella feel tiny, encircled in their vast shawl of greenery. They were different to the South Downs back home, those long ridges of chalky grassland that spelled a welcome when she returned from a trip, filling her with freshness and possibility.

These New York hills were something altogether different. They hemmed her in, as if they were sucking the breath from her and transpiring it as yet more wetness in the awful, muggy heat of the late July afternoon.

These New York hills made her feel watched.

A trickle of sweat worked its way down the hollow of her back.

'Ugh.' She shuddered.

'Push!' Jack commanded from his own swing.

'Your turn, Olly,' Bella said.

'But . . .'

'Just do it.' She pulled back and swung herself up, pointing her feet in front of her, silhouetting them against the hazy sun.

'Shitting hell,' Olly said. But he got up and pushed until Jack was giggling and soaring, his small legs catching the arc of each upward swing at the same time as Bella, so they hung together for a second each time in the dense air.

Bella and Olly had reached something of a truce since the day before – a practical step based on the fact that they were rather thrown together on Trout Island. In their usual manner, no words had been spoken about this – the ability to communicate silently with one another being one of the more socially acceptable aspects of their connection.

'Looks like we've got company,' Olly said, nodding over to the trees by the graveyard. Bella squinted across the shimmering tarmac and saw three boys, a little older than Olly and herself, leaning on a couple of shady headstones, swigging from bottles of Bud and passing a smoke around. One of them pushed a basketball from hand to hand, rolling it along the dirt.

'Mmmmmmm . . . Reefer . . .' Olly said, sniffing the air like a tracker dog.

'Calm down, drug fiend,' Bella said. 'Do you think they're OK? They look a bit sketchy to me.' The boys were dressed almost identically in dirty baggy T-shirts, massive shorts and baseball caps. Despite the beating, sweltering sun, all three had preternaturally pale, malnourished skin. And they were eyeing Bella, Olly and Jack like a pack of territorial mongrels.

'Are you worried we've taken over their "turf"?' Olly teased. 'Do you think it's going to be Sharks and Jets or Crips and Bloods?'

'They might have guns,' Bella said, trying not to move her mouth too much in case her lips could be read.

'I doubt it. Look at them. They're just a bunch of yokels,' he said. 'Observe and learn.' He gave Jack one last big push and wandered over the playground, hands in pockets, towards the boys.

'Olly!' Bella said. But it was useless trying to stop him. Olly just did things like that. He had no sense, and no reserve. Usually, though, he had charm enough to wangle himself out of the sticky spots this approach got him into. Their father had a similar way with him, but it tended to be so unctuous it embarrassed his offspring. They also got very peeved that the same delightfulness was rarely on display once the family doors were shut and there was no outside audience for it. With Olly, Bella thought, it was more ingrained, more in his bones than merely manufactured for public show.

Being the opposite of her brother in this way, Bella at once admired and was exasperated by his get-up-and-go. Sometimes it also made her feel like a complete mouse.

'What a moron,' she said to Jack, who giggled. But she had to admit she was impressed as Olly shook each of the boys' hands, introducing himself and pointing out his sister and brother over by the swings. Then he selected a gravestone to sit on and accepted a beer and a toke on the joint.

'For Christ's sake,' Bella said.

'Christ sake,' Jack echoed, shaking his head in imitation of his big sister.

'Well, that's the last bit of help I'm going to be getting from Olly this afternoon,' she said. 'Do you want a lolly?'

'Lolly!' Jack replied, nodding vigorously.

Bella slipped off her swing and lifted Jack from his.

'Hey sis, you off?' Olly yelled across the playground.

'What does it look like?' she called back. She heard the other boys snigger. 'Don't forget Dad wants you home by four,' she added, hoping to bring him down a peg or two.

'Whatever,' Olly said. The sniggering grew into laughter and they all high-fived him.

How on earth does he do it? Bella thought, bending to retrieve Jack's buggy.

They crossed the road and went past the theatre building. The doors were closed, but Bella could hear show music from within. Someone – it had to be James – shouted 'AND one and two and three AND one.' Then he clapped his hands and yelled, 'No, no, NO!'

A large version of the awful poster for the musical had been pasted on a board outside. Bella looked at her watch. She had kept it on British time, so she had to do a couple of calculations before she worked out they had exactly two hours before the show began.

'Sounds like a bag of shite,' she said to Jack.

'Bag of shite,' he giggled.

'Wash your mouth out young man. Do you want to get into the buggy?'

'No,' Jack said. 'I want my lolly.'

So, very slowly, stopping to inspect every ant and cricket that crossed their path, they headed off in search of a lolly. They reached Main Street, which was, as ever, deserted. To their left stood a small fire station. Bella wondered if its proximity to the theatre had anything to do with the choice of subject matter for the musical. It was staffed, a sign proclaimed, by volunteers drawn from the Trout Island Community, although there didn't appear to be anyone around at the moment. So when the siren went off for real, Bella imagined, people would pour out of all the houses, pulling on yellow coats and hats, slinging their axes and life-saving equipment over their shoulders, like in a movie.

Despite the lack of cars on the road, Bella decided to cross at what looked like a zebra crossing in front of a clapboard church whose noticeboard proclaimed in stuck-on plastic letters: *For the road to heaven, turn right and go straight.*

Yeah, right, Bella thought, taking Jack's hand and stepping off the kerb. Out of the blue, a dun-coloured car appeared on the road. Perhaps it was because it was a similar colour to the tarmac or perhaps it was because she hadn't heard the engine over the ever-present electric hum of the cicadas, but Bella just didn't see it until she and Jack were on the road. Confident it would stop – she was on a zebra crossing – she carried on leading Jack across, but the driver blasted the horn and sped straight at them, showing no sign of slowing down. Bella only just managed to snatch Jack out of its path.

The driver – invisible behind tinted glass – let the car window down just enough to stick an arm out, extend a middle finger and yell 'Asshole!' before roaring away. It was a gravelly voice, one that had no doubt seen too many cigarettes, but it was unmistakably the voice of a woman.

'Blimey,' Bella said. 'You OK, Jack?'

Jack nodded, speechless.

'Perhaps the zebra crossings aren't the same here as back home.'

Looking both ways this time, she led him across the road and they mounted the steps to the steep pavement some five feet higher than the other side.

The path was uneven and cracked, pushed up by roots from giant trees in the front gardens lining the road. Bella was glad Jack had decided to walk and she didn't have to negotiate this surface with the buggy. She held tightly on to him in case he toppled over.

They went on, past the library and a couple of junk shops,

including one that seemed to have some interesting old clothes in it. Bella noted it for a future visit, perhaps with her mother. Another, shoddier shop had a badly painted sign declaring it to be a 'Consignment Store', whatever that was. On its veranda was a selection of sit-in toddler toys, a grubby playpen and a forlorn Wendy house, so old and scruffy they didn't divert Jack for one second from his lolly quest.

Bella made a mental note of all of this for the photo essay she was going to make about Trout Island. She wished she had remembered to bring out her camera. The house was close enough for her to run back and get it, but it was so hot, and she had Jack, and it all seemed too complicated. She was actually completely exhausted. If it weren't for her watch calculations she'd have no idea of the time of day, whether it was morning or evening. This feeling, of being on the very edge of being stoned, was jet lag, she supposed. She didn't much like it.

'Look, Bella. Lollies!' Jack had spotted an ice-cream poster stuck to the inside of the next shop window. A mangled dump of a place, its woodwork was dirty and unpainted, but it had a sign that read 'deli' in an incongruous red neon scrawl above its door. The word brought to Bella's mind some little boutique in the North Laine of Brighton selling eye-wateringly expensive Parma ham and buffalo mozzarella. When she went in, she found that, inside as well as out, this deli was a rather different proposition. Down one side of the long, dark and dusty shop was a vast chill cabinet sparsely populated with plasticky hams and great, rectangular blocks of cheese. The floor was taken up by five long shelves with packets of non-perishable foodstuffs dotted around them.

'How you doing?' A voice came from the gloom behind the counter.

Bella couldn't make out if it was male or female. As her eyes grew accustomed to the darkness after the scorching sunlight outside, sight of the person who had spoken made her none the wiser.

'Fine, thank you,' Bella said. 'How are you?'

'I'm good,' the person said, inclining his or her head and smiling on one side of his or her mouth. Bella decided it must be a girl, probably about her own age.

'Do you have ice lollies?' she asked.

The girl guffawed like a leaky tap with an airlock. 'Do I have *what* now?' she said, once she had recovered her breath.

'Ice lollies. You know.' Bella mimed licking something.

'Popsicles, you mean.' The girl spoke to her as if she were backward. 'Where you from with that accent?'

'England.'

'You that English family with the theatre? Staying in the Larssen place?' The girl made a face on the word Larssen.

'How do you know?'

'Word gets around.'

'I told her,' a voice came from somewhere even further inside the store. Then the speaker emerged from behind one of the dusty shelves, his arms full of Diet Coke bottles.

He was the most beautiful boy Bella had ever seen.

'You must be Bella, right?' he said, leaning against the end of the shelf, his blue, blue eyes on her.

'Yes,' Bella said, hoping the blush she could feel wouldn't show on her heat-reddened face, while at the same time wishing her face wasn't quite so heat-reddened.

'I'm Sean,' he said, putting his load down on to the counter and extending his hand. 'I'm an intern at the theatre, helping James. Sent out to get supplies.' He nodded at the bottles.

'Hi,' Bella said, almost jumping at the shock of static that passed between them as they shook hands. For a moment, she hung suspended by his gaze.

'Lolly!' Jack said, pulling at Bella's skirt.

'Hey little guy, let me help you out there.' Sean led them over to an ancient freezer with sliding doors in the top. Then he lifted Jack up so he could choose his treat. 'You just got here, right?' he turned and said to Bella. She wasn't sure, but was he blushing too?

'Yes.'

'Do you like it?'

'What?'

'Here. Trout Island.'

'It seems nice. A bit quiet . . .'

'Things usually hot up once the show's on.'

'I want that one!' Jack said, pointing to a box out of his reach, deep within the bowels of the freezer.

'Right you are,' Sean said. He put him down and reached for the chosen treat. As he bent forward, Bella noticed the clean waistband of his underwear just showing above his belt, and a sweep of smooth, brown skin beneath the hem of his T-shirt.

'Have you come up from New York City?' Bella said, twirling a strand of hair around her forefinger.

The girl leaned over her counter at the other side of the shop and snorted. 'He wishes! He's lived here all his life! Ain't ya, Sean?'

'I'm afraid I have,' he said, handing Jack a lolly almost as big as his head. 'But I've been to other places. Unlike some people I could mention around here, Charlotte,' he said, leading them back to the counter to pay. Jack held his prize aloft like a light sabre.

'That's Charley to you, faggot,' the girl said, not unpleasantly.

'You'll have to forgive my friend,' Sean said. 'She's a little overfamiliar, what with us going to school together for twelve years.'

'The two class weirdos. That'll be one fifty to you, sir. You got five dollars,' Charley said, taking the bill Bella had handed to Jack, who always insisted on paying.

'You coming to the party tonight?' Sean asked.

Bella nodded. Her stomach flipped over.

'There's your change,' Charley said, handing it over with her eyebrows raised so high they almost disappeared into her short, spiky fringe.

'See you tonight,' Sean said, touching Bella lightly on the shoulder as she left.

'Sure,' she said.

And all of a sudden, Trout Island looked a little more interesting.

Ten

LARA TRIED TO WORK ON HER BUSINESS PLAN BUT SHE couldn't find any conviction; it all felt to her like so many words she was making up and pulling out of thin air. Was there a point in your life, she wondered, when you were grown-up enough to have a game plan? Or did everyone blindly muddle from one thing to another like she seemed to?

She ended up spending her precious free hour lying on the dusty sofa in the sweltering living room, one arm thrown across her eyes. She wondered if she had the energy for the evening ahead, with the show and the party afterwards. Perhaps an ibuprofen would do the trick. Or a glass of wine or two? Just to give her a bit of a perk-up? Normally she wouldn't contemplate daytime drinking, but her body was telling her the sun was way past the yardarm in England. So perhaps, just this once, she could bend the rules.

As she lay on the sofa, fighting the urge to get up and pour herself a drink, she also did battle with her irritation with Marcus. Apart from the bulgy dress incident, the fact he was just lying around on this, his last day off, was exasperating. She breathed in slowly, reminding herself that as well as being eleven years older than her, he was also naturally less energetic, so she should make allowances. But it was hard to imagine how it was possible to be less energetic than she felt at that particular moment and still have a pulse.

She jumped up, steadying herself against the dizziness caused by such a quick change in position, and went through to the kitchen to pour out a tumblerful of Yellowtail Merlot from the large bottle they had failed to finish the night before. Then she returned to the dusty sofa and stretched out, enjoying the instant relief the alcohol gave to the knot of tension in her neck.

The dashing Marcus she met seventeen years ago had been the soul of vim. He had been charming, funny, considerate, and, above all, hell-bent on having her. Seeing her beautiful daughter now, she realised what she unknowingly possessed when she was younger, and the power it must have wielded over him. Youth was surely wasted on the young, she thought.

She had been popular among the actor drinkers at the Dirty Duck, and would often join them on the other side of the bar, after her shift had ended, for regular lock-ins. There was a lot of drinking back then. One morning, after a strenuous all-night session, one of the actors heard the *Grandstand* theme tune on the pub TV and came to the dreadful realisation that it was Saturday lunchtime, there was a matinée, and he, a lead, was due on stage in half an hour.

It was a wild time.

But Lara wasn't like the other girls working in the town, happy to jump into bed with any of the bright young stars of the stage. Something of an arty outsider at school, she had been disdainful of the boys around her, who seemed too dull, too crashingly normal to pique her interest. As a result she came to Stratford a virgin, took her time settling into the rhythm of the place, and it wasn't until she met Marcus that she got around to sleeping with anyone.

Not that he was exactly a star. He was 'playing as cast', which meant, he said in the Indian restaurant in Stratford that was the setting for their first date, he was under contract to stay with the company for two years to do whatever roles they chose for him. So far, he had been the First Gravedigger in *Hamlet* and a Forester in *Love's Labours Lost*.

It was a step down in terms of parts, he said, cracking a poppadum and dipping it into some fearfully hot lime pickle. He had done a couple of leads at the Bristol Old Vic Studio, a smallish 'but plot essential' part in a Chekhov on the West End and an on-off stretch as a character's wayward brother in *EastEnders*. But a stint at the RSC, he said, after he had recovered from the pickle with a swig of Kingfisher, would get him in there in the theatre world. He was, he was certain, beginning to make his name.

Lara had found it all terribly exciting. His stories made her ache to be part of that world, part of his world. And, naturally and inexorably, she had fallen for him.

If only, she thought, draining her glass and thinking about getting off the sofa to fetch another, she could get that feeling back again.

She was just mobilising herself when the door burst open and Bella and Jack appeared. Bella looked wrecked by the heat, as melted as the ice cream slicked down Jack's front and all around his face.

'Wow, you two look like you've been having a bit of a time,' Lara said, slipping her glass unseen down the side of the sofa and making a mental note to retrieve it later. 'You'd better get cleaned up before we go.'

'What time is it?' Bella said, a hint of panic discernible in her voice.

'Half three.'

'Shit. Can I have a shower?'

'If there's hot water. I'm not sure how it works.' Another question for James. 'What about the mess you've got your little brother into?'

'Can't you clean him up, Mum? Please? I've got to get ready.'

'It's a whole hour you've got. What's the rush?'

'You wouldn't understand.'

'Try me.'

'Oh God, Mum.' Bella turned and flounced out of the room, slamming the door behind her. Her every gesture, every drop of her exasperation, Lara recognised. At once depressing and enthralling, it was as if she were her own mother, confronting her teenage self.

'What's got into your sister, then, Jacko?' Lara said, taking him by his sticky hand and leading him through to the kitchen sink to sluice the ice cream from him.

Jack shrugged. 'She's wacko, Jacko.'

'Certainly is. Did you have a nice time at the playground, then?' she asked, peeling off his sodden, filthy clothes.

'Yes. I like that big boy, too,' Jack said, shivering with pleasure as his mother rubbed a soaking wet dishcloth over his sweaty little body.

'What big boy?'

'He helped Bella with my lolly.'

'Ah,' said Lara. A big boy. Bella was so like herself she should have guessed without Jack having to grass her up. She lifted him out of the sink and rubbed him down with a tea towel.

Half an hour later, after Bella had vacated the shower, Marcus disappeared into the bathroom to have, as he put it – and despite the fact that he was growing a beard – 'A shit, shave and shampoo'.

Lara made their bed, then sat on the edge of it. With Jack leaning on her leg, watching her closely, she tried to draw a straight line of kohl on her upper eyelids. Just as she thought she had succeeded, Olly burst in and made her jump, jerking her hand up into her eyebrow.

'Sorry, Mum,' Olly said. He was noisily chewing a wad of gum, his mouth open.

'Where have you been?' Lara got up to fetch a cotton wool ball from her cosmetics shelf in the side room.

'I met some guys. Hey, cool wardrobe room thing.' Olly had followed her and stood looking around. He looked far more impressed than the large cupboard warranted, and this made Lara suspicious. She turned to inspect her son.

'What guys?' she asked, peering at his bloodshot eyes. 'And what did you do with these guys?'

'Oh, you know, just hung out.'

'Breathe,' Lara said, standing on tiptoe and pulling his face down towards hers. But all she could smell was the strong mint of the gum. 'Have you been smoking?'

'Mother,' Olly blustered. 'However could you cast such aspersions?'

The turn of phrase, the avoidance of an answer, Lara had seen it all before and she knew what it meant. He was stoned. She sighed and went back to the bed to fix her eye. There was no point in arguing with him about it now, but she was disappointed. That was one of her expectations of the summer dashed before it had even begun – the hope that getting Olly out of Brighton would also get him out of his daily weed habit. He didn't know how completely she had rumbled him, but as the person who emptied his pockets of torn Rizla packets and dusty empty baggies she had a pretty clear idea what he was up to, and she had observed him closely, learning the signs.

She had tried to talk him out of it, giving him the lectures about dope sapping his ambition and how the new forms of product were unknowable in their strength and potential to induce psychosis. All she got back from Olly though was a patronising 'Relax, Mum, I'll grow out of it,' and, 'What do you expect? I'm a sixteen-year-old Brighton boy.'

But she knew he lied about the extent of his use, and she hated lies.

'Don't let your father see you're stoned,' she said, applying new make-up to her eye.

'I'm not stoned, Mum,' Olly said, believing his own fiction so strongly he managed to sound exasperated with her.

'And go and get changed.'

'But—'

'No buts. You've got grass stains all over your backside. I shudder to think what you've been getting up to. Did you pack a second pair of jeans?'

'No.'

'Well, you'll have to wear shorts then. You've got fifteen minutes. Off you go.'

Olly tutted then turned and went to his bedroom.

'Bugger,' Lara said, as Jack reached up and batted her hand, causing her to wreck her eye make-up yet again.

By quarter past four, Marcus had assembled the Waylands on the two living-room sofas for a briefing. The afternoon heat buzzed, adding steam to the dusty air so it plastered itself all over any exposed skin. Lara had experimented earlier with propping open the front- and back-door fly screens to coax a little air into the place, but the house soon filled with black flies and buzzing mosquitoes. The Waylands were already so covered with insect bites that, as they sat there together, the predominant sound in the room was of nails scratching skin. It wouldn't do to encourage more creatures in to drink their blood.

But, bleeding and blistered lumps aside, the family looked fine. Both twins had caught the sun and already appeared polished and in holiday mode. Bella had on a tiny cotton lawn smock and Olly, who was strumming his guitar, wore surfer shorts and the Hawaiian shirt Lara liked him in so much. Marcus had chosen the contentious Paul Smith shirt for the evening, and Jack looked sweet in a Chinese brocade shirt and shorts she had found in a charity shop back in Brighton. With her finally straight eyeliner, the Boden thing and amber necklace, Lara thought she completed the Wayland cast well.

'What a handsome family,' she imagined people might whisper as they sauntered past.

'So then,' Marcus said as they sat in a line facing him. 'Olly, can you put the guitar down for a minute? Thanks, mate. As you know, James is my old tutor.'

'We know, Dad,' Olly sighed, as the guitar landed on the floor with a twang and a clatter.

'And his partner is Betty. Who is, as you've probably guessed, a man.'

'Why's he called Betty then?' Olly said.

'It's complicated. But all you need to know is she'd rather people referred to her as a woman,' Marcus said. Standing with his hands behind his back, he looked like his own father, a military man who didn't have it in him to take his only son seriously. 'And I want you to do so too.'

Olly smirked.

'And that look on your face is exactly why I'm telling you this now, young man,' Marcus said. 'So we don't get another display like we did the night we arrived.'

'What do you mean?' Olly spread his palms out, protesting his innocence. 'I didn't do nothing.'

'I didn't do anything,' Marcus corrected him. 'The way you behaved was bordering on the homophobic, and I won't have a son of mine being like that.'

On top of pleasure at how her family looked, Lara added the novel sensation of pride in her husband. Her eldest boy was such a force of nature she was rarely able even to start addressing his behaviour. But here Marcus was, meeting him head on. She tried not to mar the moment with wishing he did it more often.

'I was only joking,' Olly said.

'Well, it was in very poor taste,' Marcus said. 'I won't have any of that tonight. The Wayland family is on public show here and I want you to be as polite and as charming as I know you can be. You will laugh at the jokes and applaud the songs, whatever you really think of them. And if you fuck up, big boy, you are going to be grounded in this house until you prove you know how to relate to people in a social situation.'

'Wow,' Olly said.

'I think he means it, Oll,' Bella said.

'Damn right I mean it,' Marcus said, smoothing down his shirt-front. 'Right then. Lesson over. Ladies and gentlemen: shall we go to the ball?'

He went out of the front door to the street and the family followed him. Lara had just glimpsed a slice of the old Marcus, the part of him she was hoping to rediscover this summer. Perhaps it was having the lead role that gave him this confidence. Whatever it was, it seemed the stakes were high for him in Trout Island, and he was pretty determined to succeed.

Lara was pleased. She liked a bit of drive in her man.

Eleven

THE SUN SNAKED TOWARDS THE WEST OF MAIN STREET, lengthening the Waylands' shadows as they made their way to the theatre. But it was still hot, and, even before they had covered the five hundred or so yards lying between them and their destination, their clothes began to wilt and stick to their bodies.

From her position at the rear, Lara observed her family. Tiny Bella and long Olly were bickering about something or other. At the front, Jack skipped along hand in hand with his father, talking constantly. From the tone of Marcus's interjections – 'really?' and 'you don't say' – she knew he wasn't listening to a word the boy was saying.

For a moment, Lara saw them as if she weren't there – as if a part of her was still only halfway across the Atlantic, not yet fully arrived. She looked at them all and imagined they were getting on very well without her. It felt rather comforting.

She stopped, stretched out her arms and yawned, opening her eyes and mouth as wide as she could, drinking in the warm, tree-scented air as if it were a medicine to stitch her back together.

'Stopping?' Marcus turned and asked.

'Just taking it all in,' she said.

'You really should've had a nap this afternoon,' he said. 'You've been on the go all day.'

'Look, the library,' Lara said, as they approached the white, Doric-columned building.

'*Wow*,' Bella said. 'The *library*.'

'That really is the lowest form of wit,' Marcus said.

Lara climbed the stone steps up to the entrance and tried the door, but it was locked. An A-board stood on the porch, bearing an ineptly executed poster. If they ever decided to stay on in the typographically impoverished Trout Island, she thought, she wouldn't be short of business opportunities. The poster listed library events for the summer and she bent closer to read the tiny, curlicued script.

'There's a children's show every Thursday,' she called down to the others, who had stopped on the pavement beneath her. 'This week it's *Foxy Loxy and Chicken Licken*. We'll go to that, Jacko.'

Jack gave a cheer.

'I think he'll enjoy that more than he's going to like tonight,' Bella said as Lara rejoined them on the pavement.

'Come on now, it's going to be marvellous,' Marcus said, as they turned into the street where the theatre was. 'And look: the whole village is out!'

Indeed, First Street was lined with cars. Groups of people milled on the lawn outside the building. Some were dressed, incongruously for daylight hours, as if they were going to the opera. The women wore long skirts and blouses, the men shiny suits. Others were more casually turned out in what a department store might label 'leisurewear'.

Moving on to the grass, into the blue shade provided by the theatre building, was like entering a garden party. All around people laughed, greeted, kissed and shook hands. A couple of elderly women, stationed behind two tables, were doing a roaring trade in baked goods: brownies, big slabs of cherry pie and what looked like carrot cake. Lara wondered how it was possible to eat a great hunk of cake in this sweltering heat.

'I could kill a beer,' Marcus said, leading them all up to the end of the porch, where a lone old man in a green sun visor was selling cans from a coffin-sized cooler box. But when Marcus asked, the man laughed, revealing impossibly white and even teeth.

'Heh, hell, don't let Martha hear you ask that,' he said, gesturing to the larger of the cake ladies. 'We've been dry in Trout Island for the best part of a hundred years.'

'Dry?'

'No alcohol sales allowed, sir.'

'But I'm sure they had beer in the shop,' Bella said.

'Well now, they managed to push that through last summer, I'll grant you,' the old man said, scratching the lemon-yellow sleeve of his polyester shirt. 'But Martha ain't having none of it. Says that's what brung all the trouble last year, the beer.'

'Trouble?' Olly said.

'With the young folk,' the old man said. 'Some shenanigans with a gun, a hunting party gone wrong, you know the kinda thing. But you're not from round here, are you? Not with them accents.'

'We're from England,' Lara said.

'You don't say? Well now, you wouldn't happen to be acquainted with a fella called John Whitely, would you? Lives in London.'

'Waylands! Darlings!' James swept along the porch and put a hand each on Bella and Olly's shoulders. 'Now then. Is it acceptable with you young ones if I take your mama and papa inside? I need to have a word. Hiram, would you please set these youngsters here up with a can each of their favourite soft beverages? It's on the house, darlings.'

'You'll pay us back?' the old man asked James.

'Of course. At the end of the evening.'

'Just make sure you do. Martha don't like things not tallying. Now,' he said, turning to the young Waylands. 'What can I tempt you with?'

James put one arm around Lara and the other around Marcus and steered them towards the theatre entrance.

'I've got some lovely chilled Prosecco inside,' he whispered when they were out of earshot of the refreshment salespeople. 'Contraband.'

He led them into the foyer, which hadn't yet opened to the public, and Lara immediately felt the relief of the air-conditioned interior.

'It smells wonderful in here,' she said.

'Beeswax,' James said. 'Our marvellous volunteer front-of-house team make sure all the wood panelling is beautifully polished for an opening night. These things are important in Trout Island.' He sat at the desk by the front door, exhaled deeply and stretched back, running his pudgy fingers through his long, thinning hair. With the air out of him, he looked exhausted.

'How's it going?' Marcus said.

'Don't ask. We may get through tonight, but it'll be by the skin of our teeth. To be honest,' he lowered his voice, 'and swear you'll never repeat this to a soul: I'm rather looking forward to working with Mr Bill S's fine verse after doing battle with Betty's book.'

'But you've got a lovely big audience,' Lara said, leaning back against the smooth, cool wood.

'Oh yes. They're very loyal. And they're pretty forgiving most of the time. It's not as if we have much competition. We're the only theatre for about forty miles. For some of them we're the first theatre they've been to. And for many we're likely to be the last.'

'What about the library shows?' Lara asked.

'Well, my darling. I would hardly classify that as *theatre*.' James fluttered his eyelids. 'What's the matter, Marcus? Cat got your tongue?'

'You mentioned something about wine?' Marcus said, forcing a smile.

'Oh, please forgive me. Brain like a sieve right now.' James got up and swanned across to the other side of the foyer, where he opened a cupboard to reveal a mini-kitchen. He reached a chilled bottle out of the fridge, popped the cork and poured three flutes of bubbling, straw-coloured Prosecco. While he was doing this, Lara stole a glance at Marcus. He looked like he wanted to run away. She really hoped, for his sake, the show was going to be all right tonight.

'There we go,' James said, passing round the cold-clouded glasses.

Lara let the biscuity liquid prickle down her throat to pick her up after her afternoon glass of red.

'Lovely,' she said.

A door underneath the sweeping, polished staircase burst open. The calm of the pre-show foyer was shattered by a towering six-and-a-half-foot figure – all black lace, high hair and startling crimson lips – brandishing a spiralled dress of boned black satin.

'Betty darling. Prosecco?' James drawled.

'Can you talk some mother-fricking sense into that be-Jesused bitch?' Betty threw the satin spiral across the floor, where it landed at James's feet, sending a ripple of dust-motes into the beams of evening sunlight that sliced into the room. The voice was smooth, dark and Southern, a Blanche Dubois intonation to match the bedroom furniture back in the Waylands' grimy home from home.

'Oh not still,' James sighed. 'I thought we'd done with *that*.'

Betty acknowledged Lara and Marcus with a slight, lip-pursed incline of the head. 'Hi. I'm Betty. You must be Marcus and Lara. Charmed to meet you.' She nodded and turned back to James. 'Madam says she can't sing in it. Says she can't *breathe*. I told her it's just a matter of control. This is exactly the same style of dress I wore in *Marguerite* at the Cavern Club Theatre in Silverlake. Sang in it six nights and two matinées every week for an eight-month run. It's just she's put on so much fricking *weight* since I measured her and now the damn thing's too tight.' Betty stooped and picked the spiral up, holding it against her own piece-of-string form. 'Besides which, there's no alternative. She's got to wear it. Oh, James, sweetie, would you go and tell her? I've had it up to my tits.'

James puffed out his cheeks, took the dress from Betty, and went through the door under the stairs.

'And *he's* started now, too. Says his shoes pinch. I'm giving up on the lot of them,' Betty grumbled, following James down the stairs. 'I tell you, James, honey, this is the last time I'm working with this bunch of—'

The door slammed behind them, mercifully cutting off Betty's last word and leaving Lara and Marcus alone in the foyer. For a moment, the only sound was the faint mechanical click of the ceiling fan as it circulated and cooled the air, making welcome goosebumps prickle on Lara's arms.

'More wine?' Marcus said, going over to the bottle and pouring them both another glassful.

'Cheeky,' Lara said. 'So that's Betty then.'

'Yep.'

'Formidable.'

'Indeed. The musical's supposed to be her life story, with a few flourishes.'

'I shouldn't imagine she'd need too many.' Lara suddenly felt very pedestrian standing there in her flattering Boden thing. Like a daisy in front of an orchid. She took a gulp of her wine then slowly climbed the stairs leading up the side of the foyer, surveying the framed posters of past Trout Island Theatre Co. productions that lined the wall.

'These are really all quite hideous,' she whispered to Marcus who came up to join her. They were all the same style: literal, stiffly posed photographic treatments of the plays' subject matter. *Hamlet* had a man holding a skull, *Hedda Gabler* a woman holding a gun. Unsurprisingly, the typography was a mess – Lara spotted seven different fonts on one poster, including the dreaded Comic Sans.

'Someone's put a lot of work into them,' Marcus said, trying to sound positive.

'And the repertoire's very ambitious. Do you think I should offer to help out with the graphic design?' Lara said.

'Do you think you ought, though?' Marcus asked, wincing.

She looked at him and willed him not to get downhearted. '*Macbeth*'s going to be great,' she said.

'Oh yes. Undoubtedly.'

'Can I help you?' A voice in the foyer beneath them made them both jump. They turned to see a rotund young woman standing behind the foyer desk. She had long, straw-blond hair that reached down to her not inconsiderable buttocks. 'It's just,' she said, a stiff little smile stuck in the mass of her face, 'you're not supposed to be in here yet.'

'Oh, James let us in,' Marcus said, going back down the stairs.

'Oh! You must be Marcus Wayland,' the young woman said. 'I can tell by your accent. Welcome to Trout Island.' Wiping her own hand on her straining jeans, she reached out and shook Marcus's. It looked to Lara as if she was trying to stop herself from curtsying. 'I'm Alyssa Smith. Front of house manager.'

'Pleased to meet you.' Marcus beamed. 'And this is my wife, Lara.'

'Pleased to meet you.' Alyssa nodded in Lara's direction. 'Now if you'll excuse me, I'm opening up in five minutes and I have to get my ticketing system set up.' She gestured to their glasses. 'You can stay here until you finish your wine. We need to be a little discreet about that . . . I know James thinks it's completely lame,' she rolled her eyes. 'But there are a few ladies here tonight who feel rather strongly about the booze issue.'

'We've met them,' Marcus said.

'I just love your accent. I'm gonna bug you till I learn it!' Alyssa said.

Lara and Marcus stood to one side, sipping their drinks, while Alyssa took two long, convoluted answerphone messages concerning ticket reservations. No one left their surnames. The assumption seemed to be that Alyssa would know who Kenny and Laura and Marsha and Hank were, and in fact she did. She dutifully wrote down the contents of the messages with a purple Sharpie pen, sticking the tip of her tongue out of the corner of her mouth as she worked. Then she opened a drawer in the desk and pulled out a metal cash tin, which she opened with a key from a large bunch on a curled wire attached to her otherwise redundant belt. Inside was a pile of green cardboard tickets.

'What happens if you get more bookings than you have tickets?' Lara asked.

'We just tell 'em to come on back the following night. Except for some of the weekend people, they don't usually mind. They don't have much else to do round here. Excuse me and glasses away now.' Alyssa bustled round the desk and opened the front door, revealing a smiling, expectant queue of the largely white-haired audience.

Olly was near the head of the line, towering over the ladies in front of him. He looked exasperated.

'Mum,' he said loudly, as he came through the door. 'Where the hell did you get to?'

One of the ladies turned and tutted at his choice of language and attitude.

If only she knew the half of it, Lara thought.

'We've been stuck out here with Jack and he's had an accident,' Bella said, manoeuvring herself and her little brother out from behind an elderly man in a cowboy hat.

'Oh, poor mite,' a woman with jelly arms said as Bella handed him through the crowd.

'It's runny, Mum,' Jack said, holding on to his bottom.

'Poor you.' Lara took him by the hand and led him through into the toilet with the changing mat. Jack had a delicate stomach, and any variation in diet, or even water, could lead to upsets. Luckily his underpants had caught the worst of it, so she took them off and cleaned him up the best she could.

'I'll get rid of these,' she said, balling up his pants, 'and you can just wear your trousers and go commando.'

'Cool,' Jack said.

She wrapped the offending item in paper towels and went back out into the foyer.

'Excuse me, Alyssa,' she said, motioning to the stinking bundle she held down at her side. 'Is there anywhere I can leave this?'

Alyssa wrinkled her nose. 'There's a dumpster round back,' she said, pointing. 'Just be sure and close it up after or the racoons'll get in.'

Leaving Jack with Olly and Bella, Lara went outside and round the building. On the other side of the large dustbin she could see two actors, a man and a woman, sitting on an old sofa by what must be the stage door. They were leaning against one another, smoking. Lara crouched down slightly, so she couldn't be seen.

'Well I don't give one shit,' the woman was saying. 'I've told my agent I'm never going to come up here again, even if they did manage to pay me properly.'

'I know, honey, I know. But we've got to give it our best now we're here. It wouldn't be professional otherwise.'

'How dare she tell me I got fat. Did I get fat, Brian?'

'June. You know you aren't fat. You have a beautiful body. You know I love your beautiful body.'

'Oh Brian.' June blew away her smoke and leaned in towards him, cupping his head in her hand and pulling his face towards hers. They locked mouths and Brian's hand worked its way into June's dressing gown, exposing the most enormous, round and rigid breast Lara had ever seen. He twirled the nipple between his thumb and forefinger, as if he were one-handedly rolling a short cigar.

A tall good-looking boy appeared in the stage doorway and coughed into his fist to alert them to his presence. They unglued their faces to look up at him, but Brian's hand remained firmly on June's exposed breast.

94

'Yes, Sean?' June asked, drawing on her cigarette and looking up at him.

'Just to let you know, June and Brian, that the house is now open and this is your fifteen-minute call. I guess you didn't hear it over the tannoy.'

'I believe it's customary for stage management to address us as Miss Tarpin and Mr Weinberg,' June said, flaring her nostrils. 'For our calls.'

'Now you two get your asses inside and into costume.' Betty appeared behind Sean, moving him aside. 'I have loosened the dress for you tonight, *Miss* Tarpin, so you have absolutely no excuse for bum notes. And *Mr* Weinberg, I would thank you mightily if you removed your hand from Miss Tarpin's appendage and – uh – ceased from corrupting my sweet innocent assistant here.'

'Ain't nothing he ain't seen before.' Another actor – thirty-something and all Italian handsomeness – sauntered past Sean and ruffled his hair. He threw himself on the sofa, nearly on top of June, and lit a cigarette.

'Please, ladies,' Betty cried. 'Are we going to do any acting tonight, or are we simply going to smoke?'

'This is a genuine choice you're offering?' The Italian leaned back and exhaled, squinting his eyes up against the smoke.

Betty sighed deeply and shook her head. 'I expect you to be standing by, with your costumes on, at the five.'

She turned and went back into the theatre.

'You told him, Tony,' Brian said, finally taking his hand away from June's breast.

'Asshole,' Tony said to Brian. Then he took one last drag on his cigarette, stamped it out on the bare earth and disappeared inside the building.

'Come on, honey,' June said, getting up and adjusting her dressing gown. In doing so, she managed to flash everything she had at the stage manager. It looked to Lara like a deliberate move, but the young man remained remarkably composed.

He watched the pair go inside, then he moved smartly around the sofa, picking up the empty drinks cans, cigarette butts and plastic cups that the actors had just left there. Lara felt like she had stooped behind the dumpster for too long, so she lifted the lid and threw her bundle in, where it landed with a clatter.

'Oh, hi,' Sean said, looking over at her.

'Hello,' Lara said. 'Sorry, I didn't mean to—'

'No, that's fine. You have to be Bella's mom.'

'I am. How did you—?'

'I met her in the shop earlier on. You're very like her.'

'I'll take that as a compliment,' Lara said, smoothing her hair. So, then. This was the 'big boy'. He had the bluest eyes she had ever seen, and a smile to melt a young girl's heart. She hoped Bella wouldn't lose her head, though. 'Quite a handful you've got there,' she said, motioning to the stage door.

'You're not kidding. June and Brian are a total nightmare. I'll be glad to start working with a saner cast.'

'They're not in the Shakespeare?'

'No, thank God. They're strictly musical theatre.'

Lara was silently relieved on Marcus's behalf. 'Are you stage-managing *Macbeth* too?'

'A bit, but I'm also on stage,' he said. 'Just Ross and the Doctor. Nothing great, but it's all experience.'

'So you want to act?' Lara felt like she was interviewing a prospective son-in-law. An actor was not what she hoped for her daughter.

'Of course. I'm off to Juilliard in the fall. I'll be leaving Trout Island at last.' He leaned past Lara and put the rubbish he had collected into the dumpster, on top of Jack's underwear.

He really was very handsome indeed, Lara thought.

'Sean? Where's my Sean?' Betty bustled out of the stage door. 'Oh, you're with little *Mamacita*. Hi, honey.' She went to Lara and kissed her on the cheek, as if they were the best of friends. 'Have we got a surprise for *you* later on.'

'So I heard,' Lara said.

'Have you got any idea what it might be?'

'Not a clue.'

'My lips are sealed, honey.' Betty put a manicured finger to her lips. 'Now come along, Sean, my darling, this show won't run itself, you know. We *need* you.' She put a hand round his shoulder and guided him in.

On her way back to the foyer, Lara decided not to tell Marcus about what she had just witnessed. But it had shown that Betty had style and wit, so perhaps she and James had managed to craft a work of substance.

As it turned out, they hadn't.

Set Me On Fire! held few pleasant surprises. It was a predictable rags-to-riches tale of a Southern girl who – through a mixture of sheer determination and an encounter with an angel who assured her she would become famous – fought her way up past brutal boyfriends, unscrupulous managers and downright rude hick-bar audiences to Stardom. Lara was certain Betty's real story was far more interesting than this anodyne song-and-dance fest suggested, not least because, unlike the character in the play, she wasn't actually a girl.

As Pearl, the lead character baggily based on Betty, June Turpin was at least thirty years too old at the beginning, when she should have been sixteen. Her costume, a loose, raggedy dress and plaits, drew a guffaw from Olly that June, from the fleeting dagger stare she shot his way, clearly heard.

The rest of the audience, however, loved *Set Me On Fire!* The dances weren't the worst of it, Lara had to admit, and each piece was met with a near standing ovation.

The clapping was the only part Jack enjoyed, so Lara had her work cut out keeping him quiet and still during the other bits. A veteran of taking small children to theatres, she had packed three small toffee lollies, which went some way to keeping him busy, or at least quiet, unlike his big brother who seemed unable to sit still.

'Could you please stop fidgeting around?' Marcus whispered, leaning across Lara and tapping Olly on the knee.

As the house lights came up for a well-earned interval, Lara looked sideways at Marcus. He was visibly fighting hard to maintain the illusion that this place was going to be the making of him.

'Oh my,' a woman with an immaculate shiny white bob said to her companion as she squeezed out of her row of seats fanning herself with her programme. 'Wasn't that just *something*?'

From the Wayland family seats near the front of the auditorium, Lara looked around at the audience as they moved out of the theatre. There were no New York agent types to be seen. Apart from a couple of dragged-along teenagers emitting a truculence even more finely honed than Olly's, there was hardly anyone in the room under the age of sixty.

The Wayland family were the last to remain seated, a little out of place in their youth, Englishness and suitcase-crumpled clothes. As the last old lady waddled out of the exit – bound, no doubt, for the cake stand – Lara felt the back of her neck prickle, as if someone were standing right behind her.

She turned in her seat and looked at the empty auditorium. The banks of brand-new red velvet seats stood blank-faced and tipped up. Then a slight movement drew her eye to the shallow balcony at the very back of the room. Supported by ornate metal pillars, it spanned the width of the room. The angle from her seat to the platform was such that she couldn't pick out much, but as she looked up Lara saw the tall outline of a man silhouetted and haloed from a house light directly behind him. She couldn't be certain, but she had the feeling his eyes were right upon her. As soon as she saw him though, he stepped back into the shadows and out of her sightline.

'Did you see that?' she said to Marcus, who had finally stood up.

'What?'

'There was a man . . .' She pointed to the balcony.

Marcus looked. 'Probably the lighting operator.'

'Probably,' she said.

'Or you're seeing things. Wouldn't be the first time. Now then, who wants a slice of pie?' Marcus said.

On their way out to the cake stand Lara looked up at the balcony again, but there was no one there. Perhaps Marcus was right. Even with her contact lenses in, her Mac-strained eyesight didn't do too well in dim light; more than once she had found herself greeting complete strangers in theatre bars.

Out on the lawn, the first act of a glorious, golden sunset was kicking off, and the still air was full of bugs cruising the audience for bloody snacks.

'Look how black the trees are,' Bella said to Lara, pointing at the ridge of outlined maples on top of the hill behind the village. 'I wouldn't want to be up there now.'

'Bllllairrrr Witch.' Olly loomed over her.

'Piss off.' Bella pushed him away from her.

'It's a different world indeed,' Lara said, feeding a slice of pie to Jack and trying to stop it spilling down the front of his Chinese jacket. The 'cherry' filling was too impossibly red to be anything other than permanently staining.

'So Waylands, how do you like our little show?' James sashayed up to them and put his arms around Bella and Olly. Marcus gave Olly a subtle but stern look.

'It's great,' Olly said inscrutably.

'Lovely costumes,' Bella said. 'Aren't they, Mum?'

'Who did them?' Lara asked.

'Betty. Betty is a marvel.' James beamed, buoyed by the extravagant praise he had been receiving from other audience members. 'She does everything: the writing, the musical direction, the costume, the set design.'

'Why doesn't she perform any more?' Olly asked, and Lara wondered if he was being polite or very clever and very cheeky.

'Stage fright,' James whispered. 'A bit of a breakdown. But we don't talk about it.'

'How sad,' Lara said. And she thought for a moment of her own lost potential – from *the* actress of the Sixth Form, to wife and mother in little over a year. What could she have been had life not intervened?

'Anyway, *avanti*!' James clapped his hands. 'Ladies and gentlemen, please eat up your pies now. The show will recommence in five minutes. I don't want a crumb left!'

A murmur of laughter passed through the audience, then they set to work on what remained on their plates. A red-faced Alyssa appeared at James's elbow.

'Uh James, could I have a word, please,' she squeaked. 'In the foyer.' She turned and marched back into the building.

'Coming, Alyssa my pet. Oops. Looks like I'm in trouble with the lady of the house,' James whispered to Lara and Marcus. 'She's not keen on my impromptu announcements. Thinks it's her job. God, she's so *stern*.'

'He's in a good mood tonight,' Olly said as they watched him scuttle across the lawn.

'The audience seem to like it,' Marcus said, swigging back a can of soda. 'God this so-called beer is vile. What sort of root do they use, I wonder?'

'Come on, let's go back in,' Lara said, scooping up Jack who was leaning against her legs, on the verge of falling asleep.

The second act dealt with the happier half of the fictionalised Betty character's story. She found the love of her life – James, presumably – made it big on Broadway and was stopped by strangers asking for her autograph. The finale had a sequinned June Turpin ascending on a glittering cut-out moon, supported by – so the programme informed Lara – a fully uniformed phalanx of Trout Island's volunteer fire fighters.

'What would happen if there was a fire during the finale?' Lara whispered to Marcus.

Then June Turpin opened her mouth to sing the final song, the theme tune of the show that all the music had been leading up to.

> *You! You set me on fire,*
> *Couldn't get any higher,*
> *Don't know no one flyer,*
> *Now sir, be my sire . . .*

These lyrics, and the sight of the already out-of-kilter actress further destabilised on a dangling moon, set Olly off on a choking giggling fit. Thankfully, the backing music belting out from two speakers at the front of the stage was so loud only Lara noticed.

At the end, the large cast lined up on the small stage and took their bows to rapturous applause. People around the Waylands stood up and called out their bravos.

'Stand up,' Marcus hissed, getting to his feet.

'What the—?' Olly said.

'Stand up, or I'll never, ever give you any money ever again,' Marcus said.

The family all stood, even Lara, who had a sweaty, sleeping Jack pressed into her shoulder.

'Bravo!' Marcus boomed, clapping his hands up high above his head. 'Encore!'

'Please God, no,' Olly muttered.

Betty sashayed on stage and the applause doubled as she dropped into a curtsy. Looking round at the strait-laced audience, Lara wondered how they could so adore someone who was quite so out of the ordinary. Perhaps a little of the famous New York City liberalism had reached up here. Or perhaps they thought the glamorous Betty-woman was for real. And who was to say she wasn't? Betty and James believed in her, and wasn't it part of the American dream that you can be whatever you want to be, do whatever you want to do?

If only that dream had stretched over east to Stratford-upon-Avon in the early nineties, Lara thought.

She watched Bella redden as the young man Sean came on stage to present Betty with an enormous bunch of red roses. Sean stepped back, and Lara was certain he caught her daughter's eye as he did so. Then Betty gestured stage left and James came on slowly, holding out his hands. He leaned forward and kissed Betty, and the two of them beamed out at the audience, who gradually brought their applause to an end.

'Ladies and gentlemen, boys and girls,' James said. 'Trout Island Theatre wants to thank you for your patronage. You will know that our marvellous community theatre receives but a pittance in funding for all the activities we put on for you and your neighbours. We do hope you enjoyed the show. And we hope that, if you did, you will tell your friends. I'd also like to remind you that in three weeks' time we will be opening our production of William Shakespeare's Scottish Play. Our star, Marcus Wayland, is with us tonight, all the way from England. Marcus, stand yourself up.'

Marcus stood, turned and, with as much dignity as he could muster, bowed. The audience applauded once again, then James hushed them so that he could continue.

'As you know, we don't charge for tickets, but we do ask that if you enjoyed our show, please put your hands in your pockets and give what you can to our actors on your way out. They will be standing at the back with hats to receive your donations. No amount is too small, but . . .' and he paused for the audience to smile back at him, 'no amount can *possibly* be too large.'

Once more, the audience applauded as the actors jumped down off the stage and positioned themselves by the back door, holding hats out for dollar bills, twenties, fifties and even cheques for larger sums.

'How humiliating,' Olly said.

'It's an old tradition,' Marcus said loudly. 'I think it's marvellous.' Then he was swallowed up by a crowd of ladies who all wanted to meet him to find out if he was from London, and whether they would know him from the movies.

He was in his element.

Lara and the children wandered outside. She hoped another glass or two of wine when she got to the party would pick her up, but finding any enthusiasm for the night ahead was hard work. Even the thought of the promised surprise – which she supposed would be something camp and lame, some sort of British-themed foodstuff perhaps, or an unwearable hat made by Betty – didn't help.

'I need to sit down,' she said to Bella and Olly.

So the wife and children of the Wayland family sat on the disabled ramp at the theatre entrance, waiting for the husband and father to be free. They watched the audience leave, then, in effervescent groups, the cast. They waited the best part of forty minutes.

Twelve

JAMES AND BETTY'S FARMHOUSE STOOD A COUPLE OF miles outside the village. James had said that the Google directions were useless, so he provided them with a sheet written in his own inimitable style.

They first managed to overshoot the correct turning, travelling as far as a reservoir penned in by a rusty dam so vast it was quite out of proportion with the surrounding countryside. At this point – James would surely have mentioned such a landmark in his endlessly annotated instructions – they realised they had gone too far, so they doubled back. Coming from the opposite direction the turning was plain to see. They got on the right road, which swept out to the west and curved round the bottom of a hill. Then, as directed, they turned along an unmetalled track that climbed slowly upwards. They passed a couple of houses, but mostly they were surrounded by trees and bushes.

A deer bounced across the dusty road ahead of the car. Marcus slowed down.

'Where there's one, there's often . . . ' As he spoke, a second, smaller deer scurried in front of them. '. . . another.'

'It feels like we're going into the deep, dark forest,' Bella said. 'I'm not sure I like it.'

'Nonsense,' Marcus said. 'This is nature raw in tooth and claw, that's all.'

'Red,' Olly said from the back.

'Eh?' Marcus said.

'It's "nature red in tooth and claw". Tennyson.'

'Well, guys. That makes me feel *so* much better,' Bella said, squinting out of the car window.

'It should be along here, just after that yellow post, in the clearing,' Lara said.

'Where all the cars are parked? For the party?' Olly said.

'My, you two are on whip-cracking form with the old sarcasm,' Marcus said.

They drew up at the far end of the twenty or so cars which, in their variety – from a dented red pick-up truck to a brand new Porsche Carrera – signified the mixture of fortunes embraced by actors' lives.

'Verrry nice,' Olly said as they passed the Porsche.

They turned up the driveway and came across one of the most beautiful houses that Lara had ever seen. Hidden from the road, it was, like most of the buildings back in the village, constructed in the Greek Revival style. But, unlike the village houses, this had been beautifully cared for, painted an immaculate powder blue with cream windows and soffits. A wide veranda skirted the visible part of the house and, in the setting sun, it appeared to float on the vast meadow they had to cross to get to it. But most thrilling was its position on the top of a hill that swept down along an expanse of grass, flower and vegetable beds to a pond at the bottom, with forest lurking beyond that. At the far side of the garden, listing as if it might collapse any minute, was a tumbledown barn.

'No one goes in there, OK?' Lara said.

'Wild horses wouldn't drag me,' Olly said.

There was quite a crowd. People milled around a fire pit or lolled on blankets on the ground, drinking wine and talking. The sound of laughter and the smell of meat on charcoal carried the hundred or so feet to where the Waylands were making their way across the front garden.

'How did they all get here so quickly?' Marcus said.

'You were ages, Dad,' Olly said. 'We thought the old dears had eaten you up.'

'You have to charm 'em.' Marcus winked.

'WAYLAND FAMILY!' James burst from the crowd like a giant sail, wearing yet more floating white. The chatter stopped and everyone turned to look up at them. Then they broke into a round of welcoming whooping and applause.

'Bloody Americans,' Olly said.

'Damn theatricals, you mean,' Bella said. She was scanning the crowd, probably, Lara thought, looking out for that Sean boy.

'Zip it, you two,' Marcus said. Putting his public smile on, he led his family to James and the mêlée.

'Darlings,' James said, again encircling Marcus with a bearhug and sweeping them on towards the house. 'What on earth kept you?'

'Dad had to meet his public,' Olly said.

'And we got lost,' Lara said. 'This is amazing.' They had approached the fire pit, a coffin-sized hole in the ground full of white-hot cinders and covered by metal grilles laden with sizzling fish and meat.

'Isn't it?' James said. 'Betty dug it last year, and we've had so many parties around it. We have scallops, shrimp, buffalo wings, burgers and sausages. And of course, the corn is high, so we have our local seasonal delicacy.' He pointed to a vat full of water and sweetcorn, complete in its husks. 'Soaking means we don't burn.

'But oh my, what am I thinking, introducing the food before the people? Have you met June and Brian, my two fabulous stars for the musical? And here's Frank, Josh, Shelley, Dana, Nicholas, Dave, Dave and Dave, Sarah, Anne, Tony, Ed, Tot, Peter, Martha, Sylvester, Madonna – no, not *that* Madonna. And Nancy, Darius, Oleanna, Jose, Sol, Johnny, Helene, Janette and Brianna; then there's Cara, Stacey, Tipper, Madison, Megan, Taylor and Selina.'

'I'm not sure if I'll remember everyone's names straight off, but pleased to meet you all,' Marcus said.

'Hi!' The crowd chorused, holding up their glasses.

'As you were, everyone,' James said, steering them towards the porch. 'They're mostly musical cast. A few are in the Scottish Play but we've got a new lot coming up in a day or two for that. We like to mix it up.'

'Where's Betty?' Lara asked.

'Oh, she's inside with Trudi, fussing over the salads. Now then, Waylands,' James said, 'are you ready for your surprise? I can't contain myself any longer.' He opened the fly-screen door to the kitchen, which was mostly taken up by a table laden with bowls of salad and baskets of bread. Betty was over by the sink, slicing a watermelon. She wore a long lurex halter-neck that could have been worn by Bianca Jagger at Studio 54, but had covered it with a floral fifties pinny.

'Darlings.' She put her knife down, took off her apron and hugged and kissed each one of them, a rather stiffened Olly included. 'Is it time, then?' she asked James.

'It's time,' James said.

'Trudi, honey, we're going to need that champagne now,'

Betty said, and for the first time Lara noticed the woman over the other side of the table. Bulky and dark-haired, she had a scar across her face as if someone had sliced open her right cheek from the corner of her mouth to her ear. Trudi nodded a silent welcome to the Waylands, put down the cutlery she had been wrapping in a napkin, then went over to the walk-in fridge, from where she extracted a silver tray set with a bottle of Dom Perignon, tall, slim flutes and four cans of Diet Coke.

'Thank you, Trudi my darling,' Betty said, taking the tray from her. 'Could you just finish wrapping up the silverware, my sweet?'

'You don't want me in the parlour?' Trudi asked, her accent and timbre almost exactly the same as Betty's.

'We're fine, thank you, honey,' Betty said.

After a moment's hesitation Trudi nodded then returned to her task. She had strange eyes, Lara noticed. Like a lizard's.

'Right then, Waylands. Are you ready?' Betty said. 'Come this way, *mesdames et messieurs.*'

She led them across a cool, echoing hallway to a set of double doors which James, who was slightly ahead of them, flung open to reveal a huge living room. The blinds were drawn against the dusk, but, thanks to the light of a large fish tank running down almost the entire length of one wall, Lara could make out the figure of a man sitting, legs crossed, in a chair on the far side. Betty put the tray on a side table and James shut the doors behind them.

'Hello, Marcus. Hello, Lara.'

And at once, Lara's stomach turned and lifted itself somewhere into her throat. She didn't need the man to stand and unfold himself to his full height. She didn't need him to come forward into the pool of light spilling into the room from the hallway. She didn't need to see the still razor-sharp cheekbones, the deep-set eyes that seemed to look out from somewhere else, the dark hair that curled around them.

She knew him.

Bella gasped.

'Fuck me,' Olly said under his breath.

'Stephen Molloy!' Marcus yelled into the hiatus. 'What the devil are you doing here?'

'Shh, shh.' James fluttered around turning on a couple of lamps. 'We can't let them *all* know he's here.'

Lara breathed in and out slowly, trying to force her heart rate down. Her runner's trick. Time was bought for her by her husband, who now had his arms clapped around Stephen Molloy, holding him in a bear-hug, his face against his chest he was that short against him.

'Fuck me,' Olly said again. 'Is that really Stephen Molloy?'

'It is,' Lara said in a small voice.

'The one Dad knows?'

'What does it look like, moron?' Bella said, her eyes like saucers.

Stephen Molloy was still clasped in Marcus's embrace but he was looking at Lara. She forced her knees not to buckle. The room, which she had initially thought to be air-conditioned, seemed to have become unbearably hot.

'Lara.' Finally released from Marcus, Stephen went over to her and took her hand. 'It's been a long time.' His touch was like a homecoming to her.

'I know Stephen and Marcus go back a long way,' James said to Lara, putting his arm around her and enveloping her in a cloud of Halston for Men. 'But I think you met him back in the day too?'

'Yes, we knew each other,' she said, glad of the excuse to break eye contact with Stephen.

'It's been a hell of a long time, though, eh?' James went on. 'I mean, you've seen Stephen, obviously, we all have. But he hasn't had a sniff of Wayland for, what is it now?'

'It must be seventeen years,' Marcus said, reaching his hands up to Stephen's shoulders, examining his face.

'So you haven't met the children, then?' James said. 'Let me then acquaint you with the three lovely Wayland offspring: Bella, Olly and little Jack.'

'You must be the twins,' Stephen said, shaking hands first with Bella then an uncharacteristically silent and awestruck Olly. 'I think last time I saw your parents they had just got the happy news about you. I didn't know about this little chap, though,' he went on, bending and holding out a hand to Jack.

Unlike James, Stephen had hung on to his British accent: a thick Mancunian streak ran through his vowels. This surprised Lara. For the last few years she had only seen him doing American parts, and had somehow thought his celluloid voice an extension of his own. She wondered whether the rest of him had remained the same, too.

'Our happy accident,' Marcus said, ruffling Jack's hair, and Lara wished he would shut up. 'My God, man, it's great to see you. Small world.'

It was strange how pleased Marcus was to see Stephen. He had followed the other man's stellar career in a borderline obsessive way, joking off-handedly about how Stephen must be fucking the right sort of people, or that it was down to the luck of the Oirish. Lara had even overheard him roaring to his actor cronies, when they had gathered round to watch one of Stephen's early films on afternoon TV, that he had more talent in his little finger than Stephen Molloy had in his entire body.

Not true, Lara had thought from her Apple Mac in the corner of the room.

'I've got a place nearby,' Stephen said. 'A sort of bolt-hole. I know James and Betty from LA, and I give a bit of support to the theatre company.'

'A bit!' Betty said, wedging the champagne bottle between her thighs and popping the cork. 'It's somewhat more than a bit.'

'And when James told me you were going to be his Thane, well.'

'This is for you, Stephen.' James handed him one of the Coke cans. 'And I've got some for the kids – or are the twins OK with a drop of champers?'

'Of course they are,' Olly said.

'It's great to see you all,' Stephen said. He seemed genuinely happy – not a look he tended to wear in his work, where he was generally cast as the dark and brooding hero.

'To old friends!' Betty said, holding her glass high.

'Old friends,' the Waylands said, clinking glasses with Stephen's can.

'Such a coincidence,' Marcus said.

'Small world indeed,' Stephen agreed.

They all drank, then looked around at each other, lost for words. Bored, Jack wriggled away and went over to investigate the fish tank.

'Well then,' Stephen said, smiling and breaking the silence. There was something about him that seemed to draw everyone's breath. Perhaps it was fame, Lara thought. But she remembered him having this effect even before, in the Stratford days. Certainly on her.

'I'm afraid I have to go and prepare the kitchen for my guests,' Betty said. 'James, would you give me a hand?'

'But—'

'Honey.'

James sloped off after his partner. Again there was a silence in the room, set against the chatter and murmur of the people outside. Someone was strumming a guitar, and a woman sang an improvised melody around the chords. Stephen sipped his Diet Coke, looking at each one of them in turn, but his gaze kept returning to Lara. She noticed he was bouncing on his feet slightly, jiggling like a racehorse just before the off.

'Shall we go outside?' Marcus asked Stephen. Lara knew that, apart from anything else, he must be dying for a cigarette.

'I don't think so,' Stephen said, smiling. 'I like to keep a low profile.'

'What do you mean?' Lara said, looking up at him and realising she had to tilt her head at exactly the same angle she used to speak to Olly.

'It's just no one – other than James, Betty, Trudi and yourselves now – knows I'm here. I'm sort of tucked away.'

'Oh yeah,' Olly said, pointing a finger at Stephen. 'You had that breakdown and went into hiding.'

'Olly,' Bella hissed. 'Uncool.'

Stephen smiled and looked down. 'It was a bit like that. But I wouldn't believe everything you read in the papers.'

'You had that stalker,' Olly said, as if he had scored a goal. Stephen looked up and smiled straight at him.

'I did. Well remembered.'

'Olly, that's enough mate,' Marcus said.

'No, no. It's OK. It's better you know why I need my presence here to be secret. Not even my agent knows where I am. I was getting too much unwelcome – and quite alarming – attention back in LA, so I'm taking some time out, until things settle down. There *was* a stalker, yes, and it was very frightening. I needed a break, so James and Betty helped me out by suggesting that I come here.

'I appreciate it'll be hard to keep this quiet,' he went on. 'Especially for you guys,' he said to Bella and Olly. 'But I know your folks from way back and that kind of friendship is a rare thing for me these days. I had to come by here after the show and say hello. But I must ask you not to mention me to anyone. If you don't, I'm sure we can have a great time together this summer. I've got a really nice place out in the forest, a swimming pond, woods. It'll be fun. If you do let it out though, well, it could be rather awkward for me. I need to know you can keep my secret.'

Lara saw the challenge of this request register with her elder two children. She wished, for their sakes, she had been given the opportunity to decide whether they would be able to deal with the situation before they were plunged into it. There was no going back now, though; she hoped they were mature enough to cope.

'Sure, man,' Olly said at last, high-fiving Stephen. Bella nodded, still wide-eyed. She hadn't blinked once since Stephen had revealed himself.

'Well, that's great, then,' Stephen said. 'Look. I mustn't keep you guys – they'll be wondering where you've got to.' He nodded towards the garden. 'I only wanted to stop by and say hello – the champagne and that is down to James and Betty. They're such soft hearts. But please, come over for dinner on Monday night. It'd be good to have company. I'll email you directions.'

'That'll be great,' Marcus said. 'But you can just give Lara the address, and she'll Google it.' He had his tobacco out and was rolling a cigarette.

'You can't Google my place,' Stephen went on, draining his can. 'Like I said, it's under the radar.'

'Wow,' Bella said. 'I thought you could Google anywhere.'

'It takes a bit of organising, but it can be done,' Stephen said. 'Anyway, good to see you all again. Lara, do you want to give me your email address?'

'Sure,' Lara said. 'You lot go on ahead; I'll be out in a minute. You go out with Daddy, Jack.'

'I haven't finished looking at the fishies, though,' Jack said from over by the tank.

'You're all right with the little 'un?' Marcus said, cigarette to his lips.

Lara nodded.

Grateful to be signed off, Marcus led Bella and Olly outside. The double doors slammed shut behind them.

'Do you have a pen?' Lara said, looking up at him.

'Lovely family,' Stephen said.

'Thank you.'

'I haven't got any myself. Kids.'

'No. I sort of know that.'

'Yes. I'm pretty much public property.'

'But you must have had an amazing life.'

'It's been a ride. But in the end, it's just a job. Well paid and interesting. But still just a job. And it takes over every aspect of your life.'

'Yes,' she said, holding his gaze.

'I envy Marcus,' he said.

'You do?' The dim light in the room hid the hot blush that sprang to her cheeks.

'I'm lucky. I know that. I have a house here, a house in LA – lovely, up in the hills, you should see it. A brownstone in Manhattan and a house back home, near Manchester. But none of these places is home. The house back in the UK – I've owned it for thirteen years. Bought it with my first big pay cheque, with some sort of idea that I wouldn't lose touch with my roots.

I've spent probably thirty nights there in total. I still have stuff in boxes there, waiting to be unpacked. Two years ago I had some guys round to do some decorating – paint the hallway, that was it. They thought I had just moved in. And now I'm hiding on my own out here in the middle of nowhere. Why wouldn't I envy Marcus?'

Stephen stepped forward, took her hand and smiled. His fingers felt cool and dry in hers. She could tell without looking that they were as long and slender as they always had been.

'Shall I tell you something?' he said.

'Go on.' She tried to ignore how right his hand felt in hers.

He swallowed and fixed his eyes on hers. 'You are the big what-if of my life, Lara. Not a day goes by without me wondering what might have happened if we . . . had I not had to leave.'

Lara listened to his words with growing dismay. Because with them he was voicing the very thoughts she had fought over the years to push to the back of her mind.

'You shouldn't have left, then,' she said.

Jack came across the room and tugged her arm. 'There's a big ugly fish down at the bottom, Mummy, look.'

Thirteen

BELLA STOOD ON THE PORCH, REELING FROM HAVING BEEN so close to Stephen Molloy.

Through her father's work she had met a couple of sort-of famous actors. Two *EastEnders* regulars once came round for dinner – she had been too young to benefit from her dad's own appearance. And there was that guy from the oven cleaner adverts, and a stage actor she had never seen working, but whose name cropped up frequently in the *Guardian* arts pages, and who she heard on the radio from time to time.

But Stephen Molloy was in a different league. He was super-famous, one of Hollywood's most bankable stars. Despite his reputation for transforming himself with every role, people recognised him all over the globe; he had legions of adoring fans. And of course she, like everyone else, knew all about the stalker – the story had been well covered in *Heat, Grazia* and those *Daily Mail* showbiz web pages she found herself guiltily drawn to when she should have been doing her homework.

She knew also that her father had known him once; he had always referred to him as 'the one who made it', or 'that lucky cunt Molloy'. But she never, ever thought she'd get to meet him.

The worst part of it was, though, that she had to keep quiet about it. What was the point of meeting a movie star unless you could tell everyone?

Her father was on the other side of the lawn, smoking and chatting with some actors. She could hear his laughter above all the other voices. Olly had gone off in search of beer and, no doubt, a sneaky cigarette of his own. Standing up there alone, she drained her champagne, enjoying the way it made her head feel, as if the bubbles were whizzing around her brain. As she scanned the crowd for one particular face, she tried to remember what else she had read about Stephen Molloy. Wasn't there some sort of gossip that he was gay? He was often photographed with this or that actress on his arm, but he had never settled down and the word was it was because he preferred the men. Perhaps he did. Perhaps that was why he seemed to be so close with James and Betty.

Then she felt a touch on her shoulder. She wheeled round and Stephen Molloy was forgotten.

'Hi,' Sean said. 'I thought you'd never turn up.'

She glanced up at him and pushed a stray hair back behind her ear. Unable to meet his eyes, she looked down and smoothed out her dress, wondering if she had chosen the right thing to wear. Her short, floral cotton smock was about the only approaching-smart clothing she had that she could bear in all this heat. But it made her look too young. She glanced over at the other people on the lawn, lit now by what must be thousands of fairy lights strung from tree to tree. There were a multitude of styles on display. Some women wore vintage sundresses, others long, floaty numbers. A couple were in jeans with tunic tops. Whatever they wore, they all looked as if they knew what they were doing – the opposite of how Bella felt.

'Would you like another drink?' Sean said, putting his mouth close to her ear.

'OK.'

He steered her down the steps and into the throng.

'What's that smell?' Bella said, picking up a lemony scent that threaded through the crowd.

'Citronella. You can't be out here without it. Keeps the bugs off. Want some?' Sean handed her a small vial from his back pocket. 'Dab it on your pulse spots.' They stopped and he watched her as she placed dots of the oil behind her knees, inside her wrists, at the base of her throat. 'Now you're invincible. Come on, let's get those drinks.'

He led her over to the other side of the fire pit where there was a large, circular wooden table, on which stood two old zinc tubs full of ice, beers and bottles of white wine.

'I'll have a beer, please,' Bella said.

He picked out a bottle, twisted the top off and handed it to her.

They found a vacant patchwork quilt on the outskirts of the crowd. He sat next to her so their arms touched. She hugged her knees close and hoped that the citronella hid the slight sweaty tang she detected from her own body. She was desperate to tell him about Stephen Molloy – not least because it would give her something to talk about and she felt particularly tongue-tied – but she knew she couldn't.

'I've never been to England,' Sean said. 'What's it like?'

'Small. Crowded.'

'I've never been to any other countries except for Canada,' he went on. 'Where do you live? London?'

'Brighton,' Bella said. 'By the sea. Straight down from London.'

'Show me,' he said, reaching in his pocket. He got his iPhone out and moved even closer to her so she could see the screen.

'You've got reception?'

'Nah. Can't get it anywhere for miles around here. I've jumped on James and Betty's Wi-Fi.'

'There we are,' she said, pointing at their house on Satellite View, in among the stripes of terraced streets that radiated up from the sea towards the open expanse of the Downs. Stroking the screen, Sean zoomed in.

'You're right by the ocean,' he said. They were so close now, their cheeks practically touched. Bella could feel the sweep of his long eyelashes and there was this swooning sensation going on somewhere inside her, as if she were opening up and letting go at the same time. But she tried to keep talking as if this were the most normal thing in the world.

'If it's the same picture, you can see our washing strung up across our back garden.'

'Cute,' he said, putting his arm around her so he could get even closer to the screen. Bella glanced up. There were people right near them, but no one was looking.

'And that's our car, out in the street there.' Bella broke away and took a deep swig of beer. Home, and all it meant to her, seemed so far away. Even more so when it was relegated to tiny satellite pictures on a screen. The thought made her feel utterly liberated. If it weren't for Olly . . .

Sean sat back too, so they were once again close to one another. Bella caught the scent of him as he moved, a mixture of soap, swimming pool and something else, a little like fresh sweat, but not at all off-putting.

'Shall I show you round?' he said. 'James and Betty's place is pretty cool.'

He jumped to his feet and offered his hand to help her up, but he held on as he led her down the lawn, past a grid of eight small vegetable and flower patches. Dancing Chinese lanterns on poles marked a path between the beds. The aniseed smell of basil filled the air as they brushed past the plants, only to be overtaken by the heady fragrance of a bed of pink and red roses. The voices of the party diminished in a slow cross-fade with the love songs of the crickets in the meadow beyond.

The lanterns dipped down towards, then encircled, a wide pond, which seemed to boil and shiver in the early evening light. At the far side stood an enclosed seat, made of half a wooden rowing boat stuck erect into the ground. Bella looked at the ridge beyond the end of the garden. It was outlined by a faint orange glow, the sun's last gesture of the day. The moon was already up behind the house, and the three light sources – sunset, moon and lantern – lifted the shapes around them, making them appear more than real in a way that reminded Bella of the Salvador Dali poster she had Blu-Tacked to her bedroom wall back home.

'Beautiful light,' she said.

'Beautiful.' Sean stopped and looked at her.

Then Bella started as a sudden strange sound erupted from the pond, like a ghost jumping up and down on abandoned floorboards. It grew and grew, joined by other, similar sounds, until the crickets could no longer be heard. It sounded like the old barn was falling down.

'Oh my God. What's that?' she said, turning to him, her hands on her ears.

'It's just bullfrogs,' Sean laughed. 'Come and see.'

They tiptoed down to the edge of the pond.

'Look,' he whispered, squatting and pointing.

Bella craned forward and, as her eyes grew accustomed to the greys, greens and browns of the water, she picked out first one frog, then another and another. Some sat on lily pads and rocks, some were just heads, ballooning out of the water.

'A frog chorus,' she said.

Their eyes met and this time Bella held his gaze. Her insides, which had been on the very verge for the last half-hour, finally turned right over. She couldn't breathe. In the strange light, his irises were the colour of forget-me-nots, with dark flecks that seemed to draw her further in until she felt hypnotised, like a rabbit in a trap. He moved closer and she closed her eyes . . .

'Hey, Sean, buddy! Don't do anything I wouldn't do!'

They jolted apart and looked over to the other side of the pond, to the boat-seat, where the voice had come from. The glow of a cigarette being lit revealed an Italian-looking man. Bella guessed he was quite old, over thirty at any rate. She recognised him from the play.

'Hey, Tony, you asshole. What you doing? Spying on me?' Sean said. The way he spoke, he sounded like a different person.

'It's all cool, man.' Tony stretched his legs so they protruded from the shelter of the seat. 'You kids just do what you gotta do. Don't mind me.' He folded his arms and continued to sit there, smoking and chuckling to himself. A smell of weed wafted over towards them.

'Asshole,' Sean muttered under his breath. 'Come on, Bella.' Taking her hand, he led her up the dip, away from the pond.

'You takin' her off to the corn, boy?' Tony called. 'For a roll in the husks?' A guffaw of marijuana-fuelled laughter chased them up the slope.

'Who was that?' Bella asked when they were out of earshot.

'Tony Marconi,' Sean said. 'Prick.'

'Was he on *The Sopranos*?'

'Yeah. Prick.'

'Steady,' Bella said, smiling at him.

'Sorry. But he thinks I'm a joke just because I'm from 'round here and not come up from the city.'

'That's not very nice.'

'No.'

'I don't think you're a joke,' she said.

They had reached the open doorway of the listing barn. The darkness of the interior was criss-crossed with beams of moonlight that filtered through the wide gaps in the wooden walls, catching the edges of piles of ancient agricultural machinery that had long ago been put to bed. It looked artificial, reminding Bella of the set of one of Marcus's plays that she had been dragged to see. *The Cherry Orchard*, that was it. A faint but distinct animal smell rose from the ancient remnants of straw in the rickety stalls on one side of the building. A sharp gust of wind would probably be enough to bring the whole lot down.

'Come on,' Sean said, stepping in.

'Is it safe?' Bella asked, remembering what her mother had said.

'Sure. I've been here a load of times.'

Putting all of her better instincts aside, Bella had no choice but to follow him, to step on to this hazardous stage. Sean drew her in, out of the doorway, took her in his arms and bent towards her. At last they kissed.

Bella felt the world swirl as she closed her eyes. The excitement that had burned inside her since meeting Sean earlier that day finally radiated outwards, so she didn't know where she ended and he began.

His arms were around her, working their way up and inside the back of her short dress; his flesh was on her. She just wanted to be picked up and carried away wherever he took her. She felt him hard against her as their bodies pressed together.

'Bella, what the fuck?'

They jumped apart, as if the current that held them together had suddenly been reversed.

Olly stood swaying in the doorway, his mouth working silently. He looked as if he were on the verge of exploding.

'Mum sent me to get you because the food's ready and I find you in here. What the fuck are you doing?' He glared at Sean.

'It's cool, man,' Sean said, holding up his hands.

'No it isn't "cool", "man".' Olly strode up to Sean and put his face right up against him. He had a strange look in his eyes, as if he were slightly possessed. Bella had seen it before, and she didn't like it.

'Olly, this is Sean,' she said, 'he's—'

'Someone you know pretty well already, by the look of it,' Olly said. 'Get out of here, Bella.'

'You're not my keeper.'

'Mum said we're not to go in here.'

'Like you listen to what she says.'

'Jonny's going to know about this.' Olly said, lunging forward to grab her arm, the sinews in his neck standing out as he reached.

'Fuck off.' Bella slapped him away. 'And it's not Jonny that gives a shit, anyway, is it, Olly?'

Olly leaped again for his sister.

'Leave her,' Sean said, positioning himself between them.

'Listen, mate, you can stay right out of it.' Olly shoved him aside with both hands.

'Stop it, Olly!' Bella said, running to Sean, who had fallen on to the dirt floor.

'Bella! Olly!' Marcus boomed from somewhere out in the party. 'Grub's up!'

Bella turned to Olly. 'He'll go crazy if he finds us in here.'

'Get out, then,' Olly said. He pulled her away from Sean, who had picked himself up and was brushing straw and dust from his clothes. Though younger and not so strongly built, Olly was taller than Sean. That, and the force of his jealous outrage, gave him the upper hand. He jabbed the older boy in the chest. 'And hey, you, "man". If I catch you creeping on my sister again you're going to regret it.'

'Olly! Bella!' Marcus thundered again.

'Yeah?' Sean said.

'Oh, yes,' Olly said. Then, with one final prod at Sean, he went to stand in the barn doorway, his jaw still twitching. 'Bella?'

Bella hesitated. She didn't want to follow her brother, but she had little choice.

Because they had once been so close – too close – Olly believed he owned her, and she didn't know how she was ever going to get away from him. He refused to see what they did back then as wrong, beyond any boundaries – if Olly *had* any boundaries, which she doubted. He couldn't realise that, if they were to survive, he had to let her go. Two years she had put up with him using Jonny as a human shield on her and she had had enough.

And although she could put up a fight, there was something about him when he was like this that really frightened her. His force of will was so strong it seemed he would stop at nothing to get his way.

'Go on, Bella,' he had said to her when they were younger. 'Just this once.' She hadn't stood a chance. It hadn't been just the once, either.

And just right now he was clearly off his face, too, which didn't help.

She wanted to stay with Sean, but she had to get out of the barn and go to her father who was calling for her. More than anything, she was scared; she had to separate Olly and the boy she had just kissed and quite possibly fallen in love with.

Her decision made, she followed her brother. As she joined Olly on the threshold of the barn, she turned back and Sean smiled at her.

'See you again,' he said, and she sighed with relief. He was a fighter.

'Not if I catch you first, mate,' Olly said, pointing at him and pulling Bella away.

'You're being a total twat, Olly.' She tried to shrug him off as they crossed the lawn.

'I'm going to tell Dad,' Olly said.

'No you're not. I've got a lot more I can say about you if you do. I'll start with the fact that you were smoking weed and drinking beer when you should have been helping me look after Jack. And then I'll go on.'

'Fuck you,' Olly said.

'For God's sake,' Bella said, and stamped off, away from her brother to answer yet another one of her father's calls.

Fourteen

THE FISH HAD BUSIED THEMSELVES IN THEIR SPARKLING tank, oblivious to whatever was going on between the two adults watching them, while the child prattled on, telling his mother the name of each and every one of them.

'I promised Betty I'd be out of here before the food gets served up,' Stephen had said, breaking away to scribble something on a small yellow card pulled from his breast pocket. 'Here's my email address. Send me yours.' He handed the card to Lara, then he bent towards her.

It had been a brief kiss, but it was on her lips.

And as Lara stood in the kitchen snipping herbs, having been roped by Betty into helping with the finishing touches to the meal, she could still feel it. It made it very hard for her to concentrate on what Betty was saying.

'When we bought it, it was in as much of a state as the barn.' She was, Lara supposed, talking about the farmhouse. 'But in a *very* distant past life I was a carpenter, so I know my way round a piece of wood.' She was whacking half a pomegranate with a wooden spoon, making the seeds pop out and pink juice spatter all over a green platter of couscous salad. 'We've got a place in the city, down in the East Village, although we never go there in the summer. It stinks in August. But the winters up here are harsh. The snow reaches right over the porch. Sometimes it's just good to feel the warmth of other people, the kindness of strangers. Just to be able to walk round the block to a nice bar, see a show.'

'So you close the theatre in the winter?'

'Oh yes. No one goes out round here in the dark months, unless they positively have to. They just stay in and get cabin fever. There's a lot of indoors drinking, and very little else.'

'It's hard to think about it being like that here. I can't imagine it being anything other than sweltering.'

'Believe me, sister: it can freeze your balls off. Ain't that right, Trudi?'

Trudi nodded from the sink, where she was working through a pile of washing-up.

'Are you from round here?' Lara asked Trudi. The servant status Betty conferred on the woman made her feel awkward.

'She has an apartment down in the village,' Betty said. 'Without Trudi, this whole theatre would grind to a standstill. She practically runs this place for James and me. And,' Betty's voice dropped to a whisper, 'we lend her to Mr Molloy.'

'Though he don't want me doing stuff 'round the house.' Trudi turned to smile at Lara, her stolid face suddenly animated. 'He likes doing all that hisself. He just wants me to run errands for him.' She pushed a greasy strand of dark hair behind her ear with a hand adorned with nails so badly bitten they made Lara wince to look at them.

'Betty, will you ever get out here and join us?' James said, striding into the kitchen. 'The grill is done and all we're waiting for is you.'

Betty stopped her whacking and looked sideways at him.

'You men,' she said. 'All you want to do is put food in your bellies. But what you don't understand is that it has to be a feast for the *eyes* as much as the *mouth*. We'll all be out in just one minute.'

'Well can I at least have Trudi? I need a hand with the meat.'

Trudi looked over to Betty, who nodded her assent. Wiping her hands on a tea towel, she bustled off after James.

'What an extraordinary person,' Lara said.

'Trudi Staines. She's had a life,' Betty said. 'Would you believe she used to be a burlesque dancer?'

Lara couldn't believe it. Weren't burlesque dancers glamorous? Trudi was the opposite of all that.

'Fell on hard times, poor lamb,' Betty said, rinsing her hands and going over to open the refrigerator door. 'Trouble with the law and all. There but for the grace of God . . .' She reached in and rummaged. 'Oh my, a half-full bottle of champagne.' She winked at Lara. 'Would you like a glass to pep you up?'

'Am I so obviously in need?' Lara brushed the last pieces of oregano from her hands then lifted her fingers to her face to take in the smell.

'Oh honey,' Betty said, handing her a brimming glass. 'Seeing him again has quite unmanned you, hasn't it?'

Lara looked sharply up at her.

'Let's just say, my darling,' Betty went on, catching her eye, 'I know that he was very much looking forward to meeting you again, after all this time.'

'Was he?' Lara said.

'Oh yes,' Betty said, tipping her glass back. 'Stephen and I are very close. He's like a son to me. But don't you worry. I haven't breathed a word. Even James doesn't know. I, of all people, appreciate discretion. Gossip is so destructive, don't

you think? The only important thing in this life, honey, is love.'
She reached over and laid a hand on Lara's shoulder.

The champagne felt sour in Lara's throat as she swallowed.

'Now then.' Betty clapped her hands. 'Where's that little
boy of yours?'

'He's still in there with the fish. He's fascinated.'

'Well, why don't you go in and get him, and then we can all
go out and join the others.'

Lara did as she was told, feeling overwhelmed by Betty's
authoritative, maternal manner. She had never been on the
receiving end of anything like it before. Certainly not from the
gin-soaked vessel of disappointment that was her real mother.

The food was duly served up and Lara managed one scallop.
Her appetite seemed to have deserted her.

More used to spending her evenings at home with her
children, she didn't much like parties. Particularly parties full
of strangers. And in any case, she was too distracted to push
herself out there and make conversation. She knew she should,
to propagate the Wayland image, the myth of the jolly, perfect
English family – if only because by doing so she would perhaps
be more able to believe in it herself.

But she couldn't do it. Seeing Stephen felt like having a stick
thrust in her bicycle wheel. The years that had passed, the lives
they had lived apart from each other were like two divergent
paths that she had thought would never meet again. And now
here they were, not so far apart after all.

Luckily Jack, who was asleep in her lap, had her pinned to
the porch rocker so she had an excellent excuse for not joining
in. Instead she sat there, keeping an eye out for her family. As
all too often seemed to be the case recently, Bella and Olly had
clearly had some sort of spat. While Bella mooned about in a

hammock, her brother worked the crowd in the same way that Marcus might, striking up conversations with the younger actors, clapping one or two on the back then moving on to the next group. Even by his own standards, he was exceptionally animated. She saw him go over to two boys with a guitar and in no time he was playing the thing himself while the others looked on and nodded with approval. But from time to time, he would pass by Bella, lean over and have a couple of words in her ear. From the look on her face, she didn't like what he was saying.

Lara looked out for that lovely boy Sean and found him hemmed into conversation with James. She noticed that every now and then he glanced over at her daughter and on one occasion Bella's eyes caught his. She hoped Olly wasn't getting in the way with his stupid loyalty to that weak yes-man Jonny. But if he was, it upset Lara that Bella was being so compliant. She did wish her daughter wasn't so passive, that she'd show a bit more gumption.

Passivity in a girl was the path to disaster, and if anyone knew that, she, Lara Wayland, should.

Fifteen

'DO YOU THINK YOU SHOULD DRIVE?' LARA SAID, AS Marcus lurched across the front lawn, slurring farewells to his new friends.

'I'm fine,' he said.

Lara wasn't so sure, but as she could hardly walk straight herself, he was their only option.

The party was still going full tilt. Supervised by Betty, a couple of the younger actors had set up some speakers on the porch, and people were dancing to the Rolling Stones, their long shadows twisting and twirling in the moonlight. But the Waylands, still on British Summer Time, had begun to droop, and now they straggled towards their car, leaving the others strutting and whooping along like a lawnful of Mick Jaggers.

They turned into the lane where the cars were parked, and the bushes masked the throb of sound from the party, plunging them alone into the insect-clattering night.

'Look,' Bella said, pointing up. The sky was navy velvet, the stars stuck up there like sequins, stabbing the darkness with their glitter.

'Look!' Olly said, and a collective Wayland breath was held as they watched a light move from one side of the sky to the other.

'A meteor,' Lara said.

'I think you'll find it's a shooting star,' Olly said.

'Aren't they the same thing?'

'Oh no, they're very different,' he said, 'I think you'll find.'

'You're so full of shit,' Bella said. 'They're the same.'

'They're not.'

'Fucksake,' Bella sighed.

'Can we unlock the car, please?' Lara said. She was carrying Jack, who was still fast asleep, and her arms were beginning to hurt.

'One second,' Marcus said. 'Just stop and breathe in, everyone. Did you ever have anything cleaner in your lungs? Aren't you glad I brought you all here?' He put an arm round Lara's shoulders. 'Isn't this perfect?'

But Lara only felt as if she was half there.

'Come on then,' Marcus said at last, twirling the car keys round his finger. 'Let's get back to the dust palace.'

He fired up the engine and opened all the windows. 'Might be some interesting wildlife at this hour,' he said. Then, after driving a slow couple of hundred yards along the lane, he switched off the headlights.

'Marcus, switch them back on!' Lara said.

'Why? It's not as if there's any traffic,' he laughed. 'I've always wanted to do this.'

'But we'll end up in a ditch,' Lara said.

'Stop it, Dad,' Bella said.

'Go for it, Daddy-o!' Olly took off his seat belt and stuck his head out of the open window.

'Olly, get back inside. This is really dangerous, Marcus.'

'Don't be such a bore, Lara,' he said. 'Live a little.' Then he, too, poked his head out of the window and whooped.

Lara gripped the sides of her seat. The darkness closed over them like water. They might have been heading over the brink of a cliff, for all they could see. The car engine was so expensively silent that the only sound was the tyres as they rolled over stones and gravel in the lane, and the reflected blue glow of the dashboard turned Marcus's gleeful face into a rictus mask.

A movement somewhere in front of them, out in the lane, drew all their eyes towards it. Two beady dots, at about the height of a man, glittered starlight at them.

'WHAT THE FUCK IS THAT?' Olly yelled.

Startled, Marcus flicked the headlights on and they saw the rear ends of a doe and her fawn scurry into the hedgerow.

'It's only a deer, Olly,' Marcus said with exaggerated calm, although he had clearly been rattled.

'And look – we could have hit that,' Lara said, pointing at a car parked about twenty yards in front of them. If they had continued in the dark, they would have met it head-on.

'Shit,' Marcus whistled.

'Why do you never listen to a word I say?' Lara said.

'Because I'm a bad, bad boy, Lara. That's why.'

The car didn't appear to be attached to any house – there weren't any on this stretch of the lane, and it was too far away from James and Betty's place to have anything to do with the party. As they rolled past, they saw the driver's window was down.

'My God, there's someone in there,' Lara said. She couldn't make out the features, but it looked like it was a woman, and she appeared to be watching them through dark glasses. 'Sorry about that,' Lara said, leaning slightly out of the window. 'My husband was being an idiot.'

The woman didn't stir.

'She didn't hear you, Mum,' Bella said.

'Creepy.' Olly shuddered.

'Let's get out of here.' Marcus put his foot down and drove as fast as the rocky lane would allow him, towards the main road.

'What the fuck was that all about?' Olly said.

'Perhaps she'd had an argument with her husband,' Lara said.

'Perhaps she was a witch doing spells.'

'Do you think she's OK?' Bella said, looking back.

'Do you want to go back and check?' Olly said.

Marcus swung the big car into the tarmac drive and round to the back of their temporary home.

'Oh my God,' Bella said as they opened the car doors. A rush of stifling night air swamped them, carrying with it the pungent rubbery musk that seemed to lurk in every crevice of this place. Only this time, the stink was intense.

'You can almost see that smell,' Olly said.

'It seems to be coming from over there.' Bella pointed back to the road.

Marcus stepped cautiously along the driveway to investigate.

'Oh no,' he said.

'What?' Bella said, her hands to her face.

'Come and see.'

Leaving Jack asleep in the car, Lara joined the twins and, like soldiers on a manoeuvre, they crept towards the road.

'Yuck,' Bella said, holding her nose.

'What's black and white and red all over?' Olly said as they bent over to examine the mangled corpse of a roadkill skunk.

'So that's what that smell all over the place is,' Lara said. 'That's going to stink for days. Can't we get rid of it now?'

'And put it where?' Marcus said.

'And then Dad would stink too,' Bella said.

'Who said it was going to be me moving it?'

'Perhaps the neighbours will know what to do,' Lara said.

'It's too late now. Let's leave it till the morning, then we'll ask around if it's still there,' Marcus said.

'That's all right for you to say,' Olly said, 'Mr "my bedroom looks over the back". What about me and Bella? If we open our windows, we're going to suffocate. And we'll suffocate if our windows are closed, too, won't we, Bells?'

Bella grunted and looked away, ignoring her brother.

'Put the fans on,' Lara said. In each room there was a noisy pedestal fan, possibly the only new items in the house.

'All night?' Bella said.

'No, just till we go to sleep, then we can turn them off,' Olly said.

'Twat.'

Just then, Jack, who was out of sight in the car, screamed.

Lara pelted towards him. The car door was open, which was odd. She was certain she had shut it.

'What is it, Jacky?' she said, running round to undo his straps. She picked him up and he buried his head into her shoulder.

'There was a nasty lady,' he said, muffled by her sleeve.

'What nasty lady?'

'A nasty lady,' he wailed, lifting his head so that his mother could hear every syllable. She looked around.

'Look, Jack, there's no one here. It's all quiet. There's no nasty lady. You must've been dreaming.'

'Poor wee Jacko,' Marcus said, coming up and stroking his head. 'Did you have a nasty dream? Let's get inside, eh?'

Olly went in first. As he switched on the fluorescent kitchen light, something scurried from the table to the floor, rebounded against the counter and ran for cover back under the table. Bella yelped.

'What the hell was that?' Marcus said.

'Who left those cereals out?' Lara said. The Reese's Puffs had been overturned and whatever it was that had scuttled away had spread peanut-butter-flavoured corn puffs all over the kitchen.

'Look, it's a squirrel,' Bella said, peering under the table.

'That ain't no squirrel,' Olly said, joining her.

'It's not a rat, is it?' Marcus said, staying well away. Since coming face to face with one in a stream when a child, he had always had a thing about rats.

'Look, you take Jack up and shut the hall door on the way,' Lara said to Marcus. 'We'll sort this out.' She handed the whimpering little boy over to his father.

'Will we now?' Olly said. But she could see the trace of a triumphant smile on his face. He was going to be brave while Marcus chickened out.

'I want Cyril Bear,' Jack said, pointing out towards the car.

'Mummy'll bring him up in a bit, won't you, Mummy?' Marcus said, clearly desperate to get upstairs.

'I promise,' Lara said to Jack, kissing his hair. 'Night night.'

The three bolder Waylands got down on their knees and cornered the little beast to examine it. Then Lara burst out laughing.

'What is it, Mum? What?' Bella said.

'If my cartoon watching doesn't let me down, our "rat" is a chipmunk. Look!'

The small creature levelled its shining eyes at them one by one, as they leaned in under the kitchen table. It was still chewing the last remnants of its breakfast cereal feast, moving its swollen cheeks around like tiny balloons under its tawny fur. The three stripes down its back bristled as it made itself look as big as possible, its long, skinny striped tail bushing up in feeble imitation of a squirrel.

'Hey, Alvin,' Olly said.

'Deer, skunk, chipmunk. It's like we've wandered on to the set of *Bambi*,' Lara said. 'Be careful, I don't know if they bite.'

'He can't be all that dangerous. He's tiny,' Bella said.

'But remember Dad, the stream and the rat,' Olly sniggered. 'It could damage us psychologically for life.'

'OK, we'll lure him out with Reese's Puffs,' Lara said. 'You two stay down there, and make sure he doesn't disappear under the cooker.' She got up and laid a trail of cereal to the back door, hooking open the fly screen so he had a clear run. But the chipmunk stayed put, guarding its ground against Bella and Olly.

'I think he's had enough to eat,' Bella said, kneeling back and looking up at Lara.

'Watch out, stupid,' Olly yelled, as the little creature, seeing its opportunity, broke away from its spot under the table and made a break for the cooker. Olly dived across the floor like a goalie and managed to get there first, lying right across the gap between the base of the appliance and the floor, barring its way.

'Eurgh,' he shuddered as the chipmunk barrelled into him then ricocheted away to be shooed by Lara and Bella over the worn lino to the back door, skittering across the round cereal pieces and scattering them like ball-bearings as it went.

'Shoo,' Lara said, slamming the door behind it.

She turned to see her two eldest children looking at her, their eyes shining in triumph.

'Man, that floor's a mess,' Olly said, brushing crushed cereal from his sleeves.

Indeed, the room looked as if someone had whirled around it like a cereal-flinging dervish.

'We should clear it up now,' Lara said. 'Or we'll end up with a menagerie of critters in here.'

'What I don't understand,' Bella said, as she set to work with the dustpan and brush that Lara handed her, 'is how that cereal got out of the cupboard. I'm sure we left nothing out when we cleared up lunch.'

'I know. I was unusually impressed,' Lara said. 'Perhaps Marcus got it out.' It wasn't unlikely. Marcus was famous for reaching things out of cupboards to snack on, then not putting them away.

'And what I don't get, right,' Olly said, 'is how that little chipmunk guy got in here. I mean, he opened the door, climbed up to the cupboard and got the cereal out?'

'There must be some sort of hole somewhere,' Lara said. 'Perhaps under the house. Have you noticed how it seems to be standing up on a sort of stone wall? We'll take a look tomorrow. Right. That's the floor done. Bedtime now.'

'Thank Christ for that,' Olly said, and disappeared upstairs immediately.

Bella hugged herself. 'I don't want to sleep in this house tonight.'

Lara knew what she meant. But she was so exhausted by the roller-coaster evening that she felt if she didn't get to bed soon, she might pass out. To reassure Bella, she led her through the house as she wedged chairs up against the outside doors.

'I'll get the keys off James tomorrow, or get some bolts fitted,' she said, as she tucked Bella into her bed. 'And we're going to scour the place from top to bottom, clean out all the gloomy bits. Are you up for helping?'

'You bet,' Bella said. She looked very tiny lying there, as if she were six again. Lara switched on the fan, and the air in the room started to move.

'Is everything OK, Bell?' Lara asked. 'Between you and Olly?'

'He's just being a bit of a twat, that's all,' Bella sighed.

'What about that boy? Did you see him tonight?'

'What boy?' Bella said quickly, and Lara remembered she wasn't supposed to know about Sean yet.

'Sorry. I'm a bit confused. A few too many bevvies.'

'There's no boy,' Bella said, turning her back to her mother, dismissing her.

'I'll leave all the bedroom doors open and the hall light on. It'll be like we're in the same room.'

Lara tiptoed across the landing to Olly's room to see if he was all right, but he was already fast asleep, lying on his back, his big feet sticking out of the bottom of his bed-sheet and his young man's chest naked to the night. His fan was on, and she could see little goosebumps where the cool air caught him. How different in every way he and Bella were, and how proud she was of both of them. They amounted to two-thirds of the best job she had done in her life.

She was just crossing the landing to her own room when she remembered her promise to Jack. Cursing, she went downstairs, unwedged the back door and crossed the yard to the car. After ten minutes of searching, she had to concede defeat. Cyril Bear was not there. Jack must have left him at the party.

On her way back through the kitchen, she caught sight of the blue vase of roses. She bent over them and breathed in deeply to catch their scent, which seemed stronger in the still of the hot night. Then she looked again. Weren't there more flowers here than before – many more? She shook her head, trying to focus. She had encountered so much oddness since arriving in Trout Island.

No. Her wine mind must be playing tricks on her.

Tiredness pulled at her eyes. She went upstairs to the bedroom, where Marcus was already snoring, and Jack was curled up on the little nest she had made for him on a mattress on the floor. Although he was asleep, he was clearly too hot, so she got rid of two of the three blankets Marcus had laid over him, thinking about how she'd have to deal with the fallout over the missing bear in the morning. Then she threw off her clothes and slipped, wearing only her underwear, into the bed beside her husband.

She lay down and tried to sleep, but now the scenes of the evening intruded, playing underneath her eyelids, peeling away like the skins of an onion. First, all the animals, then that woman in the car. And finally she was down to the kernel, the thought that coloured everything else.

Stephen Molloy, looking into her eyes and telling her she was the biggest *what-if* of his life.

And then that kiss.

What on earth was she going to do about that?

Sixteen

BELLA'S NIGHT WAS PUNCTUATED BY DREAMS OF GIANT chipmunks lurking in dark corners while she and Sean tried to find an unoccupied attic for some kissing. Just before she woke, the woman in the parked car leered close to her, opened her mouth, and let out a series of pulsing, halitosed roars right into her face.

She would have sprung from her bed had her sheets, tangled after her disturbed night, not knotted her to it. The sound that had woken her was in fact her fan as it rotated on its white plastic foot, wheezing after its nightlong exertions.

She rubbed her face, grinding sweaty dust into her skin. She was glad they were going to clean this horrible house today. It helped her deal with the gloominess she felt about what had happened the night before with Sean and Olly.

Slipping her feet into her flip-flops, she stumbled across the floor and heaved up the window, letting the grassy morning air thread into the stale bedroom. It also brought with it a lingering touch of skunk, but it appeared that someone or something – a bear, or a wolf perhaps – had removed the corpse in the night, leaving nothing but a bloody smudge on the tarmac.

Looking out on the empty street, Bella wondered how somewhere so dead could produce a boy like Sean. But something was going on outside. A sign of life. Someone was running towards the house. She pressed her nose against the fly screen.

It was only her mother though, in cycle shorts and a too-tight vest, sweating her way along the pavement. She appeared to be having a conversation with herself, or possibly she was talking to the rather incongruous big black dog that loped along beside her. Bella tried to push away her embarrassment at witnessing those jiggling maternal breasts and thighs, that red face plastered with sticky hair. She was glad no one else was around to see it all. Unless, of course, the whole street was full of people who were, like her, imprinting their faces with fly-screen mesh.

Pulling on her dressing gown, she went downstairs. Everyone else was still asleep, even Jack, thank goodness. As the only other early riser, she knew she would be lumbered with him in the mornings if her mother wanted to go out for dawn jogs.

'Hiya.' Her mother burst in through the back door, all panting and sweat.

'You've been for a run.'

'Good work, Sherlock.' She bent forward with one leg extended, stretching out her hamstrings.

'What's with the dog?'

'Oh, he's my new chum. Looks out for me on my run. Fancy a cuppa?'

'I'll do it,' Bella said, reaching for a saucepan. 'Where did you go?'

'End of the village and round the school playing fields down by the river.' Lara was now bent forward straight-legged, with her face against her knees. 'Oh,' she said, straightening up, her face even redder than before, 'did you know there's a swimming pool down there?'

'No!' Bella said, suddenly interested. She loved swimming, and it was so hot here.

'And it seems it's free to use, and open all day,' Lara went on. 'A nice young man working down there told me. Name of Sean.'

'Oh.' Bella looked at her mum. So she did know. She had thought as much last night.

'He was getting it ready for the day, but it opens at eight, if you'd like a quick – and I mean quick, because I need your help – morning swim before we get stuck in here.'

'I might do that,' Bella said. She didn't know whether to be pleased that there was a pool and that Sean was down there, or annoyed that her mother not only knew what was going on, but had also gone up and talked to him when the few clothes she was wearing were striped with sweat.

'But have a cup of tea and something to eat first,' Lara said. 'Keep me company.'

By half past seven, Bella was tripping along the bumpy pavement to the school, her bikini on under her shorts and T-shirt, her towel in the maroon duffel bag she wore slung over her shoulder. She went to the playground and looked over the ridge on which it stood. A dirt path led down to the baseball and football pitches below. She supposed that was where her mother had meant the swimming pool was, so she set off down the slope. As she turned a bend she got a whiff of chlorine – a smell that always filled her with both the anticipation of diving into the blue and a desire for the vending machine hot chocolate Lara always bought her after their regular trips to the Prince Regent baths in Brighton.

At the bottom of the dip, across an empty car park and surrounded by a seven-foot-high chain-link fence was a perfect blue rectangle of a pool. To one side stood a small brick building with three doors in it, on the other a sandpit, a couple of picnic benches and some white plastic chairs.

The place appeared to be empty. The only sound Bella could hear above the crickets rubbing their legs in the morning sunshine was the pool pump whirring and reverberating around the edges of the hollow.

She traced along the fence and found a gate, but it was padlocked. A sign at the side said that opening hours were '8 a.m. until 6 p.m., seven days a week, May thru August, except thunderstorms'. Underneath this followed a long list of forbidden activities, which included diving, consuming alcohol, running, rough play or horseplay, eating or drinking in the pool area or bringing in glass or plastic that could shatter. The sign went on to tell visitors not to swim alone, not to swim if they had had diarrhoea in the past two weeks or if there were thunderstorms, and always to have a cleansing shower before bathing. Bella wondered if she would be let in, as she was clearly on her own.

The water, so close and yet so out of reach, was driving her crazy. Even at this hour, the heat had already built to something incredible. The sky was so blue it almost made a noise, and she could feel the sweat trickling down the backs of her legs.

'Hello!' she called through the fence. 'Hello?'

A door in the outhouse opened and her heart leaped as Sean's smiling blue eyes met hers. He wore baggy swimming trunks and nothing else. She couldn't help noticing how his tanned chest was smooth and firm.

'You came,' he said.

'Yes.' She beamed at him through the fence.

'And no brothers?'

'Still asleep. Olly doesn't ever wake up till eleven in the holidays.'

'Come on in,' he said, unlocking the big old padlock that kept the gate shut. 'It's usually pretty quiet first thing. Then all the moms come down with the little kids around nine.'

'This is great,' Bella said, her eyes on the water. She couldn't think of anything else to say. 'And it's completely free?'

'All the villages around here have a pool and we high-school students man them during the summer.'

'What's this?' She motioned to the brick building.

'That's where you get changed. We don't allow poolside changing.'

'So many rules.'

'Ah, we're pretty relaxed really, believe me. We just have the signs up so no one can sue us.'

'Which one do I use?' Bella asked.

'Excuse me?'

'Which changing room?'

'Well, that's the women's, but why don't you use the lifeguard hut as you're a special friend. It's more spacious and private. Bobby, the other guard, isn't coming in till later today because he has an orthodontics appointment.'

'Do you think I should?' Bella asked.

'Course you should. Go on in,' he said, opening the middle door for her. 'I've got to skim the water now.'

As Bella's eyes adjusted to the relative darkness inside the hut, she picked out a desk and chair and a load of life-saving equipment hanging on the wall. To one side was a shower stall, and to the other a row of pegs, on which hung a rucksack and some clothes, presumably Sean's.

Bella went up to the jeans dangling from one of the pegs and buried her face into them. She could smell him, and the tang of bonfire from the night before. She closed her eyes, and let the tingle in her body reach through to her fingers.

She peeled off her sawn-off shorts and T-shirt, and adjusted her bikini. Taking her towel out first, she bundled her clothes into her duffel bag, hanging it up next to Sean's things. It felt like staking her claim on him.

'First take a cleansing shower,' she recited the rule she had seen on the notice outside the gate, and, reaching into the shower stall, she turned on the tap. At first the water gushed out icy cold, making her gasp as it hit her arm, but soon it heated up and she stepped inside, letting it spray over her and wash away the sweat from her short journey through the village.

The tap still running, she wiped her eyes and opened them to see Sean standing there, watching her. She smiled at him and nodded. He stepped into the shower and took her to him, wrapping his arms around her body and pressing himself against her.

'Now, where had we got to last night?' he said, then bent to kiss her. Bella gasped as his hand reached up and under her bikini top.

'Is this OK?' he said.

'Go on,' she said and pulled him closer to her; his erection burned into her belly. The shower water dissolved them together as her hands reached under his swimming shorts, hooking them down so he sprang free against her. Helped by him, she wriggled out of her bikini bottom.

'Did you lock the door?' she asked.

'And the gate,' he said.

He lifted her up against the wall. She looped her feet around him and welcomed him, letting his touch, inside and out, erase the traces of shame left by what she and Olly had done when they were younger, the thing no one else, not even Jonny, had done with her since.

About bloody time, she thought.

Bobby arrived just as they were coming out of the lifeguard hut. He was clearly not pleased to see the pool still shut and a small queue of mothers and toddlers in sunhats at the gate. He let everyone in, smiling and greeting them by name, then waddled over to Sean and Bella.

'For fuck's sake, McLoughlin you faggot, what the fuck do you think you're doing?' Bobby said, his post-orthodontist, Novocained mouth sloping down the right-hand side of his face.

'Hi, Bobby,' Sean said, smiling. 'This is Bella. She's from England.'

'Hi,' she said.

'Hello,' Bobby said, without making any eye contact at all.

'How did it go at the orthodontist?' Sean said.

'I am not happy,' Bobby said. 'I've gotta wear these fucking braces, look.' He gurned to reveal an expanse of ironmongery surely too large to fit into such a small space – as if someone had tried to cram the George Washington Bridge into a pomegranate. 'How am I going to get pussy now, McLoughlin?'

'I apologise for my co-worker,' Sean said to Bella.

'Let's get the show on the road.' Bobby shuffled off to the lifeguard's hut.

'Sorry, Bella. Gotta work now.' Sean touched her arm, brushing her breast as he drew his hand away.

'I think I'll hang around a bit. Have a swim. That sort of thing.'

'There's nothing I'd like better.'

Bobby re-emerged and took up his position at the shallow end of the pool, opposite Sean. Bella dived into the cool blue water. As she surfaced, Bobby blew his whistle.

'No diving,' he said, as if he were bored with the complete stupidity of people who dared to swim in his pool.

Bella swam a couple of lengths, loving the feel of the water as it streaked along her limbs. Then she pulled herself out and pushed her hair back so it slicked over her head. She looked over at Sean, who was busy overseeing the small children who now filled the pool like so many maggots in a tin.

He turned his gaze over to her, and their eyes locked for a second. Bella smiled at him and he smiled back. She thought perhaps this was what love felt like.

'McLoughlin! Eyes on the game!' Bobby shouted from his seat, his high-pitched voice echoing above the laughter of the children ducking for quarters thrown by their sun-lounging mothers. Sean shrugged an apology to Bella, and looked back towards the middle of the pool.

Bella went into the hut to get her duffel bag. Then she laid her towel on the scrubby grass at the water's edge and stretched out in the sun like a cat that had got the cream, the early bird and its worm. Her body felt different. She wondered if she looked any different. She hoped not; she couldn't bear to think what Olly would say – or do – if he found out what she had been up to.

She got her copy of *Wuthering Heights* out of her bag. Alongside her plans for the photo-journal – which she kept thwarting by forgetting to take her camera out with her – another summer resolution was to start reading around her AS level books for next term. She didn't hold out much hope for this one – she preferred modern American writers.

Oh, but it was hard to concentrate. She shielded her eyes

from the sun and, as she spied on Sean up on his high lifeguard ladder, she had to restrain herself from pulling him down off it and back into the shower.

Was it right that they had done it so soon after meeting? As far as sex went, for Bella the boundaries had been blurred a long time ago, in the separate tent she and Olly shared when their mother took them camping. Lara had been far too preoccupied with her new baby Jack to notice anything odd going on; she just saw what she wanted to see.

'Olly and Bella live in each other's pockets,' was what she said, proudly, to her friends. Then she'd go on about their 'special connection'.

But Bella had felt sick and ashamed and knew that what had happened was wrong. This, with Sean, though – however premature it might look from the outside – seemed to be nothing but right.

She returned to her book, but her eyes kept blurring over the words. Her hand turned the page, but her mind couldn't stay with Lockwood's first encounter with his landlord in that buffeted, bleak landscape. She was lying by a pool in New York in the twenty-first century. How on earth was she supposed to connect with all that stuff from the past? And, oh, she couldn't help it. She looked up at Sean again, at that dark, curled hair that she had wrapped her fingers in and held on to . . .

'Bella! There you are! Mum's going mental.'

It was bloody Olly. He had spotted Bella through the fence and now he was calling right across the pool, his accent and his scolding tone causing every head to turn. Bella looked up and saw some of the mothers – all scrubbed complexions, no make-up and middle-aged before their time – look at each other and tut as Olly dragged Jack all the way around the pool towards her.

'Want a swim, want a swim, want a swim,' Jack chanted, tugging at Olly's hand and leaning dangerously close to the water.

'Shut the fuck up, Jack,' Olly said, causing a collective intake of breath in the pool enclosure.

Bobby blew his whistle and pointed at Olly. 'No cursing.'

'Chill, dude,' Olly said.

'Shut up, Olly,' Bella hissed.

'Oh look,' Olly said, seeing Sean, who sat coolly eyeing him from the shallow end. 'So this is where lover boy hangs out. Should've guessed.'

'Give it a break,' Bella said, under her breath. She really didn't want him making a scene.

'And Bella in her itsy-bitsy bikini.' Olly leaned over Bella and snapped the strap on her top.

'Stop it!'

'Mum's *incandescent*. You said you'd only be gone for a quick swim and that was hours ago.'

'Shit.' Her promise to her mum had slipped so far out of Bella's mind that it shocked her.

'Anyway, she says might as well forget about the morning now. But you'd better be around this afternoon to help her clean up. You've got to look after Squirt now, so she can get on. He's been a right pain in the arse too, because we can't find Cyril.'

'Why can't you look after him?'

'Things to do, people to see. And I had him all morning.'

That Bella doubted. He looked like he had fallen out of bed a minute ago, all uncombed, unwashed and bum-fluffed round his chin.

Olly handed Jack to Bella, who sat up and pinned him between her knees so that he couldn't escape to the water.

'She says you're not to let him in the pool on his own, *do* put his sun cream on after and *don't* take him in without his armbands on. The stuff's all in here, and there's a snack which he's to have in about an hour.' Olly threw a bag at Bella. 'She says meet them in the diner for lunch at one. All the poofs and ponces are going to be there. Ta-ta.'

He turned on his heel and left, giving Sean the finger as he passed behind him. If it hadn't been for the seething mass of small bodies in the water underneath Sean's platform, he would probably have pushed him in. But even Olly wasn't that psycho.

'Want a swim,' Jack said, trying to escape from her legs.

'All right. Just hold on a sec.' Bella blew up the armbands and fitted them on him. Taking him by the hand – she loved the way he slipped his index finger into her fist – she led him to the shallow end, to get him into the water.

'No unapproved flotation devices!' Bobby blew his whistle and clambered off his ladder, lumbering over to prevent Bella from letting her little brother go in the knee-deep water wearing dangerous English armbands.

Thwarted, Bella thought. As ever.

Seventeen

'WE'RE DUE TO TAKE THE CAR BACK THE DAY AFTER tomorrow,' Lara said.

'We can't afford to keep it,' Marcus said.

Lara looked up at the wooden ceiling-fan as it swept round and round, stirring up the bacon-scented air in the Trout Island Diner.

'How will we manage though, out here without a car?'

'Something'll turn up.'

The time was quarter past one, and there was still no sign of the kids. Lara tried to relax. It was a rare moment when she and Marcus were together without anyone else around, but she was having difficulty finding things to say to him as they sat over two cups of horrible percolated coffee.

'This is disgusting,' she whispered to Marcus.

'Shhh.'

'Isn't America supposed to be the home of good coffee?'

The diner was furnished with chunky pine tables and chairs, with vinyl-padded booths running down one side, where Lara and Marcus had been seated. Near to them sat an elderly man with a glass of lemonade who looked up and nodded when they walked in, but who had since returned to his tractor catalogue. There were only two other customers: a young man in double denim slumped on a bar stool at the counter and a large woman of indeterminate age, dressed entirely in shades of brown – including a tan baker boy cap – who sat with her back hunched towards them over by the rear wall.

'You must be the English folks then,' the waitress said as she handed them two laminated menus.

'That's right.' Marcus leaned over, turned on his smile and held out his hand. 'Marcus Wayland, pleased to meet you. And this is my wife, Lara.'

'Well hello! I'm Leanne,' she said, patting her matted blond curls. 'The others should be here any minute.' She bustled off to her spot behind the counter to carry on her business of drying cups with a pristine tea towel.

Marcus had arranged with James to join the cast of *Set Me on Fire!* for lunch. Part of the Trout Island Theatre Company deal, to compensate for the low pay, was that the actors had one meal a day in the diner and the company picked up the tab.

Lara scanned the menu, which seemed to offer little else beyond fried meat, refined carbohydrates and sugar. 'There's nothing here I really want to eat,' she said. She also had not the slightest appetite after the shock of the night before. Even her run had failed either to steady her nerves or to make her hungry.

'Come on,' Marcus said. 'When in Rome.'

'I'd be happy to tackle a Roman menu. But what is all this? Biscuits? With gravy? Sounds vile.'

Lara was, it had to be said, in a foul mood. She was cross at Bella for disappearing to the swimming pool that morning, at Olly for not waking up until gone ten, and at Marcus for sitting around with his script when he had been the first to agree that a massive clean-up of the house was needed. And all of this mess of family now stood underscored by Stephen's *what-if*. With those words came the hint of an alternative life which, had it not been for four cells joining and splitting, might have been hers.

She had tried to work her irritation out on the house. So the kitchen was now clean enough for food preparation, the wooden floor and paintwork in the vast, dusty living room had been washed down and the rug-painted Chekhovian floorcloth beaten into submission over the porch banister.

She had been on her knees, rolling it up to take outside, when Marcus wandered in from the porch swing seat, script tucked comfortably under his arm, to get a glass of water.

'Aren't you getting a bit carried away?' he had said.

But the undercurrent to the day had been, and remained, Stephen Molloy. She had always suspected that when he left so suddenly he had taken a piece of her with him. Now she realised his departure had simply put a part of her to sleep, to lie dormant all this while. And that part had been just woken up. Not gradually, like a princess after a long sleep, but slapped to consciousness, like a baby pulled blue from its mother.

Everything now was coloured by that awakening.

She saw, for example, that the reason she hadn't let Marcus touch her recently was because she couldn't bear the lily-livered sight of him. The way he had behaved when she had told him of her recent, blighted, pregnancy – banging his head, crying, not even considering the possibility she might want to let it continue into a baby – had led her to view him less as a man and more as another child that she had to look after. And she couldn't make love to a child. That would be wrong in every way.

The bleeding had provided a good excuse. Every night she would slip into bed beside him in her armour of underwear, pads and long T-shirt. Even now, as the flow seemed to have stopped, she hoped to spin it out for a couple more weeks.

But today, in the glare of Stephen's *what-if*, she couldn't imagine how she could ever touch Marcus again.

She watched him across the booth as he read the diner menu, a sunburned pinkness vibrant between his freckles and gingery beard growth. What once had been confident and attractive in him had decayed into a sort of paranoid vanity. She remembered his wooing of her – she so young and he so apparently sophisticated and seasoned. She so believed he could show her the world in all its glory that she handed herself entirely over to him.

How she had adored him. His hair seemed full of flame back then. After their fourth month together, he got down on one knee and proposed to her. And she had accepted. Just like that, swept away by the romance of it all. The wedding followed in under four weeks.

Lara realised now that she should have asked herself why, at thirty-one years of age, Marcus hadn't shown a bit more sense.

It was only at their small, almost secret, registry office wedding – Lara hadn't invited her parents who, having met Marcus just the once, had amply implied that he was too old and not good enough – that she discovered the truth.

His old school friend Rufus played best man. It was the first time Lara had met him. Where Marcus's public-school demeanour had mutated into a generic actorliness, Rufus, a barrister in London, had retained every ounce of plummy hooray ingrained into him at Stowe.

'I'm so pleased for you both,' Rufus said at the budget reception in the Dirty Duck as he kissed Lara tipsily on the cheek. 'I thought he was doomed to bachelordom after Sophie.'

'Sophie?'

'You don't know about Sophie? Oops,' he said, throwing a peanut into the air and catching it in his teeth. 'You'd better ask Marcus. Me and my big mouth, eh?'

'Who's Sophie?' she asked that night as they lay in bed in Marcus's digs. They could afford neither the time nor the money for a honeymoon, since Marcus was in the middle of a run.

He quite literally jumped.

'Who told you about Sophie?'

'Rufus.'

'The *bastard*.'

'He didn't mean it. It just sort of slipped out.'

'My arse it did.'

'Who is she, then?'

And, reluctantly, Marcus told her about the girl he had lived with since drama school and who, just eight months earlier, had left him for a younger man, an actor in the play she was starring in.

'It was bloody at the time,' Marcus said, aiming for sympathy. 'I even thought about finishing it all. But,' he added quickly, 'in the end it was a good thing. Because if it hadn't been for her going off with that little prick upstart, I wouldn't have met you, and we wouldn't be here now.'

Lara might have been only a green nineteen, but she could see how things stood, and she had to hold her hand from slapping her forehead for being so stupid and so naive. Over the next couple of weeks she tried to convince herself that Marcus had fallen head over heels in love with her, but she couldn't escape the thought that she was in fact his way of telling Sophie that he didn't care, and that he could pull a young one too. Lara was just his rebound option.

And it was just at that low point that the youthful Stephen Molloy came to Stratford, to join Marcus in the lower ranks of the Royal Shakespeare Company.

'Ah, here they are,' Marcus said, looking up from his menu as the buzzer in the diner door sounded and Jack pulled Bella in, followed by Olly. From the look of it, the twins had been arguing again.

'Where on earth did you get to?' Lara asked, moving along to make a space for them.

'I went to find Olly—' Bella started, but her brother cut in over her.

'Lover boy was at the pool, in fact,' Olly said, sitting down next to Marcus. 'She couldn't drag herself away.'

'That's such bollocks,' Bella said.

'Fella on the map?' Marcus smiled up at her. 'Watch out you don't follow in your mother's footsteps, or you might wind up with someone like she got stuck with me!'

Bella said nothing and sat down, at the opposite end of the table to Olly.

'He's caught the sun,' Lara said, looking down at Jack's bright red cheeks.

'I put sun cream on him after our swim,' Bella said. 'Olly should have put it on him before he took him out.'

'Jesus,' Olly said.

'Well hello there,' Leanne the waitress said, bringing a pitcher of icy water and three more menus to their table. 'Pleased to meet you. How you doin'?' She filled everyone's glasses.

Bella and Olly both just sat there, not responding, glaring at the red-checked vinyl tablecloth. Olly's fingers drummed against the table top.

'Stop that,' Marcus said.

'They're all good,' Lara said to Leanne, feeling she had to translate and intervene on behalf of her moody offspring.

'Cool! I'll be back in a second to get your order before those other guys arrive and the kitchen goes crazy. Just whistle when you're ready.'

'Mum, he dumped Jack on me and disappeared,' Bella said, once they were on their own again.

'Oh, Olly,' Lara said.

'I was hanging with my homies,' Olly said.

'Excuse me?' Marcus said in an exaggerated English accent.

'My dudes,' Olly went on.

'Morons, you mean,' Bella said. 'They look like a bunch of hillbillies.'

'Keep your voice down, Bella,' Lara said, looking around. 'Cultural sensibilities.'

'Whatever,' Bella said.

'Now then, what are you lot having?' Marcus clapped his hands together. 'Blueberry stack, bacon and maple syrup? Pizza burger and home fries?'

In the name of research they each ordered a different dish from the menu. Leanne was just making her way across the diner with their plates when the door burst open and the place suddenly sprang alive with the sound of actors high from release from a morning notes session.

'I can't believe James didn't notice that corpse,' someone said.

'I'd rather stick *pins* in my eyes,' another person shrieked.

'Watch out,' Marcus said. Then he got up and swept across the room towards James, who was resplendent in a vintage rose satin smoking jacket over his customary white linen, a tan leather satchel bulging with papers and books tucked under his arm.

'James darling,' Marcus said. 'How were the notes?'

'Theatre bollocks alert,' Olly muttered as Leanne put five laden plates down on the Wayland table.

'Thank you,' Lara said.

'You're welcome,' Leanne said, casting a stern eye over the twins, who were, it was clear, not doing politeness today. On her way back to the kitchen, the crowd of Trout Island players hailed her with the familiarity of tourists greeting natives.

'There's nothing green at all here,' Bella said, looking at the food.

'So *that's* what biscuits are. Sort of savoury scones,' Lara said, poking at the fluffy white objects on Olly's plate.

'They'd better be savoury, with all that chicken on the side,' he said.

'I put a rocket up their arses,' James said to no one in particular. He took his place on the banquette next to theirs, and the other actors filled the remaining booths. 'Waylands, did you meet Tony Marconi last night? He's your Banquo, and he's Heavy Dan in the musical.'

'Ah, so this is your daughter then, Marcus?' Tony said, shaking Bella's hand. 'We met last night, remember? Down by the pond?'

Bella blushed and looked away.

'And didn't I spy you at the pool this morning while I was doing my fifty laps?' he winked. 'Hanging out with our best boy?'

'Too right you did.' Olly leaned back and unsmilingly watched his sister squirm.

James stretched his arm up and waved. 'Leanne, my darling, do you think I could have a coffee? Thank you, my sweet.'

Lara thought she saw the shoulders of double denim guy at the counter stiffen at the sound of James's camp twang.

'Oh my Gawd, darling, what in hell's name is that?' Betty said, pointing to Lara's plate as she squeezed in next to her. Today she had on a combination of lumberjack shirt, baggy Levis, five o'clock shadow and full high hair and make-up. She looked like Jane Russell on testosterone.

'It's supposed to be macaroni salad,' Lara said. 'But it looks more like a plate of curdled mayonnaise.'

'Trout Island Five, here you come,' Tony Marconi called over from his seat among a group of excitable young actors.

'Trout Island Five?' Lara said.

'The number of pounds an actor gains working a show here,' Betty explained. 'We earn in calories.'

'You don't happen to know if we left Jack's teddy bear at your place last night?' Lara asked her.

'I couldn't tell you. The place looked like a bombsite when we left it this morning,' Betty said. 'I'll ask Trudi to keep an eye out – she's working her magic there all day today.'

'Can't we cancel tonight? My head,' the tousle-haired boy next to Tony said, his heavy eyelids drooping over bloodshot eyes.

'Doctor Theatre, darling,' James said. 'You'll be marvellous. Thank you, Leanne, thank you sweetness,' he said as Leanne went around the tables pouring glasses of iced water.

'You all drank far too much last night, children,' Betty said. 'You need to show a little more restraint. A little self-discipline.'

'That's easy for you to say,' a long slender girl who looked like a young Natalie Wood said.

'And what is that supposed to mean?' Betty drew herself up and took a regal sip of her water.

'You've had all those years of being the wild thing,' the girl said.

'All those years? All those years? What is that supposed to mean?' Betty said. 'You don't know the half of it, honeys. I have worked harder with my little finger than you have with all your bodies put together. Discipline is my middle name, sister.'

This set Olly off sniggering and Betty's nostrils flared. It was hard to tell if she had meant her outburst as a risqué joke or a serious telling-off. Lara didn't much understand theatre people, and all this noise and clamour was too much for her. She wished she were back alone in the dusty house, daydreaming and putting things to rights.

'Well then, ladies. Let's try to be civil, shall we?' James said. Then he stood up and addressed the room. 'Is everyone ready to order? May I remind you we have six hours exactly until you are back on that stage. Do *not* overeat, dancers!'

Leanne was joined by another woman who emerged from the kitchen door wiping her huge hands on her apron. The two of them worked the room, taking the orders. The second woman shuffled around, grey pop-socks wrinkled around her bloated purple ankles, stringy salt-and-pepper hair pulled back in a ponytail, revealing a grey neck. Lara didn't feel much like eating anyway, but the thought that this might be the cook put her off her macaroni salad altogether.

'Olly, will you pull yourself together, mate,' Marcus leaned forward and hissed at his ostentatiously bored and twitchy-looking son. A tiny vein bulged in his forehead and Lara was again reminded of Marcus's father, who was equally red-headed and similar in stature. Her joke to friends was that he and Marcus were so alike she didn't have any surprises in store for her. She always followed this, however, with a silent prayer that she wouldn't end up like Marcus's mother; a desaturated little mouse, thin as paper, run ragged by her overbearing husband.

But of course she wouldn't end up like Moira Wayland. She had none of that pale blood in her veins. Her own mother, though, made an even worse template for her older self. The thought that she had the power to make her own future, independent of either genetic legacy or other people's expectations, hadn't struck Lara until very recently indeed.

'How are you liking our little village?' Betty asked her.

'It's very pretty. The heat's a bit of challenge.'

'We're building up to a storm. It's like *The Tempest* here in August. Gets so you can't bear it, then the rain and the thunder and the lightning come and you can actually *breathe*. Until the next one gets going.'

'Let it come down,' Lara said.

'I like what you're doing there, Lara dear,' Betty said with a wink. 'But let's not get too carried away with our Scottish Play quotations. It's not awful good luck. Now then. How're the digs?'

'Fine,' Lara said. 'A bit dusty, but we're giving it a good scrub.'

'Oh,' Betty said, a note of disappointment in her voice. 'We paid some guys to clean it just a couple weeks ago.'

'I suppose if it's standing empty the dust just settles quicker,' Lara said. 'I wanted to ask, though: could I get rid of the carpet in the hallway?'

'Carpet?' Betty frowned.

'The one with the stain? I'd like to pull it up.'

'I don't remember any carpet in that house, honey,' Betty said. 'But then I've just been all about *Set Me On Fire!* for the past three months. I've barely noticed anything else. But sure, if it's stained, just rip it up.' She waved her fingers in the air. 'The owner said we could do what we want with the place.'

'Thanks,' Lara said. 'And,' she hesitated a second, 'thank you for the flowers. They're beautiful.'

'Flowers?' Betty said, raising an immaculately shaped eyebrow. 'Not me, honey.'

Lara frowned, and pondered this.

'How did you like our little musical, Olly?' James put one elbow on the table, rested his chin in his hand and swerved into Olly's personal space.

'Um . . .' Olly muttered.

'He thought it was great!' Marcus boomed. 'Didn't you, mate?'

Olly mumbled an assent.

'And Olly usually *hates* the theatre,' Marcus went on.

'Load of bollocks,' Olly said under his breath. Lara hoped she was the only one to hear this.

'How are you feeling after your little surprise last night?' Betty asked Lara as the rest of the food arrived and Marcus and James settled into an animated discussion about staging ideas for *Macbeth*.

'Fine,' Lara said. Even if she trusted Betty, which she wasn't quite sure she did, giving voice to anything right now would start to make it real, and she certainly wasn't ready to do that.

'When are you going to his place for dinner?'

'Tonight,' Lara said, wondering again just how much Betty knew.

'It's so delightful, getting old friends back together,' Betty said, clasping her hands to her chest.

'Of course, June and Brian are far too grand to step down to the diner,' Tony was saying at the next table.

'We'll have none of this divisive talk, thank you, Mr Marconi.' Betty wagged a red-taloned finger at him.

'Well, Jesus, Betty. It's hardly in the spirit of the thing.' Tony looked down and admired his own tattooed bicep.

'Really, honey. Do you blame them when you can't find anything other than a *wife-beater* to dine in?'

'Meow,' the tousle-haired boy said.

'June and Brian carry this show, and they need to take it easy in the breaks,' Betty said with one eyebrow raised.

'Yeah. Slooow and easy,' Tony said, winking at Bella and once more making her blush.

'Oh, Oh, Ohhh . . .' The Natalie Wood lookalike did a slow, operatic rendition of an orgasm.

'That's quite enough now, young Nancy,' Betty said. 'If it was good enough for Dame Nellie Melba, it's certainly good enough for our June.'

'Who's Dame Nellie Melba?' Olly said. Even if he had wanted to join in this banter, he wouldn't be able to. He was all at sea with it.

'I'll tell you about it later,' Lara said.

'You all set?' Leanne took away the Wayland plates. 'Didn't you like the macaroni salad, honey?'

'It was lovely,' Lara said. 'I'm just not all that hungry.' She noticed that Olly, too, had barely touched his food, which was quite remarkable. The heat must have killed his appetite.

'Sure honey,' Leanne said. 'Now. Can I get you dessert? We've got apple, cherry or blueberry pie, with or without cream or ice cream: strawberry, chocolate or vanilla.'

'Trout Island high five!' Tony reached over and slapped Olly's hand.

'No dessert for cast and crew!' James stood up and clapped his hands. 'You have ten minutes exactly, ladies and gentlemen. And then we return. To doom or glory!'

The woman in the tan baker boy cap at the back of the diner got up and walked across to the counter, where she paid her bill. Lara only caught a glimpse of her face as she turned to go

– it was mostly hidden beneath the cap, a large pair of oval tortoiseshell sunglasses and a chequered tan and turquoise silk scarf.

'Who's that?' she whispered to Betty, as the woman crossed to the door.

'No idea. Never seen her before in my life.'

But Lara thought she saw a tiny frown flicker across Betty's pancaked forehead as her eyes followed the back of the woman and the glass diner door swung shut behind her.

Eighteen

AFTER THE HEAVY LUNCH, MARCUS TOOK JACK OFF FOR A
nap. With a little cajoling, Lara enlisted the help of Olly and
Bella in clearing up the house. By the middle of the afternoon,
every surface downstairs had been thoroughly washed and the
front hallway carpet ripped up.

'Think of all the dead bits of skin on it,' Bella said as they
lifted it, releasing a cloud of dusty stink.

'All the dog shit that's been trampled into it,' Olly went on.

'All the baby piss.'

'Thank you, children,' Lara said, carving at the stained
middle section, which had stuck fast to the floor beneath. A
bowelish tang seeped out as she worked on it, and it became so
bad it made her gag. She ran out to the porch, retching.

'Women are such sensitive creatures,' Olly said, finishing off
the job for her. He seemed to have brightened up now he was
doing something disgusting.

'Make sure you wash your hands afterwards.' Lara held a
tissue to her nose as she came back to oversee the removal of
the carpet.

'God, I wonder what that stain was,' Bella said, wrinkling her nose.

'I'd rather not know,' Lara said.

'I bet someone was murdered here,' Olly said.

'Don't,' Bella said.

'No, look. Blood goes all dark like that when it dries.'

'Mum, tell him to stop.'

'Oh do stop, Oll. You're upsetting your sister.'

'Diddums,' Olly said.

Lara got the twins to help her cart the stinking carpet round to the back garden, where they dumped it in a far corner. To keep them apart she sent Bella to work in the bathroom and Olly to the upstairs landing, then she got to her knees and scrubbed the hall boards with bleach until the fumes made her feel dizzy. She wondered, as she worked, whether Olly might not be right about the origins of the stain. Since she had arrived in this house, something in this hallway made her want to pass through it as quickly as possible, with the hairs on the back of her neck standing up. It was all she could do to stay in it long enough to clean it. Now the thick, black murk that had covered everything swirled in her bucket, turning the water viscous; she hoped the place would feel lighter.

The heat of the afternoon dried the floor almost instantly. With the front door still propped open from taking the carpet out, and the dappled sunlight filtering through the lush canopy of trees in the front garden, the hallway looked nearly crisp, like an advertisement for the New England lifestyle.

But the illusion was instantly smashed by the bang of a mop being flung to the wooden floor upstairs and Bella's cry of 'Just leave me ALONE!' followed by her footsteps thundering across the landing and the slamming of her bedroom door.

'What's going on up there?' Lara climbed halfway up the stairs.

Olly stormed out of the bathroom, a wet cloth in his hand.

'She's such a fucking—' He paused, searching for the right word, his fists clenching and unclenching. Tears pushed at the corners of his eyes.

'I can't stand any more of this,' Lara said. 'Have you finished up there?'

'More or less,' Olly said, glaring at Bella's door, wiping his nose on the back of his arm.

Lara leaned on the banister and looked up at her fuming son. What on earth was going on between those two? For the past couple of years, their relationship had become increasingly strained. Since arriving in Trout Island, it seemed to have taken a quantum leap into near warfare.

When she thought of Bella and Olly, it wasn't as they were now, this battling two-headed beast. No, Lara's image of the twins had the pair of them, aged six, holding hands, knee-deep in grass at some campsite or other, grinning up at her and waiting for the next bit of fun. They were so close back then, living as they did in each other's pockets. What had gone wrong? She wondered whether the arrival of Jack and the subsequent diversion in her attention had anything to do with it. A more comforting thought was that all this tension marked a necessary step to adulthood – a growing apart, a separation from one another. But it was so disruptive; she wished it didn't have to happen.

'Oh, sod it. Take a break. Put the cleaning stuff away,' she said to Olly, 'and you're free to go.'

Olly picked up his bucket and mop and flopped down the stairs. As he passed Lara, she put her hand on his arm.

'What is it, Oll? What's the matter?'

'Nothing,' he said, shaking her off.

She followed him through into the kitchen.

'Come on. I'm not an idiot. What's up with you and Bella?'

'She's being a slut,' Olly muttered, emptying the dirty water from his bucket into the sink too quickly, so it backed up and splashed down his front. 'Shit, fuck, wank, piss.'

'Because she likes a boy?' Lara said.

'You don't know the half of it.'

'Oh come on, Oll. Cut her a bit of slack. Look,' she said, getting a tea towel and kneeling to wipe the pool of water from the floor round Olly's feet. 'If this is out of some absurd sort of loyalty towards Jonny, you're wasting your energy. They couldn't have gone on for ever. They were far too young. Believe me, it's better to be as free as possible until you're much, much older.'

'You know that's bollocks.' Olly narrowed his eyes down at her. 'You and Dad met when you were only a little bit older than us. You're not going to say that was wrong, are you?'

Lara stood up and cupped her lower lip to blow some badly needed air up to her perspiring face. 'No, but . . .'

'Anyway, it's not fucking about Jonny.' Olly put the bucket down on to the ground and kicked it. 'He's a creep, this Sean.' He spat the name out. 'He's only after one thing.'

Lara burst out laughing. 'Oh, Olly, I didn't have you down as such a *prude*. Don't you think Bella's able to look after herself?'

'No. Not really.' Olly levelled his eyes at her.

'Aren't you being just a bit sexist?'

'I know what she's like.'

'Hah!' Lara and Olly turned to see an indignant Bella standing in the kitchen archway, her arms crossed.

'Shit.' Olly dragged his hands up through his hair, pulling the skin of his face back and up like a tight mask.

'Leave me alone, Olly. Just leave me alone,' Bella said quietly – almost, Lara thought, as if she pitied her brother.

'Perhaps I just fucking will, and then we'll see what happens,' Olly said. He stormed through the kitchen arch, bumping quite deliberately into Bella on his way, then he banged out of the front door, letting the fly screen slam behind him as he flew on to the street.

'Be back by five,' Lara called after him.

In the silence that followed, the house seemed to sigh in relief.

'Twat,' Bella said, rubbing her arm where Olly had banged it.

'He's an angry boy.'

'Tell me about it.'

'Just don't do too much to provoke him, will you, Bella? Be kind.'

'I'm going for a swim,' Bella said, avoiding Lara's eye. Then she ran upstairs.

'Be back by five, remember, Bella. We're going to Stephen's.'

Lara stood on the front porch watching her daughter head off along Main Street, swinging her swimming bag over her shoulder. Without Olly she seemed carefree, relieved even. Sunlight flashed through breaks in the canopy of trees, lighting her up, making her glitter.

Lucky thing, Lara thought. To be so young, with everything in front of you. And, despite all she had just said to Olly, a tiny voice deep within her urged Bella to be careful, not to lose her head, and not to make the same mistakes she had.

But wasn't getting pregnant with Bella and Olly one of those mistakes – binding her as it did to Marcus, and forcing Stephen to do the honourable thing and step aside? Yet no amount of turning the clock back would have her scrubbing them out as she had her poor last baby. Life was so complicated. And she feared that the summer ahead, in a reversal of her initial hopes, wasn't going to simplify anything.

Lara took up her cloth again and started washing down the wooden panelling under the stairs in the hallway. Using her fingernail to get the dirt out from between the grooves, she noticed that one of the gaps was slightly bigger than the others. She got a knife from the kitchen and levered it down into the space. In a couple of minutes, she had prised open what she saw now was the door to an understairs cupboard.

She opened the door wide and felt around inside for a light switch. Finding it, she flicked it up – the opposite to the European way and one of those tiny differences which made her feel like she was living in a looking-glass world.

The light from the bare bulb revealed a flight of makeshift wooden steps leading down into more darkness. This surprised Lara. Earlier in the day she had checked the underside of the house to see if she could find out how the chipmunk had got in. There were no breaches or holes in the floor, nor in the yard-high skirt of rough wall that the building stood on. But, as she saw now, some sort of cellar lurked underneath the central section of the house.

Holding on to the stone wall to her right, she edged down the steps. A welcome coolness greeted her after the heat of the afternoon, and it drew her in. As she descended, a sweet, cloying scent joined the earthy, mushroom smell of the cellar. Lara had caught hints of it before, in the living room, which was directly above her. Reaching round the wall at the bottom of the stairs, she found another switch and flicked it on.

The earth-floored cellar was about the size of a double garage. The undersides of the floorboards upstairs served as a ceiling, and the walls were of the same rough stone as the chimney breast in the living room. An old worn armchair squatted on a filthy rag rug in the middle of the room, beside it a low table bearing a dirty glass and a plate. Lara went over to have a closer look and saw ancient crumbs on the plate and greasy fingerprints on the glass, which had reddish crystals inside it as if a drink had been left there to slowly give itself up to the stale air. A small bed covered in tattered blankets stood against the far wall, looking like someone had just got up and left it unmade. Tools – a shovel, a rusting saw, a collection of hammers and a large axe, hung from hooks driven into the stones, and, attached to a metal ring on the wall, two lengths of chain spilled across the floor towards the bed. Welded on the ends were what appeared to be manacles. The place stank of the grave.

Goosebumps spiked Lara's arms. She turned to get out, but her shoulder caught the corner of a low shelf she hadn't seen, bringing a jar tumbling down to the ground where it smashed, splashing her legs with its contents of grey, vinegary pickles.

The sudden noise and the unexpected wetness caught her in the throat and, with a rush, she found her legs carrying her up the stairs faster than she thought possible, out of the cupboard and towards the front door.

'What's the racket?' Marcus stood at the top of the stairs, rumpled from sleep, his boxers gaping obscenely.

'There's a hideous cellar down there,' Lara said, leaning against the wall, trying to breathe.

'A hideous cellar?' Smiling, Marcus thumped down the stairs and peered through the door. A vinegary odour wafted up the cellar stairs, mingling with the other, graveyard miasma.

'Jesus. It's like *The Evil Dead*,' Marcus said. 'You didn't go down there, did you?'

Lara nodded. 'I wish I hadn't.' She told him about the tools, the hooks, and the bed and chair.

'Tell you what,' Marcus said, shutting the door firmly. 'I'll get a hammer and nails from the theatre and we'll bang it shut to make sure no one can get in there. Or out . . .' He let his hands float up like a Vincent Price vampire.

'Don't,' she shuddered.

'Seriously, Lara. Forget about it. It's just a pile of junk in a cellar. Come on, old bird. Let's make the most of Jacky's snooze and have a cup of tea out on the stoop. You go and have a sit down. I'll bring it out to you.'

It could be the sign of a possibly overlong marriage that the first thought for an unexpected half-hour to yourselves is to sit down and have a nice cup of tea, but, after her trying day, Lara welcomed the unasked-for act of kindness.

She went out on to the porch and sat on the creaky old swing seat. The grime she had cleaned from the house felt as if had been tattooed into her skin, infecting her blood. She wished that, instead of going to Stephen's for dinner, they could have a quiet evening in, relaxing with the kids on the smelly old sofas, watching a DVD and wiping out the day with red wine.

She let her head fall forward and moved it gently from side to side, rolling out the ache at the base of her neck caused by looking down and scrubbing.

The truth was that she couldn't face up to what was going on inside her head. That was how she operated, and she knew it. Running in the morning and collapsing in the evening with too much wine was her way of anaesthetising the big questions. She was a fan of the quiet life.

But seeing Stephen had dislodged simplicity. She had moved from the middle of a safe but worn-out lawn to the edge of a sharp precipice. And now she stood on the brink, trying to resist the urge to jump. Not going to Stephen's tonight would be the same as taking a guarded step backwards.

The past twenty-four hours had, she realised, been coloured by a feeling of unease, as if a creature had lodged itself somewhere beneath her solar plexus and now, foetus-like, attempted to stretch its limbs.

She pushed herself more vigorously on the swing seat, to try to dispel that image from her mind.

If it hadn't been for Marcus, she would be eighteen weeks pregnant by now. She realised that, for the first time, she actually felt relieved she wasn't. It had been a close call, though. On the day of the procedure, she had sat in the little park across the road from the clinic, counting the petals of a rose she had ripped from its thorny stem, rolling them over in her fingers and inhaling the sweet scent that reminded her of the perfume she used to make with water in a blue plastic flask when she was a child.

'I don't think I could deal with another baby,' Marcus had said, sitting beside her.

He hadn't *dealt* with any of the others, though. They had impinged in no way whatsoever on his life. He had trolled the same argument out when she found herself pregnant with Jack. It was convenient for him to blame the lack of professional respect he commanded on the fact that he had been lumbered with offspring so early on. He chose to forget that he had been thirty-two when they were born, which hardly qualified him as a juvenile first-time father.

But it was a good excuse.

'And just as you're getting yourself back together after Jack,' he went on, stopping her hand as she tore the rose petals into tiny pieces. 'Your work, your body.'

'But I hate my work,' Lara said.

'You're just saying that.' He patted her knee and she wanted to knock his head off.

He did have a point about her body. After the twins, the shape she had only recently grown into snapped back into place by itself. Which was just as well, because the day after the births Marcus had to go to Manchester for a stretch of six weeks which only saw him come home tired, twitching and with a bag of washing late on a Saturday night. He was off again by Monday lunchtime.

After Jack it had been completely different. Even at thirty-three she was still one of the youngest at her antenatal classes. Nevertheless, it had been a struggle that time to rediscover her abdominal muscles and lose the sheath of fat built out of a craving for condensed milk swirled over tinned peaches in sugary syrup.

That was when the running kicked in. She started on a campaign of physical self-improvement, a focusing on goals of percentage of fat versus lean tissue and body mass index calculation that allowed no room for questioning any other aspects of her life.

With hard work, it had taken her six months to return to her pre-Jack weight. But her skin hung in folds at her breasts and belly, with silvery deltas of stretch marks. She looked passable in clothes, and Marcus seldom cast his eye in her direction when she was between underwear and bed, so he didn't know any better.

But Marcus's body-argument had held little sway as she had sat in the park inhaling the rose scent clinging to her fingers. This most recent pregnancy had already melted all that hard-won body tone. From the moment the hapless sperm hit the unlucky egg, she had eaten as if she were the subject of a TV documentary about people who need cranes to get them out of bed. Whole loaves of doughy white bread, and plastic-wrapped cakes meant for a family found their way down her throat. It had been this increase in appetite – far more than a period late even by her irregular and tardy standards – that had sent her to the chemist to buy a pregnancy test. The pink line that shot across the window in the plastic stick immediately after she had dipped it in her hormone-laden pee had done little to curb her appetite. Instead, she redoubled her calorie intake and took days off work, phoning in with tales of flu, to lie supine on the sofa, eating and watching people tear each other to pieces on *The Jeremy Kyle Show*.

She had toyed, back then, with the idea of not telling Marcus till it was too late. But when he returned at the weekend – he had a minor role in an Ayckbourn at Southampton – to his credit, he noticed the change. Or perhaps it was the number of Mr Kipling wrappers in the recycling. In any case, she was rumbled. And rumbled was how it felt; as if falling pregnant had only been down to her. In fact it was he who refused to wear condoms, relying instead on an inexpert withdrawal method. She supposed she could have taken the pill, or at least some sort of control. But the former felt unnatural and, given the rare occasions on which contraception was needed, over the top. And she really had no idea how to do the latter. Throughout her life, control had been something of an abstract concept.

So began a month of a tripartite wrangling with him, her conscience and her body. And it ended, there in the rose garden, with him frantically painting a positive future for her, one where she was free, and Jack was at school full time, healthy, happy and brought up with all the advantages of having only much older siblings and not having to share his parents' affection with another, younger, brother or sister.

Even as he spoke and stroked her hand, she knew his motives to be entirely selfish. He didn't want to be tied down even further, didn't want to be made to feel any more inadequate as a provider.

In the end she had let him lead her to the clinic, where they signed her in, dressed her in a blue surgical gown that did up at the back, sedated her and put her in a waiting room full of women unable to acknowledge even their own presences, let alone those of anyone else. Then, when the time was right, she was taken to an antechamber, positioned on a gurney and given an intravenous anaesthetic. The next thing she knew she was being shaken awake by a kindly but efficient nurse, crying dry-mouthed and uncontrollably, with a sanitary towel packed up between her legs.

When she got back home, silent and shaking, her eating didn't abate. Quite the opposite in fact. And now here she was, creaking on the swing seat, wondering if it could cope with the extra stone she was carrying. But the running was going to help, and the upside of seeing Stephen again was that since then she had hardly managed to eat a thing.

Once more she felt that dirty relief. How would it have been, meeting Stephen after all those years, yet pregnant again?

'Nice cuppa char,' Marcus said, bringing two mugs out on to the porch. 'Budge up.'

She moved along the seat to make space for him. His Dior aftershave – used for aesthetics rather than function, since he was growing a beard – tickled her nostrils.

'Someone's made a great job of the shower,' he said. 'I actually feel cleaner after using it.'

'Good.' She sipped her tea. It tasted disgusting. Lipton's

had been the only reasonably priced brand in the supermarket – a tiny box of PG Tips cost over five dollars – but it was grey and weak.

'Are you all right with going to Stephen's tonight?' she said. Thinking about the termination had stirred up her irritation at Marcus and she felt like skating dangerously.

'I'm looking forward to it.'

'But you're always a bit iffy when he's on the telly.'

'Actorly pride. You have to pretend to despise commercial success. It's part of the job. No, me and him go back a long way.'

'I know,' Lara said.

'And us not staying in touch is as much down to him as it is me,' he said, tucking a strand of hair behind his ear.

Lara nodded.

'It'll be good to find out what he's been up to over the years,' Marcus went on. 'We've got a lot of catching up to do. He might even be interested in what I've been doing.'

'Oh look. It's Dog,' Lara said. The big black Great Dane lumbered up the front lawn and sat at the base of the porch steps looking up at them, panting, his tongue lolling.

'Dog?' Marcus covered his nose and mouth with his hands.

'A friend I made on my run.'

'Don't let it up here.'

'Don't worry,' Lara said. Marcus was really very allergic to dogs. 'He looks thirsty, though, eh boy? Stay there.' She held a firm index finger up to the dog, stood and went into the house.

'Don't encourage it,' Marcus said, but Lara chose not to hear him.

In the kitchen, she leaned over the edge of the sink and put her whole head under the stream of surprisingly icy water, hoping it would percolate into her mind and wash it clean of poison.

Then shaking her head, like Dog might after a swim in the river, she found a bowl and filled it.

On the way back, she paused in the front hallway and, masked by the fly screens, watched the scene outside.

Dog confronted Marcus, who leaned backwards, pinned to the swing seat by his own fear. It was a stand-off.

Dog's eye, cast upon Marcus, seemed to be saying one thing to him. Lara saw it clearly.

'You are to blame for everything.'

If only Marcus could open his eyes and read the truth that was being shown to him. But then, Lara thought, perhaps it was too late for that.

She carried the bowl of water to the grateful animal and broke the spell.

Nineteen

SO THIS IS LOVE, THEN, BELLA THOUGHT AS SHE SCUFFED down the dusty track to the pool. This feeling in the pit of the stomach, this hunger that couldn't face food, this tingling in her fingertips. Even Olly's obscene suggestions – which were, she had to admit, not wide of the mark of what she and Sean had actually got up to – and the unveiled threats he had made as she tried to scrub the bath clean couldn't obliterate the wonder of it all.

Sometimes she wished Olly didn't exist. Her life would be a lot simpler.

But when she got to the pool, Sean wasn't there. His shift must have ended. She swam ten lengths with her eyes open, just in case he appeared, then she lay on her towel, feeling the sun warm every exposed nerve of her body.

In place of Bobby and Sean, two tanned and golden girls sat up on the lifeguards' ladders, chewing gum, looking bored and, Bella felt sure, smirking at her and her English pallor. What sort of match was she for them?

Sean had probably been after a shag and nothing more. And now he'd had it, he'd probably ignore her.

She strove to believe her gloomy thoughts, to wear them as an armour against rejection, but something in her knew she was wrong. She screwed her eyes shut and tried to get lost in the red and purple floaters that blossomed behind her eyelids. Then a shadow passed over her and a shock of cold water splattered on her belly. She opened her eyes hopefully. But it wasn't Sean.

'For fuck's sake, Olly!' She rubbed away the wetness, which she now realised came from his hair as he stood over her, dripping and grinning.

'Don't doze off,' Olly said. 'You might miss lover boy.'

So, Bella thought, Olly had regained his composure, and now, by standing dribbling over her and relegating Sean to a joke, he was attempting to make up. This was typical of him. He could turn on a pin. He was, she often thought, completely mental.

'Come and dive for quarters,' he said, standing over her, one hand on his hip.

'Get out of my sun,' she said, not stirring. She noticed that, behind him, the lifeguard girls were sizing him up, their immaculate eyebrows raised, their sly glances cool and unimpressed.

'You're not in there, in case you were wondering,' she said, nodding towards them. She shielded her eyes from the sun that flooded her face as he turned to look at the girls, who had returned to surveying the pool.

'I am not the slightest bit interested anyway,' Olly said. Then he let a tiny smile slip over his lips. 'Come on, Bell. Come and play.'

'Oh, for Christ's sake,' she said, getting up.

After an hour of diving for quarters, they decided to go home, a truce of sorts established between them. But as they reached the end of the steep dirt track up from the pool to the school playground Olly saw his friends, sitting on the bonnet of a battered turquoise convertible, smoking something.

'Yo, homies,' he said, raising his hand in greeting.

'There we go then,' Bella sighed.

Leaving her brother behind to get up to no good, she skirted across the lawn at the front of the theatre, her skin tingling from too much sun. She had swimming-pool water sloshing around in her ears, so at first she didn't hear when Sean called out. But he ran and caught up with her, tapping her on the shoulder and making her jump. Thinking it was Olly, she swung round ready to cuff him.

'Steady,' he said, smiling at her, tall and beautiful and just, well, perfect in every way. 'I saw you passing. I can't stop, I've got to set up for the show, but I just wanted to say hi.' He reached out and put his hand on her arm, and she surprised herself by putting her hand up to his dark curly hair and pulling him down to kiss him.

'The walls have eyes here,' he said, drawing her behind a tree. 'Is your brother around?'

'Smoking weed in the playground.'

'He's really going native, isn't he? Hey you. That was good this morning, wasn't it?' he went on, pulling her towards him and smoothing her hair. 'You're really something, did you know that?'

'I bet you say that to all the girls.'

'There are no other girls,' Sean said. He kissed her neck then put his lips to her ear. 'I think I'm in love,' he whispered, and Bella shivered, with the feel of his breath so near to her, and the near-ecstasy of the moment.

'Sean! Will you get your arse inside here right now!' James, who couldn't see them, was standing in the theatre doorway with a large glitter-ball in one hand and a thick coil of rope in the other.

'Uh-oh. Gotta go. You free tomorrow morning?'

'Yes.' She nodded.

'Meet me at the end of the village by the corn and flower stall about ten,' he said, pointing along Main Street. 'I'll take you to my cousin's pond. We can swim there.'

'Great,' she said.

'SEAN!' James yelled. 'I need you YESTERDAY.'

'Gotta go. Laters then.' Sean bent and kissed her right on the end of her nose, then leaped off towards the theatre. Bella pressed herself to the tree, the rough bark rasping beneath her fingers and along every fibre of her back. She slid round to watch Sean's broad shoulders and beautiful slim hips as he bounded up the steps towards James, who had put the glitter-ball down and was waving a schoolmasterly finger at him.

He thought he was in love, he'd said.

She knew it.

But what in the world was she going to do about Olly?

Twenty

'HOW REMOTE DO YOU HAVE TO BE?' OLLY ASKED FROM
the back, leaning sideways against the car window. They had
been driving out of Trout Island for over half an hour into the
densely wooded countryside.

'It's certainly out of the way,' Marcus said, as he skittered
the big car along dusty, unpaved roads. 'Stop banging your leg
into my seat, mate, will you?'

'Whatevs,' Olly said, transferring the imaginary drumbeat
that seemed to be driving his nervous system to his fingers.

'Are you sure this is right?' Bella peered up from the picture
book she was reading to Jack to keep him quiet. Since Olly had
reminded him about his missing Cyril Bear a fuss had been on
the verge of being kicked up.

'Absolutely,' Lara said. She had her laptop on her knee, and
was following the beautiful hand-drawn map Stephen had
emailed to her. It wasn't ideal, but they didn't have a printer in
the house. She kept the top part of the file tucked away beyond
the reaches of the screen, because he had entitled it *For Lara –
the route to me.*

They carved up the unmetalled lane into the forest. From time to time, they passed mailboxes, sentries to side-turnings that disappeared off into the trees, the households they guarded only hinted at by the names on custom-built signs: 'The Walters!' or 'O'Malleyville'. Olly pointed out that several of the mailboxes were peppered with what looked like bullet-holes.

The hedgerow that smothered the landscape hung low in all its late summer weight. Lara recognised golden rod from her own garden. But here it grew wild, as abundant and invasive as cow parsley at home. She thought she spied that, too, although it could have been hemlock. The greenery made Lara feel suffocated, and she wondered what it was like for Stephen, living this far out in nature. If their digs back in the village made her uneasy, then to be out here with nothing but hidden creatures and gun-toting hillbillies for company would be a nightmare for her. Sleeping at night would be very difficult.

Then, as if pushed by an unseen hand, they burst out from the canopied forest on to a grassy plateau where an immaculate red barn stood sentinel by a big, white farmhouse. On the porch of the house, two Adirondack chairs sat cosily angled towards a large and pristine pond, overlooking a jetty with a small rowing boat attached to it.

'I didn't realise we'd got so high up,' Lara said. Trout Island, which she could make out in the valley beneath them, nestled like a doll's-house village. A range of hills folded up and behind the specks of houses, fading out into a purple mist in the distance. Lara thought perhaps, if forced, she could bear to live up here, in this house, by this pond and this barn. Everything would seem possible up here.

'Is that it, then?' Olly asked.

'Leg, seat, mate,' Marcus said.

'Chill,' Olly said, once more relocating his drumming to the window.

'He's got ants in his pants,' Jack giggled.

Lara stared at the map again. The clearing was well marked, the outlines of house, barn and pond drawn and coloured by Stephen. But the road continued on.

'It's a couple more miles down there.' Lara pointed to a track leading off beyond the pond and back into the leafy arcade of the forest.

'Down the other side of the mountain,' Bella said.

'I'd better not touch a drop tonight,' Marcus said. 'If we're ever going to find our way back.'

'I'll drive,' Lara said.

'No, no. You relax and enjoy yourself.'

Eventually, after much bumping and skidding on loose rocks and rubble, they arrived at a fenced-off driveway behind an unmarked set of gates.

'This is it,' Lara said. Marcus cut the engine and they all looked up at the fence and gates, crowned by coils of barbed wire. 'This is Stephen's land.'

'Fort Knox,' Olly said, whistling between his teeth.

'But we have the code,' Lara said, getting out of the car with her laptop and locating a keypad recessed into a small metal cabinet at the side of the gates. Feeling the sweat spring instantly to her skin, she punched the numbers Stephen had written beside the map – 'today's code' was how he described them – into the keypad, and the gates swung slowly open. Marcus drove through and, as Lara passed in behind the car, they closed behind her.

'Now, keep going, and, after about half a mile, take the left fork,' Lara said, after she had got back into the car. The loose road grated under the wheels of the Chevy as it descended steeply past a wild meadow and an overgrown pond full of reeds and lily pads – no neat boats or jetties here. The left fork took them into a thicket of tall, broad-leafed oaks.

'Where's the damn house?' Olly said. He had opened his window, letting heat and dust seep in as he stuck his head out, craning to see into the trees.

'Look!' Lara pointed. Right in the middle of the forest, where you would expect it to be most densely packed with branches, a sizeable house stood at the centre of a clearing. They had not immediately seen it because it was almost camouflaged by its woody exterior of dark oak. Broad and sleek in a minimal style that whispered taste and money, the building was skirted by a raw wooden deck.

Marcus bounced the car up to rest by a closed garage that had two tennis-racquet snowshoes hanging on it. He switched off the engine and they all sat there for a moment, enjoying the silence and stillness after the crunch and bump of the journey. Then the door on the deck opened and there was Stephen. Tall, slim, long-legged, he stood at the top of a short run of steps, his hands in the pockets of his linen jacket, smiling in their direction.

Lara swung her aching legs out of the car. Sitting still for so long after her morning run had solidified them. She straightened up and took Jack from Bella, who had helped him out of his car seat. Then they crossed the rough grass to the house, where Stephen waited for them.

'Welcome.' He bent down to shake Marcus's and Olly's hands as the Waylands climbed up to meet him, then he kissed Bella and Lara on the cheeks. He was impeccable, Lara thought. No one would have suspected anything. He smelled of leather and pepper, exactly the same as she remembered.

'Hello, young Jack.' He stroked the little boy's cheek like a father. 'Come on in, everyone. Well done for finding me.'

'You're pretty tucked away,' Marcus said.

'Believe me, it's intentional.'

Stephen led them into an open-plan space with a high wooden ceiling. What Lara noticed first was the welcome coolness. Unlike their digs, this place had efficient air conditioning, stirred through the rooms by ceiling fans. A professional-looking kitchen occupied the first area they came to. A vast battery of heavy saucepans filled a shelf along the entire far wall, and Lara counted twenty different black-handled knives held to an oversized magnetic rack. Something in the oven smelled delicious – of meat and wine and garlic – yet all the surfaces were clear. The only other sign of any culinary activity was a pile of clean washing-up by the enormous double kitchen sink. So Stephen was a cook, and a tidy one at that – unless he had staff. But Lara remembered that strange Trudi saying she didn't do stuff round the house for him, that he liked to do it all on his own. She wondered what Marcus's place would be like if he lived alone.

A long oak table stood in the dining area; a large black wood-burning stove and two enormous, embracing sofas dominated the living side of the space. Classily worn Persian rugs softened the dark wooden floors and bookcases lined every wall, the few gaps between them filled with contemporary artworks. Bella and Olly ranged around like toddlers in a room full of new toys.

'Is that a Pollock?' Bella said, going over to a long, splashy piece of colour.

'Yep. And that's a Kline,' Stephen said, pointing to a block of black and white.

'Alice Neel,' Bella said, moving to a painting of a pregnant woman lying on a bed. 'I love Alice Neel,' she explained to Stephen. 'I went to the Whitechapel show with school.'

'I usually go for Abstract Expressionism,' Stephen said. 'But there's something about her . . .'

'What's this?' Olly said, pressing his nose up against a glass cabinet set into the wall. Inside, various stuffed birds perched in little stage sets of what Lara supposed were their natural environments. She went up to Olly and gazed in beside him. There was the bright blue bird she had seen on her run, and a hummingbird, suspended in flight beside a model of a flower.

'Bird taxidermy,' Stephen said. 'You can pick them up in antique stores all round here.'

'Cool,' Olly said, popping a piece of gum into his mouth and chewing furiously. Lara saw Marcus bristle at this. He had a rule about chewing gum.

'And that one's mine,' Stephen said, pointing to the blue bird. 'Roadkill. I found her on the way up here one day and had a go myself. It could be better. Drink, anyone?'

'Yes please,' Lara said. She was reeling from the surprise of this place. While the man wiping invisible crumbs from the kitchen work surface was both the Stephen she had loved and the Stephen Molloy of Hollywood fame, a lot of what she saw here – the art, the cooking, the books – had taken her unawares. These were habits and tastes he had picked up since they last met. Continually seeing him in the media, she'd had the impression that, accent apart, he hadn't changed in the slightest.

'What's your poison?' Stephen said.

'Do you have any red wine?' Lara asked, perching on the back of one of the sofas.

'And for me, please,' Marcus said.

'Guys, take a look in the fridge and take your pick,' he said to Bella and Olly. 'There's pop and there's juice. Can you get me one of those organic colas while you're at it?'

'You're not drinking?' Lara said. This, too, was new.

'Alcohol doesn't agree with me,' Stephen said. 'Or rather, it agrees with me too much. I had to put up quite an argument against it.'

'You don't mind if we do?'

'Not at all. It's a bit like passive smoking – quite a vicarious pleasure for the abstainer.' He poured two large glasses of red wine and handed them to Marcus and Lara. 'Try this. Francis Ford Coppola makes it. Not personally, of course. I'm told it's very good.' Lara felt his knuckle graze hers on the handover. 'Smells delicious, anyway.'

'Just one,' Marcus said. 'Then I'll stop.'

Stephen picked up a tray with a couple of bowls of olives and crisps on it and led them outside, through a fly-screen door that slammed shut behind them like a pistol shot, making Lara jump. Bella and Olly followed with Jack in tow, and they all sat at a weathered wooden table. Lara noticed how the curved back of her chair cupped her. It fitted her perfectly.

Jack pulled away from Bella and climbed on to Lara's lap, curling into her and twirling his finger in her hair. In the stultifying late-afternoon heat his squelchy body was almost too much for her to bear, but she didn't have the heart to push him away. She focused on the trees at the perimeter of Stephen's lawn. Their branches stood still, with no dapple or flutter in their foliage. The air had a filthy yellow tinge to it and the cicadas bored into her skull with their electronic whirring. She looked down and noticed a small black fly working its way up her arm.

'There's a storm in the air,' Stephen said. 'We have spectacular weather here.'

'Ow,' Olly said, slapping his calf. 'Little shit bit me. Ow. Again.'

'Cry baby,' Bella said.

'No see 'ums,' Stephen said, opening a slim drawer in the table. 'You really can't see them, but they give a nasty little nip. Here.' He threw a small bottle to Olly. 'Spray that on and pass it round. It'll keep the bugs off.'

They took turns to cover themselves in a citronella fug.

'What an amazing place,' Marcus said. 'How did you find it?'

'I built it,' Stephen said, offering round a bowl of olives. 'Not with my own hands of course. I bought this woodland, had the clearing made and built the house from the trees that were knocked down. All the stonework – the chimney and the central part of the house – comes from a small quarry on the land too.'

'That sounds so holistic and simple. So environmentally sound,' Marcus said, leaning forward rather too intensely.

Lara, struggling with Jack, who was pulling at her wine-holding hand, hoped Marcus wasn't going to spend the whole evening gushing. Keen to demonstrate his lack of issues about Stephen's success, he could easily go overboard. He didn't do moderation very well.

'It sounds like that, doesn't it?' Stephen said. 'But when I came to see how they were getting on mid-build, it looked like a scene out of a documentary on the decimation of the rainforest. They had to dig all these trenches through the trees to run the water from the spring and put in the septic tank. And I wanted the electrics buried too, so that meant even more digging.'

'Are you here permanently?' Lara said. Jack was now rubbing his head against her side, spreading snot over her green linen top.

'Until at least next summer, if not longer,' Stephen said. And, for the first time since they had arrived, he looked her directly in the eyes.

'What about your films?' Olly butted in.

'They can wait,' Stephen said. 'There are more important things.'

'Like avoiding stalkers,' Olly said.

'You could say that.'

'Oh Jack!' Lara said, as Jack finally managed to upend her glass, adding wine to the snot-trail on her front.

'Let me get you something,' Stephen said, standing up and heading back into the house.

'I don't think he wants to talk about the stalker, mate,' Marcus said to Olly once Stephen was out of earshot.

'Just making polite conversation,' Olly said.

'Just leave it, right?' Marcus said. 'And take the fucking gum out.'

Stephen came back out with a damp piece of kitchen towel and handed it to Lara. Again, for a second, their hands touched.

'So Trudi said she helps you out here,' Lara said to try to earth herself.

'Trudi?' Marcus said.

'You know, she was serving the meat at James and Betty's,' Olly said, helpfully drawing Trudi's scar line from lip to ear on his own face.

'Ooh, yes. Ouch,' Marcus said.

'She looks well rough,' Olly said.

'Olly,' Marcus said.

'That's because she's had a rough life,' Stephen said. 'She used to be a dancer, got into drugs and things descended from there. Spent five years inside.'

'What for?'

'Fraud, I think. Anyway, she found God, put on fifty pounds and when she got out Betty scooped her up – they used to work in this cabaret in the East Village together, and they're from the same part of Tennessee. She installed her in Trout Island as one of her charity cases. When I came here, Betty couldn't imagine how I would cope on my own, so Trudi was sworn to secrecy and loaned to me whenever I need a hand. I *don't* ever need a hand, but I send her off on the odd wild goose chase from time to time, just to keep everyone happy.'

'Mummy, I'm bored,' Jack said, banging his head against Lara's chest.

'Jack. That's so rude! I'm so sorry for my rude, rude son, Stephen,' Lara said.

'Sons,' Marcus corrected her, a stern eye on Olly.

'Well, it is pretty dull, listening to grown-ups go on and on. Would you guys like to take Jack out into the backyard?' Stephen said to Olly and Bella. He pointed to a grassy meadow that skirted round the side of the house. 'See if you can find any snakes?'

'Euch,' Bella said. 'No thanks.'

'Snakes!' Jack said, jumping off Lara's lap. 'Come on, Lolly.' He tugged at his big brother's hand.

'Take a stick,' Stephen said. 'There's a couple leaning against the wall by the back door.'

'Come on, weed,' Olly said to his sister.

'Oh God. All right then,' Bella said, getting up and following her brothers. 'But I'm not doing anything without a stick.'

The three adults watched the children as they tiptoed through the long grass, taking each step with enormous care, peering down to look at their feet in case they got snake-lucky.

'Great kids,' Stephen said, pouring more wine into Marcus's and Lara's glasses.

'You don't know the half of it,' Marcus said.

'I envy you,' Stephen said to Marcus.

Lara looked up from her dabbing, but his expression was neutral.

'But you've been the lucky one,' Marcus said.

'I think not.' Stephen turned to Lara. 'We should really put that top to soak,' he said. 'Or it'll be ruined.'

'It's fine, honestly. Please don't worry.'

'No, I'll find you a shirt to change into, and we'll get some stain remover on it. It's a beautiful top. You don't want to ruin it.' He looked at Lara for just one second, then he stood up. 'I'll be back in a tick.'

'Great guy. Nothing's too much trouble,' Marcus said, after Stephen had gone inside.

'He's certainly very kind.' Lara put her head down and rubbed the back of her neck, where the sweat had gathered at her hairline.

'I'd rather be inside in the air conditioning, though,' Marcus said.

They sat in silence, sipping their warm red wine in the stultifying heat. Somewhere in the distance, Lara heard a rumble of thunder. A tightening at her temples told her the storm was nearly on them.

'There you go,' Stephen said, coming back out through the fly screen, letting it snap shut behind him. 'You can roll the sleeves up. I hope it's OK.' He handed her a Prada man's shirt covered in a subtle geometric print. 'It should go with your trousers. Look, the colour here –' he pointed to the background, a dark olive green – 'is the exact shade. Give me your top when you've changed and I'll put a spot of Vanish on it.'

Lara took the shirt, amazed not only at his kindness, but also at the way he had noticed what she was wearing and the thought he had put into choosing the colour.

'Use my room to change in,' he said. 'Just go up the stairs and take the first right.'

She went inside and again the damn fly screen slammed shut behind her, making the skin on her face prickle with shock. The ceiling fan turned, cooling the interior, and whatever was cooking in the oven made the place smell like coming home. Stephen had a real touch; there was comfort here, and order. And for a man to have a bottle of Vanish, let alone know how to use it, astounded her. If she didn't know better, she would have given more credence to the 'Stephen Molloy is gay' rumours that buzzed from time to time around the celebrity gossip magazines she read in her dentist's waiting room. But here he was, welcome – if rare – proof that a straight man could be domestically competent.

'*What-if,*' he had said.

Wasn't she just getting carried away? What though, she thought as she climbed the dark, polished wooden staircase that turned on a square in the centre of the house, what if she hadn't found out she was pregnant by Marcus? What if the twins had never happened?

She stopped on the half-landing and held Stephen's shirt to her face, closing her eyes and breathing in the scent of him. He had been the love of her life. She had known it back then, and she realised now that she knew it still.

But then things might have gone differently had they been able to stay together. She remembered a story about a pre-Monica Lewinsky Hillary Clinton driving into a gas station where she was served by an ex-boyfriend. 'Imagine,' the guy said. 'If we'd married, you would have been the gas station guy's wife.'

'If we'd married,' Hillary corrected him, 'you would have been President of the United States.'

Lara would probably have been a reverse Hillary, holding Stephen back while Marcus went on to be the star. But perhaps everyone would have been happier like that?

She continued up the stairs and found Stephen's bedroom. The scent of him was strong in there, and she closed her eyes, breathing him in. A big, king-sized bed, perfectly made up with crisp linen, stood in the middle of the far wall. Beside it on one of the bedside tables was a pile of books, novels mostly: Roth, Bellow, Updike.

She peeled off her snot- and wine-stained top, thinking she would just quickly change, then make her way back down-stairs. But she needed a pee, and there was an en suite bathroom so immaculate it could have been in a five-star hotel. The toiletry items on the open shelves – aftershave, shaving soap, razor, toothpaste – were evenly spaced, each one turned to show its best side. Two towels were neatly folded over a metal radiator, and the rest were wound up in a wooden recess in the limestone wall, their clockwise-curled faces like a nest of fluffed-up ammonites. She marvelled at the man who lived in this way.

As she sat and peed, she noticed a row of pill bottles on top of the tall spotlit mirror over the sink. When she was done, she stood on the toilet lid and looked at them.

In amongst the vitamins and herbal supplements, she saw a plastic bottle of Xanax, a blister pack of Valium and a bottle of Prozac, which she shook and found to be half-empty. Not so surprising in America, even for a Brit, she supposed. She jumped down. Poor man, she thought, all on his own out here, with only his art and his books and his pills for company.

Looking in the mirror, she took off her bra and washed her underarms with Stephen's soap, patting them dry with his towel and anointing them with his deodorant. She didn't want to sweat on his lovely shirt. Then she replaced everything back where she found it, positioning it exactly.

Back in the bedroom, she buttoned up the cool cotton shirt. It was too big for her, of course, but not ridiculously so. Stephen was tall, but he was slim, so she felt less swamped than on the few occasions when she had worn Marcus's clothes. She remembered a time in Cambridge when, drunk, she had fallen from a punt wearing a white dress that turned transparent when wet. With a little persuading, Marcus had given her the shirt off his back to cover her modesty, and in return had received a nasty dose of sunburn. She had felt particularly lost in that shirt.

She looked at herself in the full-length mirror on Stephen's bedroom wall. He had been right. The colour went beautifully with her olive linen trousers. She rolled up the sleeves and undid another button at the neck.

Picking up her soiled top, she moved towards the bedroom door. But something held her back. Without really meaning to, she sat on what she knew would be his side of the bed and opened the drawer in the bedside table.

For a second, her heart stopped. Inside, right on top of everything else, was a photograph. Smiling up at her, her bob its original undyed black, her skin as yet unlined, her slim arm around a beaming Stephen, was her own nineteen-year-old self. She picked up the photo and peered closer. She was wearing that red floral crêpe dress with the slightly puffed sleeves, the dress she remembered living in that summer. From the angle of her other arm, she must have been taking the photograph, pointing the camera back at herself and her lover. Behind them the billowing tops of an ancient woodland outlined a blue sky and a green meadow.

She remembered that day as if it were yesterday.

Marcus was in rehearsal from early morning, going straight into an evening performance of *Henry IV, Part One*. Not being in the *Henry*, Stephen was free, and he wasn't called for rehearsal either. So, grasping their opportunity, they hired a car and drove south towards the rippled grassland of Dover's Hill, near Chipping Camden, where they ate strawberries and drank champagne before tiptoeing off to make a nest among the oak trees that had watched over that land since Norman times. And there, on that Gloucestershire hill riven with Iron Age workings, they made love properly for the first time.

Afterwards, they lay wound together, making plans for their future. She would tell Marcus that it was all over; they would disappear from him and move to London. She would go to drama school while Stephen worked and looked after her. And then they would be actors together and live in a house in Camden with its own front door and a long Persian carpet running along the hallway.

It was a remarkable day for many reasons, but most particularly because, for the only time in their short and intense affair, they were not involved in any sort of subterfuge – at least, not once outside the Stratford-upon-Avon town boundary. While affairs were commonplace in the incestuous theatre community there, they were usually between actors living away from their spouses. For Lara, barmaid promoted to wife of a company actor, cavorting publicly with someone else would have been unthinkable. So her liaison with Stephen had to be secret.

It was mad – she knew it at the time – but it had been unavoidable. Had she been older, more embedded in her marriage, had she not heard about Marcus marrying her on the rebound, she might have been better equipped to resist Stephen. But she knew back then, from the moment that he walked into her bar and looked at her, that he was bound for her.

If only they had met a year earlier. If only she hadn't married in such haste. She looked at the photo and reminded herself that, even then, the twins were secretly dividing their cells inside her. Even when she first met Stephen they had been there. The dates proved it. She had gone over and over this point.

And had she and Marcus repented at leisure? It hadn't been so bad, had it? The worst thing was the mourning she went through when Stephen left.

She had blundered into the Garrick Inn, light-headed and nauseous, not sure of how it was going to go with him. The doctor had assured her she was ten weeks pregnant. She had been seeing Stephen for eight, so she knew that the baby – she had no idea at that point about it being twins – was Marcus's. She slipped into the seat beside Stephen in the smoky back bar. He grabbed her hand underneath the table.

'You look beautiful today,' he said. 'Especially beautiful.'

She closed her eyes, looked down, breathed in deep, then levelled her gaze directly at him and told him what was on her mind and in her womb. The blood drained from his face.

'You're sure?' he said after what seemed to her like her entire lifetime.

'Yes.'

'Sure of the dates?'

'Yes.' Fat tears rolled down her first-trimester flushed cheeks. She hadn't dared to imagine what might happen at this meeting.

'But I could bring it up as my own,' he said, taking her hand now above the table. 'No one need ever know.'

Outside – and she didn't know why she could recall this detail so clearly – a convoy of vehicles with sirens went by, stopping all motion in the pub, making it impossible to talk, filling the bar with disco-flashing blue lights.

But what if it turned out to look like Marcus? she thought. Stocky, red-hair genes coursed through his entire family. How on earth would Stephen – tall, slender and dark – ever pass off a mini-Marcus as his own?

'I have to tell Marcus,' she said in the lull that followed the siren cacophony. 'I would never, ever forgive myself if I didn't.'

Stephen sighed as if he, too, saw the impossibility of their situation, then he put his hands across his face. Lara sat and looked at him, feeling like a tightrope walker with no safety net beneath her. When he eventually looked up, his eyes shone hot with tears.

'But then you'll be bound to him for ever, and I'll just be in the way,' he said.

'It could work . . .' she said, fiddling with the beer mat, which she had peeled into thin, curled strips.

The bar seemed to be closing in on her; the dull tang of nicotine caught in her throat and made her feel sick.

'I can't do it,' he said finally. 'I can't break up your family now there's a baby to think about as well.'

'No—' she said, reaching again for his hand.

'I'll disappear,' he said. 'I'll disappear, and you'll never see nor hear from me again.'

During that evening, she had ill-advisedly drunk two pints of Guinness, and he more pints of Abbot than she could count. In the end, they found themselves walking along the river, away from the theatre, killing time until Marcus's show finished; she had arranged to meet him after seeing Stephen to tell him she knew not what.

As they reached Shakespeare's church, he stopped and drew her into the bushes, where they had an inglorious, weeping, farewell fuck. Afterwards she stood up and brushed the bits of old leaf and twig from her brown corduroy skirt – again, the details she could recall shocked her – and she railed at him, called him a coward, demanded that he stayed to fight for her, to love her. How on earth could he throw away what they had?

'We belong to each other,' she said.

'I'm gone, Lara,' he said, looking down, his palms spread upwards. Then he leaned towards her and kissed her one last time before disappearing into the shadows. Leaving her shafted in every way, in the dark, all alone, feeling like a part of her had been sliced away without anaesthetic.

If only his promise that she would never see him again had held fast. But after wresting him from the clutches of his RSC contract for 'psychological reasons', his impressive agent got him a job in a no-budget, quirky thriller set in the Shetlands. The film went on to become that year's unexpected indie hit, winning the big prize at Sundance and launching the phenomenon of Stephen Molloy on to the world stage. And there he was, everywhere, in her face all the time.

Time passed though, and with it a measure of healing took place. She came to her senses a little. The twins, who taught her a new kind of love, kept her busy, too. She arrived at the conclusion that you win some and you lose some. Battling with the contradictory feelings of infatuation and exasperation her two babies inspired in her, she was usually too taken up to follow his all-too-public progress. And she convinced herself that, with his full and starry life, Stephen would have forgotten all about her anyway.

But his confession at the party, and now this photograph, made her realise that his departure must have been more painful for him than she had imagined. She wondered whether he had kept the photo to hand since they had parted in Stratford. Or had he just dug it out of a long-forgotten box in a corner of his attic once he knew she was here in the same town as him?

She looked back at the photograph of her young self, wondering what she would tell her if she had the opportunity. *Had* it been so awful, staying with Marcus? Her feelings about her husband ebbed and flowed, but wasn't that normal? Sometimes she could persuade herself that she loved him. Others she would find herself daydreaming, plotting elaborate escape plans that shocked her with their detail. She would empty their bank account, disappear, reinvent herself and get a little job in a shop to pay the rent on a simple bedsit. Or she would engineer an affair with someone inconsequential, then make sure Marcus found her in flagrante, thereby putting the onus on him to eject her. She sometimes found herself casting around the bus on the way to work, looking for candidates. He'd do, she would think. She wondered sometimes how it would be if Marcus were suddenly to die – keeling over from a heart attack, perhaps, or in one of those planes that fell out of the sky. Would it be sorrow she felt? Or would it be relief?

She opened Stephen's bedside drawer a little further to put the photograph away. But her hand was stayed by what she saw nestling there, only just visible under a pile of ironed linen handkerchiefs: the handle of a revolver.

Lara lifted the handkerchiefs to one side and bent to examine the gun, the first she had seen at such close quarters. Why would Stephen have it here, beside him in his bed? Perhaps this is what people did in America, especially if they lived too remotely for anyone to hear them scream, or so far from a police station that by the time the cops arrived, an intruder hell-bent on harming you would have been able to do whatever they pleased.

She touched the gun with the tip of her finger and shivered as she pushed out of her mind a picture of Marcus cowering in front of its barrel, flinching as it fired . . .

But this was rural Trout Island, where no one ever locked their door. Not downtown Detroit, or Chicago. Surely you didn't need guns out here.

'Lara?' Marcus called up the stairs. 'Are you OK up there?'

The sudden intrusion of her husband's voice made her jump. She replaced the pile of handkerchiefs, put the photo back exactly as she had found it, closed the drawer and picked up her dirty top, readying herself to go downstairs. She felt as if she had opened Pandora's box.

'Jesus, I thought you'd been eaten by a wild beast or something,' Marcus said as she turned the corner of the staircase. He stood in the hallway with another full glass of red wine in his hand.

'I'm fine,' he said, seeing her glance at his drink. 'The food'll mop it up.'

'Where is everyone?'

'Stephen's gone to help the kids. They're complaining they can't find any snakes.'

'Is it safe?' Lara said. 'Should they be actively searching them out?'

'He says there's only one poisonous snake around here and even that doesn't kill you. The copperhead or some such. Come on,' he said. 'He poured you another drink – over there, by the counter.'

Taking her wine, Lara followed Marcus on to the back deck, blinking in the light outside after the dark interior of the house. The back garden was an overgrown scrubby meadow ending in a hen house with a pile of logs neatly stacked up against it. Squatting by the side of the woodpile, Stephen and

Olly poked at something with a stick. Bella hung back, holding on to Jack.

Lara noticed how Stephen took the same stance as her son. Mirroring, wasn't it called? An attempt at winning someone over by making gestures similar to their own. It seemed to be working, too. Normally offhand and distant with adults, Olly was chatting with Stephen as if he were his best friend. Or perhaps it had more to do with the fact that, as the famous film star, Stephen had a better opportunity to win her son's favour than most.

'It slid in there, Mum.' Bella winced. 'It's about a metre long and hideous . . .'

'It's not dangerous,' Olly said.

'Look!' Stephen stepped backwards, away from the woodpile, brandishing the snake on the end of his stick. Curling itself up and lashing its head around wildly at whatever had dislodged it from its cool hiding place, the creature was every bit as long as Bella's estimate. It looped up and off the stick and everyone jumped backwards.

'Whoah,' Olly said. And he and Stephen bent as one to watch the snake make its quicksilver retreat across the meadow, towards the trees.

'Suits you,' Stephen said to Lara as he straightened up, his hand resting on Olly's shoulder.

'What?'

'The shirt. The colour's really good on you.'

'How much land have you got here, then?' Marcus asked, looking around him. The meadow was about the size of a football pitch and beyond it thick forest rose on all sides. A couple of tracks, big enough for a suitably rugged vehicle, disappeared into the darkness of the trees.

'Around five thousand acres,' Stephen said. 'Mostly forest.

But if you go down thataway,' he pointed to the track to their right, 'I've got a pond that's great for swimming and fishing. I'll take you over there one day in the Wrangler. Or we can walk. It's about a mile.'

'I'd love to walk there,' Lara said. 'And swim.'

'We'll do it,' Stephen said.

A rustle in the trees behind them made them all jump. Lara saw terror flash across Stephen's face as he swung round to see what had made the noise.

'Look, Jack, another deer!' Bella said, pointing out the receding white rump. 'And a baby deer.'

'It's called a fawn,' Olly said.

'Baby deer,' Jack said firmly.

'It's just a deer, then,' Stephen said to no one in particular. Only Lara seemed to read the relief in his remark. Then he turned and smiled at Marcus. 'More wine?'

By the time they sat down to eat, the sun had gone down behind the wooded hill, spreading a spidery gloom over the house. Stephen switched the lights on low and lit candles around the table. Then he opened the windows to let the air, which was cooling with the approaching storm, circulate through the room. With it came a resinous smell from the heat-sweltered trees, giving the lofty space the feeling of a cathedral after the swinging of the censer. But the pressure in the atmosphere made Lara feel dizzy, as if she were about to implode.

Stephen served up the stew – venison, he said, that he had shot and prepared himself. Perhaps, Lara thought, that explained the gun, although wasn't hunting more usually done with rifles? As they passed round the plates, the lights in the house flickered and somewhere, not too far in the distance, a deep roll of thunder rumbled, making the glasses on the table shiver.

'Not long now,' Stephen said.

'What's it like being so famous?' Olly said, tucking into his stew.

'Olly,' Marcus said, accepting Stephen's glass refill.

'No, it's a good question, Olly.' Stephen sat down and rested his elbows on the table. 'It's not something I ever wanted or planned. It just sort of happened. As an actor, you tend to say yes when someone offers you work. You're never really in control. And my work just took me in this direction. Of course, I've earned good money, and I can buy whatever comforts I could ever need in this world, but I've paid the price. So many things that you're able to do are impossible for me now. For instance, I can't just go out to the shops, or for a walk, or get on a plane. If you like, it's a sort of gilded prison.'

'It's true. I never wanted the kind of fame you've got,' Marcus agreed, spraying a fleck of half-chewed deer on to the table.

Liar, Lara thought. Being Stephen-Molloy-famous was exactly what Marcus had been after his entire professional life. He had positively bristled with pleasure when people stopped him in the street after the *EastEnders* part. He loved being pointed at by the general public.

'I'm far happier as a jobbing actor,' Marcus went on, shovelling in another mouthful of stew. He was slurring, running his words into each other as he did when headed towards the rollicking drunkenness he was capable of. Lara cursed. She should have known better than to assume he was going to be responsible. She had certainly drunk too much to drive, so now here they were, neither of them able to safely get their family back to their beds for the night. And with a storm on the way as well.

'Listen,' Stephen said, seeming to read her mind. 'If you guys want, you can stay over. Make an evening of it. I've four guest rooms, and the beds are all made up. Driving down to Trout Island is hard enough in the daylight if you don't know the way, but in the dark, in a storm – and this one is settling in for the night, according to the weather reports – it's a recipe for endlessly circling round and round the mountain, before you even start to worry about trees being brought down.' He stood up and got the wine bottle again.

'I don't know—' Lara began.

'That would be great!' Olly said.

'But—' Bella said.

'Cheers, mate,' Marcus said, clapping his arm around Stephen, who was topping up his glass. 'I'm a little over the limit already, if truth be told. And my call's not till two.'

'I need to be back by ten tomorrow morning,' Bella whispered to Lara.

Stephen smiled at Marcus. 'Don't mention it. It's just great to see you again. It can get pretty lonely hiding out here.'

'Why?' Lara asked Bella.

'I'm meeting someone . . .'

'Lara? What do you say?'

'We'll be back in time, I promise,' Lara reassured her daughter. She thought about the dark, unmade roads between where they were now and the dusty, smelly house back in the village and felt relieved that they were going to stay put. She was aware that staying here, in Stephen's home, was dicing with danger, putting herself in temptation's way. But what could really happen with all her family around her?

'Thank you Stephen,' she said.

'Good. That's settled then. Seconds, anyone?' Stephen said.

'Yes please,' Marcus said. 'That was delicious.'

'You did your GCSEs this year?' Stephen asked the twins after he had served Marcus.

'Yep. Just finished,' Bella said.

'And what next?'

'Um, I'm off to college to do Art, Textiles and Photography.'

'Good girl,' he said.

'She's a proper little artist, our Bella,' Marcus chipped in.

'And what about you?' Stephen turned to Olly.

'I'm doing History, Politics and Economics.'

'More of an academic, then?' Stephen said.

'Oxbridge material, he's been told, *if* he sticks at it,' Marcus said, messily tucking into his second plateful. A corona of red sauce bloomed around his plate.

'So tell me where you stand on the government cuts,' Stephen said, turning to Olly.

Stephen carried on, drawing the children out. Even Jack was quizzed about his favourite TV characters and was delighted when Stephen revealed that he was the voice of a cartoon robot he particularly liked.

'If you come and visit me in LA I can take you on a tour of the studios where they make it,' he said, and Jack clapped his hands with glee.

Lara didn't think her children had ever talked so much at table. Usually people without children of their own didn't really know how to address anyone under twenty, and those who were parents often seized the chance for adult conversation and ignored the kids. So Bella, Olly and Jack would sit silently eating and, at the earliest opportunity, they'd slope off. But not so here.

Dessert was peaches with blueberries and maple syrup from Stephen's trees. He had won Olly and Bella so fully that, without asking, they helped him clear the plates. Then they all sat down as he made coffee – grinding the beans by hand and using a cafetière – and put a bottle of port on the table.

'Can I have some, Mum?' Olly asked, leaning back in his chair and placing his hands behind his head.

'Course you can, son,' Marcus said, pouring him a glassful.

'Would you like some too, Bella?' Stephen said.

'Yes please.'

Stephen got up and brought the bottle over to her. As he leaned past Lara to pour the drink, his shirt brushed her cheek and her vision flickered in the candlelight.

A flash of lightning lit up the windows, followed, seconds later, by an ear-splitting clap of thunder.

'It's nearly here,' Stephen said. 'I'll get a few more candles ready. Storms usually mean power cuts.'

'Really? I'd have thought they'd have sorted that out in this, the richest country in the world,' Olly said.

'The infrastructure's a complete mess here,' Stephen said. 'Every time there's a storm, the electricity cuts out. The roads are terrible. Have you driven down either side of Manhattan? There are better roads in Kinshasa. Believe me, I've been there. They had big floods here about six years ago and they're still rebuilding the bridges. In the meantime the rivers have flooded again and no one has done anything to prevent it happening in the first place.'

'I have to say I was pretty shocked at the dilapidation around Trout Island,' Lara said, allowing the warm port to trickle down her throat. 'I'd expected America to be far more padded from all that.'

'It's the collapse of capitalism in motion,' Stephen said.

'Ah yes,' Marcus laughed. 'You were a bit of a Trot, weren't you, I seem to remember.'

'People have just upped and left their houses,' Stephen went on. 'They can't afford to keep them, can't pay their mortgages, can't sell them. Now the banks own them, no one wants to buy them, and they're slowly returning to the earth. Look at Detroit – large parts of the city are reverting to the rural. People are growing their own food in the empty yards around their neighbourhoods because they can't afford to shop any more. If you're sick, you run up bills of millions of dollars and your insurers will refuse to renew your policy. If you're a poor young person your best career prospect is being shot at in Afghanistan. Now they're trying to look for natural gas round here and the extraction process will involve chemicals that get into the water table and pollute us all. It's the vested interests of the powerful against the tiny voice of the people. That's how it is, here. Welcome to America.'

'Wow. Why are you here then if you hate it so much?' Olly said.

'Olly!' Marcus said.

'No, he's right,' Stephen said. 'I often ask myself that. Apart from the fact the work's here, this country, like it or not, is the nearest I've been to calling anywhere home since I left my mum's house in Manchester when I was sixteen. She's dead now and I've got no siblings, no cousins, nothing. If I belong anywhere, I belong here.'

'Why don't you do something about it then? You've got loads of money,' Olly said, emboldened by being treated like an equal.

'I'm in survival mode,' Stephen said, looking levelly at him. 'Sometimes, whatever you believe, you've just got to look after number one.' Then he looked down at his hands, and Lara thought how beautiful he was as the candlelight caught the edges of his cheekbones, working with his words to lay his topography bare.

Again, the lightning flashed and almost immediately the thunder rolled like a bad Foley effect. The room fell silent. Lara felt the sweat prick at her back. One by one, the people at the table brought their drinks up to their mouths, as if in slow motion.

Then, with a sudden release, the rain started. It rattled on the roof and battered at the windows, pouring as if someone had turned on a thousand taps above the house. An adrenaline flash of lightning coincided simultaneously with a shuddering thunderclap.

Stephen got up to shut the windows, to stop the rain flooding in.

And then the lights went out.

Twenty-One

AFTER SHE HAD PUT JACK TO BED, LARA CHECKED IN ON the twins, who had a room each and bedtime reading supplied by Stephen: for Olly a book of Byron's poetry and Bella a monograph of Alice Neel. Then she went down to join Stephen on a covered porch at the back of the house, where he sat in the light of an oil lamp, looking out at the night. The storm still raged outside, flattening the grass, filling indentations in the ground and turning them into puddles that threatened to become ponds. Marcus, who had finished off the port and half-emptied a bottle of Maker's Mark, lay conked out on the sofa, his snores competing with the thunder in their ability to set Lara's nerves on edge.

'Who'd have thought the old sky would have had so much water in it,' Lara said as she sat down, slightly apart from Stephen on a cushioned swing that was the only available seating.

Stephen smiled and looked up at the murky sky. 'I wish it was a beautiful night,' he said. 'It's like a piece of heaven here when it's still and clear. We'd have built a bonfire. It's shooting star season too, though of course you have to be out on the open land round the front to really get the full panorama. Once I saw one arc right through the sky. I swear it landed. I swear I heard a bang and saw a flash. But then again, the mind can play tricks.' He stopped suddenly and turned to her. 'Tell me you're happy.'

'What?' Lara said.

'Tell me you're happy with him.'

'Of course I am,' she said, shifting in her seat. 'Of course I'm happy.'

'I need to hear that,' he said, searching her out. But Lara kept her eyes firmly on the streaks of rain that, caught in the glow cast by the oil lamp, looked like slashed silk, whirling in the wind. 'I need to hear that, because if you're not happy, what was our sacrifice worth?'

'I love my children,' she said, drawing her arms around herself, hot again despite the chill misted into the air by the rain. She wanted to run away, into the stormy forest.

'And you love him?'

She hugged herself tighter and closed her eyes. She didn't want to hear this. Despite everything, she had never allowed the words to be spoken out loud.

'It wasn't fair, what happened,' he said eventually. 'We were too weak. Too conventional. I thought I was doing the honourable thing. But had I been bolder, I would have fought for you. Guns at dawn. Bella and Olly: they could have been mine, you know.'

Lara looked sharply up at him.

'I could have raised them as my own. They wouldn't even have known.'

'Stop this,' Lara said. 'This is all in the past. We can't change it now.'

He reached across the swing seat for her hand.

'I need to go now,' she said, getting up. She suddenly felt protective of Marcus, sorry for all he stood to lose. She needed to go through to the house and wake him, to walk him upstairs and climb into bed beside him, with her clothes on and her hands over her ears.

'Don't go,' Stephen said, standing and reaching again for her. He caught her arm and drew her towards him. He was much taller than her, almost a foot taller, and she wouldn't have been able to resist him even if she had wanted to. She looked up at him as he took her hands.

And there it was. The part of him that had lodged so firmly in her DNA long ago thrummed inside her, as if she had never known anything different. She felt his heartbeat through his palms, heard his breath as if it were her own.

If it hadn't been for the crash of a nearly empty bottle of Maker's Mark hitting the floor, sent flying by Marcus's foot as he shifted his position on the sofa, who knows where Lara and Stephen would have ended up. But the sound sprang them apart. Then, distracted, they went indoors to clear up the glass, the whisky and Marcus, who was messily, blearily awake. By then, Lara had regained her senses enough to touch Stephen on the cheek and shake her head as she whispered goodnight to him. He placed the oil lamp in her hand and pointed her in the direction of the bedroom she was to share with her husband.

'I'm sorry,' he said, leaning in close to help her as she hoisted Marcus's arm around her shoulder to lead him up the stairs. 'That was mad.'

Placing the lamp on a table by the bed, she tumbled Marcus in between the sheets and went into the small en suite bathroom, where she took off her shoes and trousers, splashed her face with cold water and removed her contact lenses, avoiding her own gaze as much as possible.

She felt stirred up, sick, excited – the same as she used to when she was forced by her parents to attend weekend riding lessons. Her fear of horses – all so impossibly huge against her own, runtish height – and the threat of something going really, badly wrong, always saw her spending Saturday mornings on the toilet, jodhpurs round her ankles, not sure if she wanted to empty her bowels or throw up. She knew now that for a young girl, when sex seems nothing more than a remote and messy thing adults do, that feeling was a trial run for desire.

She moved to the bedroom window to close the curtains, but found herself held there, her myopic eyes searching out some sort of form in the darkness. Tiny splashes of water sieved in through the fly screen and chilled her burning skin. All she could make out was a velvety blue, where trees and creatures and God knows what else lurked. She was just about to break away when, without warning, a sickening fork of lightning shot straight down into the lawn, shocking the entire back garden into illumination. As Lara flinched from the window – she had heard that lightning could strike right into houses – her weak eyes picked out the blurred form of a woman, standing in the rain at the edge of the forest. But, as the almost simultaneous clap of thunder battered her eardrums, everything plunged back into darkness.

Lara rubbed her eyes, which still held the imprint of the figure. She squinted up to the fly screen and held her breath, trying to force her eyes to work better. But she could see nothing. No movement in the inky black, no sound except the rattle of the rain on the roof above her head, and no more lightning to show her anything else or to make sure she wasn't mistaken.

She closed the curtains and went to her side of the giant bed. It was stupid to trust her eyes when there couldn't logically be anyone out there, up here, in this weather; she couldn't see more than ten feet in front of her without contact lenses. And that, with the storm, the flash and the senseless state she was in, must have led her to see things that weren't there.

Ridiculous. What a ridiculous evening altogether.

She blew out the lamp and slipped in between the sheets, huddling her arms around herself on the very edge of the bed, burying down into Stephen's shirt, which she still had on. She could hear Marcus snoring where he lay, six feet away, on his back, his ginger curls splayed around him like the mane of a drugged lion.

What now, she thought. What now?

She had no idea. The only thing she was sure of was, as if it had been in that smashed whisky bottle, the genie was now out there, roaring about with the thunder and lightning, and there was very little chance he was going to put himself away again.

Twenty-Two

THANKS TO ALICE NEEL, BELLA DREAMED OF DISTORTED women hurling babies over their rippled shoulders and bubble-fat twins rolled over and over on a crumpled bedspread. The lightning flashed her half-awake from time to time, and an insistent grunting and scratching somewhere beneath her window gave her an insomniac hour with the duvet pulled over her head, trying to convince herself it was forest wildlife and not some madman clawing his way up the wall to her room.

The whole unsatisfactory night was crowned when she woke at five and lay in the watery dawn light, unable to get back to sleep in case she missed her opportunity to be in Trout Island in time for her date with Sean. She didn't know whether it was then, in her morning doze, or before, that she heard footsteps on the landing outside her room.

At eight, delicious smells finally pulled her from her bed and downstairs to the kitchen area, where Stephen, his back to her, stood working at the stove in running shorts and a close-fitting T-shirt.

'Morning,' she said. Stephen jumped.

'Sorry,' he said. 'You took me by surprise.'

'Smells good.'

'There's tea in the pot.' He motioned to the centre island counter, where a knitted cosy sat on a squat, fat teapot. 'I've never got into that American habit of starting the day with coffee. Need me PG Tips first.'

'Cheers.' Bella poured herself a cup in one of the hand-thrown mugs he had put out.

'You're the first up,' Stephen said, returning to his frying pan, which Bella saw contained thick pancakes. 'After me, of course. I like to get out for my run before it gets too hot.'

'Mum runs, too.'

'Does she? That's new.'

For a moment, Bella couldn't quite believe she was here, in Stephen Molloy's kitchen, as he cooked breakfast. Even though he was old enough to be their father, she and her friends all had a bit of a thing for him. Unlike her dad, he clearly looked after himself. He didn't have even a hint of an old bloke's beer belly, and his shoulders were as toned as Sean's.

But then again, it was his job to stay fit. Whereas, she supposed, her father was more of a character actor so it didn't matter too much what he looked like. And what would it be like for her if he *were* as good-looking as Stephen? Wouldn't it be, to say the least, a bit embarrassing having all her friends mooning about over her dad? No, she was glad she had comfortable, average Marcus for a parent.

'Did you hear the porcupine in the night?' Stephen said. 'He comes and gnaws at the deck-post just under your window. Makes a hell of a racket.'

'So that's what it was,' Bella said. 'I thought you only got porcupines in Africa.'

'Yeah, sorry. I forgot to warn you.'

Bella perched on a tall bar stool at the island counter. 'Food smells great.'

'I thought I'd treat you to a great American breakfast.' Stephen stopped and smiled at her. 'God, you're like your mother.'

'So they say,' Bella said, feeling slightly awkward. 'Did you know her well when she was younger?'

'Yes.' He turned back to his cooking, lifting out one batch of pancakes and pouring another into the pan. 'I knew her a bit when she was first married to Marcus. Look,' he said, tipping a handful of blueberries on to the puddles of batter. 'Fresh eggs laid this morning make the best pancakes; the berries add sharpness and sweetness. I just picked them from my patch over the top of the hill.' He motioned through the window with his spatula. 'Maple-cured streaky bacon, fried to a crisp as is proper, and the whole lot topped off with a pat of whipped butter and more of my maple syrup.'

'Wow,' she said. 'If I carry on with food like that, I'll be the size of a house by the time I leave.'

'I very much doubt that,' he said, looking her up and down.

'Morning.' Lara appeared on the half-landing above the kitchen. She was showing every second of her age – her eyes were bloodshot and puffy and her voice croaked. A hangover, Bella supposed. The parents had been packing it away the night before.

'Oh hi.' Stephen smiled up at her, and for a second Bella wondered if he had once held a candle for her mother. But she dismissed it out of hand. Her parents were married when he knew her. He'd just said so himself.

'Have we got electricity again?' Lara asked.

'It's all restored,' Stephen said. 'Anyone else showing signs of life?'

'I do need to be back by ten, remember, Mum,' Bella said.

'Jack's up and in with his dad, so it's only Olly to get up now.'

'Help yourself to tea, Lara. It's pretty fresh,' Stephen said.

She poured herself a mugful and went to stand at the open dining-area window, where she breathed in deeply. 'It's so fresh out there, after the rain. Less hot too, I think. Don't you?'

'It'll warm up again pretty soon,' Stephen said.

Lara turned and smiled brightly at Bella. 'Why don't I go and wake Olly up, then you and me can slip outside for a turn around. Get some fresh air.'

'All right.' Bella shrugged. Her mother didn't seem able to stay still for a moment.

'Tell them upstairs breakfast will be ready in half an hour,' Stephen said as Lara headed up the stairs. 'I've got a stack of pancakes to make, but they keep well in the stove.'

Bella watched him work. 'Don't you ever get lonely out here?'

'Sometimes,' he said. 'But then, after LA, it's quite welcome really.'

'It must be fun out there, though.'

'Believe me, Bella. It's mental.' He smiled at her. 'The best of times and the worst of times. There's always someone watching you, wanting a piece of you.'

'I think I'd quite like that.'

'You wouldn't. Believe me.'

Bella looked at him. She wanted to ask him more about his life in LA – who his friends were, what he did, where he went. And she burned to know the details of that breakdown and his run-in with the stalker. But it was all too indelicate. She wasn't like Olly.

'But,' Stephen said. 'I'm really, really glad you guys are here for the summer. It'll be great just to do normal stuff with you lot and your mum. There's loads to do hereabouts if you know where to go. I'll be your guide.'

'Sounds good,' Bella said. Being shown around by a movie star would be quite a treat. She wondered, though, how he'd manage it without anyone spotting him.

'That was hard work,' Lara said as she came back downstairs. 'Like raising the dead. Come on then, Bell.' She linked arms with her. 'Take me outside.'

'See you in a bit,' Stephen said, as they went out the back door.

'You'll have to guide me,' Lara said. 'I didn't come prepared for an overnight stay so I haven't got my glasses or any more lenses.'

The sun had already heated up the wet greenery, creating a haze around them, like the steam room at the Prince Regent pool, Bella thought. The air hung heavy with the smell of damp humus while the insects cranked up their din for another day.

'This grass is so coarse,' Lara said. 'Not at all like the mossy stuff back home.'

They wandered over to a vegetable plot in a sunny spot by the lawn's edge.

'Look at the courgettes.' Bella bent down to reveal a mottled fruit half hidden by a prickled leaf. At its end a yellow flower hung, at an early stage of shrivel. 'There's thousands.'

'That's what you call a glut,' Lara said. 'And look – is that basil and tomatoes? We really should sign up for an allotment when we get back.'

'Well don't count on me to help you,' Bella said. 'I don't like getting muddy.'

'It's nice to dream though. Isn't it? About growing things?'

Bella looked at her mum and noticed she had a tear on her cheek. 'You all right there?'

'Oh yes. It's just me hormones.' Lara picked a basil leaf and rolled it between her fingers, then held it up to her face. 'What are you doing so we have to be back by ten, then?'

'Meeting someone.'

'Is it that nice boy from the party?' Lara asked as they crossed the lawn to a garden bench in front of a fire bowl.

'Yes.'

'Where are you going?'

'Swimming.'

'Where?'

'At his cousin's place.'

'Lovely,' Lara said, sitting down on the bench. 'Is it far?'

'I don't know.' Bella sat down next to her mother.

'Is he driving you there?'

'Possibly.'

'Well tell him to take great care. And if he drinks anything, refuse to get in the car.'

'Mum . . .'

'I mean it. You're precious cargo.'

She always said that.

'And just—' Lara went on.

'Just what?' Bella was beginning to get irritated.

'Just make sure he takes care of you. And be careful.'

'I can take care of myself, Mum.'

'I'm sure you can. I felt the same way as you when I was your age. But I was perfectly capable of making mistakes. And I did. Believe me.'

Bella stood, picked up a stick and poked at the cinders in the fire bowl. Still damp from the rain, they had the smell of a burned house drenched by firefighters' hoses.

'Just keep your head, Bell, OK?'

'Let's go back in,' Bella said, lobbing the stick up into the mist, where it turned itself around to land with a whip-crack on the grass near the trees.

'I'm going to stay out here for a bit,' Lara said. 'Give me a shout when breakfast's ready. And help Stephen lay the table or something, OK?'

'I really don't need you to tell me to do that, Smother.'

'I know.'

Bella left her mother sitting hunched up, pulling the shirt Stephen had lent her around herself as if she were cold, gazing at where the fire would have been. She was in an odd, pernickety sort of mood this morning. It got on Bella's nerves, the way she wouldn't just let her get on with things. She was nearly seventeen, for God's sake. If she wasn't old enough to look after herself by now, she never would be.

She went back into the house to help the film star lay the table and serve up his pancakes and bacon breakfast.

Twenty-Three

BY NINE THIRTY THE WAYLANDS WERE BACK AT THE TROUT
Island house, where Dog awaited them on the lawn. Taking
Jack's hand, Marcus skirted around, keeping as much distance
between the creature and the allergies as possible. When Lara
opened the front door a blast of rotten-sweet air hit her, as
warm as if she had opened an oven. The stench of the house
seemed stronger than ever.

Apart from Bella, who ran upstairs to get changed, they
were all, for one reason or another, at a pretty low ebb. Olly
grabbed his guitar and slumped on the sofa in the stifling living
room, strumming out a plaintive Beirut song. Jack flopped
around, whining about the heat.

'I'm going to the garage to get some Diet Coke,' Marcus
said, grabbing a ten-dollar note from Lara's purse. It was his
favourite hangover cure: a couple of ibuprofen washed down
with a can of what he called 'the shit-coloured nectar'.

Lara kicked off her clogs, found some fresh contact lenses,
sorted Jack out with his colouring books then headed for the
kitchen to get a bowl of water for Dog. She was just about to

cross the floor in her bare feet when she realised it was covered in smithereens of smashed glass and splats of red wine. Marcus must have had a drink before they went out – for Dutch courage, perhaps? – left it half drunk, and somehow it had got knocked off. Now she had sour wine, splinters of glass and a trail of ants to contend with. Tiptoeing around the carnage, she fetched the dustpan and brush.

As she squatted to reach the last shards of glass, Bella appeared in the kitchen doorway, looking so lovely in her striped jersey vest dress and flip-flops that Lara felt a slight catch in her throat. She had her camera bag slung over her shoulder, and her sunglasses perched on her head, holding her hair back from her face.

Lara got up and gave her daughter a hug. She had only just started to have to reach up to embrace her, and it still felt strange, as if some sort of tables were being turned.

'Do be careful, Bell,' she said.

'Sigh,' Bella said, rolling her eyes.

'All I'm saying is keep your heart and your head. Be safe.'

'I'm going swimming, Mother. In a pond. It's not as if there are weapons involved.'

'You know what I mean.'

'Oh, Ma, do back off,' Bella said. But it was good-natured enough for Lara to feel able to kiss her on the cheek. 'I'll be home by suppertime,' she said, rubbing the spot where Lara's lips had touched and turning to go. Lara went to the kitchen archway to watch her cross the living room, her little dress flipping to reveal the backs of her perfect legs.

'Be careful, Bella,' Olly said in the deep, whispering voice he used to imitate his mother at her most earnest. He placed his hand over the guitar strings and gave her a look that was decidedly unmaternal.

'Fuck *off* Olly,' Bella said to her brother. Then she slipped out of the door and was gone.

'I tend to agree with her,' Lara said.

'Jesus,' Olly said, and bent his head to his guitar again to play something a bit less laid-back.

It was a testament either to Jack's concentration on his colouring or to the everyday nature of such scenes for him, that he didn't bat an eyelid throughout this exchange.

As Lara at last filled the water bowl for poor, patient Dog, she thought perhaps she should make another attempt to talk with Olly. She was just carrying the full bowl through the living room when a ferocious barking from Dog made her jump and spill water down the front of Stephen's shirt, which she was still wearing. She had left her linen top at his house and wondered if it was still soaking in Vanish. If so, the colour would have leached out of it by now.

'Can you go and see what's up?' she asked Olly as she went back into the kitchen to dab at the shirt.

'Fuck's sake.' Olly threw his guitar down, lurched up and got the door. 'Dude,' Lara heard him say in an altogether different tone. The greeting was followed by the slap of young male palms. Returning to the living room, she peered through into the hallway. Framed by the door, two baseball-capped shapes slouched in low-slung trousers.

'What's happening, dude?' one of them asked.

Olly looked over his shoulder then turned again to his guests. Their voices fell to a murmur as he leaned against the door frame, discussing something. Lara strained to hear what they were saying, but it was too quiet.

'Hang there a second,' he said, as he turned to go back to the living room. Lara darted into the kitchen. She didn't want him to think she had been eavesdropping.

'Hey Mom,' Olly called. His voice had a strange colour to it – a slight American accent already. 'I'm off with the guys. Cool?'

'Um, OK, then. Cool.' She went through to the hallway to be introduced to the 'guys', but before she got there Olly had followed his new friends out on to the porch, slamming the front door behind him so violently it made the painted-in window frames rattle, and the rotten stink of the house whirl about her.

Watching the boys lope away down Main Street, Lara finally gave Dog his water. Then she went back to the living room, sat on the sofa and closed her eyes. At least they were both making some friends, she thought. At least there's that. Then her mind moved from her children to what had happened the night before between her and Stephen and she shivered. But she had to fold all of that away. She had told him no, and he had apologised, and that was that.

It just wasn't fair that she had found Stephen here. Of all the bastard tricks fate could play on her.

A shadow fell over her.

'Coke?'

She opened her eyes and saw Marcus standing in front of her, offering her a cold red and silver can.

'I didn't hear you come in,' she said.

'I'm trying to move a bit more lightly,' he said. 'I know it annoys you, my blundering about. And this house is a bit of a drum.'

'I'm honoured,' she said, taking the can. 'It's stifling in here, isn't it?'

'Tell you what. Let's go outside while Jack the lad's so engrossed in his colouring. There's a nice breeze out front.'

'OK.' She held out a hand for him to pull her up.

'Stephen was right, you know,' Marcus said, looking at her.

'What?' She turned away to hide the redness that had crept up the sides of her cheeks.

'That colour is really good on you.'

'Well, isn't this nice?' Marcus said as they stretched out on the swing seat. He lifted his legs round to rest in her lap. Dog sat on the lawn, looking up at them.

'Good boy,' Lara said.

'I don't want him in the house,' Marcus said.

'Don't worry. Stay, boy,' Lara said, and the dog stretched out and lay down, resting his head on his front paws. 'Have you managed to ask anyone about a car yet?'

'I've asked,' Marcus said. 'Nothing definite yet.'

'We're going to have to do something,' she said, but she knew she'd end up having to sort it out herself.

They sat there swinging in the heat, swigging on their drinks.

'I wonder if we'll ever get used to this closeness,' she said. A new layer of mugginess had placed itself over the fresher storm-cleared day. Lara felt the sweat trickle down the backs of her knees where they were weighted down by Marcus's legs. Every pore on his face was pink, open and glistening.

'What time do you start today?' she asked him.

'Two. James and Betty said they needed a morning off before they throw themselves in again. It's only going to be a read-through. Nothing too strenuous, thank God.' Marcus slugged back the last drop of Coke from his can and crumpled it in his fist.

'One show opened, then straight into rehearsal for the next. It's full on for them, isn't it?'

'Only for the summer months. Otherwise they just potter about, more or less.'

They sat, swinging slightly, watching nothing happen on the empty street. Dog, who had fallen asleep, whimpered and changed position.

'Could you live out in the middle of nowhere do you think?' Marcus asked. 'Like him?'

'I don't know.' She brushed a strand of hair out of her eye. 'I don't think I'd be too good if I ever had to be on my own. Too scared.'

'Do you want to know a secret?' Marcus said, putting his hands behind his head and stretching. 'When I first saw him at that party I thought I'd be too jealous to cope.'

Lara held her breath. 'How do you mean, jealous?'

'Of his success. He got up there and I didn't.'

Relieved, Lara made a move to protest, but he held up his hand to stop her.

'It's true. I work, but I barely make a living, and no one is obsessed enough to actually stalk me. But do you know? I really like the guy. I'd forgotten about that, not having seen him in person for so long. I really like him.'

'That's good,' Lara said.

'And, in a way, I feel sorry for him. He might be one of the biggest stars in Hollywood, but he hasn't got half of what I've got. He hasn't got all this.' Absurdly, Marcus gestured towards the house. But Lara knew what he meant.

'It's taken me all this time to realise it, but I am far, far, luckier than Stephen Molloy.' Marcus reached over and took her hand. 'And,' he went on, rubbing his finger up against her palm in the way she found so irritating, 'who knows? If my agent manages to pull out the stops we talked about before I left, well then, some big Manhattan casting guy might well come up here, see me give my Mr Mack and say, "That's the ginger cunt for us."'

Despite the weight in her heart, Lara laughed.

'I've got a good feeling about this job. The lead in the Scottish Play! So many great lines. I might end up having it all with icing AND a cherry on top. You never know.'

'You never know . . .' she said. Her gaze trailed off to a vanishing point at the far end of Main Street. That was one thing you could say for Marcus. His optimism rarely deserted him.

'Mummy, I'm bored.' Jack slopped through on to the deck. 'I'm hungry.'

'I'd better get on with the old lines,' Marcus said, swinging his legs off Lara and reaching for his bag, which lay on the porch where he had dumped it when they arrived.

Lara got up and let herself be led by her youngest son, back into the kitchen.

Twenty-Four

MARCUS WAS AT REHEARSAL, BELLA AND OLLY WERE OUT, Jack was asleep and Lara had some free time to get on with her business plan. Instead, she tidied up. She marvelled at the mess her family could create in just a couple of days. Because she hadn't yet designated a place for laundry, Bella, Olly and Marcus had gone native, leaving dirty underwear, stinking socks and T-shirts on the bedroom floors, dumped where they had been taken off. She thought there might be enough washing to justify a trip to the launderette, which James had told her was along Main Street, beyond the turning to the theatre.

As she went around the rooms picking things up and putting them in a bag, she tried not to think about Stephen and what was going to happen next. If she put it away to the back of her mind, the issue might resolve itself with no effort from her. But the imprint of him on her body was hard to ignore. Every step she took seemed to have a new significance. She felt his presence in the walls of the room, watching her every gesture, weighing it with his eyes.

She felt this as she lay on her front on Bella's floor, stretching her arm under the bed to retrieve a pair of knickers. Under his imagined gaze, it was more a dance movement than a domestic manoeuvre. As she dragged the knickers towards her, a piece of paper caught on them. Kneeling up with her find, Lara saw it was an old photograph of a girl, aged about twelve, unsmilingly confronting the camera. She was dressed in what Lara supposed must be nineteen forties' clothing. Turning it over, she saw someone had written 'Jane' on the back.

Lara brushed the dust from the photo and propped it up on Bella's window frame.

'Mummy!' Jack shouted from his bedroom, marking the end of Lara's time to herself. Now she had a long, hot afternoon stretching ahead, with only Jack for company.

'How about a trip to the launderette, Jacky?' she said. 'I'll just get changed first.' She wanted to add Stephen's shirt to the wash, although her motive for doing so – if it was clean, she would have to take it to him – made her feel slightly ashamed of herself.

She gave Jack a book to look at while she took a shower in the little roll-top tub. As the icy water drew the heat from her body, an unprecedented clarity of thought hit her. She was going to have to tell Stephen to forget about it all and leave her alone. This family she had was more important to her than anything else in the world, and she had to put them first, before any selfish desires of her own.

Everyone – most people – would be happier if things just remained as they were.

She climbed out of the bathtub and towelled herself dry, averting her eyes from her reflection in the cloudy old mirror propped up against the tin-panelled wall opposite. The last thing she wanted to look at now was her sagging body with its mapped-out evidence of recent and distant pregnancies.

The twins. *What-if—*

She shook her head. What an awful thing a nagging doubt is, like a seed buried deep, always threatening to push up a shoot and break the earth.

She cleaned away the remnants of mascara that had melted, panda-like, around her eyes. Then she smeared on some moisturiser and re-blackened her lashes. Putting on fresh underwear and pulling on her inky linen dress that always looked better for being crumpled in a suitcase, she bundled up Stephen's shirt, added it to the laundry bag then set off, Jack in the buggy, to find the launderette.

The murky heat had settled into a yellow haze so thick Lara felt she had to fight her way through it to get along Main Street. The village looked weighted down by the afternoon. As she passed the deli, a man exploded out of the door, nearly banging into her. Without stopping he jumped into his car, which he had left empty, idling at the side of the road, and roared off.

'How can anyone be in such a hurry in this heat?' she asked Jack, who looked round at her and shook his head sagely.

After the turning to the theatre they found themselves on an unexplored stretch of Main Street. The road carried on past an unmanned roadside flower and corn stall and more houses in ever-increasing states of dilapidation. Then she came to the sign James had told her to look out for. Peeling and hand painted, it was of such an impressive vintage it could have been on sale in one of the antique shops up by the library. 'Laundromat' it said in a curly, hand-lettered script, and underneath there was a picture of two children hand-washing clothes in a zinc tub, bubbles flying up around their ears. At the bottom of the sign was an arrow pointing down a dusty driveway that turned sharply behind a derelict house. Lara hoped there were more than zinc tubs for her to do her large bag of washing in.

In the low shed tucked away at the end of the driveway, she

was pleased to find ten large washers and five tumble dryers. Apart from one load flopping about inside a dryer, the place was deserted. Lara stopped to look at the browns, creams and taupes of the clothes as they rolled around. The heat inside the laundromat made it almost impossible to breathe and Lara cursed as she felt her armpits dampen – she had forgotten to put deodorant on after her shower. It seemed a waste of effort to sweat in your clothes while you were doing the washing. For a moment she thought of stripping down to her underwear and chucking the dress in as well.

She bundled her laundry into a machine, fed its slots and drawers with quarters and powder then turned to Jack, who looked like a butter pat in his buggy. 'Shall we go outside and read this book?' she said, getting a copy of his current favourite, *We're Going on a Bear Hunt*, out of her bag.

'No,' said Jack.

'What do you want to do then?' They had an hour until the washing was done and she didn't want to go all the way back to the house to have twenty minutes before they had to set out again.

'I want the swings,' Jack whined. 'And I think I'm going to die of hot.'

He puckered up his sweaty little face into a scowl. Lara looked around at the laundromat. It was nearly as grim as their house, with cheap plastic laminate walls and scuffed lino floor. Lara wondered who on earth would run such a place in a village like this. Tucked away and shielded by trees, it was the perfect spot for a misdemeanour. Jack was right, Lara thought. The swings would be far better than hanging around here.

He claimed to be too exhausted to walk, so she wheeled him outside, reckoning they could cut across the school grounds at the back to get to the playground. Just as they were crossing the car park, a vehicle swung down the lane and round the blind corner. Lara yelped and dived with Jack into the hedgerow. If she hadn't reacted so quickly, the car would have clipped his buggy, or worse. The car screeched to a skidding halt.

'Steady on,' Lara said as she picked herself up.

The woman driver got out of the car, muttering something to herself. Ignoring Lara and Jack, she strode into the laundromat, a flash of beige and a tan and turquoise silk scarf that Lara recognised from the diner the day before.

'How rude,' Lara said loudly to Jack, hoping the woman heard. 'She could have killed us.' She wondered if she dared go inside and confront her. But then, no more than a minute later, the woman marched back out of the laundromat with a stuffed bag. Her eyes were hidden behind a big pair of sunglasses, but her mouth looked mean and bitter. The woman slung her laundry into the back of the car, jumped in and reversed in an arc, screeching the tyres before speeding away, leaving behind a smell of burning rubber.

'Extraordinary,' Lara said.

'Nasty lady,' Jack said.

'Very nasty lady,' Lara agreed.

To the left of the car park, a path led down a grassy hill towards the school playing fields. It looked to Lara like a good short cut, but the buggy would have to stay at the top. After a brief negotiation with Jack, she folded it and left it under a bush. Then the two of them half-walked, half-slid their way down the slope, crossed the football field and climbed up the other side to the playground.

Lara pushed Jack on the swings, chatting and prattling with him as she tried to work out what had just happened. The driveway to the laundromat was wide enough to accommodate pedestrians and a vehicle, and anyone in their right mind would take it slowly round that bend. Even so, the driver had had plenty of time to clock Lara and Jack and avoid them. It was as if she had driven straight at them on purpose. But why?

Perhaps she had been dazzled by sudden sunlight. The clouds had scattered in the last half-hour and, from time to time, the sun shot out in the gaps. Lara tested her theory by first glancing up at the sky then straight ahead. Sure enough, her pupils took a short while to adjust. So it was a couple of seconds before her vision cleared and she realised she was looking at a tall man, a stranger, sitting in a sort of gazebo at the far end of the playground.

Lara felt a prick of unease. She had thought she and Jack were alone. The stranger's face was almost hidden behind a curtain of long blond hair and a baseball cap pulled low over his aviator-shaded eyes, but she had a strong feeling he was looking straight over her way. This was confirmed when he smiled and raised his hand to wave. There was something odd about him, which put Lara's instincts up. He was wearing too many clothes for such hot weather, and he just didn't seem to fit into himself. If Lara were casting a psycho in a movie, he'd get a recall.

She looked away from the man, pretending not to have noticed him waving, and considered her situation. The playground was right on the street, with houses all around and the theatre just across the road. There were plenty of people nearby to hear if she screamed.

'Who's that, Mummy?' Jack asked, pointing as he swung up high.

'Shhh. Don't point, darling,' Lara said. Then she saw, with a note of alarm, that the stranger had got up and was heading towards them.

'Let's stop now, Jack, eh? We could go and see Dad at his work.'

'Yay!' Jack said as she grabbed hold of his swing to still it. Then, picking him up, she turned to leave.

'Hey there!' the man called as he quickened his pace across the playground to catch her up. He had a strong Southern accent. 'Wait up there, now.'

'Sorry. I don't think we've met,' Lara said, resigning herself to stopping and facing him. She had little choice. If this man *were* dangerous, she'd never outrun him, and if he were just being friendly, she would appear rude.

'Sam Miller,' the man said, putting his hand out to shake hers.

'Hello. Lara Wayland,' Lara said, looking at him.

Jack giggled, wriggling out of Lara's arms towards the man. 'Stephen,' he said. 'Why are you in fancy dress?'

'Rumbled,' 'Sam Miller' said in a familiar Mancunian twang. 'Out of the mouth of babes, eh?'

'Stephen?' Lara laughed with relief. 'What on earth are you playing at?'

'How else do I get around?' he said. 'I've spent years in wardrobe and make-up. Might as well put the knowledge to work.'

'But why like *that*?' Lara said. 'I thought you were a lunatic coming to abduct us.'

'People tend to keep their distance from Sam Miller,' Stephen laughed. 'They don't tend to ask too many questions.'

'It seems like an inordinate length to go to,' Lara said, realising how stupid she had been. Under the four or five external elements of the disguise, it was clearly Stephen looking back at her.

'It's a nice change from everyone staring because they think they own a part of me. I just need a break from all that, and although this may seem crazy, it does work, you know.'

'I can't really take you seriously with all that on.'

'I'm glad I bumped into you,' he said. 'I keep thinking about our conversation last night and I wanted to say sorry.'

Lara shot him a warning glance, inclining her head towards Jack, who had her by the hand, pulling her towards the theatre.

'Oh dear,' Lara said. 'I promised him we'd drop in on Marcus.'

'Do you like ice cream, Jacko?' Stephen bent so his eyes were the same level as the little boy's.

Jack nodded and smiled, his freckles dancing up and down.

'Well I'm going to take you and your mum to our local ice-cream shop: the best in the whole county.'

'Wow!' Jack said.

'It's called Pretty Fly Pie . . .' Stephen told him as he got up. 'And it is really something. My car's over there.' He pointed to a dented red Wrangler parked outside the theatre.

'We have to drive?' Lara said, thinking about her laundry.

'Yep. It's about ten miles thataway.' Stephen pointed west.

'And that's local?'

'Welcome to America.'

When they stopped by the house to pick up the child seat, Stephen rolled down the top of the Wrangler, much to Jack's delight. Then they set off, the wind in their hair, out of the village in the direction that Lara had taken on her run. Instead of turning along the river once over the bridge, they went straight on, out into the countryside. They zigzagged steeply up a hill and down the other side, where they crossed a gargantuan, six-lane freeway on which they counted just three cars and one lorry. An empty gas station stood at the side of the road, dwarfed by an incongruous, thirty-foot-high illuminated Sunoco sign. Apart from a small trailer park, it was the first building they had seen since leaving Trout Island.

'How much longer?' Lara yelled over the roar of the Wrangler and the rush of the air. She was amazed Stephen's wig had managed to stay on.

'Nearly there,' he said. 'Look out for the pie.'

They took a right after the freeway bridge and crawled through a village that looked like a mirror image of Trout Island, different only in that it lacked the grandiose presence of the theatre building. They picked up speed and covered another couple of miles of the wilds until they came to a wooden cut-out of a giant winged pie.

'Pretty Fly Pie . . .' Stephen said, turning into a gravelled car park in front of a red-painted barn. Over the doorway, another sign proclaimed '. . . and darn dream ice cream'.

'It had better be darn dream,' Lara said. 'It's got a pretty heavy carbon footprint.'

'Believe me, it's worth every ounce.' Stephen reached Jack out of his car seat. He went to put him down, but Jack clung to his neck. The three of them looked every bit the family as they crossed the car park.

The barn doors led them into a vast airy space, unexpectedly full of people sitting at mismatched tables and chairs, eating pie and ice cream. Some played chess on boards painted on the table tops; others pored over jigsaw puzzles. There was produce for sale, too – a wooden stall in the doorway bore a display of Pennsylvania peaches so ripe that the air tingled with their downy scent. A rack of baskets stood to one side, brim-full of sweet corn, the yellow kernels still dewy underneath the papery husks. There were piles of organic tomatoes of all shapes and sizes, and every sunset colour, as well as blueberries, tiny strawberries, basil, courgettes and peppers. To the back of the barn rows of wooden shelves offered honey, preserves, maple syrup and chopping boards made from local timber by someone called Wally Woodshop. Along the side wall, though, was the holy grail they had come in search of: thirty different flavours of home-made ice cream.

'They make the ice cream and pies here, all the vegetables are organically grown round the back, and most of the other stuff comes from within twenty miles, so you don't have to feel too guilty,' Stephen said.

Lara picked up a peach and inhaled. It was almost liquid in her hands. Jack scrambled down from Stephen's arms and made a beeline for the ice-cream counter. Lara found tears coming to her eyes, simply because this place was so lovely. She looked up at Stephen, who was watching her with a smile on his face.

'It's reet great 'ere, lass, in't it?' he said.

Lara put the peach down and looked around. 'It's perfect.' She smoothed over the lurch his look had set in her stomach by joining Jack at the ice-cream counter to help him choose.

'I want them all,' Jack said, holding on to the counter, pulling himself up on tiptoe so he could see.

'Well, I don't know about that,' Lara said, 'but perhaps you could choose two?'

As she helped Jack make the difficult decision, she felt Stephen standing close to her.

'Hey, Sam, how ya doin?' the plump man behind the counter said.

'Just fine thank you, Jim,' Stephen said, putting on the gallant Southern accent he had used in the playground. 'I recommend the sundae for the little guy,' he said to Lara in the same voice. 'The chocolate sauce is to die for. It's on me, by the way.'

'Why, that's very kind of you, sir,' she said, curtsying like a belle. 'You seem to be a great connoisseur of the menu. Do you come here often?'

'All the time,' he said, and Lara thought of Stephen driving out here on his own, in his absurd disguise, and sitting and eating ice cream. Did he do a jigsaw to pass the time? Did he find a chess partner?

Eventually, decisions were made, and the patient, pleasant Jim got a fancy, scallop-shaped dish and doled on to it one enormous scoop each of cookie dough and peanut butter ice cream. He moved over to the back counter with a surprisingly balletic step and pumped two dollops of warm chocolate sauce on top.

'Sprinkles?' Jim turned to ask Jack.

'Sprinkles.' Stephen nodded.

'There's so much,' Lara said, taking the dish for Jack.

'Don't worry,' Stephen said, still in his American accent, 'I'll help him out.'

'Any more for any more?' Jim stretched his full lips into a cherubic smile.

'I'll have one of these.' Lara pointed at the low fat, no sugar water ices at the far end of the counter.

'Are you sure?' he said. 'These are so much nicer.' He waved his hand along the counter at the fuller, billowier tubs full of double chocolate, Hershey Bar, butter almond and maple fudge.

'Go on, little lady,' Stephen said. 'You don't need to watch your figure, surely?'

'You old charmer, you.'

In the end, she settled for a cone of pumpkin on the grounds that she had never tasted it before. Stephen had strawberry cheesecake and toffee cookie crumble in a dish like Jack's with maple cream on it.

'I've tried them all now,' he said, with some satisfaction.

While Stephen paid, Lara and Jack turned to find a table.

'Oh!' Lara stopped in her tracks. Coming through the doorway, hand in hand, their attention so wholly focused on each other they might have been the only people in the world, were Bella and Sean. He cradled her hand as she lifted a peach for him to smell. She pointed out the corn and he picked out a yard-high stem of basil, presenting it to her like a bouquet. It was almost a parody of young love, and for a moment Lara felt a stab of jealousy.

Then Bella turned to look at the ice cream and saw her mother and little brother standing there, gawping at her.

'Mum?' she said. 'What are you doing here?'

'What does it look like?' Lara said, licking her ice cream, which was beginning to dribble down the cone on to her fingers. It was delicious, a muted sweetness of pumpkin riding a little cinnamon on an almost powdery texture.

'Ice cream, Bell. Nice,' Jack said, scrambling on to a seat, already with more chocolate sauce round his mouth than he had in his dish.

Bella towed Sean up to their table. 'Mum, this is Sean.'

'I know. We've met,' Lara said, smiling up to him. 'I thought you were swimming in a pond.'

'Well we were,' Bella said. 'But we started to get pruney, so Sean brought me here. Isn't it cool?'

'So you drove here,' Lara said. 'I hope you wore a seat belt.'

'Hi, I'm Bella, Lara's daughter?' Bella reached across her mother and held out her hand to Stephen, who had joined them and was wiping the chocolate from Jack's face. He took her fingertips, then leaned over and whispered something in her ear. Bella's eyes widened as she stood back and looked at him. Then she smiled. 'Oh yes,' she said. 'Now I see it.'

Stephen held his finger up to his lips.

'Hey, "Sam",' Sean said.

'You know?' Bella turned to her boyfriend, open-mouthed.

'I thought only James, Betty and that Trudi knew?' Lara said to Stephen.

'Well, Sean sort of rumbled me round at the farm once. But he's a good kid. I'd trust him with my life,' Stephen said in a low voice.

'And you have every reason to,' Sean said seriously.

'I wish I'd known. You don't know how much it hurt not telling you,' Bella said to Sean. Then she turned back to look at Stephen's disguise. 'Too weird.'

'So: do you kids want to treat yourselves?' Stephen said more loudly, now in his Sam voice. He reached in his wallet and handed them a ten-dollar note. 'Go on, guys. It's on your Uncle Sam.'

'Thanks, Sam,' Bella said.

Lara watched as they went over to the ice-cream counter. Sean showed the flavours to Bella, resting his hand on her waist so that she was close to him. The way Bella turned to him, the look in her eyes as she spoke, and the new shape her mouth took as she listened to what he said told Lara more than she wanted to know about just how far this friendship had progressed. She sighed as she finished off her ice cream. So soon after meeting, and with Bella so young. She was in deep – anyone could see that. Lara braced herself. The best she could hope for was that her daughter had her heart broken, or broke a heart herself. Anything else would be unthinkable, this young.

'Remind you of anyone?' Stephen leaned forward and whispered to her, in his own voice.

* * *

Lara bought a basket full of produce. She invited Sean and Stephen back to supper, which she had already planned to be pasta with fresh basil and tomato sauce, and local pecorino on top, followed by a Pretty Fly blueberry pie. After a moment's hesitation involving an agonised glance at Bella, Sean accepted, but Stephen said he had to get back to feed his chickens. They drove back over the hill in convoy, Stephen with Lara and Jack in the lead, Sean and Bella following behind in his car, which Lara noted with relief was a sensible, not-too-old Nissan.

As they climbed the steep hill on the other side of the freeway, Lara remembered she had to stop by the laundromat. When they got back to Trout Island, she asked Stephen to pull over. She ran out to tell Sean and Bella, who had tucked in behind them, to go back to the house while she went with Stephen to pick up the washing.

As before, the laundromat was completely deserted. Lara got the buggy first, lobbing it into the back of the Wrangler. Then she went into the shed. The machine she thought she had left her laundry in was empty. Thinking she must have made another supermarket-car-park-type mistake, she checked all the others, but they too contained nothing but their shiny stainless-steel drums. She looked into the tumble dryers, thinking perhaps that someone had, with the best of intentions, moved her washing on, but there was no sign of it. And the plastic laundry baskets were all empty, too.

Perturbed, she looked for a phone number on one of the crude notices dotted around the place. They were full of misspelled instructions like DO NOT OVERLODE THE MACHINES, and CHECK ALL POKETS BEFORE LODEING. CUSTOMERS ARE LIBEL FOR BLOKAGES. Then she found a small, handwritten sign tucked down underneath the washing powder dispenser, which gave a contact IN CASE OF MALFUNTION. Lara scribbled the number on her arm.

'Bastards,' she said as she went out to the Wrangler. Stephen was sitting in the back, reading *We're Going on a Bear Hunt* – which he must have got out of her bag – to Jack. 'Someone's taken all our washing. Someone's nicked our laundry.'

'That's weird. Kids?' Stephen said.

'Or perhaps Olly or Marcus came and got it?' Lara said. 'Though I doubt that.'

'Nasty lady,' Jack said.

'You're right, Jack,' Lara said. 'Perhaps it was the nasty lady.'

'What nasty lady?' Stephen turned to face her.

'Some idiot nearly ran us over as we came out here this afternoon,' Lara explained as she climbed into the Wrangler. 'But I'm sure it couldn't be her. What would she want with all our clothes?'

'What did she look like?' Stephen moved forward into the driving seat.

'I didn't really see her. Sort of brownish, middle aged-ish. Angry. She whacked her car down the lane, nearly ran us over, swore at us then went in there.' Lara pointed at the laundromat. Then she turned back to Stephen and noticed his eyes had darkened.

'It's my fault,' he said.

'What?'

'Nothing.'

'No. What?'

He broke away and put his hands behind his neck, bowed his head and sighed. 'Strange things happen around me,' he said.

She put her hand on his shoulder. 'Look, don't worry about

it. There's probably some simple explanation. I'll call this number when I get back,' she pointed to the scrawl on her arm, 'and I'm sure we'll trace it. If someone in the village starts wearing Olly's *Made in Brighton* T-shirt, we'll have our man. Marcus will be cross about the Paul Smith shirt though. Oh damn,' she said, remembering. 'Your shirt was in there, too.'

'Don't worry about that. I've got hundreds,' Stephen said. 'But I'll be sure to get your top back to you as soon as possible, given the reduced clothing situation.' He started the engine. 'I'd better get you back. Marcus will be home in a few minutes.'

'You seem to know his rehearsal schedule very well,' Lara said, putting on her seat belt.

'I have my sources,' he said, smiling.

He drove them slowly round the block to the house. Stopping in the street, he got out and helped Lara get her shopping from the back, then he lifted Jack out, detached the car seat and put it on the front deck.

'I'll see you soon, Lara. Very soon.' He touched her shoulder, leaned in to kiss her on the cheek, then jumped back into the Wrangler and sped off.

Lara stood there waving, her shopping at her feet. Her cheek burned where his lips had touched it. A breeze shook the maples that towered around the house, rattling their leaves so for a second they were all she could hear. Hadn't she resolved, just this morning, not to see Stephen again? And hadn't she just spent the whole afternoon with him, drawing Jack into it all as well?

Then she saw Marcus at the far end of Main Street, the unmistakable shape and colour of him as he loped along, a heavy satchel on one shoulder, a cigarette in his hand. The low, late afternoon sun illuminated his hair, making him look as if he were on fire. From the spring in his step, he must have had a good day at work. He looked strangely complete, as if he at last belonged in the space he took up in the world.

'Daddy!' Jack said, running towards his father.

And here am I, she thought. His Lara, contemplating murdering all of that happiness.

Twenty-Five

BELLA LAY IN THE DARK IN HER SWELTERING BEDROOM, listening to the whine of a mosquito as it homed in on her skin, adding to her agitation after an awkward evening. One of the fly screens had a small tear, and when she went out the night before she must have left the light on. So she had to spend a good half-hour before getting into bed creeping about with a sandal, squashing the wily insects that had found their way into the room in bloody splatters on the mildewed wallpaper.

The drone of this last remaining mosquito stopped and she felt the prick as its proboscis pierced the flesh on her belly. Holding her breath, she lifted her hand up high and brought it down on herself with a slap. She rubbed the grainy remains of the creature between her fingers. If she turned on the light she would see her own blood, ample motive for the killing. But she just couldn't be bothered to lean over and fiddle with the annoying switch.

The downside of not having the mosquito buzzing around was that she could hear Olly more clearly. He was writing a song, which meant he was making a racket, singing in that gruff wail of his that irritated her so much. It sounded so false, as if it were manufactured expressly to annoy her. He was, he had declared at the uncomfortable supper table the Waylands had shared with Sean, setting to music a Byron poem from the book Stephen had lent him. So now she was plagued with Olly's voice, in the room next to hers, droning on.

> 'Like me in lineaments: her eyes
> Her hair, her features, all to the very tone
> Even of her voice, they said were like to mine . . .'

'Shut up,' Bella groaned into the dense darkness of her room. She knew his game exactly. She hadn't studied the Romantic poets without learning about Byron's goings-on with his half-sister. This was Olly, typically, trying to ennoble what had happened between them. He'd done it before, back home, swaying stoned at the top of the stairs when their parents were out, blocking her way, jabbering on about how in Bali fraternal twins used to have to marry because it was assumed they had already had sex in the womb.

Any sort of intellectual justification made it all right for Olly. But Bella felt only shame. She wanted to forget all about it, to make it something only she knew. But how could she, with him knowing it too? With him in her face all the time?

Olly finally finished his 'songwriting'. Bella tried to breathe the tension in her shoulders down, out through the tips of her fingers and on to the wrinkled bed sheet. She forced her mind to empty its trash, trying instead to fill it with the good things.

It was so hot her chest felt blocked. Another storm was on its way. She 'felt it in her waters', as Marcus would say. She wasn't going to waste electricity by turning on her fan, though. That afternoon, after their wonderful skinny dip and everything else – she gave a hum of pleasure at the memory of that *everything else* – Sean had driven her from his cousin's remote pond into the town with the unpronounceable name he said was of Native American origin.

All the shops had their doors open to the stifling air, yet inside they were like fridges. She and Sean tried to work out how much energy all the shops across America wasted chilling their customers so they had to carry warm clothing, even when temperatures outside soared. It was obscene. Sweating in her bed was Bella's personal direct action for climate change. She thought with a smile that if she had another body in there beside her, she would be even hotter and her protest even greater.

Fat chance of that with her brother around, though.

And there she was, thinking about Olly again, allowing him to poison her brain. She ran back again over the evening's events, and, not for the first time, she groaned.

She lifted up her sheet and let it fall down, wafting air over her that was, if not cooler, at least not stagnant.

Everything Sean said at the table Olly did his best to do down with little underhand remarks and snarky comments. Sean hadn't risen to the bait, but she could tell he was upset.

'You could have knocked me over when I bumped into the pair of them in Pretty Fly Pie . . .' her mother had said.

'Lucky it wasn't me bumping into you,' Olly muttered with his head angled so only Bella and Sean could hear.

And Marcus had been so *gushy*, forcing wine on to Sean, asking him about his plans for the future, interviewing him as if he were a potential son-in-law. It was excruciating. But it was inevitable with Marcus, she supposed. He always liked to dole out the Wayland charm offensive when they had guests. And he was particularly full of himself that evening because his read-through had gone so well.

But her mother had been acting oddly too, knocking back the wine, smiling at them with this stupid look in her eyes, referring to them both as 'you two' and making little jokes about holding hands and billing and cooing. It had taken all of Bella's strength to stop herself withering away in embarrassment.

Then there had been the detailed list of which bits of her underwear had gone missing in the stolen laundry. And what was that about? Bella sat up and tried to pummel some life into her lumpy pillow. Her favourite sundress and an irreplaceable bra, gone for good, nicked by some pervert because her mother had swanned off with Stephen Molloy and forgotten all about them. And now her parents had turned it into some big joke.

She scratched at the lump made by the mosquito. At least she'd get some new clothes out of it. That's if she found a decent shop out here in the middle of nowhere. The only place she had seen in the unpronounceable town was the grimmest shop in the world, called Fashion Bug, which seemed to sell nothing but lime and pastel polyester.

She cast around for other positive things to think about. The *everything else*, of course. And Sean. Beautiful Sean. When they said their goodbyes on the porch, he had even said how much he liked her parents, how cool they were, how he hoped to see a lot more of them.

They had kissed – with less abandon than earlier at his cousin's pond, but still enough to kindle that flame he had set burning in her. He wound his fingers in hers and they made plans to meet again the next day.

But then, of course, bloody Olly had blundered out of the front door and straight into them, making them jump apart.

'OH GOD,' Olly said. 'I'm SO SORRY. I didn't realise you were out here SNOGGING.' Then, his face set in an ugly sneer, he shoved Sean away from her, making him stumble down the porch steps.

'Olly, get in here this instant!' Bella heard her mother call from inside.

'I thought I told you to stay away,' Olly hissed, jumping down, grabbing Sean by the collar and pushing his face right at him. Then, louder, he called, 'Coming, Mother,' and went back indoors.

Bella winced as she remembered Sean brushing himself down, trying to conceal his anger behind a set jaw.

'What *is* it with your brother?' he said.

She couldn't say anything of course. She was utterly stifled by Olly. And her parents, come to that. She had no space in her family. She couldn't wait to leave home and get away from it all.

She closed her eyes and again tried to clear her mind of the lot of them, tried to wind back to the picture of Sean, smiling down at her as he held her hand, but it was impossible. Olly's face kept leering in, prising them apart.

Sean must never know what had gone on between her and Olly. It made her feel so dirty. She would die, quite literally, from shame.

And then the unmistakable whine of another mosquito started up by her ear, as if it had been sent to make this night a *total* misery for her.

It just wasn't fair. None of it was at all fair.

Twenty-Six

'I THINK I'D LIKE TO ASK JAMES IF, AS WELL AS HAMMERING up that hideous cellar, we can get some locks put on the doors,' Lara told Marcus as she cleared away the breakfast things. Her head ached with a cheap wine hangover and her hands seemed disconnected from her body.

'What on earth for?' Marcus said, looking up from the online *Guardian* he was reading on Lara's laptop.

'After the launderette thing. I'm not so sure there aren't some weirdos around, and I'd rather we could lock the doors.'

'I'll mention it today,' Marcus said, but in a way that meant he'd do nothing of the sort.

'If you're not going to do it, let me know and I'll ask him myself.'

'Didn't I just say I'd ask him?'

'What are your plans this morning?' Lara plunged her hands into the sink to tackle the washing-up. Marcus's rehearsal didn't start till after lunch. If he said he was going to sit about and learn his lines, she thought she might explode.

'I think I'll look at me lines,' Marcus said. 'Steady, old girl,' he added as a plate slipped from Lara's hand on to the floor, smashing into several pieces. 'What are you up to?'

'There's that kid's show at the library,' she said, scooping up the bits of broken crockery. 'I thought we'd go along to that. Jack and me, at any rate.'

'Tell you what,' Marcus said, shutting the laptop and stretching. 'Why don't I come with you? Let the lines go hang for an hour or two. It'd be good to be out together, just the three of us.'

'OK then.' Lara swirled the foamy dishwater round, trying to get an ancient stain out of the bottom of a coffee cup. She didn't know what irritated her more: that Marcus hadn't noticed she had smashed the plate on purpose, or that he hadn't offered to take Jack on his own, giving her an hour to herself. She might as well give up on the business plan. It was never going to get written.

'Has that launderette guy got back yet?' Marcus said. He was concerned about what he called 'that exorbitant shirt'. Lara had phoned the number on her arm when she got in the night before, and, after an answerphone greeting in a Russian accent so heavy she couldn't make out a word, had left a message and the house number.

'Did you hear the phone ring at all this morning?' she asked Marcus.

'Nope.'

'Then he hasn't got back. I'm going to have to go shopping. Olly's got practically nothing to wear.'

'Can't we claim it on the insurance?'

'We will, but we won't get the money for ages.'

'Well let's not go too crazy with the new clothes, eh?'

* * *

By quarter to ten, they were on their way to the village library, Jack bowling on ahead. Lara and Marcus walked together, but they didn't touch. Like many long-married couples, used to having their arms taken up with babies, buggies, shopping and small children, they had lost the habit of hand-holding.

There had been another storm in the night, which had washed reddish-brown mud down the grassy banks to their side, creating puddles in the warped and cracked paving stones. Jack stepped in a puddle a lot deeper than it looked, and the water soaked over the tops of his trainers and seemingly upwards into his eyes as, feeling the cold clam of soggy socks, he started to bawl.

'Oh come on, Jack,' Marcus said in his stern father voice. 'It's only a bit of wet.'

'Sit on that wall,' Lara said, 'And I'll sort you out.'

'You spoil that child,' Marcus said in a high, Pythonesque voice. 'You're making a rod for your own back.'

Lara knew he was having a laugh, imitating her mother – she and Marcus had made a mutually unfavourable impression on each other on the few occasions they had met. But behind all that bluster was what he really thought. She took off Jack's sopping socks and wrung the water out of them. 'Let's go barefoot.' She winked at Jack. 'Then you can splash to your heart's content.'

'Recipe for disaster,' Marcus went on in the same voice, and Lara wished he would stop.

They arrived at the library and climbed the steep stone steps that mounted the bank up to the picture-perfect building. Entirely symmetrical, with four columns supporting a gabled porch, it was backdropped by tall, green trees and sparkled in the morning sun.

Undermining this fine façade, someone had tacked a laminated, clip-art-adorned sign to an A-board in the street, telling passers-by that 'FOXY LOXY and CHICKEN LICKEN are right here this A.M. at 10 a.m. and EVERYONE is WELCOME!!!!!!'

'Bloody hell,' Marcus muttered.

'You didn't have to come,' Lara said. 'Now, let's get ourselves together, Jacko.' She made him wipe his feet on the bristled mat on the library porch, setting his shoes and socks out in the sun to dry.

Inside they were greeted by a shiny woman sitting in front of a bank of wooden box files. A rack of rubber stamps stood before her, poised for action.

'Hello,' she said, standing up and extending her right hand. 'You must be Marcus and Lara Wayland. And this is?' She bent forward and beamed at Jack, who stared back up at her, sucking his thumb.

'This is Jack. Say hello, Jack,' Lara said.

'Hello,' Jack said, edging behind Lara.

'I'm Tina,' the woman said, shaking their hands. 'Trout Island librarian. And don't ask how I know who you are. I know everything and everyone that's going on round here.' She laughed, waggling her head in a strange, sideways motion. Although she couldn't be more than forty, she was dressed in a voluminous patterned shirtwaister that bypassed vintage and shot straight into frumpy.

'We've come to see the show,' Lara said.

'Well, I thought you might've. Come on in, come on in!' Tina ushered them behind the bookshelves to the children's section. A group of women and their offspring sat perched on ten or so rows of tiny wooden chairs, facing a table on which there was a plywood cut-out of a jug, two dozen giant eggs in a basket, and some heads of sweet corn. Behind this arrangement stood a canvas screen, painted with green hills that overlapped and disappeared into a cartoon-clouded blue sky.

'There you are. Now,' Tina said to Jack. 'While you're in here having *fun*, I'll just make you out a card so's you can pick up some books before you leave. What's your address? You're staying at the Larssen place, aren't you?' she asked Lara.

'That's right. Number one-four-six.'

Tina grimaced and turned to go back towards her desk.

'Why did she make that face?' Lara said as they looked for seats.

'Do we have to do this?' Marcus whispered.

'No turning back,' she said, and they slid into the back row. Jack immediately started to complain that he couldn't see anything. Lara suggested he sat on the cushions at the front.

'Come with me, Daddy,' he said, tugging at Marcus's arm.

'Go on,' Lara said. 'I'll stay back here.'

Marcus allowed himself to be dragged down to the front. With some difficulty, due to his jeans being too tight at the knees and waist, he sat on a cushion and folded his legs into the same crossed position as his son to keep them out of the performance area. Sitting there like that he looked as much a little boy as Jack. The two of them simultaneously smiled back at her and put their thumbs up.

'Hi.' A woman a few chairs away from Lara extracted her hand from the small child who clung to her side and extended it in greeting. 'I'm Gina. I've not seen you here before.'

'I'm Lara. And that's Marcus and Jack. We're here with the theatre company.'

'You're English!' Gina said, with delight. 'My husband's a Brit.'

'Really?'

'We live just next door to the library. This is Bert.' She gestured to the child, who now had his face buried in his mother's shoulder. 'He's awful shy, aren't you, Bert? And his sisters Gladys and Ethel are down in front. You must come for coffee after, if you're free.'

'I'd love to,' Lara said.

'I hope this programme's all right,' Gina leaned over and whispered. 'They're usually not very good. Quit your noise now, Bert!' she said to her silent son. 'Show's about to start.'

A skinny woman in a blue milkmaid outfit strutted out from behind the screen, clucking like a chicken, swooping her hyperthyroid eyes from side to side. The children in the audience whooped with laughter.

'Today,' she said, 'I'm going to tell you the very sad-indeedy story of Chicken Licken and Foxy Loxy.' She spoke slowly, as if the children were halfwits and needed time to consider every syllable. 'Does anyone *know* the story of Chicken Licken and Foxy Loxy?'

A couple of hands shot up in the audience.

'I do!' a large bespectacled boy in the front row said.

'No?' Chicken Milkmaid said, ignoring the boy, whose hand was up so high he was nearly bursting. 'Do you *want* me to tell you the story of Chicken Licken and Foxy Loxy?'

'Yes!' the children yelled, sitting up straight, waiting.

'I'm going to need some help then,' she said, beaming round at everyone.

'Me!' The large boy shot his hand up again, followed by all the other children in the room.

A lot of business followed while Chicken Milkmaid cast the various characters from the audience. The boy in the front wasn't chosen and started complaining loudly to his mother, who sat behind him, commiserating. Marcus turned and rather publicly grimaced to Lara.

'Told ya,' Gina whispered. 'Not very good.'

When all the chosen children were dressed up, masked and armed with their lines on pieces of laminated card, Chicken Milkmaid turned back to the audience, smiling like a loon.

'Well now, I think we're missing someone, aren't we, children? We've got' – and here she carefully pointed out each costumed child as she recited their character's name – 'Hen Len, Cock Lock, Duck Luck, Drake Lake, Gander Lander, Goose Loose and Turkey Lurkey. But who are we missing?'

'Foxy Loxy!' the large boy said, putting his hand up again, his hope reignited.

'That's correct. Foxy Loxy,' she said, for the first time acknowledging him. The boy took this as a sign to get up and join the others on stage, but Chicken Milkmaid halted him with her outstretched palm. 'Wait,' she said. 'We need someone REALLY big and REALLY frightening to be our Foxy Loxy. Now then,' she went on, raising her finger to her mouth like Shirley Temple. 'Who shall we have?'

'ME! ME!' the poor boy said, nearly combusting.

'I think . . . we'll have . . . YOU, sir.' And she pulled Marcus up by the hand. Jack whooped.

'Here's our scary Foxy Loxy!' she cried. 'And look,' she said, picking up a strand of Marcus's hair. 'His tail is just the right colour. What's your name, sir?'

'Foxy Loxy?' Marcus said. Every part of his body signalled that he wanted to run away. He didn't know what to do with his hands.

'No, good sir, your real name?'

'Marcus. Marcus Wayland.'

'Gor blimey, we've got a limey,' Chicken Milkmaid

chirruped in a Dick Van Dyke Cockney accent. Gina raised an eyebrow at Lara, who wanted the floor to open up and swallow Marcus. This was the worst form of torture for him. It cut deeply into his vulnerability, exposing the veins of self-doubt beneath his blustery veneer.

'Poor man,' Gina said.

Chicken Milkmaid snapped a pointed fox nose on to Marcus's face. Then she tied on a badly fashioned mask, which circled his face with red fur and gave him tall, pointed ears. She gave his dignity a final blow with a little checked waistcoat and a walking stick. If it hadn't been so grotesque it would have been funny.

There followed an excruciatingly repetitious enactment of what was never an exciting story in the first place. When it became clear that several of the performing children couldn't actually read the lines they had been given, even the keenest and least critical young members of the audience grew restless.

'I coulda done it a million times better,' the kid in the front complained loudly to his mother.

'I know, honey,' she said back.

Poor Marcus had to stand silently throughout this. He tried to look nonchalant, giving the odd smile and thumbs-up to Jack, but it clearly took all he had.

When it came to his line 'Come along with me and I'll show you the way,' which he was supposed to follow with a *Bwah hah hah hah* of an evil laugh, he didn't do it with enough verve and gusto to satisfy Chicken Milkmaid, who made him repeat it over and over, ramping it up each time.

And Lara realised this is how it would be if she were to leave him. He'd be up there, ridiculous to the world, cuckolded, usurped by Stephen Molloy not only professionally but in his personal life too.

Could she do that to a man she once loved?

Then she gasped – out loud, so that Gina looked over at her – because, for the first time, she had thought of her love for Marcus in the past tense.

It was done, then, she thought, a heavy feeling in her belly. Stephen Molloy or no Stephen Molloy, continuing with Marcus would be like flogging a mortified fox.

'So, you'll come for coffee?' Gina asked when the Foxy Loxy ordeal was over. Released from the stage, Marcus had fled back home to his lick his wounds and learn his lines and Jack was busy selecting a pile of picture books with which to while away the afternoon.

'God, yes please,' Lara said.

Twenty-Seven

GINA'S HOUSE MUST HAVE BEEN BUILT AROUND THE SAME time as the Larssen place. It had the same rickety air to it. But inside, it told a whole other story. Where the Waylands' digs echoed with stifling emptiness, this home was darker and cooler, bursting at the seams with all the clutter of life. Piles of books and papers clustered on every surface, three racks of freshly baked cookies stood on the kitchen table, and the living-room floor was littered with toys and DVDs. It had the same spicy damp smell of the other house, though, and, as with everywhere else in the village, a skunk lurked within stinking distance.

As they walked over from the library, Gina had told Lara about how she home-schooled her children. All three were tall and skinny like their mother. Where Bert was still and painfully shy – Gina seemed unable to put him down in the presence of others – Gladys and Ethel, his eight- and ten-year-old sisters, were boisterous and constantly in motion. Once in the house, they scooped Jack into their angular arms as if he were a large doll, and took him upstairs to play.

Lara knew instinctively she had found a friend in Gina – so much so, she had to fight the urge to sit down and tell her the whole Stephen story. But of course she couldn't even mention his name. Everything, but everything, had to stay secret.

'How are you finding Trout Island?' Gina asked, using her Bert-free hand to set the coffee pot on the stove.

'We've only been here for a few days,' Lara said. 'But we really like it. It's so beautiful round here.'

'Isn't it?'

'How long have you been here?' Lara asked.

'I was born on a farm just outside of the village,' Gina said. 'But I've done my travelling. I ain't just a hick.' She had a way of delivering her words as if each sentence were the punch line to a joke.

'And your husband. You say he's English. Where's he from?'

'Coventry. Do you know it?'

'I grew up not too far from there.' Thinking of her up-bringing as an only child on a private housing estate on the outskirts of Leicester put a metallic taste in Lara's mouth. Her memory of those days was there was nothing much to remember, just mundanities: waiting for the bus in the rain in her embarrassing private-school uniform; long, dull Sunday afternoons spent in front of the TV with the central heating turned up too high. Her childhood seemed green-tinged, like a faded Polaroid.

So from an early age, she had cast around for a means of escape – first it was books, then it was theatre. But the most effective route, as it happened, turned out to be men. By marrying Marcus so young and so secretly, she had ensured that her disappointed parents – who muttered darkly about all that money spent on her education being wasted – had more or less lost interest. They had met the twins three times and Jack just the once, and Lara was far from heartbroken about this.

Gina poured the coffee and they sat at the table in the airy kitchen. Every wall was hidden by the children's paintings. Other handiwork covered the horizontal surfaces: papier-mâché dinosaurs, galleons made of Lego and an electrical circuit construction that resembled some sort of bomb. The whole house seemed to be given over to the children. Lara watched Gina sipping her coffee, Bert curled into her side like a comma, and thought her strong, pretty features looked rather worn out.

'So, why do you home-school?' she asked, cradling her mug. Gina made an excellent cup of coffee.

'The village school sucks. They make them pledge allegiance to the flag every morning, then they teach them all the wrong stuff at completely the wrong pace. They never have time for anything creative.'

'Looks like you do, though.'

'Oh yeah. I'm a bookbinder by trade, so I guess I'm a little bit arty,' Gina said.

'I'll send my daughter down to visit. She's bound for art school, we think.'

'You have other kids?'

Gina was interested to hear how these urban British teenagers were coping with the quiet life in Trout Island. Lara mentioned Sean, and Gina agreed with her that he was a really nice kid, which confirmed Lara's own instincts. However, when she told her about Olly's friends – whose names, she had gleaned in a monosyllabic conversation with him, were Aaron, Brandon and Kyle – Gina sucked her teeth.

'Problem?' Lara asked.

'Well, they wouldn't be my friends if I were sixteen!' Gina said.

'Go on . . .'

'Out here in the country there's always those kind of kids. Same now as when I was at school. They come from big, poor families – chaotic, a little dirty. Mom's on her own, or as good as, and too busy scrabbling around making a living to keep much of an eye on them. I mean, they don't have much of a chance. They flunk out of school as soon as they can, then they just hang out all day, doing nothing, getting high, getting into bits of trouble.'

'And these boys are like that?'

Gina nodded.

Lara decided to have a few words with Olly when she next saw him to make sure he wasn't getting waylaid. But she suspected that the part of Gina that made her take her children out of mainstream schooling also might lead her to make those sorts of judgements. The main thing about these boys, surely, was that they came from poor families. It would do Olly good to mix with kids like that, so he could see a different side to American culture, and realise how lucky he was himself.

So long as he kept his head.

She thought perhaps she might take a turn around the village next time he was out with them, to see if she could find out what he actually did with his new friends.

'And how are you getting on in the house?' Gina said, making the same face as Tina the librarian had. She got up to reach down some plates from an open shelf. 'Cookie? Glad and Eth baked them this morning.'

'Oh, go on, then. I'm going to get so fat here,' Lara said,

biting into one. It was perfect – chewy and maple-sweet, with a bit of walnutty earthiness underneath.

'If only I could gain a couple pounds,' Gina said, knocking her hip bone with her fist. 'I eat like a pig all day and I just get bonier and bonier.'

'Lucky you,' Lara said, chewing. 'I wanted to ask. Why did you make that face when you mentioned the house?'

'Face?'

Lara showed her the expression. 'And you sort of shuddered just now.'

'Oh. Oh, sorry. It's only, you know, with the history and all that.'

'History?'

'Oh my God. You don't know, do you?'

'Don't know what?'

Gina slapped her forehead with her open palm. 'Forget it. Forget I said anything. I'm such a klutz.'

'You started, so you've got to tell me now.' Lara sat back and folded her arms, waiting.

'Oh God. You promise you won't freak out?'

'I promise.'

Gina chewed on her cookie, then set her mug down on the table. 'Well, that place has been empty for, what now, nearly five years?'

'OK.'

'It's hard to sell a house like that.'

'Like what?'

'OK, then. This guy Larssen lived there for it must have been sixty years. I remember him from when I was a kid. He kept himself to himself, went around in the same pair of baggy old pants all that time, done up with string. He'd walk all day, for miles, just round and round the village, talking to himself.

He was real stinky. We all used to laugh at him. Well, kids can be cruel. He had the house full of dogs. Let them poop all over the place.'

'I thought I smelled dog.'

'Your imagination's working overtime.' Gina laughed. 'It was years ago. So, in the middle of one summer, Larssen stopped walking around. We noticed, but we just reckoned he was sick or something. But those dogs, they just howled away day and night inside the house. And the smell – which was pretty bad in the first place – started getting worse. In the end, Andy Schmidt, who used to live next door, just couldn't stand it any more, so he goes round and, getting no answer when he knocks, he breaks the front door down.

'The first thing meets him is the smell. Rotten, mixed up with dog-shit. Smell of hell, he said. Then, as the door swings open revealing the hallway, he sees it.'

'What?' Lara asked in a small voice.

Gina put her hands over Bert's ears. 'What remained of old Larssen,' she whispered. 'After the dogs had finished. They reckon he must've fallen down the stairs, broken his neck and the dogs, not having anything to eat . . . well, you can guess . . .'

'How horrible.' Lara thought of the stain on the carpet and her stomach turned.

'And that's not all,' Gina said.

'No?'

'Andy Schmidt goes right ahead and calls the police, and, while he's waiting, he rounds up the dogs and ties them to the porch. He said they were quite docile, like they were ashamed of what they had done. But when he takes himself back inside to take one last look at old Larssen he hears the thumping coming from under the stairs.'

'I don't like this,' Lara said, thinking of the cellar and the bed.

'I'll stop then,' Gina said. 'You don't need to hear the rest.'

'I think I do.'

'Well, eventually, Andy finds this secret door under the stair.'

'I know it,' Lara said.

'And he opens it, and this even worse stink hits him, and there's this whimpering. He finds the light switch and flicks it on, then he goes down the stairs.'

'He found the room down there.'

'Yep. He finds the room. And he finds Jane.'

'Jane?'

'Mean anything?'

'I think I found a photograph of her in Bella's room.'

'No way. That's too weird. I thought they'd completely cleared the place out.'

'Who is she, then? And why was she down there?'

'She couldn't get out. He'd chained her to the wall, like a dog.' Gina paused and took a bite of cookie.

'The manacles,' Lara said.

'The manacles are down there still? Ew. Well, we knew he had a retarded or mad or something sister, but everyone said she was in some home in Buffalo. In fact,' Gina narrowed her eyes, 'he kept her down there in the basement all that time. She was like an albino mole, Andy said. Hadn't been out of there for years. Just hugging herself, starved of course, rocking backwards and forwards, blind. Making little moaning sounds.' Gina demonstrated for Lara, as if her words hadn't been quite vivid enough.

'Horrible,' Lara said.

'So the police come in. They take Jane away and put her in a home, where she should have been all that while. Seems old Larssen didn't want to pay, so he took it into his own hands.

But it turns out he had this stack of money in the bank. Nearly a million dollars. Poor old Jane didn't last long, she was dead within a year. So all that dough he'd hung on to went to some distant cousin in Nebraska.'

'And the house?'

'It had a For Sale sign outside until this spring, when a person unnamed bought it and gave it to the theatre company. The price had dropped to almost nothing with the property crash anyhow.'

'James should have told us about all this.'

'What good would that have done?' Gina said. 'Ignorance is bliss. I wish I'd never opened my mouth.' She started on another cookie.

'I don't know if I want to stay there any more.'

'Hey, it's just a set of walls. They did a load of work on it before you arrived, too. There were vans parked outside and guys working for a couple of weeks.'

'I don't know what they did. The place was filthy when we got there. I've spent the past three days cleaning it up.' Lara thought about the carpet with the stain and shuddered. 'What happened to the dogs?'

Gina drew a finger across her throat. 'Well, all except one, which ran away while they were trying to get them into a van. Headed off up on the back road over the river and into the forest.'

'What did it look like?' Lara asked, thinking of Dog.

'I have no idea,' Gina said.

'Which house is this Andy Schmidt in?'

'He's not there any longer.'

'He moved?'

'Dead.'

'Jesus.'

'Mummy look!' Jack stood in the kitchen doorway, flanked by Gladys and Ethel. He was wearing a long, glittery dress, blond curled wig and full make-up, including turquoise eyeshadow, plastered-on rouge, and big red lips. 'I'm pretty, Mummy.'

'You certainly are, darling.' Lara scooped him up and held him close.

Not for the first time, she wondered what sort of mess following Marcus over here had led her family into.

Twenty-Eight

GINA SAID SHE FELT TOO GUILTY ABOUT EXPOSING LARA TO the story of the house and, by way of apology, pressed her to stay for lunch. Lara tried phoning to let Bella and Olly know that they'd have to fix themselves something, but there was no reply. She supposed they were either still asleep or had gone out. Either way, she and Jack wouldn't be missed.

Over lunch, Lara told Gina about her car situation, and Gina immediately offered the use of her old Volvo. 'I just haven't gotten around to getting rid of it,' she said. 'It's sitting there, doing nothing. You'd be doing me a favour.'

She took Lara into the garage down a lane at the side of her house. The rusting wreck was the same model as the Waylands' vehicle back home: same colour, everything – although this one was even older.

'She's all yours,' Gina said. 'Please, take her away.'

By the time she and Jack left Gina's house, with an invitation to bring everyone back that evening to a gathering around their fire pit, Lara had decided she needed to move out of the Larssen place. The story was too awful. She skirted past the theatre to see if she could catch James or Betty, to have it out with them in person.

Sure enough, James's little sports car was parked outside the building. Lara helped Jack up the steps to the porch and banged on the front door, which was locked.

Almost immediately, James answered her knock. He looked worn out, and his eyes were bloodshot.

'Hello darlings,' he said, kissing Lara on the cheek. 'To what do I owe the pleasure?' One of the more irritating things about him was that he normally had the energy of an overexcited puppy. To see him quite so subdued was unnerving.

'Are you all right?' Lara asked.

'Oh, you know. Just a bit overstretched.'

He let them in, sat behind the foyer desk and gestured to Lara to take the chair opposite. 'I've got extra rehearsals for the musical *and* the worry of the Scottish play. June and Brian have had a tiff and aren't speaking to each other – not even on stage – and I've got Lady M gnawing my ear off because she doesn't like her digs. I mean as if I haven't enough on my plate.' He got up and went over to the kitchenette cupboard, where he filled a kettle. 'Anyway, less of me. What can I do for *you*, Lara my love? Coffee? Mint tea?'

'Mint tea, please.' Lara had drunk too much coffee at Gina's and could hear her heart pounding.

'Well then,' James said, turning to face her. 'Isn't this nice.'

'I wanted to talk about the house,' Lara said, hearing her voice echo in the high-ceilinged wooden room. 'I've just been told what happened there.'

'Ah.' James rubbed his fingers deep into his temples. 'Hang on a tick,' he said. He pulled out a basket of toys labelled *Stay'n'Play group ONLY*.

Jack wriggled off Lara's lap, headed for the playthings.

'Betty. Are you still there?' James called down the stairs. He poured two mint teas and carried them to the desk.

'I just can't seem to drag myself away,' Betty said, coming up the stairs with a tape measure around her neck. 'Oh hello, Lara darling.' She went over and kissed her.

'She's found out about the Larssen place.'

'Oh,' Betty said. 'Oh dear.'

'Before you say anything else, Lara,' James said, 'I want you to know we had no choice. We promise to house our actors, and, in Marcus's case, we found ourselves committed to putting his whole family up too, which presented us with a massive headache. We have to rely on people offering their space for free or for very little money, and Betty and I spend months before the summer sorting out accommodation. To find someone to take all five of you would have been nigh-on impossible if it weren't for the generosity of an anonymous benefactor, who bought the house from the Larssen estate and donated it to us, thereby solving the problem you, the Wayland family, posed us.'

'But you know what happened in the house?'

'Of course we know what happened in the house,' James said.

'Everyone knows.' Betty sat by Lara and took her hand. 'But really, darling, how long ago does it have to be?'

'Why didn't you tell us?'

'What good would that have done?' James yawned, leaned back and put his hands behind his head.

'But surely you knew we'd find out?'

'I have a zillion things on my plate, Lara,' James said. 'I guess we thought if we cleared it out and cleaned it up, you would settle in, get comfortable and then, even if you did find out, it wouldn't be so bad. I mean, it's not so bad, is it? It's a beautiful house. I'm not asking you to live there for ever, just the summer. Most people would be grateful,' he added.

'That's unnecessary, honey,' Betty said to James.

'I'm just so tired,' James said, rubbing his eyes.

'I wouldn't have called the house clean or clear when we arrived,' Lara said, swallowing hard.

'You said, honey. But we did tell them to clear it out completely before they put the furniture in, didn't we?' Betty looked at James.

'And there's a load of weird stuff in the basement, and there was that disgusting carpet with the stain in it.' Lara felt quite sick now, at the thought of it all.

Betty looked at James. 'I wish you'd gone and checked.'

'Like I haven't got enough to do?' James said, getting up and striding across the room.

'I suppose you've got nowhere else to put us?' Lara said.

James laughed.

'It's just I can't bear the thought of all the misery that went on there. That poor girl.'

'Girl? She was well past middle age when they found her,' James said.

'Oh, James, that's hardly the point,' Betty patted Lara's hand. 'Tell your Aunt Betty.'

'There's this horrible feeling to the place.' Lara rubbed the back of her neck and shivered. The air conditioning in the theatre was too efficient. She wished she had brought her jacket along with her, but she hadn't thought, with the day being so hot outside.

'Say,' Betty said to James. 'How about Danny?'

'Oh God, Betty.' James rolled his eyes and put his head in his hands.

'Danny?' Lara looked at Betty.

'Danny'll help you out with the place. He's a beautiful guy, lives just outside the village. A Seneca Tribe elder.'

'So he says,' James said, picking up the mugs and taking them to the sink.

'And he does this great space-clearing ritual,' Betty continued, ignoring James.

'Space clearing?'

'Sage burning and chanting. It rids a place of bad spirits and energies. It so works. It's been passed down through his family, who used to live on this very land. Danny did it for us when we opened the theatre. I was certain we had a ghost downstairs. I couldn't stay for one minute on my own. Now I practically live down there.'

'Give me strength,' James said, splashing water around in the basin. 'Betty, honey, rehearsals start in ten minutes. Are you ready?'

'I'm always ready, James,' Betty said. She leaned towards Lara and took her hand again. 'I'll talk to Danny and tell him it's urgent. I'm sure he'd love to help you out.'

What else could Lara do? She hated all that mumbo-jumbo, those purple New Age shops full of crystals and incense. But perhaps this Danny, with his people having inhabited the land long before the houses were here, was the real deal. Perhaps, she thought, he could waft his sage over her too, cast out the spell Stephen had put over her and make things simple again.

'I'll give it a go. But don't let Marcus know. I'll never hear the end of it.'

'Well, that's sorted then,' James said, standing in the hallway and showing with his body language that this meeting was drawing to a close. 'I'm sorry if you thought we were trying to deceive you.'

'No—'

'But I hope you see it from our point of view.'

'Of course,' Lara said.

She prised Jack from the basket of toys with the bribe promise of a lolly. When she finally got him away, she turned, with him on her hip, to find James and Betty standing together, smiling sweetly at her.

'Go on,' Betty nudged James.

'I've got a vacancy for young Jack here,' James said. 'If he'd like to make his acting debut.'

'Vacancy?'

'We need a pretty chicken for the Macduff scene,' Betty said. 'Do you think he might be interested?'

'What do you think?' Lara asked Jack, who looked blankly back. 'I think you'll need to speak to his agent,' she said.

'Hello? Is that Jack's agent?' Betty held an imaginary phone up to her ear. 'Would your client be interested in a small part in the Trout Island Theatre production of *Macbeth*?'

'Scottish Play,' James shrieked. Jack jumped and looked alarmed. He stuck his thumb in his mouth and stared, wide-eyed, at James.

'Oops. We'll have to get Danny in to clear the space again,' Betty said, winking at Lara.

'I'll just confer with my client,' Lara said into her own imaginary phone, trying to distract Jack, whose bottom lip was wobbling. 'Jack, would you like to be in Daddy's play with Daddy?'

Jack looked round at her, thumb still firmly planted, and nodded, his red curls bouncing around his face.

'My client would like to accept your offer,' Lara said into her hand-phone, thinking of the acres of free time that had just opened up for her.

'Great! What are your terms?' Betty said.

'Terms schmerms. Just get Danny on to the house,' Lara said, hanging up her imaginary phone.

'Well. That's all just lovely,' James said. 'Now then, Lara and the pretty chick. If you don't mind, I have some rehearsing to do.'

'And I have a garden to tend,' Betty said.

'After you've delighted us with your costume ideas, my love.' James turned to Lara. 'I've given her the afternoon off. I have no idea why.'

He showed them to the door.

Marcus was outside on the porch, sitting on a plastic chair, his back to them as they came out of the theatre. He was angled towards a tanned woman with long, honey-coloured hair, who had one arm looped around his neck.

'Unsex me here,' she was saying to Marcus as he lit her cigarette for her, her eyes burning into his face, 'and fill me, from the crown to the toe, top-full of direst cruelty—'

She noticed Lara and stopped, looked up and smiled, leaving Marcus holding his lighter in mid-air.

Marcus turned and saw his wife and son. 'Oh, hi,' he said, tossing his own cigarette into a fire bucket by his chair. 'We were just going through our lines. Lara, this is Selina Mountford, my Lady MacB. Selina, this is Lara, my Lady Wayland. And Jack, a babe whose brains were not dash'd out.'

'Pleased to meet you,' Selina said, reaching across Marcus to shake Lara's hand.

'And you too,' Lara said, thinking how beautiful this Selina was. And didn't her arm brush Marcus as she leaned forward? Might there be something going on here?

She rather hoped there might.

* * *

Lara and Jack were just crossing Main Street when Sean's Nissan pulled over in front of them. Bella wound down the window, letting some lovely acoustic music escape into the warm air.

'Hey, Ma. Where you been?'

'Around,' Lara said.

'Hello, Mrs Wayland,' Sean said.

'It's Lara, please, Sean. Where are you off to?'

'Swimming,' Bella said. 'I'll be back for supper.'

'Be good,' Lara said. The car took off, dissolving into the heat haze.

'You're a fine one to talk, Miz Wayland,' a voice drawled behind her, making her jump.

She wheeled round to see Stephen, in his Sam disguise, standing right behind her.

'Where did you spring from?' she asked, her initial shock turning into a flush of pleasure at seeing him.

'I just happened to be passing, ma'am.'

'But I didn't see you.'

Stephen smiled and pointed to a bench, half hidden by the branches of a tree. 'I was just sitting there, passing the time of day,' he said.

Jack held his hands out to be picked up by Stephen.

'Is everything OK?' Stephen asked, taking Jack.

'Yes,' Lara said. 'Why?'

'You look a little unsettled.'

'Oh. It's nothing.' Lara's mind raced, confused by what she could tell to whom. 'I've just found out some stuff about the house we're staying in.'

'Really? What?'

'I can't say in front of—' She motioned to Jack, who was too busy trying to get Stephen's attention to notice what his

279

mother was saying. 'Some other time, when we're on our own.' She smiled up at him and felt the world tilt.

'I look forward to it.' He angled his mirrored aviators at her.

She shook her head and rubbed her eyes. 'Oh damn, and I forgot to ask about the locks.'

'Locks?'

'There're no locks on the house and I want some. I meant to ask James and Betty about them.'

'Locks are good. I'm a fan of security.'

'I noticed. Although I'm not asking for something as advanced as your set-up. And I want something on the basement door, too. Marcus said he'd sort it out, but . . .' She trailed off, because it felt like a betrayal to talk Marcus down in front of Stephen.

'I'm sure if Marcus says he'll sort it, he'll sort it,' Stephen said, putting a hand on her shoulder. 'Anyway,' he went on. 'I'm glad I ran into you, because I was wondering if you and the kids would be interested in coming to this with me.' He held out five tickets. 'It's a circus show – new circus, thank God, because they still have performing animals in the traditional type over here. They're on in a small town about half an hour south. Tomorrow evening. It's unmissable.'

'What about Marcus?' Lara said.

'Oh, it starts at seven, so he won't be finished rehearsing in time.'

'Pity,' Lara said, smiling at Stephen.

'Yes, pity.'

'We'd love to come.'

'Great.' He pocketed the tickets. 'I'll call by about five, then. We'll grab something to eat while we're out.'

He stood there smiling at her while Jack tugged at his wig.

A cicada buzzed somewhere close by. Even in this strange, slightly absurd disguise, Stephen felt special to her, precious, *hers*. She reached up and lifted his aviators so she could see into his eyes. A split second before Jack became aware of anything passing between them she stood on tiptoe and kissed him on the cheek, at once breaking and sealing the moment.

'Pushing the envelope,' he said. 'I like that.'

'I'll see you tomorrow, then,' she said, her voice catching.

'Does it have to be so long?' He handed Jack back to her.

Lara and Jack set off along Main Street. Just before she reached the village store, where she was going to buy the bribe lollipop, she turned back to where they had been standing. Stephen was there, shielding his exposed eyes from the sun, still watching her.

Twenty-Nine

IT TOOK LARA AND JACK ANOTHER HALF AN HOUR TO decide on the lolly of the day. As they dawdled back to the house, she tried to concentrate on the more benign aspects of its shabby appearance: the peeling clapboard and picturesque window shutters. But her eyes kept on being drawn back to the stone plinth the house stood on; how dark and moss-covered it was. Like gravestones, she thought.

She decided to keep what she had learned about the building to herself. It would be pointless to worry Bella and Olly, and she really couldn't face the belittling Marcus would bestow on the whole story.

As they turned on to the front path, she noticed the little thing on the decking, at the top of the porch steps.

A yellow, fluffy chick lay on its back, its stubby wings splayed, its wormlike feet pointing, like arrows, back up at its own corpse. Its neck was clearly broken. Bending to examine it, Lara was reminded of the diagrams of a twelve-week foetus in an old pregnancy book back home that she hadn't been able to stop herself looking at. It would have been about this size, she thought.

'Poor baby bird,' Jack said, squatting by it, letting his lolly drip on the ground.

Lara stood and looked along the street. The air was always filled with animal sounds – insects, dogs, the horses round the back, and wilder things. But she had not once heard the cluck of a hen, or the crow of a cockerel. In any case, this tiny thing couldn't have come very far on its own. And, from the angle of its neck, it must have been killed by something bigger than itself.

She thought of Dog. Without any real evidence, she had already cast him as the Larssen hound that got away. Was this some sort of canine peace offering, because he knew that she had found out?

She passed a hand over her eyes. Was this place turning her mad?

'Yes, poor baby bird,' she said, lifting her son up and opening the front door.

'Hello?' she called on the threshold, hoping that at least Olly might be around. But only the house greeted her, with its particularly heavy brand of nothingness and putrid stink. Only the whirring of the old fridge, as it kept itself from overheating, punctured the quiet inside. She looked down at the patch of floor on the hall landing where the stain had been. She had done a good job on that. You'd never guess that anything nasty had ever happened there.

Stepping in, Lara trod on the letter waiting for her on the doormat. She knew it was for her, because the sender had written her name on it in capital letters, in green ink. The envelope stank of stale cigarettes. Inside was a note, scrawled in the same idiosyncratic, unpunctuated hand.

HEY CHICKEN DONT COUNT YOUR CHICKENS LEAVE SM ALONE.

283

Lara flushed. Someone knew about her and Stephen. But who? Surely the only person who could have an inkling was Betty, and from the little Lara knew about her, nastiness like this was not her style.

She took Jack to her computer where she set him up with a game on CBeebies. Then she got a beer from the fridge and went outside to sit on the porch and think, looking at the dead chick as if it could tell her what she wanted to know.

Things were getting ever more complicated: the stolen clothes, the chipmunk incident; the madwoman nearly mowing them down; the Larssen thing; Bella losing her head; Olly running around with bad boys.

For a moment, a solution presented itself in high definition. She would take the children back to England, leaving Marcus here to get on with his work, unencumbered by his family. When he got back in September, she would sort things out one way or another, depending on what the distance from him had taught her, and without the complicating presence of Stephen.

She couldn't think straight with him so close.

But, even as she thought it, she knew she wasn't going to do it. She would have to explain her departure to Marcus; Bella and Olly would demand a reason, as well as quite possibly arguing that they could stay on with their father. And she couldn't have that.

But the main reason she wasn't going to leave was the main reason she *should* leave.

She wasn't going to do what the malevolent little note ordered. She couldn't leave SM alone. Not any more.

She put her hands underneath her hair and rubbed her neck. She looked at the blind-eyed houses all around her, feeling watched. It was horrible. Behind her she felt the pressure of the Larssen place and all its misery.

Unable to sit there any longer, she got up and went down the side of the house to the shed at the back, where the hummingbirds were still feeding as if nothing had changed since she watched them on that first morning. Pushing open the cobwebbed door, she peered gingerly into the dark, creosote-scented interior.

It was almost completely empty, except for a few flowerpots and – the thing she was looking for – a spade, which she picked up. She went round the back of the shed and dug a small grave in the rough grass. Then she returned to the front porch and scooped the dead chick up with the spade, taking care not to further mutilate its body.

She carried it to the hole and tipped it in. Seeing it lie there lifeless in the red soil reinforced her conviction that she had to see this thing with Stephen through. Life was short, a one-time event, and the shocking thought came to her that she had wasted sixteen whole years of her three-score and ten.

Wasted was perhaps a little strong. But even so . . .

Saying a prayer to the baby she had pulled the plug on, she covered the dead chick with a mound of soil. She plucked a chrysanthemum from a scabby bush sprouting in one of the overgrown flowerbeds behind the shed and stuck it in the freshly turned earth. Kneeling there in the dirt, she knew she had to call Stephen.

She hurried inside and dialled his cellphone number, but, not surprisingly, reception in the area being so patchy, it went straight to voicemail. She tried his house phone, but it just rang and rang. She could almost hear the bell echoing in the cool, high-ceilinged living room. There was no answerphone, but she couldn't have left a message anyway because she had no idea what to say.

Jack still happily played on the computer, but Lara felt

shredded. She needed to talk to someone. But who? She couldn't call Gina, because she couldn't mention Stephen. The only person she could think of was Betty. She punched the farmhouse number into the phone. She counted fifteen rings and was just about to hang up when a breathless voice said, 'Hello?'

'Betty?'

'Is that you, Lara?'

In a rush, Lara told her about the chick and the note. Betty made her describe it in detail – the colour of the writing, the capital letters.

'Have you told Stephen about this?'

'No. Not yet. I can't contact him.'

'Good. Don't breathe a word to him, honey. I want you to come up here to the house right now and we can have a talk. I've got iced tea in the cooler. Bring me the little letter so I can see it.'

'I've got Jack, though.'

'That's fine, sweet. I've just the thing to keep him amused.'

After a slight delay, because Jack needed a complete wash-down after managing to get most of his lollipop down his front, Lara pulled up in the lane by the side of the farmhouse.

'Hello,' she said, rapping on the kitchen door.

'There you are!' Betty called from the garden behind Lara. 'I'd given you up for lost.' She straightened up behind the tomato plants and came up the path between the vegetable beds, a trug tucked in the crook of her arm. Since Lara had seen her in the theatre she had changed into an antique silk kimono and a pair of cut-off shorts. She had tied her hair back but still sported full make-up.

'Trudi's down there. Say hello to Lara and Jack, Trudi,' Betty said. The stout upper half of the strange, scarred woman

286

appeared from behind a chaos of gooseberry plants, and she lifted her hand in greeting before bending to her work once more. 'Look at these babies.' Betty picked one of the tiny, fat tomatoes from her trug and popped it into Lara's mouth.

'Delicious,' Lara said.

'So you want to see something special, Jack?' Betty said, squatting down so she was level with him.

'The fish?' Jack said, his eyes expectant.

'Even better than the fish.'

Jack nodded and took Betty's hand. She led him inside to a recess under the stairs.

'Look,' she whispered, leaning on the banister to kneel. Jack sank to his knees, craned forward to see, then gasped with delight.

There, tucked away in the shadows, was a basket of kittens in full fluff. Betty picked one up and held it out for Jack, who looked up at Lara for permission.

'One minute.' Lara rummaged in her bag for his antihistamines and a bottle of water. 'He's allergic,' she said to Betty.

'Oh God, sorry,' Betty said.

'Don't worry.' Lara handed Jack the pill. 'I always carry these. They keep him safe for ten hours.'

Dosed up, Jack turned back to the kitten and took hold of it as if it were a piece of thistledown. It nestled into his arms like it had been born to be there. Jack looked up at Lara with such a smile on his face that she felt tears pricking at the corners of her eyes. This then was innocence.

'Coyote got the mother,' Betty whispered to Lara. She turned to Jack. 'It's feed time. Do you want to do it? Let me show you how.'

Betty went to the kitchen and returned a few minutes later with a teat pipette and a small jug of milk. She showed Jack how to tease the kitten with the milky glass tube and gently push the bulb to let the milk come down as it sucked.

'That should keep him amused for a while,' Betty said. 'Now then, *Mamacita*, come and sip ice tea and tell Betty everything.'

Lara sat at the kitchen table and handed Betty the malevolent note. Slipping on a pair of leopard-print reading spectacles, she read it, smelled it, and put it down on the table between them, wrinkling her nose.

'So. You need to be told to leave Stephen alone?' she said, not unkindly.

'Nothing's happened . . .' Lara said. 'But, as you said to me yourself, the only important thing in this life is love.' She put her head in her hands and closed her eyes. She should shut up. Talking about it just brought her one step closer to committing to it.

'Oh Lara,' Betty said. 'You and I are of a piece. We're both romantics. Do you want me to tell you about this note?'

'Yes,' Lara said into her hands.

'You've no doubt heard most of it. It's hardly been a secret. You see, things happened in LA that made poor Stephen very sick. If you're in the public eye, you attract a lot of attention and he was no different. But there was this one particular person – this Elizabeth Sanders – who became so convinced he was the one for her that, when he failed to respond to the barrage of messages she sent him, she went berserk. At first it was innocuous things like eggs broken on his car, or items turning up that he hadn't ordered. But it got worse, and then the threats started coming.'

'Threats?'

'It was awful. Real physical threats.'

'Why didn't he go to the police?'

'He did at first, but it was so slow – she covered her tracks well and it was hard to prove that it was coming from her. She kept herself hidden and they never found her, never got a description. It drove Stephen crazy. She went into hiding and continued to wage her campaign against him. Then his management, freaked by the amount of publicity the case was attracting – not good, they said, for his hard man image – made him drop his complaint, in the hope she would just disappear. But of course it just got worse. Stephen started having these "accidents". It got so he didn't dare go out. All he could do was sit and drink away the fear.'

'I thought he didn't drink.'

'Not any more. James and I were in New York at the time. When we got back to LA we were shocked at how we found him. It's hard to imagine, seeing him now, but he looked *awful*. So we smuggled him out of town and into three months of rehab in Utah, which had the added bonus of hiding him away from Elizabeth Sanders. Then he more or less came straight out here to stay with us while he searched for a place to buy. We hid all our booze at the back of the barn and only drank when he was away. Can you imagine? Like two naughty teenagers.'

'And the chick? And the note?'

Betty leaned forward and narrowed her eyes. 'I don't know how she's done it, but she's tracked him down.' She picked up the note and waved it at Lara. 'This is completely her style, if that doesn't dignify it too much. We've done everything we can to hide him, but she's found him. Did your kids let anything out?'

'No,' Lara said, hoping she was right. 'They're good kids. They wouldn't do that. They understand Stephen has to be discreet.'

Betty sat back, crossed her arms and looked at Lara. They could hear Jack cooing at the kittens in the hallway.

'Besides,' Lara said, 'there was this woman watching us just after we left your party, just after we met Stephen. And you remember that strange person in the diner? I think it might be her.' Lara told Betty about the laundromat incident. 'You thought there was something odd about her too, didn't you?'

'I never actually saw Sanders,' Betty said, frowning. 'And you're right. I didn't exactly get a nice vibe off that diner woman. But I didn't expect . . .' She fell silent, her eyes closed, their long spidery lashes casting shadows on her cheeks. Lara could almost hear her brain working.

'OK, honey,' Betty said at last, examining her beautifully manicured fingers. 'There are two things you have to do now.'

'What?'

'First, and this is most important: Stephen must not know Elizabeth Sanders has followed him out here.'

'What good will that do?'

'He is more delicate than you think, honey. If he finds out, it will kill him. I saw how desperate he got last time.'

'But she's not going to go away, is she?' Lara said.

'No. And that's where you come in.' Betty leaned forward again. 'She's obviously on your trail. I want you to see if you can work out who she is, what she looks like. Gather the evidence like a detective. And then, when we've built our case, we can go to the police and get the whole thing quickly cleared up before Stephen even knows about it.'

'But isn't she dangerous? What about us?'

Betty fixed her with a stern look. 'Lara, this is for *Stephen Molloy*'s sake.'

Lara frowned, taken aback. Betty had said his name as if he were some sort of deity, as if she should sacrifice everything for him.

'And the other thing,' Betty went on.

'Other thing?'

'I said there are two things you have to do, remember, honey?'

'Go on,' Lara said, feeling her cheeks burn.

'It's vital that *Macbeth* goes well. For the theatre, for James, for me, for Marcus. In addition to not telling Stephen about his little nemesis turning up, I urge you to exercise some caution in your dealings with him.'

'Dealings?'

Betty turned to look at Lara. Every ounce of warmth had drained from her face, so, for the first time, she looked her age. 'I don't want you to upset Marcus *in any way* until the end of the run. Is that understood? If you do, you will have me to answer to, and, believe me, I do not take prisoners.'

Lara pushed her half-drunk glass of iced tea away from her and looked at Betty. So she had been rumbled, and, as punishment, her autonomy and safety had been stripped from her. She remembered how it had been when, as a child, her views had never been taken into account about anything, when her parents, looking down at her from their adult platform, viewed her as an entirely different species to themselves, something on an altogether lower branch of the evolutionary scale. That was exactly what was being done to her now.

'So then, honey,' Betty said, standing up and clapping her hands together, her beautiful kimono flapping like the wings of a large raptor. 'Let's go and see how dear little Jack is doing with the fluffy little kits.'

Thirty

SEAN PULLED THE NISSAN OFF THE TRACK AND SWERVED ON to the spongy grass at the side of the pond. He cut the engine and turned to smile at Bella.

'Hi honey, I'm home,' he said, pulling her close and kissing her.

'Swim?' she said.

'Sure thing.'

They got out of the car and Sean fetched the blankets, the beer and the picnic from the boot. Hand in hand, they walked round to the other side of the pond, which in England would have been called a lake. Sean shook the blanket out on to the leaf-littered ground at the edge of a jetty with a round inflatable dinghy tethered to it. On their first visit to this, Sean's cousin's pond, they had drifted out on the dinghy to the middle of the water, where they had spent the whole afternoon, lazily making love, sunbathing, and swimming in among the trout and bullfrogs that inhabited the cool, stone-lined pool.

Initially Bella had been worried about being discovered, but Sean reassured her no one ever came up to the pond on weekdays. It was also five miles out of the village, two miles off the main road, and right in the middle of privately owned land, so there was no chance of anyone accidentally coming across them. By this, their fourth visit together, she was completely relaxed about being up here, lying naked on the blanket on the ground with her boy, spending the whole afternoon kissing, touching and whispering with him. It was like Eden for her.

They pulled off their clothes and ran hand in hand along the jetty to throw themselves into the water, where they made love for the first time that afternoon, the frenzied, unstoppable fuck they had been desperate for since he had picked her up from the creepy old house.

On the way, as he drove, Sufjan Stevens strumming his laid-back stuff out of the car's old cassette player, Sean had told her about the history of the Larssen place, about the old man, the cannibal dogs and the mad sister. Bella's eyes had grown large and round.

'No way,' she had said. 'That is so cool.'

'I love you,' he said, as, a little later, they lay on the blanket, the glow from their lovemaking spreading through them as they sipped ice-cold beer. A dragonfly flashed iridescence across the jade-green surface of the pond. 'I want to spend my life with you,' he whispered in her ear.

'Me too you.' Bella drew him close and held him to her breast.

Sensible, sensitive, serious and totally reliable, Sean was different from any other boy she had ever known. Had someone proposed those qualities to her before she met him, she would have yawned and pronounced them boring. But in him – well, they were anything but.

Olly had always had this idea that she and he were two

parts of the same person. He'd banged on about it since they were quite young. She had never bought into his theory, and as things got more complicated between them she had actively denied it, suspecting she could actually be a whole being in her own right.

Meeting Sean made her realise that while she was complete in herself, at the same time he fitted with her – not only physically, but with every part of her. He completed her in a way that Olly never, ever could, no matter how hard he pushed for it.

She felt warmed through, like caramel. The sun dappled on her naked skin between the broad leaves of the trees around the pond and, with the still heat, the slight wooziness from the beer, and the scraped-clean feeling of making love in the water, she found herself dozing off.

'What was that?' she said, sitting bolt upright. Something had moved in the trees, crashing through the undergrowth, startling them both awake.

Sean sat still for a moment, listening carefully, slowly scanning the forest. Then he relaxed and lay back down again, propping his head on his hand, looking at her. 'A deer,' he said, pulling her towards him with his free hand. 'Probably.'

'Or a bear,' Bella said, resisting him, sitting up and hugging her legs. 'Or a mountain lion.'

'Very unlikely. And if it was, they wouldn't come anywhere near us – they're more frightened of us than we are of them, you know.'

'Yeah, yeah, country boy,' Bella said, turning towards him. She traced the side of his face with her finger and bent to kiss him. He lifted his hand to her breast and she shifted and swung one leg over him, straddling him.

'I'm not scared with you here,' she said, easing him inside her.

'Too right.' Sean smiled up at her.

She began to move on top of him, slowly. Sean closed his eyes and put his hands on her hips.

'Oh, Bella . . .'

Then there was a great crash and four swaying figures sprang out of the trees, rifles aimed at them. It all happened so quickly it took a minute for Bella to realise that one of them was a twitching, chewing, pinprick-pupilled Olly. His face was made up with camouflage paint and his bloodshot eyes roved over the scene.

'Tracked you,' he snarled.

The insects in the grass and trees, the crickets and cicadas and katydids, all fell silent. A bullfrog plopped from the lily pad where he was sunning himself into the safety of the water, spreading ripples across the pond. Bella jumped off Sean and pulled the blanket over them both.

'Olly, what the FUCK?' she said.

'Look what we've got here, then,' Olly slurred to his companions. 'Looks like we've got ourselves some real good game.' He motioned to the three others, who slowly formed a circle around them. Bella recognised them as the gang from the playground. They were all filthy, covered in dust and sweat, and quite clearly off their faces. One, a tall, lanky boy with a shaved head and bad acne, had a joint stuck between his lips and a rucksack on his back. Another, fat and missing a front tooth, was giggling, a horrible, high-pitched snicker. The third, a short, stocky, blond boy, stood right by Bella, his grubby, bulging crotch level with her eye.

She looked up at her brother.

'What do you think you're doing?'

'Shouldn't I be the one asking that of you?' he said, reaching for the joint. His pinprick eyes bulged and his mouth worked around his words. 'What did I say to you about seeing this creep? And now what do I find you doing? Camera!' he barked, holding out his hand. The boy with the erection handed an iPhone to Olly, who took a photograph of Bella and Sean cowering under the blanket. 'We got some great footage, Bella. While you were in the pond.'

Bella roared, and sprang up at her brother. The fat boy grabbed her from behind, splaying his sweaty palms over her bare breasts. The other two turned on her and she saw the tall boy leer, revealing two sharp, pointed canine teeth.

'Sean!' she cried, but Olly had grabbed his gun again and was pointing it straight at him.

'Don't make a move, lover boy,' he said. Then he yelled at his companions. 'Get away from her, you animals. And Bella, put something on, or you'll get what you deserve.'

Bella picked up her clothes, which she had thrown off an hour before, when she was free. 'Olly, please go away,' she whispered to him as she pulled her dress on.

'I'm not finished yet,' Olly said, smiling at Sean.

'Leave him alone.' Bella threw herself again at her brother.

'Steady Bella,' Olly said, sidestepping her, his gun trained on Sean. 'It's loaded and ready to go. We don't want a nasty accident.'

'Put it down, Olly.' Bella planted herself between Olly and Sean.

'Jesus. Guys, do something with my sister,' Olly said.

'Anything?' The boy with the canines leered into her face.

'Not that, Kyle,' Olly said. 'Just get her out of the way.'

Kyle put his rucksack down and got out a bottle of Jack Daniels, which he swigged and passed on to the fat boy.

Then he pulled out a length of rope.

'This do, Olly man?' he said. Olly nodded. Bella tried to scramble away, but Kyle was with her in two paces, thumping her on the ground, his whole body on top of her.

'Careful,' Olly said.

'You just wriggle some more, little girl,' Kyle hissed into her ear as she struggled to get away from him. 'That's real nice.' He tied her hands behind her back, yanked her up and, dragging her by her hair to a tree, lashed her to its trunk.

'Don't you even look at her,' Olly hissed to Sean, as he motioned with his gun for him to stand up. 'Get him,' he said to the others. 'Let's see what he's got.'

The three boys hauled Sean up and held him, one on each arm, one round his neck, so he was splayed, naked, in front of Olly. He put up no resistance, and didn't make a sound, but he looked straight into Olly's eyes, not wavering for one minute.

'Leave him!' Bella screamed.

Olly put his gun on the ground and, getting a knife out of his belt, moved in on Sean. He placed the blade on his belly, right below his navel, and leered into his face.

'Not such a happy chappy now, are we?' Olly said, flipping Sean's penis with the blunt side of his knife. 'Not like when you were FUCKING MY SISTER, eh? I thought I told you not to touch her.'

Bella saw Sean swallow. He said nothing, but still he held Olly's stare.

'Now then,' Olly said. 'What am I going to do with you?'

'He's got a real purty mouth,' the fat boy said, laughing again with his peculiar, high-pitched cackle.

'And we always knew he was a faggot,' Kyle said, 'Right from kindergarten.'

'Fag,' the blond sneered, then he sang a snatch of 'Duelling

Banjos'. The three of them found this so funny they snickered until their eyes streamed with tears. But they didn't, for one minute, let go of their hold on Sean.

'Turn him round,' Olly said. 'Pull his legs apart.'

The others did it, roughly, and, powerless, Sean let them do it.

Olly stood there for a while, considering, looking at Sean's naked backside, splayed above his shaking knees.

'No!' Bella screamed.

'Shut it, sister,' Olly barked. Then he spat at Sean's back. 'I can't bring myself,' he said in a mincing voice. 'He's not my type.'

Again, his three cronies sniggered. Kyle passed Olly the whisky and he took a long, hard slug.

'Turn him round again, get him on the ground,' Olly said. The boys pushed Sean down on his back. Olly reached inside his pocket and got out a packet of cigarettes, a pair of gloves and a Zippo. 'I've decided I'm going to be kind to you,' he said, lighting up a cigarette. 'Not that you deserve it.' He delivered a sharp kick to Sean's ribs, bent close to his face and rubbed some dirt into his cheeks and mouth. 'I'm going to give you a warning this time, but you're lucky because you're also being taught a lesson. It's good to learn. Hold him tight.'

Kyle and the blond boy positioned themselves one at each arm. The fat boy put all of his weight on Sean's legs.

'Now, I'd say this wasn't going to hurt,' Olly said, 'But I'd be lying.' Cigarette in mouth, he pulled on a glove and knelt, his back to Bella, one hand at Sean's groin. For the first time, Sean struggled, but the others had him securely under their panting weight. Bella looked away. She couldn't bear to see their greedy, excited faces as they waited to see what Olly had in store.

With his free hand, Olly lifted his cigarette high into the air. Then he brought it down to where his other hand had hold of Sean.

'Sizzle,' Kyle said.

Sean's scream made Bella's knees buckle. Olly lifted the cigarette away and leaned back. 'Oh look, where's your little man gone now, eh?' he said. 'You made my tab go out, lover boy, with your slippy dick.' He took the Zippo again, and, bending forward he set it to work on Sean, who wailed like an animal being murdered.

Olly lifted the lighter and brought it down again. Again, Sean screamed.

'Don't you ever come near my fucking sister again,' Olly yelled. 'Or I'll fucking kill you. You hear me, creep?'

'That's enough, man,' Kyle said after Olly had applied the lighter the third time and Sean had screamed himself out underneath them.

'You won't be using that for a good while,' Olly said, stepping back. 'Let him go.' The boys moved away and Sean curled up on the ground, weeping with pain.

Olly stood up and got his gun. 'Stand up!' he shouted. Whimpering, Sean scrambled to his feet. His beautiful body seemed to have shrunk and his skin was bleached of its tan. Tears ran rivers down the dirt in his face, and his hands were clamped over his front.

'Your keys in those?' Olly motioned to Sean's jeans, which were still in the heap where they had fallen when Bella had greedily helped him off with them. Sean nodded. 'Get them,' Olly said to the blond boy.

'Now, lover boy, take your keys, get in your car, start the engine and drive. Drive away from here and don't come anywhere near my sister again. Understood?'

Sean went to pick up his jeans. 'No,' Olly said. 'As you are.'

Sean limped, naked, to his car, got in and drove off.

'And you couldn't see him for dust,' Olly laughed. Then he swung over to Bella and took her face in his hand. 'Now then, little sis, what do you think of that?'

'Bastard,' Bella spat.

'It's for your own good,' he said. He looked her in the eyes and sang, at full volume, the song he had practised the night before when she had tried to sleep.

'Like me in lineaments: her eyes
Her hair, her features, all to the very tone
Even of her voice, they said were like to mine . . .'

And he squeezed her cheeks so her skin burned with the pulling.

'Who are you?' she said, as he finished his song. She didn't see a thing she recognised in her twin brother's face.

'You know me better than anyone, Bella,' he said, his voice low.

'I'm going to tell Mum.'

'You try, and there'll be a nice little gallery going up on Facebook.'

Bella tasted the bile in her mouth.

'You got a line there, Aaron boy?' Olly asked the blond boy. 'Chop chop.'

'Yum,' Kyle said, reaching into Sean's picnic basket. 'Pizza.'

'Like your face,' Brandon said, and his laughter melted into Kyle's cackle and they all joined in, until, once more, the tears rolled down their cheeks.

* * *

After they had finished Sean and Bella's picnic and the lines of white powder had been snorted and the bottle of Jack Daniels was empty, the boys untied her.

'What do I do now?' she said, gesturing to the spot where Sean's car had stood. 'How do I get back?'

'My boys here are hunters. They know all the trails through the forest,' Olly said. 'We can provide an escort.'

And, once again, the boys laughed until they were on the ground, rolling in the dirt.

Thirty-One

'AND WHERE HAVE YOU BEEN?'

Marcus was smoking on the porch when Lara and Jack got back from Betty's. At his feet sat two drained beer bottles, in his hand a third, half empty.

'I've been up to the farm to see Betty,' Lara said, mustering an Oscar-standard performance of unperturbed normality. 'She gave us some beautiful veg, look.' She held out the basket of courgettes, tomatoes and basil that Betty, her sweetness rediscovered, had pressed upon her.

Marcus grunted.

Lara left Jack to tell his father about the kittens while she took the produce through to the kitchen. As she opened the front door, the rotten smell coming from the cellar halted her in her tracks. It was worse than ever. Determined to sort out whatever was causing the stink, she crossed over to the secret door under the stairs. But her hand was stayed by the two new pieces of wood nailed across it, keeping it shut. She turned and saw a set of keys dangling from a new lock crudely but effectively cut into the front door. Apart from seeing Stephen,

302

this was the best turn-up of a particularly trying day.

'Well done!' she called to Marcus, as she went through to the kitchen. Her mood was further lifted when she noted that the back door now had bolts at top and bottom, so the house could be completely locked.

She got herself a beer from the fridge and went to join Marcus. Safety, she thought, in numbers. Jack had finished his story and was pottering around the front lawn with a football that had somehow appeared.

'Thanks for sorting the locks,' Lara said as she sat on the swing seat next to Marcus, scanning the road for anything untoward. Something at the back of her mind wondered if life was going to be like this from now on – always on the lookout.

'What?' Marcus said without much interest.

'The doors and the basement. You took me seriously!'

'Not me.' Marcus held his hands up. 'I'd never do that.'

'You mentioned it to James though? He must've sent someone.'

'Possibly,' Marcus said, slapping a mosquito on his arm and flicking the bloody remnants on to the deck.

Lara turned to face him.

'What's up with you?'

'I'm pretty fucked off if you must know,' he said, tossing his cigarette butt into a spiky bush that grew up around the porch railings. Then he looked furiously at Lara and paused. She swallowed.

'Why?' she brought herself to ask.

'James has got it into his head that we're going to give the play the full Scottish treatment, accents, tartan and all.'

Lara was so relieved she nearly choked on her beer laughing.

'It's not funny,' Marcus said. 'It's a total disaster.'

'Yes,' Lara said, reining herself in. 'Sorry.'

'It's so naff. And James's ear is so unattuned now to any accent that comes east of Maine, that he can't tell how shit the other actors are at it. It's embarrassing.'

'Can't you just persuade him that he's wrong?'

'What do you think?' Marcus said. One of his endless peeves about his profession was that it stuck him in a position of complete powerlessness. In his worst moments he said he was no more than a piece of walkie-talkie meat that just had to put up and shut up.

'It's not been a great day for you, has it?' she said. Although, she thought, in comparison with my own . . .

'It's not funny,' he said again, finishing his beer and childishly lobbing the bottle to join his cigarette butt in the bush.

Lara sighed, got up and retrieved the bottle, putting it by the front door, ready to take in to the recycling bin.

'I'm beginning to see James in a different light,' Marcus said, reaching down to a half-empty six-pack she hadn't seen and popping the lid off another bottle. 'I used to think the sun shone out of his arse, but actually he's just a cunt.'

'Eloquently put.'

Lara sat back down next to him. The low sun bled plastic tangerine into the hazy sky, but the close heat of the day wasn't ready to let up. The only movement out on the street came from a couple of black, white and buff-coloured birds hopping on the tarmac, picking at seeds dropped from the trees above them. Oblivious to the thump of Jack's ball as he kicked it up into the air, the birds called to one another. *Chick-a-dee-dee-dee.*

Like before, she wondered if there might be someone watching them from the houses opposite. Before today, it had only been a wild imagining. But now it posed a real possibility. Or what about up in those hills looming above the village? Did a watcher lie belly-down in the grass, a pair of long-range binoculars clamped to her eyes? Lara scanned the green for a glint of something glassy.

'It's your friend again,' Marcus said and, alarmed, Lara wheeled round to see where he was looking.

It was only Dog. He trotted up the garden path and took up his usual station on the lawn, directly in front of the swing seat, so Lara and Marcus could see him.

Unhappy about her young meaty son being so close to what could possibly be a hound with a taste for human flesh, Lara flew down the steps and scooped Jack up off the grass.

'I want to play ball, though,' Jack said.

'How about a bit of CBeebies instead?' she said.

'Yay!'

'You're supposed to encourage him to play outside,' Marcus said, rolling another cigarette. 'Not drag him in front of the computer.'

'You're not the only one who's allergic to dogs,' Lara said. She knew Jack was full of antihistamines, but Marcus didn't.

'Fair point.' Marcus held up his hands in surrender. He gestured to Dog. 'He looks thirsty. Get him a drink while you're in there.'

Typical of Marcus, Lara thought, to get sentimental over Dog just as she had possibly found out something hideous about him. It was tempting to tell Marcus the full story, but she didn't have the energy to go through with it right now. Not after the day she had just endured. Instead, after settling Jack in front of the laptop, she fetched a bowl of water for Dog.

'There you go, boy,' Marcus said to Dog from the safety of his position up on the porch. 'There you go, wee laddie,' he said again in a Scottish accent. He put his head in his hands and groaned. 'I want to resign,' he said. 'I want to go home.'

'But we can't leave now!' Lara said too quickly. What might she lose if they did? 'This could be your big break, remember? Surely you can convince James he's wrong about the accents?'

Marcus shook his head. 'He's adamant. I think I'll just leave.'

'But it would be more than depressing to go back to an unemployed August at home, after all the looking forward we've done for this. I mean, until today, you thought everything was going swimmingly. If it's just about the accents . . .'

'And the kilts,' Marcus said. He stuck his lower lip out so that he looked like Jack when he didn't get what he wanted. 'And the bagpipes.'

'No.' Lara tried to suppress her smile. 'Bagpipes?'

'I don't want to talk about it.'

Having finished his water, Dog sat up and whimpered, fixing Marcus with his eye.

'He looks hungry,' Marcus said, and Lara felt sick at the thought of what might once have sated the creature's appetite. 'Have you got anything for him?'

'He knows a soft touch,' Lara said as casually as possible. She went into the kitchen to rummage in the fridge.

On the way back, Jack called her over to look at a game he had found on the website. She watched him play one round, and allowed his joyful absorption in the task to settle her.

As she went out again, a cold sausage in her hand, she heard a bellow of hearty laughter from Marcus. What, she wondered, could have lifted his bleak mood so quickly?

Lara's place beside Marcus had been taken by Selina Mountford, who swung her honey locks round when she heard the fly screen bang, her eyebrows raised over her symmetrical, strong-featured face. She was tall and athletic, really quite striking. If there were a complete opposite to Lara's small, doll-like roundness. Selina had it.

'Hi Lara,' she said, detaching herself from Marcus's side and rising, her hand held out. 'So pleased to meet you again.'

For a nation famous for mastering the casual, it seemed to Lara that Americans relied on a surprisingly elaborate code of gesture and politesse in their everyday encounters. She wondered what they had to hide. She tossed the sausage to Dog, who gobbled it up with gratitude then left, his mission accomplished. Then she wiped her hand on her skirt and greeted Selina.

'Selina's my stage wife,' Marcus said from his chair. Nothing overchivalrous or elaborate about *him*. 'Mrs MacB.'

'I know. We met this afternoon, remember?' Lara said.

'Oh yeah. Must be more pissed than I thought.' He scratched his beard.

'I was just letting Marcus know that I've solved the accent issue,' Selina said.

'Good old girl, she is.' Marcus winked to Lara. 'She had James wrapped round her lovely little finger.'

'We'll be doing it in American now,' Selina said.

'Thank God *I've* got an ear for accent, at least,' Marcus said.

Having heard his attempt at Brooklynese in the Palace Theatre, Westcliff-on-Sea production of *A View from the Bridge*, Lara was inclined to disagree with this, but she was glad the Scottish issue had been resolved.

Lara dragged up a wooden chair from the other end of the porch while Selina bent forward in the swing seat and let Marcus light her long, slim cigarette. Lara noticed her French manicure and glanced down at her own grubby nails. She would keep them that way, she thought. If Marcus saw her as shabby by comparison, it was all to the good.

'I invited Selina over for supper tonight,' Marcus said. 'What are we having?'

'I haven't given it a moment's thought yet,' Lara said, peeved at Marcus both for doling out invitations on the spur of the moment and for his automatic assumption that it was she who would plan and cook the meal. 'And Gina's invited us round for a bonfire party tonight.'

'Gina?'

'My new friend. Remember? The woman from the library?'

'With the children with the stupid names?' Marcus said, shuddering no doubt more at the memory of Chicken Licken and Foxy Loxy. 'Well I'm sure she won't mind if Selina tags along too. She's quite miserable in her digs, aren't you, lovey?'

'I am,' Selina said, nodding her glossy head. 'Have you got a corkscrew, Lara honey? I brought this,' she said, holding up a chilled bottle of Chablis.

While Lara worked in the kitchen, scratching together a meal from Betty's produce, Marcus and Selina sat on the porch and steamed through the wine. Deciding she wasn't going to be beaten, Lara got stuck into her own bottle of Sauvignon Blanc.

As she moved between cupboard and sink, fridge and table, she felt as if she had an audience. Since meeting Stephen again, she had been aware of being in his mind, in his regard. But this was more unsettling. Somewhere beyond the lens of the glassed-in porch, someone might be watching her, bearing her ill will. The way the village nestled in the dip between two hills – a feature she had previously seen as picturesque – now made her a sitting duck. This was how Stephen must have felt back in LA. Poor man. What he had to put up with.

She was grateful, whoever sorted it out, for the new locks.

The red roses in the blue vase were past their best. She

should really do something about them. Half-heartedly, she topped up their water.

To escape from the heat and steam of the kitchen, she took a break and sat on the back porch, dangling her legs over the edge like she had on the first morning. She sipped her wine, newly chilled by another top-up from the fridge, and felt the burden of the house sandwiched between her and the theatrical joviality over on the front porch. The hill at the back of the house loomed in dusky darkness and for the first time that evening she wondered where Olly and Bella were.

Out having fun, she supposed. Did she need to worry about them? Surely though it was just her that Elizabeth Sanders was watching . . .

The lone headlights of a car panned across the dark ridge at the top of the hill and disappeared, the remote sound of the cranky engine just about audible against the cacophony of dusk insects. A dog barked in the distance, regular and reliable as a heartbeat. On the other side of that mountain, miles into the forest, Stephen sat in his house. She wondered what he would be doing right now, up there on his own. She added a little prayer to keep him safe.

A loud bellow of Marcus-laughter shot up over the house – the especially throaty sort he reserved for his theatrical friends. His basso profundo was followed up by Selina's silvery trickle.

Lara hoicked a load of phlegm from the back of her throat and spat into the grass, something she usually only did when she was running. She looked at the big hire car parked across the tarmac and wondered what stopped her jumping in and driving up to be with Stephen and away from Marcus. The fact her husband didn't even have an inkling something was going wrong made her despise him even more than she had when they arrived, and, if she was honest with herself, that was saying something.

Hot, tired and filthy, Olly and Bella got back just before she served up the ratatouille-based meal she had put together from Betty's offerings. She was glad they were home, but something was not right between them. Bella seemed to be incredibly cross with her brother and refused to talk to or look at him. It was a far from unprecedented situation, though. That was the trouble with twins, Lara thought as she tossed the salad. So close they are always arguing.

If she weren't so disturbed herself, she would have tried to find out what exactly was going on with Bella, but she guessed whatever stupid sibling battle it was would work itself out without her intervention. She had enough on her plate.

In any case, the table talk was dominated by Selina and Marcus's business gossip and impressions of James in full creative flow. Selina had just finished working on a film with a director more famed of late for his strange familial set-up than for his waning oeuvre, and Marcus drew all the dirt out of her. Unusually, Bella didn't show a spark of interest in the show business tittle-tattle. Instead she just sat, morosely picking at her food. Olly seemed to be enjoying himself though.

'There's a bonfire party down the road later on,' Lara said to try to cheer her up.

'Do you mind if I don't come?' Bella said. 'I'm done in.'

'Are you all right?' Lara held her hand up to Bella's forehead.

'Probably too much sun. I just need an early night.'

'Well, if you're sure. Olly, do you want to come?'

'Yeah, OK then.'

'You could bring your guitar.'

'Cool.' He smiled. He seemed to be a bit twitchy, Lara thought. A bit all over the place. And he looked drawn. From what she could make out, he was spending all his time running around in the woods with his new friends. Perhaps he was burning off more than even he could eat.

She had a cold shower, put on her last remaining dress, then grabbed two bottles of wine from the fridge. Marcus and Selina took Jack and strolled across the road to buy more beers. While Lara waited for them she again entertained the fantasy of jumping in the car and driving out to see Stephen. But before she could even dismiss the thought as ridiculous, Olly appeared at her side, also freshly showered, his guitar slung across his shoulder.

'I really need some more clothes, Mum,' he said.

'I'm going into town tomorrow.'

'Good.'

'Do you want some gum?' He offered her a stick of Orbit.

'No thanks. And do keep your mouth shut when you're chewing. Oh look, here they are.' Marcus and Selina came out across the garage forecourt. Marcus had the beers under his arm and they swung Jack between them.

'What a happy little family,' Lara said, locking the front door to keep Bella safe.

'Eh?' Olly said.

The night cloaked Gina's back garden in a bluey blackness, but, in the middle of the lawn, a little distant from the house, a group of silhouettes glowed around a crackling bonfire. Someone strummed a folky guitar song and another person sang something bluesy over the top. Fireflies danced deadly duets with the sparks rising from the flames.

As they drew close Gina rose to greet them, introducing her lanky English husband Tom and her assorted neighbours.

So, Lara thought, these were the people of the village, the

invisibles who inhabited the world behind the fly screens. She was pleased to find she liked the look of them – all scruffy hair and worn jeans, sitting round the fire on mismatched chairs, drinking wine out of jam jars. They reminded Lara of the friends she used to go camping with when the twins were little and Marcus was away.

The Trout Islanders welcomed the Wayland party, moving around to let them into the campfire circle. In no time at all, Olly had joined the guitar playing, steering the repertoire in a more edgy direction. The last heat of the day had gone and the humid air had condensed into a heavy dew under a clear sky chock-full of stars. With the after-effect of her cold shower still on her nerve-endings, Lara huddled closer to the warmth of the flames, to the safety of the crowd.

'I hope it's the chill air making you shiver,' Gina said. 'Not lingering shock from my revelations this lunchtime.'

'I've decided not to let Marcus and the kids know,' Lara whispered. 'Too much grief.'

Gina looked at her sideways. 'Well, I won't be the one to tell them, but I can't guarantee they're not going to find out. Jaws are slack in Trout Island.'

'I'll cross that bridge when I get to it,' Lara said.

'Wine?' Gina handed Lara a jam jar and filled it to the brim. 'Hey guys,' she called over to Gladys and Ethel, 'show Jack here how to make s'mores.'

Her two daughters pulled their visitor over to a table where they skewered up marshmallows and handed them out, showing him how to toast them and make a sandwich with two Graham crackers and a lump of Hershey's.

'Now, when have you got to return that car to the depot?' Gina said.

'Tomorrow. I guess I'll get a bus back.'

'Bus?' Gina laughed. 'There's not been a bus to Trout Island in my lifetime. I'll come in and we can give you a lift home.'

'Really?' Lara said. 'That's awfully kind of you.'

'I need to go get the girls some new shoes anyhow. They just *sprout*.'

'I've got to go shopping, too.'

Gina's eyes grew large as Lara told her about the laundromat incident. It was only after she had mentioned the woman driver nearly mowing her and Jack down that she thought perhaps she had said too much.

'She doesn't sound like anyone from 'round here,' Gina said, frowning.

Lara could see her mind working.

It was a convivial evening, a welcome respite for Lara. Marcus was in his element, regaling his generous audience with his theatre tales. Selina chipped in from time to time with her own hilarious experiences. It seemed, for these people – three painters originally from Brooklyn, a folk singer-songwriter, a carpenter called John, a couple of university professors and a few home-schooling mother friends of Gina's – Trout Island Theatre Company was a lifeline.

'The place would be a cultural desert otherwise,' the folk singer said.

'Do people come up from the city to see the shows?' Marcus asked. The group round the fire laughed.

'Only if they're friends who come up to visit us,' one of the painters said. 'I mean, why would you come all this way when you've got like a hundred thousand theatres on your doorstep?'

'It's really just the community appeal,' another painter said. 'They sometimes even have local people in the cast. And that's pretty neat. If not always quite as polished as it could be, eh John?'

'I was in a show.' The carpenter held up his hands. 'And I fell off the stage.'

Everyone laughed except Marcus, who set about dealing with his growing disappointment in Marcus style by drinking until his speech slurred.

'I think we'd better go,' Lara said, after he reached for his glass and managed to tip himself out of his camp chair, ending up splayed out on the grass. The others helped her get him to his feet, and, after many kisses and handshakings and invitations out to visit and to have dinner and to swim in ponds, Lara led her family back home. Marcus slumped between her and Selina, an arm around each of their shoulders, stumbling over his words and his feet. Olly carried Jack, who was fast asleep and full of s'mores.

'This is my turning,' Selina said. 'Can I help you get him back to the house?'

'I'll be fine,' Lara said. 'Why don't you go home and get some sleep? It'd be good if at least one of you is compos mentis for rehearsals tomorrow.'

'Goodnight then, darlings,' Selina said, kissing each of them.

Lara watched her trip-trap into the shadows of the street to her lodgings, then she hoisted Marcus's arm up on her shoulder and lugged him back. Thankfully no strange packages awaited her on the deck, so, with Olly's help, she unlocked the doors and got her husband upstairs, undressed and into bed. As they pulled off his trousers, Marcus let out an enormous fart.

'For fuck's sake, Dad,' Olly said.

'Thank you, darling,' Lara said, kissing her son goodnight. Then she tucked Jack into his nest on the floor and went in to check on Bella, who was fast asleep, the covers pulled right over her head. Back in her own room, she tugged on her old sleeping T-shirt and slipped into bed.

She was just dropping off when Marcus moved over next to her and pressed himself into her back, his erection hard against her.

'We haven't done thish for a long time,' he slurred into her ear.

'There has been a reason,' she said.

He put his hands up under her T-shirt and started rubbing her breasts. He pulled her round and his bearded face rasped against hers. Then she felt the wet softness of his tongue as he tried to find her mouth. She let him kiss her briefly with his winey, ashtray mouth, then moved her face up, so it might seem to him – if he were in any condition to wonder – that she wanted him to nuzzle her neck. Then, as she knew she must, she let him slide on top of her, pinning her down with his weight, parting her legs with his fingers. He thrust himself inside her, heedless that she wasn't ready for him.

'Ah. Ah. AHHH.' After a couple of thrusts he started breathing and exclaiming loudly. The bedsprings ricocheted against one another, squeaking and screeching.

'Shhh,' she said, mindful of Jack sleeping on the floor just a few feet away.

'Ah, ah, AH,' he went on regardless. He thrust a couple more times. She just managed to wriggle herself away from under him so that, when he came, it was on the sheets, not inside her.

'I love you,' he said. Then almost instantly he fell asleep.

She lay there awake listening to his snores, fuming at him for not being more careful, and at herself for continuing to put up with this sort of thing.

Things, she thought, were going to change around here.

Thirty-Two

THE NEXT MORNING, AS SHE WAS MAKING COFFEE AND EGGS
to prise Marcus from his hangover, Lara noticed that the roses
seemed to have perked themselves up overnight. She went over
to take a closer look, marvelling at the difference her splash of
fresh water had made. But, with a skipped heartbeat, she
realised that these flowers weren't a resurrection. They were
completely new.

Lara put her hands to her face. She had locked the doors
when they went out the night before and before she went to
bed. How had these roses been replaced? Her head whirling,
she hurried out into the back garden and dumped both the vase
and its contents behind the shed.

'What are you doing running barefoot round the grounds?'
Marcus said, leaning on the door frame, managing to look at
once both wrecked and pleased with himself. He climbed down
the wooden steps and carefully stepped across the hot tarmac
in his bare feet, to put his arms around her.

'That was nice last night,' he said.

* * *

After an edgy morning, she put Jack into the hire car and set off to meet Gina for the trip into town. Olly said he had other plans and couldn't come, and Bella showed no interest in getting out of bed. Both of them said they'd trust Lara to buy them some new clothes – something neither of them had done for over five years. Thinking she must be doing something right for once, Lara left them locked in the house, with a key and strict orders not to go out and leave the place open. She ignored Olly's eye-rolling.

Gina showed them the mall first. Perched on the outskirts of town, it was beige and frigid. Most of the shops were shut down and empty.

'Daddy says the mall is a prime example of capitalism in its death throes,' Gladys said.

'Daddy might have a point,' Lara said.

'They've got a JC Penney at the end,' Gina said. 'You could look in there. We're going into Payless, see if we can find some cheap shoes that aren't too depressing.'

Lara went off with Jack, who was asleep in the buggy. One turn round the deserted floor of Penney's told her there was nothing that Bella or Olly would be seen dead in. Waiting for the others, they walked the length of the mall. There was a Radio Shack, but all the other shops that were still trading sold stuff no one could ever want or need – 'gifts' of plasticised dream-catchers, unwitty fridge magnets and vile, synthetic pot pourri, the odour of which tainted the entire building. At the far end, an army recruitment stall was doing no business whatsoever; the lone soldier manning it sat flicking through the *New York Post*. Apart from Gina, the children, and two shop assistants, he was the only other person she had seen in the entire building.

Again, she was struck by the chasm between the shiny America she had imagined from the media, and this down-at-heel reality. How brilliant of a country to market itself so convincingly to the rest of the world.

She went down a side alley and paused to look at a display of tarot cards in a shop window. As she bent to wonder at the poor quality of the design, a movement in the reflection of the corridor behind her made her wheel round, her heart pumping. Glimpsing a heel turning a corner into the main body of the mall, she rushed with the buggy to the end of the alley to see who it was. About a hundred yards away, back down near the army stall, a beige-clad woman hurried out of the sliding doors to the car park.

'Wait!' Lara called, but she was too far away to be heard. Even the soldier didn't stir.

'Hey!' Gina tapped Lara on the shoulder, making her jump again. 'Oops, sorry. We got lucky, though, look.' She pointed out the girls, who were swinging a yellow plastic bag each and looking pleased with themselves.

They went into town proper, or 'downtown', as Gina called it. She led them in convoy along a narrow Main Street lined with shops. They parked up, climbed out of their cold cars on to the sweltering pavement and got the two young boys into their buggies.

'Are you OK?' Gina went up to Lara and put her hand on her shoulder. 'You seem a little on edge.'

Lara, who had been scanning the street for a woman in a dun-coloured car, turned to her new friend and smiled.

'I'm fine, thanks. It's just I'm not used to this heat yet.'

'I know. Isn't it disgusting?' Gina made a face. 'So,' she said, looking up and down the street. 'Clothes for your big kids.'

'And running gear for me,' Lara said.

'Running. You're so crazy,' Gina said. 'Hey, girls, shall we take them to Fashion Bug?'

'Yay!' Gladys and Ethel cried. 'Fashion Bug!'

From the font used for the signage, to the merchandise – nasty pastel items in man-made fabrics – Lara knew she wasn't going to find anything in Fashion Bug for her kids. She shuddered as she fingered a shiny polyester blouse.

'Isn't it great?' Gina said, holding up a light pink shirred skirt and posing like a catwalk model.

'Um . . .' Lara said, as the two girls collapsed into giggles.

'I'm just messing with you,' Gina said, slapping her arm with the back of her hand. 'Fashion Bug *sucks*.'

'Where do you get your clothes from?' Lara asked. Gina wore loose, simple cotton dresses and the girls jaunty little shorts and sleeveless tops.

'Well,' Gina said. 'We usually wait until we go down to the city. Or we buy online. There's nothing really here for anyone other than freaks to buy. But I wanted to check out this new store, just off Main. One of the guys last night told me about it.'

She led them round the corner and, much to Lara's relief, this new shop sold skater/surfer-style clothes in fabrics she could bear to touch. She bought a couple of items each for Bella and Olly, and a new dress for herself. On the way back to the cars, Gina took her to an expensive sports shop where she replaced all her lost running gear.

'There's nowhere I can buy a couple of good, smart men's shirts?' she asked Gina.

'You're kidding me, right?'

They dropped the car off at the Avis depot on the outskirts of town. Lara said a quiet farewell to all that luxury, then they piled into Gina's people carrier.

'We're on the right side of town to go home via Pretty Fly Pie . . .' Gina said. 'It's the best ice cream this side of the Catskills.'

'I know. We've already been,' Lara said.

'Wow. You do get around, don't you?'

Lara nearly told her that she had a guide, but she buttoned her lip just in time.

Gina pulled the car into a parking place in front of the big red barn. Just before she got out, Lara glanced in the wing mirror and saw the dun-coloured car edge slowly behind them, as if the driver were looking for a parking place. The windows were tinted, but she could clearly see the outline of a woman at the wheel. Without a doubt it was her.

'Stay in the car,' Lara said to Gina and the children, who, stunned at her tone, did as they were told.

Incensed at the cheek of this person, at all the misery she had caused Stephen, Lara jumped out of the people carrier and lunged forward, yanking open the dun car door. The woman inside turned, roared, and swung her vehicle into reverse, knocking Lara flying across the gravel car park. The car spun and screeched out of the exit, nearly crashing into an oncoming vehicle as it did so. Lara scrabbled to her feet.

'I know what you look like now!' she yelled at the dust cloud that hid the car. 'I know what you are.'

'Are you OK?'

Lara turned and saw Gina, Ethel and Gladys standing in a line, looking at her, their mouths wide open.

'That's the laundry thief,' Lara said. 'That's the bitch who stole our clothes.'

'Your knees,' Gina said.

Lara looked down and saw the blood running down her shins, seeping into her leather sandals.

Thirty-Three

WHEN STEPHEN ARRIVED AT THE KITCHEN DOOR AT THE end of the afternoon, his physical presence made Lara quite giddy with relief.

'Hi,' she said, touching his shoulder.

His disguise for the outing was different from his daytime get-up. Heavy, geek glasses covered his eyes, and a battered fedora obscured half his face. A light vintage mac hid the rest of him.

'You look like a nineties art student!' Lara said, her lungs only half full of air. He looked, in fact, like he did when they first met.

'You look like the woman of my dreams,' he whispered, kissing her on the cheek. As he bent towards her, Lara scanned the darkening hill behind him for any movement or presence.

Jack ran up and placed himself between them.

'Hello, Stephen. Are we going to the circus now?' he said.

'I think we just might,' Stephen said, hoisting him into his arms. 'Now, where are your brother and sister?'

Jack pointed to the living room, where Olly sat, chewing

gum, strumming his guitar and singing a rather nice song that he had just written.

'Hey man,' Olly said, getting up and holding out a hand.

'Byron?' Stephen said, pointing to the guitar.

'From that book you lent me.'

'Good lad.'

'Bella's got some kind of bug or something,' Lara said. 'So she won't be joining us.'

'Or she's a bit lovesick,' Olly said, winking at Stephen. 'Lover boy hasn't called. Diddums.'

'Don't be cruel, Olly,' Lara said.

'That's a pity,' Stephen said. 'Do you want me to go up and have a word?'

'There's no persuading her, I'm afraid,' Lara said.

They piled into the Wrangler and, with the top down, they set off, winding along a valley into the deepening evening, past a series of phallic silos and red barns that became more dilapidated the further they went.

'Do you know why they're red?' Stephen shouted over the noise of the engine. 'The farmers used to cover them with oil mixed with blood from a recent slaughter.'

'Ugh,' Lara said. 'Why?'

'Because it looked good,' Olly said. He seemed to find this hysterical.

They turned a corner and crossed a bridge over a rocky river some fifty feet below. Then they carried on past a pristine modern low-level house, all minimal glass and oak, reflected in a board-edged pond.

'*New York Times* journalist's summer place,' Stephen said. 'A dangerous gossip. I try to avoid this road as much as possible.'

The journey continued along a flat expanse carved out by a

river and lined by fields of man-height maize, blue in the early evening light. Stephen switched on the wipers to remove the carnage of insects from the windscreen.

They climbed up out of the valley. As they approached the blind brow of the hill, a white car with go-faster stripes roared up and overtook them. Stephen hit the brakes.

'Idiot,' Lara said, her nerves creeping with the suddenness of it. 'He could have killed us all.'

'There's a lot of moronic driving out here. Kids as young as sixteen, drunk or stoned,' Stephen said. 'The only way out is by car.'

'And here we are,' he said as they reached a small town and turned into a beautifully kept Main Street of bustling cafés and restaurants. 'It's one street and it's where it all happens. The liveliest place for miles.' He found a parking spot and pulled up.

Lara got out of the Wrangler and lifted Jack from the back. From where she stood, she could see a sushi restaurant, a couple of independent coffee shops, a wholefood shop that was still open and busy, a couple of Italian places and a bookstore-cum-bar. The people milling along the streets looked youngish and hip, a variation on the crowd at Gina's place. As if to confirm this, one of the Brooklyn painters walked by, a brown paper bag of vegetables in the crook of his arm.

'Hey, Lara, how you doing?' he said, shaking her hand. 'Hey, Olly.' He nodded, then reached to ruffle Jack's hair.

Lara turned to introduce Stephen, but he had vanished.

'Well, hey then, gotta split,' the painter said. 'Hungry mouths to feed.' He indicated the bag.

He climbed into his pick-up truck and drove off.

'Who was that?' Stephen reappeared at her elbow.

'I met him at Gina's place. I forget his name, though.'

'Gina?'

'Gina. She lives just opposite the theatre?'

'When were you there?' he asked, looking at the street that rose up to their left. At the top of the slope was an illuminated white church that made Lara think of Italy.

'Last night,' she said.

'I didn't know you went out last night.'

'We were invited.'

'I see.' Stephen adjusted his hat so it came down further over his face. 'You didn't say anything? About me.'

'Of course not!'

'Good.'

He led them to a restaurant attached to the wholefood shop. 'This is a great place. I've reserved us a table or we'd never get in. The chef used to work under Mario Batali, so it's upmarket Italian with a locally sourced organic twist.'

'Bella would have loved this,' Lara said.

'Silly Bella, staying in bed,' Olly said to Jack.

A waiter showed them to their table, tucked away in a booth at the far end of the candlelit dining room. Stephen positioned himself in the shadows next to Lara, his thigh resting against hers. The nearness of him killed what little appetite she had, so she ordered a salad, and a kiddy pizza for Jack. Stephen and Olly went for pasta dishes. Stephen also ordered fresh lemonade and a large glass of Italian Sauvignon Blanc for Lara.

'Can you stop that, please, Olly?' Lara said as the waiter left with their orders. He had been drumming on the table since they sat down and it was setting her nerves on edge.

Over dinner, Stephen explained that this little town was different from the others around the area because it was home to a SUNY campus, which gave it the middle-class, liberal trappings of a university town – including moneyed students keen on having a good time. Lara rather liked the place, and indulged a brief fantasy where she and Stephen lived a bookish, anonymous life in that *New York Times* journalist's house by the lake, near this town.

Every now and then, Stephen – who, under the cover of the dim restaurant lighting, had removed his hat and sunglasses – caught her eye. And each time she felt a jump in her belly, like a small bird fluttering around her insides.

'Where's the famous Olly appetite?' Lara said, nodding towards her son's pasta, which he had barely touched.

'I'm on a diet,' Olly said, levelling a bloodshot eye at her. 'Go on, Mum, give me a sip of your wine.'

Surreptitiously, Lara let him finish her glass and Stephen ordered her another. When they were done – both Lara and Olly leaving at least half their food on their plates – Stephen paid for the meal using a pseudonymous credit card. They slipped back out on to the street, where the crowd had got bigger and younger. It reminded Lara of Brighton's North Laine on a Friday night, except the sense of being on an island surrounded by countryside gave it a more concentrated atmosphere. They passed a group of young women in pretty vintage dresses and beaten-up leather jackets, heading for a night out. Had Lara been a student, she would have liked to have gone to this SUNY campus. She would have liked this life.

They drove for a mile or so to the end of the town, where a large marquee dominated a flat river meadow. The damp warmth of the earth gave itself up to the colder night air, providing natural cooling for the motley crew milling around the box office entrance.

Fully disguised again, Stephen presented their tickets and they filed inside to a seatless central space. A live band to one side played loud jazzy rock as acrobats and performers mingled with the audience, improvising small dramas, shouting out for each other in English, Spanish, Italian and French, shimmying up posts and tumbling on the ground, through air scented by perfume, sweat and sawdust. The pressing crowd pushed Lara up against Stephen. Emboldened by the wine, she held her position, glued to his side. It was intoxicating. She could hardly bear it and, when she looked up at Stephen, his eyes were closed.

'Jack,' she called, looking round for him in the crush.

'It's OK. I've got him,' Olly said. He was holding Jack, who he had put up on a hay bale a little way away so he could see.

The last of the audience filed in and the music stopped. In a moment of silence, what had appeared to be the sides of the marquee fell away, revealing, Tardis-like, yet more tents beyond, where eight beautiful young punk-acrobats dangled from high-slung trapeze swings. The lights dimmed so only the top part of the tent was lit.

The band struck up again, a prowling bass line with snare drum, built on to by a repeated vocal line, rasped by a man who looked as if he had seen it all.

I. Will. Not. Be-Good.
I. Will. Not. Be-Good.

The instruments added to the song one by one: electric guitar, congas, sax and trumpet. By the time the brass extinguished the vocal line, filling the tent with its anarchic energy, the acrobats were describing great arcs across the ceiling with their swings, whooping and trilling.

Stephen took off his hat and shook his head in the warm tent air, enjoying the anonymity of being in an audience in the dark.

'Can I wear that, man?' Olly said, appearing out of nowhere, now with Jack in his arms.

'Sure.' Stephen smiled and passed his hat to Olly, who pulled it on low over his eyes, mimicking Stephen's stance.

'You've made a friend there,' Lara whispered up into Stephen's ear.

'It makes me very happy.' He smiled down at her.

The acrobats spun and twirled above their heads. Somehow, through leaping, flying and falling, they all came to the spotlit ground to mark the beginning of the show proper. They used the whole vast space, from tumbling over the floor in giant silver hoops to leaping across the ceiling on bungees. The spectators were ushered from one side of the tent to the other – at one moment huddled in the middle while a woman in knee pads and glitter looped herself in and out of a piece of rope, then made to form a circle around an impossibly muscled man who shouted in French as he performed extraordinary feats with a single rod of steel.

Through it all the band played their raucous music – songs about breaking taboos, about conquering loneliness and desire by transgression.

Not once were Lara and Stephen separated by the movement of the crowd. Instead, they hung back out of the light, enjoying the secret contact the darkness allowed them. But Olly and Jack roved all around the space. For one disorienting moment Lara thought the person standing close behind her, pressed into her back, his hands on her shoulders, couldn't be Stephen, because he was over on the other side of the performers, in the front, looking up. But seeing the jaw working on the gum, she realised it was Olly, transformed for a moment by the lighting and Stephen's hat. Jack was by his side.

Above them a statuesque woman in a dove-grey silk dress

swooped and arched around a static trapeze bar. She reached up into the void of the tent. Then she fell, plummeting towards the audience underneath. The crowd flinched and moved back as one, caught between the thought of catching her as she plunged down into their midst and the urge to run away and save their own skins. Lara hid her face in Stephen's sleeve. The woman's move was planned, though. She was saved, caught at the last minute by the foot she had looped around one of her ropes.

'Come to me tonight,' Stephen murmured into Lara's hair.

The acrobat hooked one strong thigh around her bar, her silk dress swung away like wings and she arched her back in victory over her fall.

'I can't,' Lara said, her mouth grazing his ear. 'I want to. But I can't.'

'Tomorrow then. Come during the day, if you can.'

Lara nodded. As she watched the boldness and beauty above her, she felt close to tears. If she had envied the lives of the girls in the leather jackets and vintage dresses, she ached to be the woman above her. She would run away and join this group of free-wheeling bodies and souls, living their lives in each others' beautiful, raggedy pockets, each week a different town, a different country, their only duty to perform with all their hearts.

The tears came, quietly, for her lost youth.

The trapeze was winched back up into the gods, and the acrobat melted down a long rope to the ground. An older man in a hat and mac not unlike Stephen's – although under his open coat he was bare-chested and wore only a pair of leggings – hustled the crowd into another formation to watch a couple perform a double-act on a loop of rope above another part of the tent. Their bodies twisted into each other, moving on top and around, the man holding the woman up in one arm. Then they flipped and she was supporting his entire weight from her leg. He jumped up and their bodies moulded to each other. Lara felt Stephen's hand as his arm circled her waist.

'There you are, Mother,' Olly said into her ear.

Instinctively, she moved away from Stephen. She had thought Olly was still over on the other side of the audience. She looked up at him. Nothing suggested that he had seen anything, but Lara realised that, walking a tightrope of her own, she had let her guard drop.

'It's great, isn't it?' she said. To her relief, Olly nodded.

'Beats Dad's boring sort of stuff,' he said, gazing on the coupling going on fifteen feet above his head. 'I want to do that,' he groaned.

'Let's get the A levels out of the way first,' she said.

At the end of the show they spilled out of the hot tent into the cooler night air, the rhythms of the band still pulsing through their veins. As they crossed the rutted grass to the car park, a couple passing them turned and stared at Stephen.

'It *is* him,' the woman said. 'I told you.'

'Hey, Olly man, could I have my hat back?' Stephen said, slipping his sunglasses on. 'Forgot I wasn't a normal person for a minute,' he said to Lara, who squeezed his arm. 'Forgot I had two heads.'

Olly pulled the hat off.

'Shit,' he said, as his curly hair snagged in an adjuster buckle. The couple up ahead had stopped, the woman debating with the man whether she should go up and address Stephen.

'Don't pull,' Lara said, but Olly yanked the hat away from his head, taking a hank of his hair with it.

'Ow, shit,' he said.

With the hat and geek glasses on, Stephen was another person.

'Well, honey, we'd better get our little guy back home to bed,' he said in his Deep Down South accent, his arm around Lara as they approached the gawping couple.

'Someone needs their eyes testing,' the man said to the woman as they passed.

'Whatever,' they heard her say behind them.

'And the Oscar for the part of the hillbilly daddy goes to Stephen Molloy,' Olly said once Stephen had started up the Wrangler.

Stephen had bought the CD of the show music and they drove under a fiercely starlit sky, singing 'I. Will. Not. Be-Good' at the tops of their voices. Jack, who had loved every minute of the show, led the way, screaming out the words and swallowing them in gurgling laughter. For the first time in a long while, Lara felt entirely encased in the moment, not wishing to be anywhere else. She continued the scene Stephen had set going back in the car park, imagining that they *were* a family, returning to their home in the forest, where they lived together. She put herself outside the car, thinking how happy they must sound as they passed noisily along the road.

'Damn lights,' Stephen said.

Lara glanced round. A car was right on their tail, so close it was almost in the back seat. Its lights were on full beam, blinding Stephen. He tried to flip the rear-view mirror into reflector mode, but he was still dazzled.

'Jesus,' he said. 'Hold on to your hats.'

The car began to overtake them, but as it did so, it edged into them, nudging them sideways. Lara looked over Stephen to their tormentor. To her horror, it was the same dun-coloured car that had nearly run her and Jack over, the same vehicle she had accosted at Pretty Fly Pie . . . Again she saw the silhouette of a woman through its tinted windows. This was Elizabeth Sanders, and it was pretty clear she was acting out her warning.

'Go away,' Stephen yelled. 'Get away from me.'

They bumped along the road, half on the tarmac, half on the verge. The bridge they had crossed on their way out loomed a couple of hundred yards away. If they carried on as they were going, they would be over the side and into the river below.

'Brake!' Lara cried, her hands gripping the dashboard, white at the knuckles. Just in the nick of time, Stephen came to his senses and floored the brakes, bringing them to a screeching halt in some gravel about ten feet away from the bridge.

With a final swerve into them, denting the side of the Wrangler and nearly toppling it, the other car swooped past them and bombed off into the night. Stephen rested his forehead on the steering wheel while the CD played on, an unstructured, atonic improvised brass section riff. Lara reached forward and switched it off, and the sound of the crickets resumed in the empty fields around them.

'Everyone all right?' She looked at her sons, both hunched-up wraiths. They nodded silently. 'Stephen?' she said, carefully laying a hand in the middle of his back.

'See?' he said at last, lifting his head and smiling. 'Load of arseholes on the roads round here.'

Lara searched his eyes to see if he believed what he was saying, if he really didn't know what was going on, but he was inscrutable. He shrugged, switched the engine on and turned back on to the road.

'Let's get these young 'uns back home,' he said, in his accented disguise voice.

'Go, Daddy, go,' Olly said, in the same Deep South tones.

* * *

When they got back to Trout Island, Marcus and Selina were on the porch, smoking. A large, nearly empty bottle of Yellowtail Pinot Grigio stood on the shabby plastic table in front of the swing seat.

'How was the show?' Marcus boomed across the front garden after Stephen cut the engine.

'Great!' Olly said, jumping out of the back of the Wrangler.

'Drink, Stephen?' Selina said, getting up and sashaying down the steps towards him.

'Shhh!' Marcus said. 'Damn.'

'Marcus,' Lara said. 'You haven't?'

'I can keep a secret, darling,' Selina said, leaning on the side of Stephen's vehicle. 'Selina Mountford.' She stretched over towards him, extending her hand. 'I *really* admire your work. I was in *Transform*, although I don't think we ever met. I was one of the Water Girls.'

'Hello,' Stephen said, lifting Jack out of his car seat.

'Oh, don't worry about me,' Selina said. 'I'm discretion itself. It's not as if I'm a civilian. I understand you have to keep a low profile. Do stay and join us.'

'I'm sorry. I've got animals to get back to.' Stephen handed the car seat to Lara. ''Bye, guys,' he said, waving to Olly and Jack, who were heading towards the house. ''Bye, Lara.' He gave her a brief, impersonal kiss on the cheek. 'Marcus,' he said, pointing a finger at him.

'Cheers, matey,' Marcus said, waving. He had got up and was leaning on the deck rail, swaying.

'Thank you, Stephen,' Lara said. 'That was a great night.'

'My pleasure.' He started the engine and took off. It was only when his tail lights had completely disappeared that Lara realised, with a pang, they hadn't made a firm arrangement to meet up again.

'Oll, could you get Jack ready for bed?' Lara said. Olly tutted and sighed, but he scooped up his sleepy little brother and carried him indoors.

Lara turned to Marcus, diverting delayed shock after the incident on the road into anger at her husband. 'You do know Stephen being here is supposed to be a secret?'

'Come on,' Marcus said, waving his arms around. 'What harm can it do to let Selina here know?'

'You don't know the half of it,' Lara said.

'What's that supposed to mean?'

'You *can* trust me, Lara,' Selina said. 'I do happen to have quite a few friends who are as famous as him, if not more so. I do know how difficult it is. I'm cool.'

'I hope you're right about that,' Lara said. She wondered how gushing up to him and outlining the small part you played in a film he starred in eight years ago counted as cool, but she let it go. 'He goes to great lengths to stay hidden. There's a lot at stake for him.'

'Oh come on!' Marcus said. 'Don't you think he's being a bit grand, a bit mysterious? Like he's built this myth up about himself, and he believes it so much and no one's telling him no, so it's all just become a bit of a game for him.'

'A game? You don't understand, do you?'

'Oh God.' Marcus rolled his eyes. 'What's he been telling you?'

'Do you know what? You don't deserve to know.'

'Look. We've all heard about the stalker business. But that's in the past and on the other side of this giant country. So steady on there old girl.' Marcus got up and attempted to put his arm around her. 'Look. I'm sorry I told Selina. Does that help? Now, do you want a glass of something?'

'Yes, do join us for a glass of wine,' Selina said, touching her arm.

Lara looked down at her toes, which she had clenched so tightly they were cramping. She wanted to slap Selina in the face, then smash the stupid wine bottle and drive it into Marcus's belly. She actually imagined herself doing this.

'I'm tired,' she said after a minute. 'And I need to go and tuck Jack in.' She wondered if she could make up a story about leaving something in Stephen's car so she had an excuse to call him, just to hear his voice again, but her imagination deserted her. 'You stay out here and enjoy yourselves,' she said to Marcus and Selina. 'Make sure you lock up when you come in.'

As she went in and started climbing the horrible stinking stairs, she heard Selina's light laugh, underscored by Marcus's low, throaty rumble. He must seem quite exotic to her, Lara thought, all plummily English, having been brought all the way from Europe to play the lead.

Well, she was welcome to him.

Thirty-Four

'SO, DANNY WILL BE WITH YOU TOMORROW AT MIDDAY for a spot of space clearing. I've called Marcus so he'll be busy and need never know. Now then. Can my little chick make a rehearsal tomorrow evening about five?'

'James, it's a difficult time of day for a chap of his age. He's not at his best.'

Lara heard James sigh at the other end of the line, as if this were just another *detail* for him to *deal with*. She hardly had the patience for this after the sleepless night she had endured. Every noise seemed to have had malice threaded through it, from the percussive barking of a dog over the hill behind the house to a creak on the stairs which, clog in hand, she had climbed out of bed to investigate at three in the morning.

'I don't know if you know, but Marcus has offered to be chaperone,' James went on. 'So you don't have to worry about a thing. You'll be free for a couple of hours. To do what you want.' A silence followed.

'OK, look,' she said eventually. 'I'll make sure Jack's worn out in the morning so he puts in a long nap, then hopefully he'll be brighter than usual at five. But not too late, OK?'

'Thank you, sweets. I'm sure it's going to all work out marvellously.'

'I'm sure it is,' she said, and hung up.

For a few moments she stared at the phone and thought about calling Stephen, to apologise for Marcus's big mouth the night before and, just, well, to hear his voice. Then, as if she had summoned it, the phone rang right before her eyes. Grabbing it, she pulled it to her ear.

'Hello?' she said.

'Don't get excited. It's only me!' Gina laughed down the other end.

'Oh. Hi, Gina. How are you?'

'I heard you went to the circus last night.'

'How on earth?'

'Simon saw you – remember, the guy from the party?'

'Right, yes. We bumped into him.'

'Was it any good?'

'It was brilliant. You should go.'

'Ah, it might be difficult with Bert. He's not so good in crowds of strangers. Anyway, talking about Bert, he's asleep right now, so I wondered if you'd like to come round for coffee?'

'I'd love to. We'll be over in ten minutes.' The twins hadn't yet surfaced, and Lara hadn't been looking forward to spending the morning with Jack like a couple of sitting ducks in the marked house.

'See you then.'

'See, they're not too bad now I've cleaned them up.' Lara lifted her skirt to show Gina her knees.

'You were crazy,' Gina said. 'You were so mad. And what I don't get is why a woman like that would be going around stealing people's clothes from the laundromat.'

Lara peered into her mug and took another bite of the cherry walnut cookie that Gladys had offered her before taking Jack upstairs to play.

'And who was the mystery man?' Gina said.

'Eh?'

'The guy Simon saw you with last night. The one he said sort of melted away when he came up to you.'

'Oh. Just an old friend I bumped into.'

'You bumped into an old friend out *here*?' Gina asked. 'That's some coincidence.'

'Yes. It was,' Lara said. They were sitting in the shade at the back of Gina's house. The sky was blue and the air surprisingly clear. A cool breeze funnelled down the side of the house towards them, and Lara reached into her bag for her cardigan. She slipped it on, folded her arms and sat back, watching the trees as they rustled in the wind.

'Am I going to get any more out of you?' Gina said, trying to catch her eye.

Lara shook her head. Looking into her friend's kind eyes, she found herself on the verge of tears. 'I wish I could tell you,' she said. 'But I can't. It's – too complicated.'

'That's OK,' Gina said, reaching over and putting a hand on her leg. 'You don't have to tell me, if you don't want to.'

'I can't,' Lara said, forcing a smile, although her eyes were brimming. 'Believe me. If I could, you'd be the first to know.'

'It's got nothing to do with a certain famous Brit actor who is "hiding" in the hills up thataway?' Gina pointed in the direction of Stephen's house.

If Gina had reached out and whacked her round the face, Lara would not have been more shocked.

Gina laughed. 'Look, honey, some secrets aren't quite as well kept as people would like to believe. Word flies around in

Trout Island so fast you can't even see it. The word grows into rumour and the rumour gets coloured in. And my house is right here, in the middle of the village, so I know everything. Just be aware of that and be careful, OK?'

Lara nodded. What exactly did Gina mean she had to be careful about, though: word, rumour or the fact that she knew everything?

Oh no, Lara thought as she and Jack walked up the garden path to the house. There was a note, addressed to her, pinned to the front door.

From the lawn, she scanned the porch for anything nasty, any stray corpses or faeces, but there was nothing. She climbed the steps to the door and grabbed the note, as if it were a nettle needing a firm grasp.

Inside, written in a familiar hand that made the blood rush to her cheeks, was the message:

Blueberry picking today? Bring kids. Pick you up at 2. Sx

She felt the familiar, digestive flutter that Stephen stirred up. It was only half past twelve. How on earth could she wait a full hour and a half?

'I'm sleepy, Mummy,' Jack said, not surprisingly, since he had spent the entire morning playing ballet school mascot for Gina's daughters in tutu, blusher and all.

'Why don't you stretch out on the swing seat?' Lara said. 'It's lovely and cool out here.'

She settled him on the porch, plumping up the cushions so he could lie fully down. Unlocking the front door, she stood in the scene-of-the-crime hall and called up the stairs.

'Bella? Olly?' There was no reply, so she supposed they must be out. A part of her she wasn't proud of hoped they would stay out, so it would only be she and Jack – who noticed less than his brother and sister – who went blueberry picking. She could get away with more that way.

In the kitchen, she cleared up the post-breakfast carnage that proved the twins had, at some point in the morning, surfaced and fed themselves. Then she took a shower and put on her new dress, the one she had bought the day before.

Remembering that she had to remove a liberal application of make-up from Jack's face, she headed for the front porch. But when she got out there, her heart jumped into her mouth. The swing seat was empty. Jack wasn't on the porch, nor was he in the front garden.

'Jack!' Lara called, dashing into the house. But he wasn't inside either. She ran out of the kitchen door and scanned the backyard and the hill beyond. He was nowhere to be seen.

'Jack!' she yelled, tearing back down the driveway to the front. A cold panic rose in her throat. She had lost her son. He had gone. He had been taken. She ran out on to the pavement and looked one way down Main Street, then the other. Apart from a distant truck slowly making its way towards her it was deserted, as usual.

She grabbed on to a streetlight and pressed her forehead against the hot metal, trying to think straight and stop the whirling behind her eyes.

'Mummy!'

She jerked her head up. Jack was running towards her along the side street across the road from her. He had some sort of long, chewy sweet in one hand. In the other was what looked like the long-lost Cyril Bear.

'Jack, STOP!' she screamed just as he reached the kerb of the road that separated them. Shocked, he obeyed her, and in doing so was saved from running out in front of the truck as it thundered between them. Looking both ways, Lara darted across the road to the little boy, who was standing, wide-eyed, on the pavement, sticky sweet and make-up mingling with the tears of shock caused by his mother yelling at him.

'What happened, Jacky? How did you get across the road? Who gave you that sweetie?' She pulled the thing out of his fingers and threw it on the ground, as if it were about to explode in his hands. 'And where did you find Cyril?'

Jack took a deep breath in and wailed, now outraged at losing his candy.

'Who was it?' Lara said. But she knew the answer already.

'Lady,' Jack said. 'That lady gave me Cyril.'

By the time she had washed the stickiness from him, both Lara and Jack had calmed down. She told him he must never, ever go off with a stranger again.

'But she's not a stranger. She's the lady.'

'Most particularly you mustn't go off with the lady,' Lara said. 'She's not a nice lady. Remember?'

'But she gave me a sweetie,' Jack said.

'And you must never take sweeties from the lady or from strangers. Understood?'

Jack nodded his red head. All clean and safe, he looked, more than ever, like an angelic version of his father. All the good without any of the infuriating.

Hearing the rumble of the Wrangler in the driveway, she glanced out of her bedroom window and saw him, Stephen, there, in the driving seat.

'Now, not a word about the nasty lady to Stephen,' she said, miming a zip over her mouth.

Jack nodded and zipped his lips in the same way.

She picked him up, grabbed her bag and set off outside to greet Stephen.

'No twins?' he said, getting out to help her.

'They're out.'

'Ah well. Take a look at that dent,' he said, showing her the side of the Wrangler. 'I'm still puzzling over why that idiot wanted to do that to us. Has everything been all right here since yesterday? Nothing odd happened?'

'Yes,' Lara said. 'I mean, no, nothing odd.'

'Good,' Stephen said, frowning slightly. 'You would tell me, wouldn't you, if something was worrying you?'

'Of course,' Lara said. 'I'll just get the car seat.' She dashed into the hall and picked it up from where she had left it the night before. She wanted to tell Stephen what was going on. But Betty's words rung in her head.

If Stephen finds out she's back, it will kill him.

Lara didn't want any more blood on her hands. Besides, she wanted to nail this woman once and for all, using her own devices.

'Where are we going to do this blueberry picking?' she asked as they drove out of Trout Island.

'My place,' he said. 'The best blueberries are on my patch.' He turned up the music he was playing on the car radio through his iPhone. It was the Smiths' 'There is a Light That Never Goes Out'. 'Remember?' he said.

She gazed at him and nodded. It had been their song.

They roared on up over the mountain, Stephen and Lara singing about double-decker buses crashing into them and dying by each other's side.

'I love that house,' she said as they passed the pristine white farmhouse with the view.

'Too exposed for me,' Stephen said. 'I need to be tucked away.'

They plunged again into the forest, until they got to his driveway. He reached into the side pocket of the car door and held out a button device. The locked gate whirred open, letting them pass, and clanged shut behind them.

'It's so beautiful here,' Lara sighed as they drew up in the clearing by his house.

'Yes.' He looked over at her.

Lara stood to help Jack out of his seat. 'Snakes!' he said, wriggling out of her arms and making for the woodpile. Unseen by Jack, Stephen put his arm around Lara and kissed her hair.

'I'm so glad you're here,' he said.

'I'm glad I'm here, too. I'm so happy to have found you again. I thought—'

'Stephen! Come and find snakes with me!' Jack bowled back round the corner and they moved apart.

'I'm going in to get the blueberry picking things,' Stephen said. 'Your mum'll come and help you.'

'All right. But you must have a stick, Mummy,' Jack said.

They were poking in the woodpile when Lara felt Stephen's hand on her shoulder.

'There you go,' he said, handing a small wicker basket to each of them.

'Carry me,' Jack said, holding his hands up to Stephen.

They wandered off along the path into the forest at the back of the house.

'We could take the Wrangler, but it's not too far and it's a lovely day,' Stephen said.

'That's fine by me,' Lara said as they climbed steeply up through dappled woodland, away from the house. As they walked, Stephen told Lara and Jack how there had once been a settlement up there, how, a hundred years ago, these hills, which were now completely wooded, were bare and cultivated, populated by smallholders trying to etch a living out of the shallow, stony soil. But the demise of the railway, which used to pass within ten miles, and the difficulties the land and the bitter winters presented for farmers, forced people away from the area. Within a couple of decades the trees and undergrowth had taken over. Lara thought of the trouble she had keeping weeds at bay in her little back garden in Brighton. How quickly the native plants must grow out in this hot, wet environment. She could practically see the ground-hugging vines creeping along the rocky ground, an inch at a time, reclaiming the path from the humans.

With every step, Lara felt herself recovering from the past couple of days. The three of them were striding out into the future, the binding strands of history and duty breaking as they moved forward.

'If you keep your eyes open, the remains of those settlers are everywhere,' Stephen said. 'See.' He pointed to an ivy-choked wall running up the hill, perpendicular to the path. 'That's an old boundary wall. If you follow it up over the top and down again, it leads to a tumbledown house. I'll take you there after we've picked the blueberries.'

'Sounds good, eh, Jack?' Lara said. The little boy, his head held high, his arms clasped around the tall man's neck, nodded. Stephen held him firmly with one arm and, using a stick he had picked up, cleared an overgrown section of path by slashing at the long, green leafy stems of some sort of willowherb. With the boy and the stick and the forest, Stephen looked as complete as he did in the Dover's Hill photograph he kept in his bedside table.

'And here we are!' Stephen said, as they reached the top of the slope and the dark green light behind the trees turned lime then blue with the sky. One more step, and they were on a grassy hilltop, bunched around with large shrubs that stood taller than Lara. Narrow pathways wound into the bushes, which were thick with dusty, blue-purple berries crying out to be picked.

Jack wriggled out of Stephen's arms and ran to the bushes.

'But look at the view,' Lara said, climbing on to a tussocky mound and turning. For a full 360 degrees, wooded hills folded into each other, fading out into the purple distance. If it weren't for five distant power lines cutting across the land on looming pylons, there would have been no sign of human intervention. For the first time for a while, Lara didn't feel as if she were being overseen.

'Pretty good, eh?' Stephen said, placing his hand on her shoulder and pointing. 'We've come from all the way down there.'

Lara closed her eyes and rested her cheek on his fingers. 'I—'

'Shh,' he said, moving his finger to her mouth. 'Come on, Jacko, let's fill these baskets up for Mum to make you pancakes.' Taking Jack by the hand, he led him off along one of the pathways, deep into the blueberry patch.

In a daze, Lara set to work on a bush, absent-mindedly filling her basket and popping the odd blueberry into her mouth, pressing its dull-sharp sweetness against her tongue. A low buzzing of flying insects joined the clatter of crickets and she prayed to be allowed to stay here, in this blueberry patch, for ever.

'Look, Mummy!' Jack burst into her daydream from behind her bush, his basket full of berries.

'That was quick,' she said, squatting down to inspect his harvest.

'He had a tiny bit of help.' Lara looked up to see Stephen

peering down at her. She stood to break the odd intimacy of the moment.

'I reckon we've got enough for breakfast tomorrow and maybe a pie,' Stephen said. 'Although I think Mummy's eaten more then she's put in her basket.' He licked his thumb and wiped a stain of juice from her lips.

'Naughty Mummy,' Jack giggled. 'Can I—?'

A sudden crashing in the bushes behind them swamped his words and made Lara and Stephen wheel round. About a hundred feet from them, a six-foot black bear stood on its hind legs, staring at them with an outraged expression. It seemed to be as startled to find them as they were to see it.

Jack grabbed Lara's legs.

'Don't make any sudden movements,' Stephen whispered, standing tall. 'Get behind me and whatever you do, don't look it in the eyes.'

'It's all right, Jacko. It's going to be just fine,' Lara said, bundling Jack behind her and trying to hold him still.

As instructed, she looked towards, but not at, the bear, keeping it in her peripheral vision. She could tell, though, that it had its hungry eyes firmly set on them. The insect life around them had stilled into silence, as if sensing the tension that stretched between the people and the beast. Although it was quite far away, the fruited stable-smell of the bear wafted towards them in the hot afternoon air. For what seemed like an eternity, nothing happened.

'Hey bear,' Stephen said, holding his hand out low, palm down. 'I'm going to talk now, Lara,' he said in a low, slow voice. 'Keep upright and stand tall. Remember, don't look it in the eyes, but don't look away, either.' He waved his arms slowly up and down and drew himself up to his full height. 'This fellow,' he said of the bear, 'probably thinks we're on his personal berry patch. We're going to show him we mean no harm and we're going to let him have what we picked to tell him sorry.'

'No!' Jack yelled. At this sudden sound, the bear began to move, looping its heavy, furred body from side to side, rotating its head and grunting.

'Quiet, Jack,' Lara said, holding him firmly behind her, pressed into her legs. 'We can get some more berries.'

'Have the berries, bear,' Stephen said, emptying his basket on to the grass beneath them. 'Now,' he said, 'we back away.' Still waving his arms and looking in the direction of the bear, he shuffled backwards, steering Lara and Jack towards the path back to the house. After they had moved about twenty yards, the bear made a move towards them.

'Stop,' Stephen said, grasping her hand. She felt his blood pulsing through his body. A bead of sweat rolled from his hair down the back of his neck. 'We're going to have to hold our ground. Get behind me.'

Lara pressed her face into Stephen's back, holding Jack tight behind her. The bear began to lope towards them, picking up speed as it went. Stephen quickly lifted his arms right up, spread his legs wide and roared so loud that the trees around them seemed to shudder. Jack shivered into Lara's legs.

To die by your side . . .

Stephen's roar stopped the bear in its tracks. It froze on its hind legs while Stephen stood his ground, his arms up, looking as big as possible. Time stretched as man and bear regarded each other. At last, the bear dropped on its front paws to nose at the spilled blueberries, as if the three humans had disappeared.

'He's met his match,' Stephen said, a small smile playing on his lips. 'He's met his bloody match.'

They backed into the forest. Only when they were out of sight of the bear did they turn round. Stephen hoisted Jack up into his arms.

'Well done, my brave little man,' he said. 'Now we have to make as much noise as possible so that if he's got any mates nearby we won't surprise them. But don't run, whatever you do.'

They climbed down to the house, shouting, clapping and yelling. By the time they got to the deck by the back door, Lara's throat was hoarse. But the adrenaline that had seized her when she was scared now mingled with the deeper thrill of having survived. Stephen unlocked the doors and let them in.

'I thought we were done for, back then.' He turned and grinned at her. She flung her arms around him and Jack and for a moment the three of them stood there, holding on to each other. After a short while. Jack started wriggling, worming his way out from between them.

'Snakes!' he said.

An hour of hunting in the back meadow yielded great treasure – a four-foot-long black rat snake, which Stephen said was extremely rare that far north. Jack clapped his hands in delight as the thing attempted to constrict the stick Stephen had looped it around.

All too soon it was time for Lara to return, Cinderella-like, to the horrible house in Trout Island, where she was expected to cook and clean for everyone else.

On the way down the mountain, Lara made use of the noisy Wrangler engine and the wind rushing through their hair to tell Stephen about the two free hours she had the following evening.

'Perhaps I could come up and pay you a visit?' she said.

He smiled, looking ahead, his hand on the wheel. 'That would be very nice indeed.'

'Wait,' he said as she jumped out of the jeep back at the house. He pressed a key into her hand. 'Back door,' he said. Then he took her arm and, using a pen from the dashboard, wrote five numbers on her skin.

'That's the code I'll set for the gate tomorrow. Just come when you can and let yourself in.'

Lara waved goodbye, then carried Jack and the car seat inside. The house was as empty as it had been when they had left, earlier in the day, before they had been chased by a bear and saved by a hero.

Thirty-Five

BELLA HEARD THE WRANGLER PULL UP AND HER MOTHER saying goodbye to Stephen, that she would see him tomorrow. The fly screens smashed open and shut and then there was the shout as her mother called up the stairs for her and Olly, who Bella knew, thankfully, wasn't in.

She sighed and pulled the bedcovers further over her head. She wanted to go back to Brighton. Or, rather, she wanted to run away. She didn't want to see her monster of a brother ever again. She hoped that no one would guess she was up here, in her bedroom.

She remembered Sean running to the car, his hands clamped over his front, his buttocks pale where his swimming shorts had been all summer, and she groaned at his humiliation and her shame for bringing it down on him. How could she face him again, after what Olly had done?

She was worried about how he was doing, but when, knowing the house to be empty, she had slunk out of her room to phone him, his mother had answered.

'Yes? Who is this please?' she had said, her voice cold,

echoing like an admonishment in what Bella imagined to be a bare wooden hallway. Bella hung up without saying anything. Of course she couldn't speak to Sean again. However much it hurt her, she had to stay away from him, because who knew what Olly would wreak on him if she didn't? He was far, far better off without her.

So that was why, when the phone had rung on four different occasions, and on four different occasions her mother or her father had called up the stairs for her, she ignored them completely, pretending not to be there.

She was utterly alone, then. She had no one to turn to. Olly held the photos over her, so public humiliation stood in her way if she told anyone. And, even if she did speak out, where would her revelations stop? Whatever she said would get her into trouble herself, Marcus wouldn't believe any of it anyway, and her mother seemed to be far too preoccupied with running around the countryside with Stephen Molloy to take any notice of what Bella was up to.

Starfucker mother.

Bella turned over and sighed again. That was it. She was done with her family. And she was done with love. Perhaps it was her own fault for letting things get out of hand with her brother when they were younger. Because now, in the face of everything that had happened, her shame hung on her in all this heat like a military greatcoat.

She thought about running away. She thought about taking one of Olly's cronies' guns and blasting his brains out. That would be the only way she would be truly free of him.

But then, she thought, wouldn't it be easier just to curl up and die herself, here alone in this stinking bed?

Thirty-Six

AS LARA POUNDED THE RIVER ROAD, THE MORNING MIST curling around her feet, she found she had a companion. Dog had popped up and was loping along beside her.

'Hello, boy,' she said. 'Come to save me from the beasts and bears and nutters?'

Dog looked from side to side, as if to confirm that he was, indeed, on lookout duty. Everything this animal did seemed to be designed to prove he was a good boy, but a part of Lara remained suspicious that he would, given half a chance, snack on her shins.

This morning, the run was a necessity for her. She had woken before dawn, in a lather, apprehensive about what she knew she was going to do that day. As she tiptoed downstairs in the pale first light, the house closed in on her, infecting her with its misery.

The night before, she had tried to wait up for Bella, Olly and Marcus to get in. But a day out in the sunshine, the exhaustion following the excitement of the bear episode, and the best part of a bottle of red wine meant that she was woken by Marcus shaking her as she lay stretched out on the sofa,

Jack pressed into her side like a sweaty little hot-water bottle.

'Come on, old girl. Bed,' he said, tobacco and wine on his breath.

'What's the time?' she said.

'Gone the witching hour.' He picked Jack up.

'Where are Bella and Olly?' She sat up, confused. She remembered waiting supper for everyone, then giving up and eating her own – what little she could manage.

'Tucked up in bed. I just checked on them. Both sleeping like angels.'

He carried Jack upstairs, leaving her sitting blinking on the sofa in the bare, dusty living room, with its fruited rotten smell.

She got up, stretched, and went through to the kitchen, where she cleared up, put the uneaten food in the fridge and checked the back door was locked, which it was. She added a new refinement to the house security, in the form of a broom and a mop wedged respectively under the back- and front-door handles. Finally she wobbled her way up to bed. By the time she got there Marcus was already asleep, so she didn't have a chance to ask where he had been all evening.

So, added to her sense of hangover, as she cantered with Dog along the shrouded river road, Lara also had a nagging notion that she was becoming a superfluous member of her family. She tried to work out whether this was a good thing or not.

They reached the barking Rottweiler which, as usual, pelted towards them, only to fall back whimpering as it hit its invisible wall.

'Ha,' Lara said. 'In your face, horrible dog.'

The run was doing its job, lifting the cobwebs from her mind, helping her to look forward to the coming evening when, for the first time in sixteen years, she and Stephen would be fully alone. She tried to think about what this meant for

Marcus, but she realised she no longer cared. The past week had been like an intolerably long foreplay, and she was ready to explode. She needed, for once, to do something genuine and true to herself. She checked her arm – the combination for his gate was still there, in Stephen's hand.

'Living a lie, living a lie,' she chanted as she jogged, using her footfall as a rhythm. She usually ran to music, but doing so this morning had made her feel undefended, so she had taken her earphones out.

Without warning Dog stopped, dropped down and snarled. Lara had to halt suddenly to avoid tumbling over the top of him. The object of his attention was a figure standing beside a car about fifty feet ahead, half hidden in the river mist.

'Hello?' Lara said. Dog shifted his shoulders and snarled again. The figure stepped towards them, away from her dun-coloured car, and, with a sick rush, Lara clocked the baker boy cap, the mousey hair, the tan and turquoise scarf.

'Stop. Or I'll set my dog on you,' Lara said.

'I know what you think . . .' The voice came loud to her, across the morning air, the kind of voice you can only get after a lifetime of smoking. Elizabeth Sanders took a few more steps forward, so Lara saw the thick, orange foundation on her face.

Dog growled.

'Good Dog,' Lara said.

'But I've come to warn you about Molloy.'

'Oh yes.' Lara said narrowing her eyes at her, her heart thumping. 'I know all about your *warnings*, Elizabeth Sanders.'

The woman folded her arms and smiled at her.

'You think I don't know what you're up to?' Lara said. 'You can't scare me.'

'I can. I *have* scared you. I scared him, too,' the woman said. 'He pushed me and I got a little *carried away*.' She laughed out loud. 'Nearly finished off the lot of you at the bridge there.'

Lara stood looking at her, safe in the knowledge that if it came to it, she would easily be able to outrun this bulky creature.

'Says he wants me off you now, but the bastard owes me and now he's going to pay.'

'He knows you're here?'

'Of course he knows I'm here.'

'He's not supposed to know,' Lara said, anger seizing her. 'It'll kill him.'

Sanders laughed. 'Kill him? He brought me here, honey.'

'You're crazy.' Lara pulled her iPhone out of its armband. 'He doesn't want you. He never has. You have this twisted idea you have some sort of relationship with him. But you don't even know him. Not like I do.'

'Oh, but I do know him. And what you really don't know is what you're getting yourself into, Lara Wayland.'

Taking her courage into her hands, Lara stepped forward with her iPhone and took a photo, right up in Elizabeth Sanders' face. Then she ran on towards the car and photographed its registration plate.

Sanders charged at her and grabbed her by the neck. She tried to get the iPhone out of her hands, clawing at it with bitten fingernails. But Dog launched himself at her, rounding her up and away from Lara, baring his fangs and snarling.

Lara moved round, away from the car. 'I've got you now,' she said, waving the phone at her. 'And, as you've done me the favour of revealing yourself to Stephen, I'm going to go to him and let him know. And then we'll call the police.'

Elizabeth Sanders bellowed with laughter. 'You are truly the silliest little girl I have ever come across,' she said. Backing away from Dog and shaking her head, she got into her car, started the engine, and looked up at Lara. 'I was trying to do you a favour,' she said, lifting her sunglasses and fixing Lara with a lizard stare. 'But it's pissing in the wind with you. You're blind. Blind, blind, blind, blind. You deserve him. You deserve each other.'

She floored the accelerator and in a second she was gone, leaving nothing but the smell of burning rubber and a deal of smoke in Lara's mind.

'Completely fucking mad,' Lara said to Dog, goosebumps on her arms. She was glad for one thing at least, though. Sanders had revealed herself to Stephen, so, at last, Lara could be open with him about her.

She returned her iPhone to its holder and, with Dog loping along beside her, she set off at her top speed, back to the horrible house.

'I'll be off then.'

Marcus poked his head round the archway to the kitchen while Lara was leaning forward stretching out after her run and trying to work out her next step.

'I thought rehearsals didn't start till eleven?'

'I'm meeting Selina for a bit of a line bash over breakfast. Great about the shirt coming back,' he said, as he helped himself to a glass of water.

'What?' Lara straightened up and saw that Marcus had his Paul Smith shirt on.

'The Russki laundromat guy got back in the end, then, I guess?' Marcus asked, putting his half-empty glass down in a puddle of wet on the kitchen table. 'Oops, I'm late. Gotta run. Laters.' He kissed Lara on the top of her head and dashed out of the front door.

As soon as he had left Lara ran upstairs to their bedroom,

where Jack was still fast asleep in his nest, and checked the side room. Everything had been changed. The medicines now sat on the low shelf where Jack's toys had been and the toys had been moved to a top shelf. The pink dress she looked so bulgy in hung on the back of the door, and there, in a neatly folded, ironed pile – in place of Jack's clothes, which had been flung on to the floor – was the stolen washing. The only thing missing was Stephen's beautiful shirt.

Horror rising in her throat, Lara ran from room to room to check that whoever had been in the house wasn't still there. Apart from the usual mess – unmade beds, damp towels heaped up on top of sheets – Olly and Bella's rooms were empty; they must have gone out early that day with their various local friends. Or at least, that's what Lara hoped.

After checking the downstairs, she locked the doors and tried to call Stephen, but there was no reply. She thought about driving up to his house right then, but what would she do with Jack? She had no choice but to stay put.

Over the morning, waiting until the moment she could drop Jack off at rehearsal and get up to Stephen's place, she tried phoning again and again.

There was no answer.

She was just picking up the phone for one more attempt when someone knocked on the front door. She edged into the living room and peered through the window to see a large stocky man standing on the porch.

'Lara? Hello? It's Danny,' he called up at the open first-floor windows above him.

She had completely forgotten that this was the day for the space clearing. Grateful for the presence of another adult, she rushed to the door.

'Danny. Thank you so much for coming.'

She didn't know what she had been expecting, but the man standing in front of her wasn't it. It would be impossible to guess his age – he could have been anything from forty to sixty-five years old. Dressed in smart chinos and an ironed cotton shirt, with a leather satchel over his shoulder and short, silvering black hair, he could easily have been an estate agent arriving to show the house to prospective buyers.

Instead she greeted a Native American shaman come to cleanse the place of negative energy.

He came into in the hallway and looked around.

'This is the worst part of the house,' Lara said. 'I can't stand it here.'

Danny closed his eyes and stood still, his hands clasped in front of him. After a few minutes, he relaxed and turned to Lara.

'Show me the other places.'

She took him around the ground floor, explaining the basement to him as they went up the stairs. Then she led him to Olly's room, where he stood on the threshold and frowned at the greying bedclothes and dirt-caked garments strewn over them.

Then Lara showed him into Bella's room, where, to her surprise, from underneath what she had taken earlier to be a heap of unmade bedding, her daughter turned her tousled head to confront them.

'Can't you knock?' she said, shielding her eyes from the dusty light that infiltrated her room through the open door.

'Sorry, darling. I thought you weren't in. Are you all right?' She went over to put her palm on Bella's forehead, but it was impossible, in the heat of the room, to gauge whether she had a fever or not. 'How do you feel?' she asked, putting her hand on her arm.

'Pants,' Bella muttered.

'It might do you some good to get up and get some fresh air,' Lara said.

'Yeah, right.' Bella pulled the sheet over her head and turned her back to her.

'Sorry,' Lara said to Danny, who was looking at the photograph that Lara had propped up on Bella's window.

'That's a photo of poor Jane Larssen,' Lara said, going over to him. 'Should I take it down?'

Danny shook his head. 'That's not the problem,' he said.

They finished the tour of the house and went back downstairs. In the living room, over coffee, Danny asked Lara about her family, where they were from and how long they planned to stay. As she answered his questions, Danny watched her and nodded, rubbing his chin between thumb and forefinger. His scrutiny of her put her on edge, as if she were gabbling on too much.

She finished and he finally spoke.

'Lara. There is a problem with this house, but it is very small, very ancient. It's almost past history. The big problem isn't with the building.'

'What do you mean?'

'The big problem is with you, Lara.'

'I don't understand.'

He put his bag on the ground and opened it. He brought out a foot-long bundle of dried twigs and leaves, all tied up with yellow cloth bands.

'What are you doing?'

He held up his hand to silence her. Using a red plastic lighter from his pocket, he set fire to the end of the bundle, fanning it until the flame took. Then he blew it out and let the smoke rise up between them. He stepped in closer to Lara, who watched, wide-eyed, as he closed his eyes and started to chant something in a language she didn't recognise. He moved the smouldering twigs all over himself first, along his arms, down and up his own legs, then he turned to her, passing the smoke more slowly over her, taking more time.

'Breathe it in,' he said to her between chants.

Lara tried to suppress the urge to cough as she inhaled the herbal smoke. It reminded her of the home-grown spliffs she and Marcus used to smoke before she was pregnant with the twins, or the awful Honeyrose cigarettes he took up for a week when he tried to quit tobacco. Whatever it was, it was heady stuff and it made her light-headed and giddy. She fought not to giggle.

After what seemed like an hour, but which could have been only a few minutes, he pulled away and stood silently in front of her, scrutinising her as if trying to read some small print on her cheek.

Eventually he spoke.

'I've done what I can. The rest is up to you.'

'What about the house?'

'I'll clear it for you if you like. It will help. But it's only you that can make the real difference.'

He stepped around the house, chanting and moving smoke through what Lara considered to be the problem areas, until his burning bundle was just a stub. Finally he took her by the hand and led her on to the front porch, where he took her into his arms in a fatherly embrace.

'Open your eyes, Lara,' he said. 'Bad things are going to happen unless you are very careful.'

She watched him gather his things to leave.

It was as if he knew.

Thirty-Seven

LARA TRIED CALLING STEPHEN ANOTHER COUPLE OF TIMES, but still got no reply, which did nothing to soothe her mounting sense of unease. After dropping Jack off at the theatre, she left a note and thirty dollars for Bella – who was still moping up in her room – and Olly – who she had not seen for days, it seemed – to get themselves supper from the pizza place. Marcus and Jack had been invited to dinner at the diner with James and Betty after rehearsal. She explained her own absence by claiming to have errands to run in town. She was pretty certain that, so slight was their interest in her comings and goings, they would buy without question such a vague and boring-sounding alibi. In any case, she would probably be home before anyone realised she had gone.

She stopped briefly as she walked to the back of the house after locking the doors and scanned the muggy yard and bushes beyond for observers. It was extraordinary how in a matter of days this had become instinct. But she was pleased now she could speak to Stephen and they could go to the police.

If she managed to find him.

She hurried to the old Volvo. Three turns on the ignition produced nothing: no sound, not even a stutter. Following Gina's liberally exclamation-marked instructions in a little brown book in the glove compartment, Lara got the 'giant great spanner from the trunk!' located the 'recalcitrant starter motor!' and gave it a 'Gawd almighty whack!'.

The unlikely recipe did the trick and, sweaty now, she turned the growling car on to Main Street. The evening was especially humid: hot, damp air pressed in on her body, and, of course, the Volvo's air-conditioning didn't work at all. Even without thinking about her own situation, there was a sense of something on the verge of happening, a storm on its way. On top of this, Lara felt a heat in the base of her belly, and a pins-and-needles sensation danced between her legs. She was on her way to misbehaviour and possibly danger, and this brought on light-headedness.

It was like she was nineteen again, off to meet Stephen in his attic digs in Stratford, where his theatrical landlady, a woman fond of fabric flowers and Judy Garland movies, made herself discreetly absent whenever her actor gentlemen 'entertained'. Lara looked back at it now as a sort of age of innocence, and although it was of course anything but, compared to what was at stake with this visit, she had some reason for doing so.

The shadow of the unanswered phone calls and the thought of what might be going on up at his house made her foot rest a little heavily on the Volvo's accelerator.

But before she got very far she was forced to stop. Someone had decided to do some road works on Main Street, and had so far got around to putting in an excessively slow-to-change set of temporary lights just outside Gina's house. As Lara sat there, dissolving on to the hot leather seats, waiting for the non-existent oncoming traffic to pass through the one lane left open on the road, she extended Stephen's *what-if* into a detailed scenario where they had brought up the twins in LA and lived a life that consisted of family evenings at the circus punctuated by untold nights of winding their bodies around and around each other . . .

A hand thumped down on the roof of the old Volvo, jerking Lara out of her daydream.

'How's the old girl?'

Lara turned to see Gina's head poking through the passenger window. By her side were her daughters.

'Oh, hi, Gina,' Lara said, breathing out with relief. 'Ethel, Gladys. I can't believe these lights.'

'I know!' Gina said. 'Jim was waiting here for three years the other day! Hey, cool – matching bag and car.'

Lara looked down. It was true, her handbag, which she had flung on the seat beside her, was the exact same colour as the car.

'Except for the rust!' Gina added.

Lara smiled. Normally she loved Gina's upbeat manner, but she was in no mood for chitchat. Also, she was pointing in exactly the wrong direction for her going-to-town alibi. Not even properly started on a double life, and here she was, already slipping up.

'Where you off to then, lady?' Gina asked, one eyebrow raised.

'Oh just um . . .' But Lara was saved by the changing lights.

'Catch 'em while you can!' Gina said, slapping the car again as it were a lazy horse. Lara cranked the handbrake and set off at a bit more of a lick than the *Dead Slow* decreed by the roadwork signs.

As she reached the turning that took her off Main Street towards Stephen's place, she glanced in her rear-view mirror to check once more she wasn't being followed in any way. To her dismay, Gina and her daughters were standing by the road, still waving goodbye to her through the wiggling heat haze. That would be typical Gina, waving and waving with her children until the very last glimpse of the person they were saying goodbye to had disappeared. It also suggested, however, that Gina was on to her.

But what did it matter, really? As she wound her way up the mountain and across the grassy plateau at the top, Lara began to detach herself from the crippling fear of consequence that had hampered her life so much.

At the highest point, where she could see for miles, the hills folded blue into blue underneath a khaki sky. Forks of lightning – so distant she couldn't hear even a whisper of thunder – stabbed at the furthest ridge, sparking a crackle of electricity through the damp flannel air. Looking west as she was, across a land vast and empty to a degree unimaginable to a European mind, Lara knew anything was possible on this earth.

She drove back into the forest on the other side, crunching off the gravel on to the dirt road that took her eventually up to Stephen's gate.

Reading the numbers from her arm, she punched them into the entry keypad. She drove in and forced herself to wait for the gate to close behind her. Then she set off – too quickly for a car with such antique suspension – along the rocky drive that led her, through the trees, to the magical house that Stephen built.

She pulled up between his dented Wrangler and the wooden garage and cut the engine. The drive up with the windows open had brought road-dust in; she tasted powdery dirt as she licked her lips. For the first time in this country, she heard absolutely nothing. The silence was so dense, it made her ears ring. Not an insect, bird or any other creature intruded.

This must be the storm on its way, then. Her vest was drenched with sweat and something buzzed behind her eyes.

Not only was it silent in Stephen's clearing. The house seemed pretty quiet too. All the blinds and curtains were drawn. Her own heartbeat thumping in her head, she wiped the sweat away from her upper lip. His car was there, so he must be around somewhere. She scanned the perimeter of the garden. Beyond the grass, the forest could conceal or swallow up anyone or anything.

Nothing, not even the stir of a branch, made the scene seem other than a photograph, or a still at the beginning or end of a film.

A flicker of lightning led the way for a low rumble of thunder. The sky darkened like she remembered in the eclipse of 1999, when she had been standing in the middle of a Sussex campsite, on her own as usual, with her two small children.

Then she heard the sound – irregular cracks and pops, like bones breaking – of the first, fat raindrops fighting their way down through the thick air to land on taut leaves.

She didn't like that the house appeared to be closed up. She fought the urge to get back into the car and drive away and forget all about it. Whatever she was going to find there, she had to go inside.

She strode over the snake lawn towards the back door, and, using the key Stephen had given her, let herself in. The door swung shut behind her. If it had been dark outside, inside the house was like a tomb. She stood still, waiting for her eyes to accustom to the gloom. Then she angled her vision across the kitchen towards the living room, where, outlined by the light from a dimmed table lamp, she could just about pick out the shape of a figure sitting on the leather sofa.

Whoever it was had a gun, and they were pointing it directly at her.

With a jab of terror, Lara heard the click of the catch coming off the gun. For a moment, she was reminded of the stand-off with the bear. But this was even more deadly.

A simultaneous flash and crash of lightning and thunder heralded the arrival of the storm directly overhead. Confused by the surge, the dim lamp flickered on full, revealing the gunman on the sofa to be Stephen.

'Stephen!' she said. 'What?'

'Step into the light so I can see you,' he said.

Carefully, Lara moved forward into the living room. Her hands lifted automatically into the air. 'Stephen, it's me, Lara.'

'Lara!' Stephen let out a great sigh and seemed to collapse in on himself. The gun clattered to the floor. Lara stayed where she was, rooted to the spot, unsure of whether to run out of the house or towards him.

'I could have shot you. I thought you were . . .' he said, pressing his fists into his forehead.

Lara took the seven faltering steps necessary to reach him, then, gingerly moving the gun to one side, she sank to her knees and grasped his hands in hers, moving them away from his face. Behind the dirt that smeared his cheeks, his skin was white. Desperation clouded his eyes. She saw him, for the first time, with his guard down, defenceless.

'I thought you were her,' he whispered.

'I know,' she said. 'I know she's here again. She's been after me since I arrived.'

'What?' Stephen's eyes flashed up at her.

'Betty told me not to tell you, that it would kill you to know,' she said, squeezing Stephen's hands tight as he gasped.

'Betty?' he said.

365

'But I'm glad you know now,' Lara went on, 'because we can talk. You're not alone, Stephen. You've got me, and we're going to make sure this Elizabeth Sanders gets sent down once and for all.'

'I'll never get the better of her.' He broke away and buried his head in a cushion. 'She's tracked me across a whole continent, like I was some sort of wild beast.'

'But look,' Lara said, rummaging in her bag for her iPhone. 'I've got evidence.' She showed Stephen the photographs she had taken of Sanders and her car.

'She got this close to you?' Stephen said, his voice tiny with disbelief. 'Jesus, what sort of danger have I led you into?' He took her face in his hands. 'Lara, if anything ever happened to you, I'd—' He stood up and started pacing the room. 'I can't believe Betty put my sanity above your safety. Doesn't she know how dangerous this woman is?'

'She wanted us to work out a way of trapping her so you didn't even know about it until it was all over. But Sanders did me a favour by letting you know she's here. You'll never believe it,' Lara said, 'she even tried to tell me you'd brought her here. She's crazy. Completely la-la.'

A roll of thunder shook the house and seemed to echo in Stephen's eyes as he looked at her. 'Don't believe a word that *creature* says. She's evil, Lara, a player of dark games. And Betty – such a meddling mother hen. Doesn't she know I can look after myself?'

'Can you?' Lara said, getting up and moving towards him. 'From the state of you right now, I'm not so sure she wasn't right to try to protect you.'

'But it's no protection at all, me not knowing. And what if something had happened to you Lara? Where would I be then?'

He had his hands on her shoulders now, and was holding

her at arm's length, looking at her. His concern, and the whirl of the moment, made her feel as if he were pulling on some cord deeply rooted between them. She wanted to ask him the details, about how he had found out about Sanders, about whether she was out there right now, lurking in the dense trees, but all of that seemed unimportant as their bodies were unstoppably drawn together.

'I have waited so long for this, Lara,' he said, his voice hoarse.

'Shh,' she said, and reaching up, drew him down towards her, so their lips touched. As he fell to his knees, she feared she might float away and never be seen again.

'Oh God,' he said, pressing his face against her belly. The noise of water hitting wood deafened as the rain battered down on the house, but all she heard was his breath as it came in short, shallow gasps.

He knelt back and, slowly and gently, took her clothes off piece by piece, revealing her more fully than she felt she had ever been before. Then she was naked, standing there in front of him. He gazed up at her, a small-boy look of wonder on his face.

'You are so beautiful,' he said. 'More beautiful than I remember even. More beautiful than I have imagined.'

Lara closed her eyes. No one had told her she was beautiful. Not for years.

He reached out and ran his hand over her hip and down her thigh, little darts of pleasure shooting into every inch of her he touched.

'So soft,' he said. 'So soft all over.' He pressed his cheek to her again, this time skin on skin, and she fell – no, she folded – to the floor.

'I love you, Lara. I have always loved you and I always will.'

That she would find herself here, being adored by him like this. She wondered if it was real. Then his hand moved between her legs and she realised how tangible, how palpable, it actually was.

'I love you too,' she said. 'I have always loved you and I always will.'

For the next hour, he didn't allow her to touch him. He worshipped every inch of her, every nook, every hidden curve. This was what she remembered. This was what she had missed. Then, when she couldn't imagine having any pleasure left to spend, he pulled off his own clothes, leaving only his vest, and, standing, gently lifted her up and on to him.

They stood there, coupled, still, full, until neither of them could bear it any longer. Then, by some unseen signal, she arched back and he followed her down on the sofa, where the frenzy began until, minutes later, they came together, him deep within her.

This, she knew, was what she wanted. She wanted him to lay himself there in her core, to become one with her, to plant his DNA inside her too-recently emptied womb.

They slid to the floor into a tangled heap, him still taking the last, electric grips and turns of her. Outside, the wind was up, driving the branches of the nearby trees against the house like a thousand scratching fingers. Another simultaneous lightning and thunderclap shook them into one final mutual shudder.

'Welcome home,' she said. And then, everything else forgotten, they fell into a brief but deep sleep, wrapped at last in each other's arms.

'Tell me how you found out Sanders was here,' Lara said a short while later as she lay on Stephen's chest, listening to his heartbeat and trying to breathe in time with him.

'Tell you what,' Stephen said, stirring. 'I'll take you out and show you what we're up against.' He stood and got dressed. Then he helped her back into her clothes, kissing goodbye to each part of her body as he covered it up.

The storm had passed far more quickly than it had arrived. When they stepped outside on to the sodden back porch, Stephen with his gun slung over his shoulder, Lara heard the distant rumble of retreating thunder. The clouds above them – partly steam rising from the trees – were clearing to reveal a golden red and orange sky, the prelude to a spectacular sunset. All around them and beneath their feet, crawling and jumping things ventured out from behind their shelters to start up their racket again. The air, washed by the rain of its heaviness, now carried the tang of newly wetted earth.

Lara felt like a baby after its dunk in the font.

'Where are we going?' she said.

'Into the woods,' Stephen said. 'We'll take this.' He picked up a torch from the boot store on the deck. 'It might be dark by the time we get back.'

'Do you think it's wise to go out there?' Offset by the glistening grass, the trees looked especially black to Lara.

'Despite what Lady Betty might think, I am more than capable of looking after us.' Stephen put his arm around her, turning her and pointing to the trees. 'I know these woods as if they were my wife. As I know you.' Lara reached up and drew his mouth down towards hers. They kissed, and she felt his hand move up inside her red vest top, on to her breast.

'Come on,' he said, his voice hoarse. 'We'd best get moving. Or it really will be dark.'

'And I said I'd be back by eight.' It was already six thirty and the drive back to Trout Island was a good half-hour.

'I'll make sure you're back on time,' he said.

'I don't want to go.'

'I know.'

They climbed up through the woods, just like they did when they went blueberry picking, except this time there was no Jack and they had their arms wrapped around each other. The rain had left the undergrowth and canopy soaking wet, drenching their legs and showering their heads as they stopped from time to time to kiss.

'What if she sees us?' Lara said. 'What if she's watching?'

'Let her. Do you know? For the first time since she started plaguing me, she has lost the ability to scare me. I feel . . .' he said, breathing in the washed air around them, '. . . I feel invincible.' He turned to her, picked her up and swung her round, laughing. 'You have made me a Superman!'

Lara believed him. How could she be anything other than safe by his side?

They moved on, up towards the summit of the hill.

'You couldn't guess,' he said, helping her over a large branch that the storm had brought down across the path, 'how unable I've been to buckle down to anything since we parted yesterday.'

'I think I have some idea,' she said.

'I kept on thinking I should be preparing for your arrival, building a bower, putting on a feast. But I also know, you and me, we don't need any props.'

He paused to pick a small wild strawberry he had spotted at his feet. He turned and put it on her tongue.

'So I've been outside, almost all the time. I've done two long runs. I chopped wood, weeded, and harvested my tomatoes. I did a bit of coppicing, mended a drystone wall. I kept myself busy to stop myself spontaneously combusting. And then I thought I'd go out and try and find that bear again. See if I could get a picture or two.'

'See if you could face him down again.' Lara squeezed his hand.

'Now then, you. I just wanted to take photographs,' Stephen said. 'But he wasn't around. So, while I was up there, I thought I'd go on, perhaps take a swim in my pond – I'll show you that very soon – and on the way I checked in on that derelict house – the one I told you about.'

They reached the blueberry clearing and stood silently for a few moments. There was no sign of the bear, or anything else untoward: no crashing in the undergrowth, no twigs cracking on the forest floor. As far as they could tell, they were on their own.

They moved on, back into the trees at the other side of the clearing, where the path zigzagged down a steep hill.

'Another half-mile and we'd be at the best swimming pond in New York State,' Stephen said as they scrunched down through decades of leaf-litter. 'Spring-fed, it's the sweetest, clearest water you'll have swum in.'

He held back a low, heavily leafed branch. 'This is what I found,' he said as he revealed a single-storey stone house on an earth terrace. There were gaps where the windows and doors had been, but the roof was still intact. A drystone wall made a perimeter around the building, and this had kept the under-growth at bay, although a maple sapling was working its way out of one of the window holes.

'Brr.' Lara shivered.

'Look inside,' Stephen said, flashing his torch through the doorway.

Peering in, Lara saw a stained sleeping bag, an old hearth

with the remains of a recently built fire in it, a litter of empty food containers and wrappers, and a half-full gallon-sized water container. On the floor, spelled out in large twig and leaf letters, and enclosed within the outline of a heart made of small stones, were the letters ES + SM. It was the dolls, though, that made the goosebumps rise on Lara's neck. Fashioned out of bird skulls, bone bits and root fibres, the bigger one had material from Stephen's shirt wrapped around it – the shirt that had had been stolen from the launderette. The other wore a piece of Lara's green top. Lara looked up at Stephen, who had come in behind her.

'I washed it and hung it out to dry the day after you first came here,' he said, reading the question in her eyes. 'It disappeared. Thought a bear had got it. I'd done a great job on the wine stain, too.'

Lara looked back down at the dolls. Each had six big thorns stuck into its torso.

'Spines from the devil's walking stick. Grows all the way through my forests,' Stephen said.

'Ouch,' Lara said. 'So she's playing Witch. How long do you think she's been in here?'

'I dropped by about ten days ago, on my way for a swim. It was completely empty. This is all new. Fuck her.' For a second he seemed to lose control, kicking at the stone heart and the bird-skull dolls, the sleeping bag and the water bottle.

'Steady.' Lara laid a hand on his shoulder. 'You're spoiling our evidence.'

He looked at her, fire in his eyes.

'She's trying to destroy us,' he said. He broke away from her and stormed outside to the gloom of the forest.

'Come out, Sanders,' he yelled, holding his gun ready. 'Come out and face us.'

But only silence answered him.

'I want to go back to the house now,' Lara said, placing a calming hand on him. The light was fading fast – the patches of sky between the trees turned from pink to grey. Even with Stephen by her side, even with a torch, she didn't fancy being out here when the final tint of light dissolved and they were slung into pitch black.

'Yes,' he said, looking around in a way that told her he, too, wanted the shelter of four walls.

Silently they picked their way through the brambles and vines that seemed to have grown up behind them since they started out.

Stephen held his gun ahead of him like a soldier moving through a jungle, like he had in his award-winning role in that Vietnam movie. Lara lit their way with the torch. Time was moving on. She should think about setting off back to Trout Island. But she didn't want to. She wanted to stay with Stephen and she didn't want him to be on his own with *that woman* somewhere out in those trees, watching him.

Also, she didn't think she could drive down that dark mountain on her own, in that unreliable car, with that fear of hers of evil eyes popping up in the rear-view mirror. It was bad enough back home, night-driving through benign, leafy Home Counties English lanes. But here, in a landscape used for thousands of celluloid nightmares, with the additional threat of an authentic madwoman on the loose, she didn't see how she would get back to the village without collapsing in dread.

So, when they reached his porch and he drew her to him and asked if she would stay a bit longer, she was quick to agree.

He unlocked the door and they both went in, but he didn't put the lights on. Using the torch, he led her to the living room and drew her down on to the big leather sofa. She held herself close to him, pressing her head against his chest.

'Tell me about her. Tell me what she did to you.'

She stretched her legs along his and listened to the rumble of his voice.

'I started getting these text messages from someone. They weren't so sinister to begin with. Flattering stuff about my work, that sort of thing. A bit weird, you know, coming from someone you don't know. But it happens. It's part of the deal you make with the devil in this game. Like not being able to walk down the street without people wanting your autograph or to talk to you. Sometimes you want them to go away, but you have to be civil. You have to be polite.

'Then the messages started getting personal – about my body, about what this person would like to do with me. I ignored them, thinking the sender would get bored and stop, but my silence only seemed to egg her on. I started finding these handwritten notes pinned to my door, written in green capitals, with the unique prose style and questionable spelling that told me they were from the same sender. I also found them on my trailer door if I was working, or tucked behind my car windscreen wipers.'

'Scary,' Lara said, stroking his beautiful forearm. Each slender muscle was distinct. The real fibre of him under her fingertips.

'Exactly.' He put his lips to her hair. 'But then the messages began to get proprietorial – the shirt I was wearing didn't suit me, I shouldn't be ordering that for my dinner at Ugo's. Things started turning up on my doorstep: bottles of whisky, boxes of chocolates, bunches of flowers, teddy bears. Teddy bears! Deliveries of pizza, books and clothing would arrive – stuff I never ordered. I changed my phone number three times, and employed a security guard at my gate, but she always managed to find a way to get to me. And by trying to block her way of course I made her angrier and angrier. The messages took a nasty turn, the gifts were less benign – tons of rotted manure dumped in my driveway, two dozen dead roses, what looked like a human turd in a Godiva box.'

'Ugh.'

'And by this point, the relentlessness and the nastiness of it was getting to me. I cancelled a dinner where I was supposed to talk because I didn't want to put myself on a public stage. I started to get really paranoid about the level of security at the studios where I was working.'

'And the police were no good?'

'They had so little to go on. She was so clever; she was almost invisible. They never once saw her. And then—' He stopped, and breathed in, steadying himself.

'And then?'

'I had a series of accidents. To an outsider each one might have looked like bad luck or carelessness – indeed that's how the police viewed them. And I suppose I was beginning to lose it. But I'm certain she had a hand in it somehow. I mean, nothing like that had ever happened to me before she turned up.'

'Like what?'

'I had a tyre blow out just after I turned out of my house on to Mulholland. On a bend on the edge of a mountain. I was lucky I didn't go over. I've got this high deck that comes off the second floor of my house, cantilevered over the valley.' He used his hands to describe the layout. 'You'll see it one day soon. You'll love it. One of the wooden steps leading up to the deck from the pool collapsed as I climbed it, and I fell, breaking my ankle. It could have been my neck. Then I got some sort of food poisoning that put me in hospital for three days. And one evening I lit the barbecue and this happened.'

He shifted round and Lara propped herself up to watch as he lifted his T-shirt and showed her his chest. Where it had once been smooth, taut and golden, now it was shiny, mottled white and purple. She reached out to touch the scarring. He held her hand on his damaged skin and looked at her.

'The police advised me to take the barbecue incident to the manufacturers. And not to drink too much champagne while cooking on an open flame. The only woman they found in LA with the name Elizabeth Sanders was tiny, eighty-nine years old and with no record at all of anything untoward. It couldn't be her. It was a made-up name, and she was untraceable.'

'Poor you,' Lara said, laying her head on his chest, running her fingertips along the ridges and valleys of the crackled scars.

' "If I can't have you then nobody can" was the message that pushed me over the edge. I was taking too many painkillers – my leg was still weak and I was undergoing skin grafts for the burns – and I was mixing them with alcohol. Very bad. I stopped going out. I became the proverbial prisoner in my own home. I felt so alone, Lara.'

'Poor you. Poor love.' Lara reached her arm up and held him tight to her.

'Betty was the only person I could talk to back then. She was a rock. She came in, found me after the overdose.'

'Overdose?'

'She did a great job of covering it up. But I thought it had got out on to the rumour corners of the internet?'

'I never heard anything about an overdose.'

'Well, let's just say I didn't see much point to my life at that time. Betty got me into rehab in Utah. Then, when I came out, she and James suggested I move over here, disappear for a while. She even found this land for me. So I quite literally vanished. Even my management don't know where I am. I never dreamed Sanders would find me. But now she's here and I've got to leave. I'll go to Mexico. Or Europe.'

'And she will have won. We have to stop this, Stephen. We need to tell the police and get her arrested, for trespass at the very least. We can do that.'

'It's true. Over here, they view crimes against property far more seriously than crimes against the person.'

'We have to stay put,' she said, sitting up and looking him in the eye. 'Whatever happens.'

'I like the sound of that "we".' He closed his eyes and rested his forehead against hers. 'Stay with me tonight, Lara.'

'What will I say to Marcus?'

'Say a tree came down in the storm, say the road is impassable. It happened before, last year. I was stuck up here four days. It's entirely feasible. I need you here in so many ways, Lara. Please.'

'So I left my bag up here when I came up blueberry picking yesterday with Jack, so I couldn't go into town because I didn't have a purse, so I had to come up here to pick it up. And then there was the big storm. You did have it down in the village?' She twirled the cord to Stephen's office phone between her fingers.

'Yes,' Marcus said. His annoyance at being left on his own in charge of Jack reached her clearly through the phone line.

'So, after the storm had passed, I set off down the mountain. But this big oak has come down about a mile away from Stephen's. The road is impassable. I came back here and Stephen rang some emergency line and they say they'll have it cleared by morning. So he's offered to put me up for the night.'

Stephen handed her a glass of wine and raised his eyebrows in question.

'That's very kind of him,' Marcus said.

Lara gave Stephen the thumbs-up.

'He's a real mate,' Marcus went on.

'I'll be back as soon as the road is cleared.'

'I'm sure you will. And what'll I do about Jack in the morning when I have to go to work?'

'Look, this is not my fault,' Lara said. She actually felt quite indignant. 'Get Bella or Olly organised. Or go round and see Gina. I'm sure she'll help.'

'All right then,' she heard him sigh. 'I suppose it's not impossible.'

'I'll see you tomorrow evening, then,' she said.

'All right. And Lara?'

'Yes?'

'I know Mr Molloy is a world-famous movie star, but hey, no hanky panky eh? Or I'll send the boys round.'

For one second, Lara wavered. Then she gathered herself. 'What, Olly and Jack?' she said. 'I'm scared.'

'Take care love,' he said. 'Don't worry about things back here. I've got it all under control.'

'How did that go?' Stephen held his arms out to her as she joined him in the living room.

'Exhausting,' she said. 'His first reaction was "how am I going to cope?". Not "poor you, take care".'

'Poor you. Take care,' Stephen said, sitting and pulling her down so she straddled him.

* * *

378

Later, they had a long bath together in a sunken tub that Lara hadn't seen before.

'I dreamed about doing this with you in here,' he said, as she lay on top of him, their bodies sliding over each other in the scented, soapy water.

'I love all of you,' he said, moving her over and kissing the stretch marks that striated the tops of her breasts, the bottom of her belly. 'I always have.'

'Don't ever go back,' he said, leading her, naked, to his big double bed. 'Don't ever go back to him.' He stretched her out and started to stroke her, gently, from her toes to her hair. She felt numb with pleasure. She had never been so adored.

Thirty-Eight

ACCUSTOMED TO BEING WOKEN EARLY BY JACK, LARA opened her eyes after too little sleep to find her face pressed into Stephen's scarred chest. It took her a couple of minutes to remember where she was, that she hadn't dreamed the last fourteen hours. She listened to his steady, satiated breathing as their body heat mingled in the cool bedroom air. Clear skies on top of a soaked forest had made the night almost chilly, but they had hardly noticed.

All Lara knew in the fresh morning light was that this was home for her, and she wanted to remain. She lay trying not to wake him as she worked it out. Jack would come and live with Stephen and her, out here in the woods, and, when that Sanders woman had been dealt with, they'd go back to LA. Bella and Olly could stay with Marcus during term time until they finished sixth form, then they would choose whether they went to university in America or England. It all seemed so simple, so obvious to her as she lay there in Stephen's arms on that first morning, in his bed.

Of course, she had broken her promise to Betty about

holding back. But Betty had been proved wrong about not telling Stephen about Sanders. It would have been far better if Lara had confided in him earlier. And even Betty with her steely eyes couldn't have stopped what was going to happen between her and Stephen.

'Hello you,' Stephen said, turning her on to her back and smiling deep into her being.

'I have a problem,' Lara said as, much later, they stepped out of the shower they had just shared. 'I can't see.'

'What do you mean?' Stephen enveloped her in a fluffy white towel that reached from her shoulders to the ground.

'I didn't bring any spare contact lenses, and I had to take my old ones out last night. I thought I had some in my bag, but I don't. I won't be able to drive without them.'

'Now why would you want to do that, though?' Stephen said, gently rubbing her dry with the towel.

Later, after a breakfast of blueberries and home-made creamy yoghurt, Stephen put on his long-hair Sam Miller disguise, picked up his gun and kissed Lara on the lips.

'Won't be long,' he said.

'Where are you going?'

'There's this package I have to pick up from the post office in the village. A very important document. I'll be back in no time. Just stay in the living room, keep the curtains drawn and don't go out.'

'I can't stay here alone,' she said, and she meant it. 'Couldn't you get Trudi Staines to fetch whatever it is for you?'

'She's not answering her phone,' Stephen said quickly. 'And I need the package now.'

'Oh,' she said.

'Poor you.' He encircled her in his arms. 'You're scared, aren't you?'

'Yes.' She smiled up at him.

'You could come down with me,' he said. 'If . . .'

'If?'

'You'll have to lie low when we get into Trout Island. And I'll have to take a bit of care. We don't want anyone seeing there's no tree-on-road situation.'

So they went down the mountain in the open-topped Wrangler and, on the outskirts of the village, Stephen pulled over. Lara climbed into the back seat, and he passed her the gun.

'I don't want this,' she said.

'You'd better take it. It's locked, don't worry.' He threw a rug over her and drove on down into the village. Lara felt claustrophobic and hot under the blanket, but it beat being on her own up at the house. The Wrangler drew to a standstill.

'We're at the post office. Stay down,' Stephen said, as he got out of the car. 'I'll be two minutes.'

As Lara lay as still as possible underneath the blanket, two familiar voices approached.

'Come on, Jacko, let's try it again. It's just like learning nursery rhymes. What is a traitor?' Marcus said.

'What is a traitor?' Jack repeated.

'Why, one that swears and lies,' Marcus replied in a pretending-to-be-a-woman voice.

'And be all traitors that do so?' Jack said, and Lara's heart contracted.

'Every one that does so is a traitor and must be hanged,' Marcus went on in his woman voice.

'And must they all . . .' Jack said. He paused. 'Yes. I remember . . . be hanged that lie and swear?'

'EVERY ONE!' Marcus roared, and Jack giggled. 'But it's swear and lie, Jacko,' Marcus said, in his own voice.

'But I was good though, Dad, wasn't I?' Jack said. 'I learned my lines.'

'Like a top pro,' Marcus said. 'Good as your old dad.'

'Look!' Jack said, his voice coming close, far too close for comfort. 'Stephen's car.'

'What?' Marcus said. Lara could smell his aftershave as he leaned into the vehicle. There was a pause, long as a lifetime. Lara held her breath and prayed Stephen wouldn't come out of the post office.

'Nah. Can't be Stephen's car, Jacko. He's stuck up the mountain with Mummy, remember? Poor old fella.'

'Look, though, Daddy. Stephen's dents,' Jack said, his voice getting further away as he squatted down to point at the crumpled side where Sanders had tried to run them off the road. For a moment Lara was distracted from her precarious situation by the sudden puzzling thought that Stephen hadn't even for one minute suspected that Sanders might be behind that trick. Or the launderette episode.

'Look, Daddy.'

Shut up Jack, Lara thought.

'It can't be Stephen's,' Marcus said finally. 'There's loads of jeeps like this one around here. And I bet every one of them is covered in scratches from all the manly off-roading their butch owners put them through. Come on, Jacko. Time to go. Or Daddy'll be late for work.'

'But . . .'

'No buts. Gina's expecting us and I don't want to be late.'

'When's Mummy coming back, though?'

'She'll be back to make your tea.'

Lara worked hard to stop herself heaving a sigh of relief as they resumed their journey towards Gina's house. Thankfully, like any doting young son, Jack had believed his mistaken father about the jeep. Lara was glad, for once, that Marcus was quite so dense.

After what seemed like yet another lifetime to her, during which she had to slowly and smoothly turn on to her back under the blanket to cool down and breathe more freely, the door opened and she felt Stephen move into the driver's seat. She heard him put some things on the front seat, then his hand was on top of her.

'Hi,' he said.

'Jack and Marcus went by,' she said, catching his hand in her fingers.

'I know. I had to wait inside till they went,' he whispered. 'Stay there until we get out of town.'

Lara held on to his hand. 'Couldn't we just nip into the house and get my contact lenses? It's too early for Olly and Bella to be up.'

'Too risky,' Stephen said. 'We've got to get out of here as quickly as we can.'

She felt the vehicle lurch as he swung it across the road in a U-turn and back towards home. Lara knew they would also be passing Gina's house and she prayed Marcus wouldn't see Stephen driving the jeep. But then again, he'd only seen him in his circus guy disguise, so probably wouldn't recognise Sam Miller. In any case, she had waded in beyond any point of return. She had to put herself in Stephen's hands. Which, of course, was exactly where she wanted to be.

There was no one she trusted more in the entire world.

Thirty-Nine

'ALL CLEAR,' STEPHEN SAID TO LARA AFTER A BRIEF SEARCH of the house for any sign of intruders. 'Are you going to be OK for a few moments? I've just got a couple of things to deal with in here.' He indicated the package in his hand and his study, where Lara had called Marcus and told him the lie. 'Then we have the rest of the day together. Help yourself.' He showed her a tall bookshelf to the side of the kitchen area. 'And here's some music for you.' He flicked through an iPod perched on a small, gorgeous wooden sound system. The room filled with Morrissey.

'More of the charming man, then?' Lara said, browsing through the bookcase.

'This is newer. *Years of Refusal*, it's called,' Stephen said, folding his arms, leaning back against the wall and watching her. 'But he speaks for us just as strongly as ever. He's got different things to say, but I always get this feeling he's telling the story of my life. You know?'

'What would Morrissey say if he knew Stephen Molloy was his biggest fan?' she said, looking up at Stephen's perfect, angular features, the glamour of him, the way he was so completely a star.

'You know what? He wouldn't give a shit. And that's why I love him.'

Lara smiled.

'I'll see you in a couple of minutes,' Stephen said, going over to her and holding her close. 'Don't go anywhere.'

'I don't think I can,' she said. 'With these eyes.'

She flicked through the spines on Stephen's bookshelves, leaning close to read the titles. There were lots of cookery books, and a couple of rows of modern poetry. At eye-level a long shelf of art books – theoretical works and monographs – stretched the width of the room. Searching though the alphabetised titles, she found the Alice Neel book Bella had looked at and loved so much. She heaved it out of the shelves and carried it to the sofa, where she propped it on her knees, squinting forward to look at the pictures.

As she flicked through the book, one page had been looked at so much it opened itself. When she saw it, Lara felt a shock of recognition. The painting on that page, of a woman called Nancy, lying on a bed with her two babies, could have been of herself and the twins when they were small. It wasn't only the physical resemblance, though that was striking in itself. The look in the woman's eyes – as if these two monsters had somehow landed in her life unannounced, to possess her – captured Lara exactly in her early days with the babies. The grey shadow looming on the white wall behind her trapped her to the bed. It was as much part of the story as the figures.

Lara gazed at the image and her eyes filled with tears. Trapped was the right word. Those babies had unwittingly built a prison for her out of duty, fatigue and love; through no fault of their own, they had sapped her and made her too timid.

But now, finally, Stephen had given her back her courage.

The door to his study opened and he stood there, holding a piece of paper, a smile spotlighting his face.

'What is it?' Lara said, closing the book and putting it on the sofa beside her.

'Something incredible has happened,' Stephen said. He held a piece of paper out to her. 'It's a lab report.' He sat down and put his arm round her, drawing her close. 'Look!' He ran his finger down a list of figures, to a block of text headed *Conclusion*. 'Read it, Lara.'

' "Based on the DNA Analysis, the alleged father, Sam Miller . . ." '

'That's me,' Stephen said.

' "Cannot be excluded as the biological father of the Child, Oliver Wayland . . ." ' Lara stopped and clasped her hand over her mouth.

'Read on,' Stephen said, holding her close.

' "Because they share the same genetic markers." I can't go on, Stephen,' she said.

He took the paper from her and carried on reading. ' "The probability of the stated relationship is indicated below, as compared to an untested, unrelated person of the same ethnicity." And below, Lara, it says this,' Stephen said, his face burning with triumph. ' "Probability Percentage: ninety-nine point nine nine four two per cent." '

'But how did you—' Lara's mind was whirling.

'I'd got this lab lined up in town for a rush job. I thought it was going to be hard to get samples, but Olly's hair in my hat, the night of the circus, was a godsend. Lots of roots.'

Lara drew away from Stephen. She felt as if her chest was caving in.

'All these years I had this suspicion . . . and this was what it was all about,' he said, taking her by the shoulders and turning her to face his own triumphant gaze. 'I wondered when you told me you were expecting, but you were so sure of your dates I put it to the back of my mind.'

'No.' Lara broke away from him again and put her hands over her eyes.

'I found out it was twins, you know. Soon after they were born.'

'If you had doubts,' Lara said, turning to him, 'why didn't you come back and tell me?'

'I wasn't in a position to do so back then. I was broke, remember? You couldn't get tests like these back then anyway.' He waved the paper at her. 'Nothing could have been proved. And even if it could, if I was wrong, what then? I did the honourable thing. I got out. I behaved like the very soul of honour. You have to respect that, Lara. But I've always wondered. And I've done my research. Do you know how difficult it is to date a twin pregnancy?'

'Yes,' Lara said in a small voice. Tears were rolling down her cheeks now.

'And if we take the fact that you're not exactly regular—'

'How did you—' She looked up at him, but he seemed distant from her, his energy making him unreachable.

'What you thought was ten weeks could easily have been just eight . . .'

'But the dating scan?'

'Even now, dating scans before twenty weeks are only accurate in about ninety per cent of cases.' Stephen recited this like a script. 'And,' he said, 'back then it would have been even less. Again, the twin thing would complicate it. I always had my doubts, you know. And then, when I saw the first photographs of Bella and Olly . . .'

'What?'

'And Olly particularly struck me. Surely you noticed how alike we are?'

'Yes. YES. STOP!' Lara said, putting her hands over her ears.

They both sat still for what seemed like hours. Eventually, Stephen took her hand.

'I thought you'd be pleased,' he said, bringing his mouth close to her ear.

'It's all such a mess,' Lara said. 'It was bad. But now it's even worse. I can't think straight, I can't even—'

'It's simple though.' Stephen laughed. 'He's got no claim on them now. It's all about us, Lara! We have so much time to make up. You, me, our kids.' He kissed her neck.

'This is too brutal, too sudden. I've got to go,' she said, tearing herself away from him and standing up. 'I need time to take it in.' All she could see now was Marcus, alone, coming back to a cold, empty house in Brighton after a terrible tour of some godforsaken play with no one to greet him, no one really to live for, the family he thought he had as good as dead.

She ran across the kitchen to the back door and turned the handle. It was locked.

'Unlock the door. Please, Stephen. Let me out.'

He stood and walked slowly towards her. 'I can't let you out there. It's far too dangerous, remember? With Elizabeth Sanders. She might strike any minute.' He took her face in his hands. 'And you can't really drive now. Not with those eyes.' He bent down and kissed each of her eyelids.

She tried to move away, but he held her too tightly.

'Not now, Stephen. I need a bit of time.'

'There's been too much time.'

'It's all been such a waste.' She looked up at him, her eyes overflowing, the tears tumbling out of them and running down her cheeks. 'All those years and now it's such a mess. The children – I can't. Their lives pulled away from them, everything a lie.'

'Shh,' he said, pulling her to him. She felt him harden against her, press into her. What was he trying to do?

'Not now Stephen. I can't – please drive me back.'

'We've only just started though. We've got so much catching up to do,' he said, his lips buried in her hair. He pulled her gently but firmly down on to the kitchen floor. She tried to move him away, but he was insistent. Then he was straddling her. His hand worked at his fly.

'No, Stephen,' she said. This was not right. It was not what she wanted.

He was on her, his hand now up her skirt, his fingers up inside her.

'You can't leave me now, you know,' he said, closing his mouth over hers. She gasped as, in one rough movement, he pushed himself deep inside her. It hurt, because she didn't want it, and he thrust so violently. Her head whirled as if she were seasick – this was the opposite of the worshipful lovemaking she had received during the night. Struggling underneath him, trying to get away, seemed only to excite him more. He was staking his claim and she no longer had any part in it.

'Please Stephen . . .' she said, but he was beyond hearing her.

'I love you Lara,' he said, over and over, until he came, again inside her.

When it was over, after he had lain, panting, on top of her, the rhythms of his breath in counterpoint to the heaves of her sobbing, he knelt up at her side.

'You don't know how much time it has been for me,' he said. As he spoke, he removed her clothes. 'Look at you. You're so lovely. I've never loved anyone else but you, Lara. You're like a disease for me. I've been waiting all this while to be with you, waiting for those twins to grow up and be old enough for you to leave Marcus. I'd never, ever, split up your family. You know that. I am chivalry, I am.'

He laughed, but there was no joy in it. 'The irony is though, by leaving you, I did just that. We could have had a happy little family, Lara. You, me, our babies. It could have been perfect.'

Naked now beneath him, her eyes screwed tight against the light that filtered though the shaded kitchen windows, Lara nodded, wretched. What happiness they had lost. Could he be blamed for losing his balance over what he had just found out? She opened her eyes and looked up at him. 'What about Jack though? Where's the chivalry in that?'

He shifted and lay down on the floor next to her, stretching his fully clothed body against her naked skin. He cradled her head next to his. She held herself stiffly against him.

'Fair do's Lara,' he whispered in her ear. 'He'll have to be mine now. After all, Marcus had my two for all those years.'

Again, Lara struggled to get away from him, but he held her tight.

'Didn't you wonder sometimes, Lara? When you looked at our boy, and he looked so like me? Didn't you ever wonder that you might have got your dates wrong?'

Lara nodded miserably. She had, but it was all too late by the time the thought struck her, and she had buried it away, far, far beneath her consciousness.

'Oh Lara. Why didn't you come and get me and tell me? Just think how happy we would have been. That was so bad of you. In a way, I suppose, you robbed us both.'

'It would have made so many people so miserable,' she whispered.

'And this is going to be *easy*?'

Still holding her down, he got to his feet. Then he scooped her up, pressing her close to him as if she were his baby. She realised, from the shuddering of his chest, he was crying.

'Oh Stephen,' she said. 'I'm so, so, sorry.' She stroked his cheek. His tears tracked down his face, along the skin of her arm and around her hip. Like a thread, tying her to him.

'Think how happy we would have been,' he said again. Holding her tight to him, he carried her up the stairs.

'I need to go, Stephen,' she said, trying to appeal to what reason he might have left.

'You love me though, Lara, don't you? You've always loved me. You said so.'

He laid her on his bed and swiftly curled up behind her, to hold her in place, as he wept into her shoulder. She could barely breathe, he held her so tightly. They lay there for a long time, his face pressed into her back and, in the end, her system shutting down after the shocks it had been subjected to, she tumbled into an obliterating sleep.

She woke much later to the phone ringing, echoing across the bare wooden house. The day had disappeared. Its final throes of light striped the room in long, slanting shards across the bedroom floor. Stephen's arms were still wrapped, vice-like, around her. The phone stopped. Then it rang again.

'That'll be Marcus,' Lara said. 'Wondering where I am.'

'I don't think so.' Stephen kissed the back of her neck.

A scream lifted into the dusk from somewhere outside, somewhere up the hill behind the house. Others joined it. In the cage of Stephen's arms, Lara tensed.

'What's that?' she said, her heart racing.

'Coyotes on the kill,' he whispered into her ear. 'Like a group of girls being murdered in a field.'

The phone stopped ringing.

'Now. I think we need a bath. Don't you?' He moved away from her and rolled her on to her back. 'So lovely,' he said, as he looked at her.

'But Jack will need picking up,' Lara said. 'They'll all be wondering where I am.'

'Don't worry, love,' he said. 'That's been taken care of.'

'What do you mean?'

'I rang James this morning and told him the tree was still blocking the road, and it's not likely to be cleared up for a couple of days. He said he'd tell Marcus. He's very good like that, James.'

Lara curled back up on to her side and looked away.

'It means we can just relax and be together,' Stephen said, as he rose and went through to run the big, round bath. 'We've got all the time in the world.'

Lara lay there and considered the slenderness of her options. Even if she managed to get out of the house, there was no way she could drive down to Trout Island. Without her contact lenses she could only see a foot in front of her. If she walked it would take hours. The only way she knew was on the road, so Stephen would be able to follow her. If she went through the forest, though . . . But there were miles of woods out there, with bears and coyotes and snakes.

The phone rang again. Before Lara got across the bed to pick it up, Stephen was there, his hand on the receiver.

'I don't think you should be answering phones, Lara,' he said. 'Leave it to the professional.' He picked up the phone. 'Hello? Oh, hi, Marcus. Yes she's fine. I think she's having a little nap. No, no.' Stephen held his finger up to his mouth as he listened to what Marcus had to say. 'It's too far to walk, no. They're very inefficient round here. We're just going to have to sit it out. Oh. That's good.' He listened a little more then laughed at something Marcus said. 'OK. Yes, cheers mate then. Yeah. 'Bye.'

Lara looked up at Stephen.

'He says Jack had a great day at Gina's and she's offered to have him overnight.'

'That's good then,' Lara said, wondering what Marcus had told Gina about where she was, and whether her friend had drawn any conclusions.

'Tub time.' Stephen picked Lara up and carried her through to the bathroom, where he put her into the hot, deep-drawn bubble bath. He didn't get in, but knelt beside her. Then, with great care and attention, he washed her, using his bare, soaped hand to cover every inch of her skin.

'I think I owe you for earlier,' he said, bending to kiss her breasts. 'I'm sorry about that. I got carried away.'

His expert hands caressed her, his beautiful mouth explored her, until, despite herself, she felt herself turning inside out.

'Stay there, Lara,' he said, getting up and leaving her while the water still lapped around her, while she still pulsed deep inside. 'I've got just the thing for you.'

Lara did as she was told, wondering what on earth he had in store for her next. After about half an hour he returned, with a bottle of champagne in an ice bucket and one glass, which he put on the console by the bath, across the room from her. She could do with a drink, she thought. There was nothing else she could do now and it was dark outside.

With his back to her, Stephen poured her a glass. Then he turned and handed it to her.

'To us,' he said.

She drank deeply, downing her glass in one. He quickly refilled it and again she drank. Almost instantly the numbing sensation of the alcohol crept over her, and her limbs grew heavy. When the whole bottle was gone he helped her out of the bath, wrapping her in a thick fluffy towel so large it trailed on the floor behind her, as if she were some sort of bride.

'Come and see.' As he led her to his bedroom, she realised she could barely feel her legs. The sheets were strewn with fresh rose petals, and crammed around the bed were vases and vases of blooms still on their stems. They weighted the air with their scent.

'A byre fit for a queen,' Stephen said.

'The roses were from you,' Lara said, her voice slurring.

'Damn straight they were,' he said, as she collapsed on to the mattress and passed out.

Forty

LARA OPENED ONE EYE AND TRIED TO FOCUS ON THE
pillow. Every part of her ached.

As she pieced together where she was and what had
happened, snatches of barely registered images flashed through
her mind – Stephen's face, looming over her, lit by a candle,
perhaps, from below. She saw orange, she saw red. She saw
him in close-up, like an owl, or a dog.

Then there she was, somehow viewed from above, juddering
so every part of her moved, a rag doll. A ribbon digging into
the flesh of her arm, rose petals crushed up against her face.
The smell, the stink of rose, of rotten rose water, seeping
through her skin, working into her bones.

She shifted on the mattress. Stephen's arm lay over her,
weighty with sleep.

Taking his wrist, careful not to wake him, she freed herself
from his embrace and swung her legs so she sat on the edge of
the bed. Her head hurt, and she badly needed to pee. But what
she noticed most of all was the pain between and around the
backs of her legs. Passing her hand over herself, to the source of
the hurt, she drew it away and found a streak of blood.

Standing, a little shaky, she turned to look down at Stephen, who was still fast asleep, smiling to himself. He seemed so beautiful there, like a dark angel. But what had he done to her in the night? She remembered drinking champagne – too much champagne – and then she could recall nothing else.

She staggered to the bathroom and leaned on the sink, examining her bloodshot eyes in the mirror. Her arms shook, supporting her weight against the basin. She noticed the red weals on her wrists.

She splashed her face, took a burning pee and levered herself on to the bidet, where she ran warm water to soothe the stinging pain. Taking his sandalwood-scented soap, she began to wash herself. She tried to formulate a plan, but her brain couldn't string any thoughts together. A movement caught the corner of her eye. She looked up. Stephen leaned against the door, gazing down at her.

'Don't stop,' he said. She lowered her eyes, ashamed. He knelt in front of her. 'Let me help you.'

'I don't know if I can,' she said as he worked his hands between her soapy thighs where she hurt the most. But, somehow, he picked her up, using that most intimate touch. Jamming her up against the door and ignoring her gasps of pain, he entered her yet again, pushing into her until she fell, sobbing, against his strong, scarred shoulder.

'Can I get dressed now?' she asked as he dried her once more after another shared shower.

'I don't think so,' he said. 'It would be a sin to cover up all that beauty.'

So she was naked as he served her coffee, eggs and toast at the dining-room table, under the great wooden fan that turned and circulated chilled air around the space. She didn't feel like eating at all, but she was light-headed and dizzy, so she forced down a couple of mouthfuls.

'So this is what we'll do,' he said, as if he were making a shopping list. 'We're going to tell the twins. You and Marcus will get a divorce, you and I will marry and we'll live happily ever after.'

'You make it sound so easy.'

'I've got something to show you.' He picked up an iPad and slipped on to the bench to sit right beside her, his hand on her thigh. He held the screen thoughtfully close up in front of her and stroked his way to some photographs.

'This is my house in LA,' he said. 'I thought we'd keep it. Do you like it? If you don't, I can always buy another.' He took her through a series of photographs of large, beautifully furnished rooms, a dark-bottomed infinity pool, and a night-time picture of a terrace hanging on the edge of a hill above the lurex sprawl of Los Angeles.

'We'll sit here in the evenings and I'll watch you drink champagne.' He pulled across another picture of a red bedroom, with a beautifully dressed oversized bed, brocaded hangings and what appeared to be an original Klimt hanging above the pillows. 'I had it decorated with you in mind. You like red, don't you? And this –' he opened another photo of a vast, more minimally furnished room, with the same view as the terrace – 'is for Olly. See the guitar.' He pointed to the wall. 'An original Les Paul. Owned by Kurt Cobain. When I found it I knew he'd love it.'

'But, when—'

'This is for Bella.' He showed her another bedroom, softer, with more pattern to it. 'She could have my Alice Neel in there. But,' he smiled at Lara, 'she'll have to keep it tidier than her Brighton room.'

'How do you know—'

'Hello beautiful breast,' he said, and bent to kiss her left nipple.

Lara's mind whirled. The food had lifted the hangover and ache that had clouded her brain.

This wasn't romance. It wasn't nostalgia. It wasn't *what-if*.

She had been so, so stupid.

'You've got it all worked out, haven't you?' she said.

'I've had long enough to think it over,' he said, drawing a line with his finger down her front, from her breast to her navel.

She tensed her stomach muscles and tried to draw away, but his other hand remained firmly on her leg. 'You've been very clever, haven't you? It wasn't coincidence we bumped into each other, was it?'

'Got me in one!' He winked at her.

'Tell me how you did it,' she said, trying to sound more fascinated than horrified, trying to buy some time.

Stephen sat back, extending his right arm along the back of the bench, so one hand held her firmly by the shoulder. The other gesticulated freely as he spoke.

'I think we've already established that I am chivalry itself.' He smiled at her. 'I've been lying low, waiting for those twins to reach their sixteenth birthday so they no longer need their cosy little nuclear family and I can come back and claim what is rightfully mine. You did say that, didn't you? When I had to go. You did say that we belong to one another?'

'Yes.' Her breath came in short, shallow gasps, but she tried to look admiring. 'I did.'

'And I was extremely lucky because, if you have a bit of money to pay the right people, it's very easy to follow what a person is doing these days. I've been keeping tabs on you, Lara Wayland.

'Poor old Marcus. His career didn't ever really happen, did it? They gave him a good review in the *Guardian* for that National Theatre young people's tour he did, but generally he doesn't even get a mention, does he? I did worry whether he made enough to support you. I even thought about slipping a few quid into your Co-op account.'

'How did you know about that?' Lara gasped. Even Marcus had no idea about her Co-op account.

'Ways and means,' Stephen said. 'Look at this.'

He picked up the iPad and searched through the photograph library.

'Look.' He held it in front of her. There she was, getting out of the car in her local Sainsbury's car park, the Brighton sea wind whipping through her hair as she reached into the boot for something. 'That was last year. This is a bit earlier. They used to send me prints. I scanned them in for my records.' He flicked to a picture of her struggling up the hill back to her house, the twins in a double buggy laden with bags. 'You'd been Christmas shopping. You really maxed out your plastic,' he said. 'Naughty Lara.'

'But I had no idea . . .'

'Course you didn't,' he laughed. 'That's the point. And then, as time went on, and these two got bigger . . .' He scrolled on to a photograph of Bella, aged about thirteen, at a bus stop in her school uniform, bending over her mobile phone. 'She began to look like you.' His finger lingered over the photo. 'Just like you. And he, the naughty lad . . .' The next image was of Olly in swimming trunks, sitting on the beach, staring out to sea, an incriminatingly fat roll-up in his hand. From the look of him, it must have been taken the previous summer. 'Well then, how could you not have suspected that I am the boy's father?' Stephen held his hands up to frame his face, assuming the exact expression Olly wore in the photo. Breaking the pose, he shrugged and smiled at Lara.

She looked down at her own hands, so tightly twisted that her knuckles had turned blue. Shame spread over her like a shroud. She had not had an inkling that her family were being trailed. Not a clue.

'But look,' Stephen said, expansive again. 'What a guy I am. I had all this evidence and *still* I waited until they turned sixteen. I'm a man of my word.' He lifted her hair to kiss her neck. 'I didn't get in the way of their exams,' he whispered into her ear. 'I wanted them to have the best start.'

'That was very kind of you,' Lara said, trying to choke her fear back down again.

'It was, wasn't it?' He laid his head on her shoulder.

'But what about Jack, though?' Lara said. The thought of her little boy brought tears to her eyes. She wished she was back home in Brighton, curled up, reading him a bedtime story in their safe little house. But then she remembered it had only *seemed* safe. Unseen eyes had been watching their every move.

'I know,' Stephen said, heaving a weary sigh and taking her by the shoulders to face him. 'But how long am I supposed to wait, Lara? When do *I* get my turn at happiness?' He smiled. 'Good job about the abortion though, eh? Or you'd be pregnant now and that would've complicated matters somewhat.'

Lara closed her eyes. She felt sick. Sick and cold.

'And I know you're not happy. Drinking wine on the sofa in the afternoon, all those arguments with him.' He stroked to another image, which, on his touch, began to play.

'I won't be angry with you if you tell me the truth,' she heard herself say from the screen in his hand.

'OK. Well, you look a little, well, bulgy in it,' Marcus's voice replied.

'*I* thought you looked lovely,' Stephen said, pausing the video and showing her herself standing in the bedroom in her tight pink dress, hurt stinging her eyes.

'How?'

'Laptop. That router I delivered was rather clever. It was as if I was sitting inside your computer. A lovely place to be.'

The router he delivered? What remained of Lara's spirit swirled away, like the last grains of sand in an hourglass.

'Poor thing, you've got goosebumps,' Stephen said. 'Here, have this.' He pulled over a deerskin from the back of the sofa. 'Fur on skin,' he murmured as he tucked it round her bare shoulders. 'So beautiful.' His hand fell back to her thigh.

Lara caught the faint, sweet tang of animal putrefaction on the pelt.

'So you knew we were coming here,' Lara said, trying to keep him talking and away from her. Despite its smell, she was grateful for the cover the deerskin offered. She drew it tight around her.

'No. Leave it open so I can see you, please,' Stephen said, arranging it so she was exposed again. 'Oh Lara. You don't get it, do you? Do you really think James wanted Marcus for his *Macbeth*? He took a lot of persuading, I can tell you. It got quite expensive!'

'Expensive?'

'Fully retractable seating, re-arrangeable into eight con-figurations. Custom-designed and covered in the costly red option. Your favourite colour crops up again.'

'You mean you bribed James to bring us here?'

'"But Stephen,"' Stephen took on James's accent and mannerisms exactly, '"we so need more accommodation for our *actors*. And the Larssen place is such a *bargain*." I'm glad you found my work so convincing. Lara,' he went on, slipping back into his own voice. 'I didn't want you and Marcus stepping into a love nest.'

'You made up the Larssen story?'

'Nope. Horrible, isn't it? But it inspired me and I worked a bit of theatre magic on the place. A nice old carpet soaked in the entrails from the doe you are currently wearing, as it happens. A couple of photographs. A bed. Some manacles.' He rolled the word round his mouth like it was a strawberry. 'I even hid a hunk of dead mama deer here down in the basement for an authentic miasma.

'James and Betty were reliably busy and only too happy to let me sort it all out for them. Not that they'd ever question a thing I do. They try to appear cool but they're really just proper little starfuckers like all the others. It wasn't exactly hard for me to retain their "friendship", if that's what you call it, to help me brew up my plan.'

'They know everything?' Lara said.

'No,' Stephen laughed. 'Only enough to make them useful to me. I knew James had taught Marcus back in the wilds of time, so I searched him out. And then the whole stalker business – which really *did* upset me, Lara – well, that proved most useful for bringing out Betty's big old maternal tits. It really got them on my side, looking after me.'

'But the stalker is still a problem for you,' Lara said. Stephen stopped, froze for a few minutes, a distant smile on his lips and one eyebrow raised, as he surveyed her. Then he jumped up.

'Oh, I don't think we need to worry about Elizabeth Sanders any more,' he said. 'Be back in a tick. Don't go anywhere.' He went into the bathroom.

What did that mean? Alone at last, Lara cast around the room for an exit. She knew all the doors were locked, and the windows were covered with secured screens. With a rush of joy she made out the unmistakeable shape of her handbag on the kitchen counter, where she had left it when she first arrived, when the world had been a different place.

Drawing the deerskin around her, she shuffled over and tipped out the contents. She scrabbled wildly through the purse, keys, pills, Ventolin and make-up, all so strange to her now, as if they belonged to someone else entirely. Finding her phone, she unlocked it with trembling fingers. But, with a groan, she realised it had no signal whatsoever. She flung it down and looked about wildly, more like a feral beast under the animal pelt than the woman she once had been. She spotted the house phone, which Stephen had put by the cooker when he was scrambling the eggs, dived towards it and quickly punched the number of the Trout Island digs into the keypad. But, to her horror, when she pressed the green 'go' button, the sound of the connection being made was relayed at great volume throughout the house.

The bathroom door flew open. Stephen rushed out, grabbed the phone from Lara and threw it into the kitchen sink, which was full of cold, soapy water. He wheeled round towards her, his jaw twitching.

'I said I'd take care of it,' he said. 'We don't need to call anyone right now. They all think we're trapped up here by that fallen tree.'

'But don't you think they'll start to wonder soon?' she said. 'They could send someone up and I could climb over the tree, or someone will come up here and check it out.'

'Now why on earth would they worry? James and Betty will be only too delighted that I've got you up here. Marcus will be enjoying being looked after by the lovely Selina and, in fact,' Stephen said, tidying up the things Lara had strewn over the kitchen counter and putting them back in her bag, 'in fact, I wouldn't be surprised if James isn't telling Marcus this instant about how he drove up here and found the tree and how impassable it was, how difficult it would be to get around it even on foot.'

Lara stood there, clutching the deerskin to her, her mouth wide open.

'Now then, I think we'd be more comfortable if we moved to the sofa. Don't you? Would you like to watch a movie?'

He steered her through to the living area. 'I don't think you need this any more,' he said, removing the deerskin from her shoulders. 'Not now you're away from that big old wooden fan.'

He sat next to her, scrolled through a list of films on his iPad and made a selection. Using the remote control, he switched on the large, flat screen TV that he had pulled up close in front of them.

The opening credits to his first-ever movie rolled on to the screen.

'I thought we'd take a tour through my back catalogue,' he said, putting his arm around her and drawing her close to him. 'Start at the beginning. Can you see alright?'

Lara nodded.

'Brilliant,' Stephen said, ninety minutes of his young self later. Lara thought perhaps she could detect the hurt he had been carrying with him when he made that first film. He was beautiful then and he certainly hadn't lost his looks over the years. But beautiful was not a word she would now use to describe him. He was not beautiful at all.

'You're tired,' he said, as he switched off the TV and stood her up, taking her by the hands. 'How about a lie-down?'

'I'm fine. I'm really good. Thank you.' She tried to work her hand free from his. She felt so exposed.

'Nonsense. Come with me. This is our life now, Lara.' And he led her back upstairs to the bedroom, where the bed stood testament to the night before, all red splattered with rose petals and her own blood.

'Lie down,' he said. 'On your front.'

What now, she thought, as she heard him move to the other side of the room. The bed shifted as he came back towards her and placed his knee close to her arm. Then he poured something wet on her back, and the smell of orange trees in full blossom assaulted her nostrils. Instantly she was pulled back to the cheap spring holiday she and Marcus had taken near Seville, when the twins were tiny. All sunlight and laughter.

It was like being kicked awake. They *had* been happy. She *had* had a good life. And now she had completely and utterly blown it.

Then Stephen's hands were on her, smoothing and kneading and pummelling her body into abeyance. As he worked on her, massaging her back, her legs and deep into her scalp, spreading oil into her hair, he told her the story of their future life together. She listened, her head heavy on her forearms, and she realised how the picture he was painting was almost identical to the one she had drawn herself, in her dreams, since she had arrived in Trout Island.

After a while, his massage became more insistent and he rolled her over to face him.

She knew she had no choice but yet again to let him have her.

Forty-One

WHEN IT WAS OVER SHE LAY ON THE BED, PINIONED BY HIS limbs, forcing herself to stay awake so she didn't miss her moment. Eventually, when his breath became slower and fuller, the sketch of a snore, she extricated herself, taking care not to wake him. She turned to look at him as he lay there, an advert or bliss, his terrible will dormant. Aided by her myopia, she once again glimpsed a sort of beauty – the arch of his eyebrow, the angle of his lip. But it was like one of those extraordinary flowers that stink of death.

She slipped out of the bedroom and tiptoed, naked, along the corridor, leaving a scent trail of sex and neroli. She opened the first door she came to and found herself in another bedroom. Her plan was to open a fly screen and drop down to the ground from the first floor.

Thinking perhaps she might find some clothes to wear, she opened a wardrobe. Inside, she found first Stephen's disguises for getting around incognito – Sam, Circus Guy: denim jackets and Day-Glo T-shirts. Behind them, causing her to pause and catch her breath, she uncovered a brown UPS delivery guy outfit. Beyond that hung a khaki uniform, like a security guard might wear in a supermarket car park. She frowned, trying to think how on earth—

But then she stopped, completely stunned by what she discovered next. Draped round the last hanger was a filthy beige woman's coat with a chequered tan and turquoise silk scarf slung around it. Dangling in front of the coat was a plastic carrier bag. Horrified, Lara reached in and found a straight mousey wig, a pair of large oval tortoiseshell sunglasses and a tan baker boy cap. She examined the wig. It was clumped together in places by clots of what looked like blood.

Elizabeth Sanders – or what remained of her – was on this hanger.

Was this what Stephen meant when he said they didn't need to worry about her any more? Lara felt sick. What was this man she thought she had known capable of?

But she didn't have time to think. She had to move. Pulling on the soiled coat, she darted over to the window and lifted the latch. It opened easily. The fly screen presented more of a problem. It appeared to be nailed to the frame. Searching back in the wardrobe, down on her knees, rummaging around the floor, Lara found a wooden baseball bat, which she grabbed and forced against the fly screen, bending the mesh outwards. She realised she needed to use more force, so, desperate now, she used the bat to knock the edges of the screen away from the window frame. After the third bang, the thing fell out and landed on the ground outside with a clatter. Lara was halfway out of the window when the door behind her burst open to reveal Stephen, naked, levelling his gun straight at her.

She had blown it.

'What are you doing, Lara?' He grabbed her and pulled

408

her back into the room, throwing her down on to the floor in front of the wardrobe so her face met the bloody wig.

'What have you done with her!' she said, tangling her fingers in the artificial hair, all thoughts of strategy draining from her. 'What have you done with Elizabeth Sanders?'

'Nothing she didn't deserve,' he said, lifting the gun so it pointed at her head. 'Now, take that disgusting coat off.'

'But what is this?' she said, as she clutched at the wig and picked up the sunglasses, which she now noticed were cracked. 'Is this just another costume? Was it you dressed up as her?'

'Take the coat off.'

Crying now, Lara shook her head.

'YOU WILL,' he roared, 'DO AS I SAY.' He reached forward and ripped it from her shoulders.

'That's better,' he said, suddenly calm again. He stepped back, took a deep breath, swung his weapon over his shoulder and leaned against the door post. 'Think for a minute, Lara,' he said, speaking slowly and calmly now, as if she were a child. 'How could I have been Elizabeth Sanders? I was driving when we were coming back from the circus and she nearly forced us off the road, remember. Nearly KILLED US ALL.' He closed his eyes and breathed in, flaring his nostrils, steadying himself. Then he smiled again and looked at her. 'Even I can't be in two places at once.'

Confused, Lara put her hands to her face and tried to blot him out of her mind.

'If you must know, Lara, the original Elizabeth Sanders did exist. But she doesn't any more. So I had to draft in another one. Someone tough and in need of cash. Unwittingly, Betty offered me Trudi Staines on a plate. She was, until recently, perfect, and I like perfect. Theatre background, expert in make-up to disguise that grotesque disfigurement of hers.' Like Olly had, Stephen drew the smile shape of Trudi Staines's scar from his mouth to his ear.

'This, though,' he bent forward to pick up the beige coat from where it had fallen when he tore it off her, 'is the genuine Sanders outfit, rescued from the original back in Los Angeles and worn by her rather overenthusiastic replacement. I'm going to have to get it cleaned up again now, which is a total pain.' He held it up to Lara, showing her mud stains on the outside, as if it had been dragged over wet ground. He then flipped it over to reveal a darker, red-brown bloom on the inside. 'That stupid bitch Betty put a proper spanner in the works, though.'

'What do you mean?' Lara's mind was racing.

'What an interfering old queen. The WHOLE POINT was that you would come to me, all like this,' he waved his hands in the air, and gave a feeble wail, 'and we'd be pushed together by the trying circumstances. But Betty stuck her big nose in where it wasn't welcome. And to make matters worse, little Trudi started showing her real colours, started getting all difficult on me, wanting more money, threatening this, that and the other. So unprofessional. What's a guy to do?'

Lara collapsed on the floor, sobbing.

'Please let me go,' she said. 'Please?'

'That's ridiculous, Lara. This could be perfect. All you've got to do is change your attitude.'

Lara scrambled to her feet and tried to make a dash for the door. Taking him by surprise, she managed to get halfway down the stairs before he tackled her, bringing them both tumbling down on to the kitchen floor at the bottom. Lara, who had hit her head on a newel post, blacked out.

* * *

It might have been a few seconds or a few hours later, she didn't know. But she woke to find a pain in her temple and Stephen out cold beside her on the floor, a cut on his cheek, like a felled action hero. She wondered briefly if he was still alive, but she didn't want to miss her opportunity again. She tried the outside doors but, as she feared, they were all locked, so she fled back up the stairs to the bedroom where she had knocked out the fly screen. Without pausing, she rolled out of the window, grasping the sill with her hands, and dropped down naked to the ground beneath. As she landed, she stumbled back against a metal dustbin, sending it clattering over. Her finger-tips, snagged on the window frame, were sore and bleeding and her head still throbbed, but none of this registered for her because she had escaped the house. She was free.

She looked around wildly, wondering what she was going to do. Then, with no more conscious thought than an animal heading for shelter, she fled towards the woods, across the grassy garden, where snakes lay in the woodpile, dozing against the afternoon heat.

'LARA!'

Without stopping, she glanced back. Stephen was staggering out of the back door, blood on his face. He was on her trail. She ran and ran, thistles tearing at her feet, brambles ripping at her skin, for the cover of the trees. Her breath came in rasping sobs, but she knew this was down to fear, not exhaustion. She could do this. She was a runner, and he was barely able to stand up.

She streamed along the path, up the hill towards the heart of the forest. Anyone watching would have thought they were looking at a fleeing wood nymph. But the satyr on her tail was not on foot. If Lara had heard anything other than her own breath, her own pounding heart, it would have been the dented red Wrangler as Stephen started the engine. She pounded the ground, the steep incline no obstacle to her. The fact she had no clothes on didn't give her the slightest pause for thought as she whipped through dogwood and alder, tripped on knotweed and dark, protruding roots. Three times she fell, three times she got up and, without stopping to brush the dirt from her sweating body, she moved on.

Running for her life.

All at once the roar was on her. She turned her head to see the monstrous red vehicle tearing up the mountain behind her, bearing up on her at an angle so impossibly steep it seemed as if it were leaping. Lara quickened her pace. As she ran, she clocked the brambled tangle of undergrowth on either side of the path. She had to do it. If she was going to get away, she had to go there.

Using the turn to propel herself, she launched off the path and into the trees and darkness, where the dazzle of sunlight was almost entirely masked by dense foliage. Her eyes took a few moments to adjust to the new conditions, but her legs kept going, flying over the bushes, shedding skin and flesh on to bystanding thorns.

And then her shin found the half-submerged, tumbledown wall, the forest secret, the leavings of a past people. Her foot, lodged in a crevice, stayed where it was as her body plunged forward. She heard the sickening crack of her own shinbone as she tumbled into the ditch at the other side of the wall, her face smashing into the dirt of a mound of newly dug earth. Soil in her mouth, her tooth cracked, her lip bitten. The world stopped and she felt a pins and needle sensation crawl over the back of her skull as she realised with a sickening lurch of horror that right up against her face was a hand. A woman's hand, with dirt under its bitten fingernails, sticking up, out of the earth.

'Oh, Lara. What are you doing?'

And Stephen was there, standing over her, his chest heaving, his stance unsteady. But he still had the strength to haul her over his shoulder and pile her into the back of the Wrangler. After that the pain of her leg, as it was carelessly lifted and shifted into the vehicle, made sure she knew nothing more.

Forty-Two

MARCUS WAS WORKING LATE AGAIN, AND HAD TOLD BELLA to get in a Pepperoni Special from the village pizza shop. At least it had forced her out of her bedroom, and the walk had made her feel a little less like death. But only a little.

It was a complete pain her mother being stuck up at Stephen Molloy's place. Her dad was too busy rehearsing to do any shopping or cooking. And as for Olly, forget it. Even though she had spent most of the time holed up in her stinking bedroom, she suspected her freak of a brother hadn't been home for over two days. He was no doubt running around in the woods, taking drugs and killing small animals. Well, she was glad. The longer he stayed away, the better.

At least she hadn't been lumbered with Jack. Gina down the road had him for this, the third night of their mother's absence.

As she reached the house she saw the dog sitting on the front lawn, in his usual position. He had posted himself there nearly all the time her mother had been away.

'Hello, boy,' she said, going over to pat him on the head. He gazed up at her with his droopy, doleful eyes, his interest piqued by what was in her big, grease-stained package.

She went inside, opened the box and tore off two slices. She carried one out, oily-fingered, and threw to the dog, who ate it in two swift gulps. Then she went back indoors, switched on her mother's laptop and tried to eat the other slice, the first thing to pass her lips since Olly had attacked Sean. It hadn't seemed right to eat. But now, although she had no appetite, she was so hungry a part of her felt like it was detaching itself from her body.

The MacBook gave its usual welcome chime and Bella typed in the password her mother thought was secret. She launched Safari and logged into her own Facebook account to check what her friends back home were up to. Looking at the flash-lit photographs of her blurry peers falling over each other at beach parties and sharing balloons full of laughing gas at summer festivals, she felt very homesick, a long way away from everything she knew and loved.

She glanced at her private messages, and quickly deleted a depressing little note from Jonny, Olly's stool pigeon, saying how miserable he was, why hadn't she been in touch and that Brighton was boring without her.

Bollocks to that, she thought.

She scanned the rest of her inbox.

She wished she could speak to Sean. She had even, on her only other sortie from the house, gone round to his place. But, thinking of his mother's voice, she hadn't been able to pluck up the courage to climb the steps to his front door. She had searched Facebook for his name, but he wasn't there. It was as if he had been deleted from her life.

It was probably just as well, she thought gloomily.

She read and trashed a couple of invitations to parties she couldn't go to, and an accusatory little missive from her friend

Kat, wondering where the hell she was. The last unread message, entitled *Lookee here*, was from someone called *Your Friend*. Thinking it was probably some sort of spam or boring game app, she nearly binned it without opening it.

Instead, she took a bite of pizza and clicked it open.

What greeted her was a series of photographs, all taken from the same viewpoint, of her mother and Stephen Molloy on the porch of his house. Frowning, Bella bent forward to take a closer look. In the first picture, they were standing close together by the door, their backs to the camera. The second showed him turning her, his hand on her back. This brought their faces round so the camera was fully trained on them. He was pointing something out to her.

Then, as she clicked through to the third image, the pizza became a dead lump of dough in Bella's mouth.

Her mother had moved her hand up to his neck, and was pulling him down towards her. In the fourth they were kissing – and, from her extensive recent experience, Bella knew this wasn't the kiss of friends greeting one another. The final image showed them locked in an embrace, his hand underneath her vest, on her breast.

The first thing Bella did after she caught her breath was to click on the link that took her to *Your Friend*'s profile. But there was nothing there. No photo, no information, nothing. *Your Friend* didn't let anyone see anything unless you became his or her friend, and Bella didn't think she wanted to do that.

'Helloo!' Someone knocked at the back door. 'Anyone in?'

Bella sat still and quiet, staring at the empty profile, as, like a game of Tetris, parts of the truth began to fall into place.

She heard the back door fly screen swing open and shut.

'Bella? Lolly?' Jack called. 'Where are you?'

'Perhaps they're out,' Gina said as Jack led her through to the living room. She had Bert clamped to her hip as usual.

Bella snapped the laptop shut and looked up just as they came in.

'Bella!' Jack said, running towards her and throwing his arms round her legs as if he were a drowning boy and she a liferaft.

'Oh, hi, Bella!' Gina said. 'You were being very quiet.'

'I was doing some emails,' Bella said. 'Sorry, I was a bit involved in—' She gestured to the computer.

'Oh, that's fine,' Gina said. 'Jack was a little homesick, so I thought we'd just take a stroll down, show him how close we are.'

'Very close,' Jack said, nodding.

'So, Tom and I were wondering,' Gina said, 'whether perhaps we could offer any help getting your mom back down from off the mountain. Marcus told us about the tree and all. Well, to be honest,' Gina sat next to Bella, and put her hand on her knee, 'I know *where* she was going and *who* she was visiting.'

'You do?' Bella said in a small voice.

'I have my informant.' Gina inclined her head in Jack's direction.

'I told Gina all about how Stephen took us to the circus,' Jack said, beaming up proudly at Bella. 'And the bear.'

'Oh Jack.' Bella put her hands over her mouth.

'Don't worry, honey. I pretty much knew everything already. Not much of the very little that happens in Trout Island passes me by.'

'Oh.'

'Jack, honey, would you get me a glass of water?' Gina said. 'I'm awful thirsty.'

417

Looking proud as punch at the task being entrusted to him, Jack nodded and strode off to the kitchen.

Gina lowered her voice. 'Tom took a diversion by there on his way into work this afternoon to check out the tree-on-the-road situation. We thought perhaps we could help. Jack misses his mommy.'

'Yes,' Bella said. She feared she knew what was coming next.

'There is no tree,' Gina mouthed to Bella.

Bella nodded and closed her eyes. 'Why are you telling me this?'

'I don't want to interfere,' Gina said, which Bella thought a bit rich. 'Which is why I haven't gone straight to your dad. But what I don't understand, though, is how a mother, no matter what's going on for her, can leave her little child for so long. From what I know of your mom, it's way out of character.' Gina sat back and looked Bella in the eye. 'If you want the truth, I'm a little worried about her.'

'What am I supposed to do about it, though?' Bella said. She thought for a moment about showing Gina the photographs, but she was too ashamed. She didn't want all of this put upon her.

'Look. Your Sean has a car, doesn't he? Can't you go up there, say you were seeing if you could help? Found the tree had been moved. Find out what's going on?'

'But . . .' Bella couldn't start to tell her about Sean. There were clearly *some* things going on in Trout Island Gina didn't know about. Like, for example, how her brother was a sadistic lunatic.

'I'd go, but I've got the children. And I'm not supposed to know. If it *is* all innocent, me going up would be a disaster. I'll mind Jack. Please Bella. I'm coming to you because your mom said you're the sensible one. Couldn't you go and check on her?' Gina asked. 'It's just I've got this quirky old feeling . . .'

'Here you are, Gina,' Jack said as he carried her water through. He tried his careful best, but he still managed to spill over half the glass before he got it to her.

'Can I – can I speak to Sean please?' Bella said, twirling the old-fashioned, curly Pinter phone wire round her finger.

'Is this the English girl?' his mother said.

'Please, I've got to talk to him . . .'

The mother hung up.

She stood at Sean's house waiting for someone to answer her knock. Eventually, she heard leather heels click along echoing wood and the door opened, letting out a cool wave of beeswax-scented air.

'Yes?' A short, dumpy woman in a grey checked dress filled the doorway.

'Mrs McLoughlin. I need to talk to Sean.'

'Don't you think you've left that rather too late?' his mother said. A serious-looking woman with short, grey hair and half-moon reading glasses at the end of her nose, she was, Bella remembered Sean saying, an accountant who worked from home. Which meant she was never away from her sentry post.

Bella grabbed the woman's hand.

'Please,' she said. 'It's urgent.'

'I cannot let you see him.' Her voice sounded clipped and hoarse. 'You've been too cruel to him. In one week, you, young woman, have turned my son—'

'Mom, it's cool,' Sean appeared, towering behind his mother in the gloom of the hall. 'Let me speak with her.'

His mother looked round and up at him, then back at Bella.

'If you—' she started at Bella.

'Thank you Mom,' Sean said. 'I can deal with this.' He held the front door open, making an archway with his arm. As his mother walked underneath, she glanced up at him, shaking her head. Sean slipped out on to the porch, closing the door behind him.

The two of them stood and stared at each other. Bella closed her eyes, the tears running down her face. Stepping forward, he wrapped his arms around her.

'I've missed you so much,' he whispered into her hair. 'When you didn't answer my calls I thought you didn't want to see me any more, that you thought me weak.'

'I was just so ashamed,' she said.

'So was I,' he laughed, his voice cracking.

'And I didn't want to give Olly any more reasons for harming you.'

'We can't let him win, Bella.'

'What did you do?' Bella asked. 'When you got back that day?'

'Ran for my bed. Hid under the sheets. Luckily Mom had gone to the city for a couple of days, so I had time to sort myself out. She doesn't know. No one knows. She just thinks you've broken my heart. Just!'

'You didn't go to hospital? I thought—'

'What would I have said?'

'How are you now?'

'Sore, still. Managing with Advil. But I'll soon be mended.'

'Thank God.'

It was only after she had buried her face in his chest and held him tight that she remembered what she had to do.

'Sean, you've got to help me,' she said, looking up at him.

'What's he done now?' Sean said, his jaw tightening.

'It's got nothing to do with Olly, Sean.' Bella held out the directions Gina had helped her to piece together using her knowledge of the area and Google Earth. 'It's about Mum and Stephen Molloy.'

Dog calmly wandered into Main Street and sat down on the heat-wobbled tarmac, right in the way of the car as they sped towards him.

'Crazy damn mutt,' Sean said, slamming on the brakes.

Dog stayed where he was, in the middle of the road, looking at them.

'He wants to come with us,' Bella said, getting out and opening the back door. Dog trotted round, jumped into the back seat, and positioned himself facing forward like an impatient VIP waiting for the chauffeur to pull his finger out.

'Strength in numbers,' Bella said.

A hundred yards down the road they had to stop again, this time because of the temporary traffic lights. While they were waiting, Gladys ran across in front of them, holding a frightened, crying Jack.

'Jack?' Bella said, poking her head out of the window.

'Bella!' Jack held his hands out to her.

'Is that you, Bella? Oh, thank Gawd,' Gladys said, perfectly adopting her mother's idiom. She was pale, and her breath came in rasps. She was having some difficulty carrying Jack, who despite being several years her junior was almost the same size as her.

'What is it?' Bella sprang out and took Jack from the girl.

'Ethel fell out of the tree house and her arm's all bent backwards and the bone's poking out and she's screaming blue murder. Mommy sent me over to the theatre to take Jack back to his daddy, 'cause we have to go to the Emergency Room, but there's no one there.'

'There's a costume fitting for the principals in town,' Sean said, getting out of the car. 'That's why I've got the afternoon off.'

'I'll take him. You get back to your mommy,' Bella said.

'Thanks, honey,' the little girl said, then she darted towards her house.

'So what do I do now?' Bella turned to Sean, Jack on her hip.

'He'd better come along.'

'But we haven't got the car seat. Mum'll go mad.'

'I somehow think that's going to be the least of her worries when she sees us up there,' Sean said, opening the back door so Bella could put Jack inside.

'Doggy!' Jack said, his face instantly brightening as he saw his travelling companion. Dog turned and gave Jack's cheek a cursory lick of welcome, then resumed his position facing forward.

The lights changed and Sean hit the ignition. Just as he was about to pull out, they noticed the turquoise convertible cruising slowly along Main Street towards them, having ignored the red at the other end of the roadworks.

'Oh shit,' he said. Bella reached over and took his hand.

In the front seats of the turquoise car were Kyle and Aaron. If she weren't so terrified, their resemblance to Laurel and Hardy would have made Bella laugh. As the boys drove slowly up to them, Aaron, who was at the wheel, lazily levelled an imaginary gun at Sean, took aim, and fired. He slowed right down as he passed.

'What will Olly say, Kyle?' Aaron said in a grotesque, feminine voice.

'I don't like to imagine,' Kyle lisped back.

'I guess we'll just have to tell him what his naughty little sister is up to again . . .'

'He won't like it.'

'He *certainly* won't like it.'

With two loud revs of the engine, the car sped away. Sean put his forehead to the steering wheel. After a moment he breathed in deeply, looked at Bella and smiled.

'No more running away. The worst part about all that for me was that I didn't put up a fight. I'll never let that happen again.'

Bella leaned over and kissed him. Then he put his foot down and they set off, up Main Street, towards Stephen's house in the middle of the forest, on the other side of the mountain.

'And what's the problem, anyway?' Bella said. 'They have no idea where we're going.'

It was only when they were too far out of Trout Island to do anything about it, when they had reached the house with the pond that Lara had admired so, that the thought struck Bella.

Despite her shock and awe at the photographs of her mother and Stephen, she had remembered to log out of Facebook. It was habit for her; if she didn't, Olly got in there and wrote something salacious or idiotic in her name. Frape, they called it.

But had she closed the page with Stephen's house zoomed in on, on Google Earth? Gina had shown her in minute detail how to find the address he had said was impossible to see on Google. If, as she feared, she had left the page open, then, far from not knowing, Olly would have a very clear idea indeed of where they were headed.

Forty-Three

THE FIRST THING LARA KNEW WHEN SHE CAME ROUND WAS that she couldn't feel her arms. Then she realised it was because they were twisted behind her back and tied together with something metal and restricting. She felt her leg, though. The pain throbbed from dull to sharp like someone turning the volume up and down on a badly tuned radio. With some difficulty she forced her eyes open.

Stephen's face hovered over hers. He smiled down at her like a benign uncle.

'Ah, you're back,' he said, stroking her hair. 'I was beginning to get a bit worried.'

She noticed the cut on his cheek was now held in place by SteriStrips.

'I'll get all the villain parts now,' he said, touching the cut. '*Scarface Two.*'

Lara struggled to get up, but even if her head didn't hurt too much to lift off the pillow, she realised she was tied to the bed with webbing straps.

'Please let me go,' she croaked.

'Oh, not this again.' Stephen sighed. 'Do you know, Lara, how many women would – quite literally, probably – *kill* to be in your position? To be here, with me? You should be grateful. I've rescued you from that stale sham of a marriage.'

'I can't feel my arms,' Lara said. 'Please. Untie me.'

'Oh, I don't think I can do that, my love. Not after your little bolt this afternoon. Don't trust you, you see. Sorry.' He bent to touch her shoulder, running his hand down to her arms underneath her. 'Oh, I see,' he said. 'You're lying on your hands. That must be uncomfortable, in fact.'

He knelt on her belly to hold her down and undid the webbing. Pushing down at the same time as rolling her over, he turned her on to her front. The sudden movement of her leg made her yelp.

'Sorry,' he said. 'Poor little leg.'

He waited for her to stop gasping. Then he straddled her and undid her hands, lifting her arms so they lay out at right angles to her body.

'Is that better?'

'Yes,' Lara said, her voice muffled by the pillow. The blood returning to her fingers actually caused agonising pins and needles, but he was right, it was better than lying on them.

'So,' Stephen said, reaching over her to the far corner of the bed. 'It's a good job I've got these. You'll be a lot more comfortable, I think.'

Lara's heart sank as she heard the rattle of chains. She felt the snap of more metal as he closed handcuffs round first her left, then her right wrist, stretching her out. He quickly jumped up and did the same to her ankles so she was pinioned, face down, to the mattress.

'Now Lara,' he said, lifting himself off her and running his hands up her legs and over her buttocks. 'I'm going to claim your undiscovered territories.'

Afterwards he lay motionless at last, still inside her, sweat on sweat, blood and tears and seed mingled. Lara had a moment to wonder where she had gone in all this. Then, mercifully, her mind shut down, taking her away from the horror that was Stephen Molloy, into a kind of oblivion.

Forty-Four

HOWEVER MUCH BELLA TRIED TO WISH THE FALLEN TREE into existence, Gina's husband had been right. The only obstacle on the road was the car-mangled body of a fawn.

Sean crunched the Nissan up the dirt track to Stephen Molloy's gate and cut the engine. Bella got out of the car and he followed.

Enrobed in the dust cloud they had created, they surveyed the obstacles in front of them. A locked, ten-foot-high gate with barbed wire on the top. A fence of exactly the same proportions and fortifications. Artificial lines drawn in the forest, stopping them dead. Apart from a keypad, which Bella pressed to no avail, she saw nothing else at the gate – no buzzer, no camera – to tell anyone inside the house they were there.

The katydids in the trees above them made their noise, drilling into Bella's skull.

'I mean, I don't see why we've come all the way up here,' she said finally.

'Don't you think you've got a right to know?' Sean said.

She looked at him. His eyes were burning.

'If I'd had a chance to stop my dad fucking around before my mom found out . . .'

'It's not my business, though.'

'It's every bit your business.'

'Is it?' She marvelled at the fire of him. She leaned against him and he put his arm around her. 'What are we going to do, then? How are we going to get in? It's like Fort Knox.'

'Local boy knowledge.' Sean held up his finger. 'We can get in from the back, cross-country. My uncle owns the land on the other side. The car will only take us some of the way. The rest we'll have to do on foot.'

'We've got Jack, though,' Bella said, turning back to look at her little brother, who, from what she could see through the dusty car window, seemed to be alternating between sneezing and talking to Dog.

'We'll take turns carrying him if he gets tired.'

They got back in the car and Sean drove along the track, beyond where the tall fence around Stephen's land turned up away from the lane and into the forest. The road came to an abrupt end five miles later at an overgrown field of maize, high up on a plateau above dense, dark, forested hills. The early evening insects fogged the air with their buzzing and biting. Bella slapped a couple of stings on her arms – more no see'ums.

'No one comes up here any more,' Sean said, cutting the engine. 'But I spent whole summers here when I was a kid, back when my uncle was well enough to farm the land. Their house used to be over there.' He pointed in the direction of a red barn that tilted at a forty-five-degree angle to the ground. 'But it was too exposed. Got hit by lightning. Kind of exploded.'

What a strange world this is, Bella thought, as she stood on that hot, wind-whipped hill, where the red soil bled colour from the setting sun and dazzled against the green of the bolted maize. Houses could explode, brothers could go psycho, mothers could defect with movie stars and she could find the love of her life.

'Where do we go now?' she said.

'South. Down through the forest, where it's so wild even Molloy wouldn't be able to put up a fence, up the other side and down again.'

It sounded like a challenge, with a small boy and a dog. But Bella comforted herself with her newly acquired knowledge that nothing was impossible.

'He says we have to hurry up,' Jack wheezed. Bella turned to see her little brother, his freckled face all allergy-distended, with his hand on Dog.

'Jack, are you all right?' Bella said. She had always assumed that her mother going on about Jack's allergies and asthma was just babying. But, looking at him now, she realised he needed his inhaler and tablets. She supposed they were back in Trout Island, with Gina.

'I'm fine,' he said, as he let Dog go on ahead of them, through the maize field and down into the indigo heart of the forest below. Bella hoped being out in the open air would help.

'Come on, slow coaches!' Jack said as he skipped off after Dog.

Sean shut the car doors, took Bella's hand and led her forward, across the field.

Before the trees swallowed them up, Bella glanced back. Sean's car, on the brow of the plateau, couldn't have advertised its presence any more strongly. If those boys wanted to find them, they had a good starting point.

Forty-Five

THEY HAD ONLY JUST ENTERED THE FOREST WHEN THE path petered out and they were left to stumble through the undergrowth. Dog forged on ahead, with Jack running after him.

'Is Dog going in the right direction?' Bella asked Sean.

'It's crazy, but yes he is.'

'Be careful of poison ivy,' Sean said, as they slid down the hill. They could hear the rush of the river at the trough of the valley below them as it tumbled over stones that had rolled down from the slopes above. 'They say it doesn't grow this far north, but I have first-hand knowledge that it's all over these woods.'

'I wouldn't know poison ivy if it hit me in the face,' Bella said.

'You'd get the idea pretty quickly. Look.' He bent to point out a harmless-looking green-leaved vine trailing its way up a tree. 'Leaves of three, let it be. If you touch that, in a day or two you'll come up with big old blisters that'll last for weeks and travel all over your body.'

'Ugh.' The forest looked so benign on the surface – like an English oak wood. But with poison ivy and snakes underfoot, bears, coyotes and mountain lions lurking behind trees, and her mother getting up to god knew what with Stephen Molloy somewhere out there, it was not as friendly as it seemed.

They waded down through shoals of crumbled leaf mould until they reached a river. Using reddish-brown rocks scattered through the water, they began to cross. Bella couldn't get that photograph of Lara and Stephen Molloy out of her mind. Could she *really* stop her mother doing whatever she was doing? She obviously *wanted* to be out there with him. Bella wondered how long they had been carrying on like that together. She remembered Stephen saying they knew each other when they were younger. Was the 'chance meeting' here in Trout Island a fake?

She stopped, halfway across the river.

'I think we should go back,' she shouted across the noise of water on rock to Sean.

'What?' he said, turning to face her.

'I don't want to go there. I don't want to find out. I want to forget I ever saw those photos. I want Dad to sort it out.'

'If that happens, you know that'll be the end, right?' Sean stepped back towards her and took her hand. 'And you'll never forget those photos.'

Bella closed her eyes and frowned. He was right. The image of Stephen and Lara was as clear as if it were lasered on the inside of her eyelids.

'Bella,' Sean said, as they balanced on a big rock in the middle of the river. 'Think about that little kid.' He nodded at Jack, who had reached the other side and was sitting on a boulder, hugging his dirty knees, Dog beside him. He looked very small, dwarfed both by the animal and by the big trees that rose behind him.

'Are you ready to let his world fall apart?' Sean said.

Bella looked down and shook her head.

'It's our duty to him – to everyone – to give it our best shot.'

Our duty, Bella thought, looking up at Sean. And, she realised with enormous relief, whatever happened, she at least would not be alone.

'Come *on*!' Jack called breathily from his boulder.

'Coming!' Bella said, jumping to the next rock.

'Also,' Sean said, catching her arm as he joined her. 'There's one thing you haven't considered.'

Bella looked up at him. A dragonfly silently passed between them, a flash of iridescent blue and green.

'Who took those photographs? And how did they know to send them to you?'

Bella bit her lip. How could she be so dumb? With the shock of the images, she hadn't given a further thought to who *Your Friend* might be. She had stupidly read them as more of the paparazzi pictures she saw of Stephen and his ilk in every magazine she picked up, as something that *just happened*. She ran through who it could possibly be. She hoped, for Stephen Molloy's sake, it hadn't been Olly . . .

'Come *on*,' Jack yelled.

Then it hit her. 'The stalker!' she said. 'Stephen Molloy had a stalker—'

'Yes, back in LA, Betty said. A real nut job.'

'You don't think?'

'Jesus.'

'Perhaps Gina's "quirky old feeling" was right,' Bella said.

'Eh?'

'Come on.'

They jumped across the remaining stones to the other side.

'At last,' Jack said. 'Let's go, Dog.'

'Hurry,' Bella said.

They took off and were halfway up the hill, scrabbling up a scree slope, when a loud gunshot echoed through the valley, stopping them in their tracks. Dog wheeled around, barking at where the shot came from, somewhere behind them.

'Quiet!' Sean hissed at Dog.

The forest fell silent. The only sound was Jack wheezing as he tried to catch his breath.

'What—?' Bella turned to Sean.

'Shhh.' He held up his hand and listened, peering into the darkening forest behind them.

Far away, on the other side of the river, they heard an unmistakable high-pitched cackle, followed by a whoop.

'Jesus,' Bella said. Of course Olly and his crew had followed them. She might as well have been unravelling a ball of string to show them the way.

'Those boys have spent almost every weekend since they were able to crawl out hunting with their marvellous uncle daddies,' Sean said. 'It was easy for them to follow our trail up the track – no cars ever go up there any more. Then, well, a new path through the maize, trampled undergrowth. We've hardly been covering our tracks.'

'What do we do?'

'We go on. We don't want them to catch us up, and if we double back, they're bound to spot us, with Jacko and Dog. Our advantage is that we're nearly at the top of the hill. Come on.' He ran ahead and scooped Jack up, swinging him on to his shoulders.

With Dog in front of them, they made quick progress up the path. Sean stooped to pick up a stick, which every now and then he threw into the trees for the animal to retrieve.

'Giving them a few detours on the way up,' Sean said. 'Slow them down.'

'Brilliant.'

'Common sense for a country boy.'

Bella would have smiled, but she was having difficulty keeping up with him. His legs were a good foot longer than hers. She knew this because they had compared them one lazy afternoon at the pond.

They tore past a tumbledown house, half smothered in moss. It looked like a face with its eyes gouged out.

'These hills used to be full of people,' Sean said.

'They seem quite busy today too.'

'Come on, Sean!' Jack said in between gasps for breath, and he tapped him with his heels as if he were his horse.

Finally they were at the top of the hill, bursting out of the trees into a sun-dappled clearing, breathless with the effort of the climb.

'Bear,' Jack said. His lower lip began to tremble.

'Is this where you saw the bear, Jacky?' Bella looked up at him.

Jack nodded and she noticed his eyes, now two little slits in his puffy, distended face.

'We have to keep Jack away from Dog,' Bella said.

'But I like Dog,' Jack wailed.

'Bear's the last of our worries. Let's move on,' Sean said to Bella. They forged on, past a tangle of bushes purpled with powdery berries. Then they plunged back into the woods on the other side and started careering down the hill, along a muddy path, sending orange salamanders slipping for cover.

'There it is!' Sean pointed to a spot of red roof through the leaves. 'Mr Molloy's shag pad.'

'Don't,' Bella said. Suddenly, the adventure of what they were doing leached from her and she thought she was going to vomit. She stopped for a second.

'Do we want to take them by surprise?' he said.

'I'd rather not.' She grimaced at the thought. 'I'd rather they had a bit of warning.'

'Snakes!' Jack said, as they reached the edge of the lawn. Coughing, he struggled to get down from Sean's shoulders. Dog steamed on ahead and sat on the porch, waiting for them.

The house looked silent and empty in the dusk. If it weren't for the old Volvo and Stephen's dented Wrangler standing outside, they would have thought nobody was in.

'You'd better stay out here with Jack,' Bella said. 'I don't want him to see anything too disturbing.'

Sean pointed to the forest behind them. 'Seeing them doing what they plan to do to me when they get here would be better?'

Bella bit her lip. 'Olly wouldn't do anything to you in front of Jack.'

'You have no idea how comforting that is to me.'

'OK,' Bella said, thinking quickly. 'I'll knock on the door and show my face first. Then we'll take it from there. Mum won't let Olly do anything.'

She went up to the door and looked for a bell. Of course there wasn't one. There was no way of announcing oneself as a visitor – why would there be when the only feasible way on to the property was so firmly barred? So she knocked gently on the door, half hoping there would be no reply and they could all go home and forget completely about coming up here.

'They'd better come quickly or we're completely screwed,' Sean said, staring up at the forest, where, not too far away, Olly, Aaron, Brandon and Kyle were audibly following their trail. Bella's boy looked like he was beginning to lose the nerve he had so bravely recovered for her.

Then Jack, whose airways had narrowed to a hair's breadth, turned purple.

Forty-Six

'WHAT'S THE PLAN?' LARA MUTTERED. STEPHEN LAY BY HER side, his arms and legs woven around her. She was still shackled to the bed, in need of a pee and a glass of water. The smell of their bodies surrounded them, but so scented had she been by Stephen, she couldn't work out which was her odour and which his. 'Do you have a plan?'

'I'm going down to the village this evening,' he said, propping himself up on one elbow and stroking her back, 'and I'm going to tell Bella and Olly that I'm their dad. I think they'll be rather pleased, don't you?'

Lara lay completely still, unable to comment. She couldn't imagine what their reaction would be, but rather pleased wasn't the first that came to mind.

'Don't worry. I've prepared the ground for them. They'll be relieved, really. Then I'll bring them up here, and we can all have tea together. Perhaps you could bake a cake.'

'I need to pee,' Lara said.

'Of course you do.' He jumped up and unshackled her ankles and wrists. Supporting her – her broken leg was useless

– he led her to the bathroom, where he stood over her as she sat on the pan.

'Let me wipe you,' he said, reaching for the toilet roll. But as he did so, there was a loud rapping on the side door. Lara caught her breath and looked up at him. He narrowed his eyes.

'Very enterprising,' he said.

'What do you mean?'

'OK, you'd better stay here.' He carried her back to the bedroom and quickly chained her up again. The knocking continued, growing ever more insistent.

At last, Lara saw a glimmer of hope. Someone had come up here to rescue her.

'Mum? Lara?'

Her heart lurched into her mouth as she realised who stood out there in the wood in the middle of nowhere, waiting at his door.

Her daughter.

'That's my girl,' Stephen said.

Forty-Seven

'IF THEY'RE IN, THEY'RE GOING TO HEAR THAT,' SEAN SAID.

'Mum!' Bella yelled again, at her wits' end. 'Lara!' She pressed her ear to the door then she stood back. 'Someone's coming,' she said, hugging her little brother, trying to calm his desperate attempts at breath. 'Hold on Jacky.'

'Bella. What a lovely surprise,' Stephen said as he opened the door, his welcoming smile incongruous, accessorised as it was by a shotgun.

'Jack's having an attack,' Bella said, looking up at him. 'We don't know what to do.'

Dog crouched, bared his teeth and snarled at Stephen Molloy.

'GET BACK,' Stephen roared at Dog, holding his hand out, ready to hit him. Such was the authority in his voice that Dog reared away on his hind legs and sloped off to the vegetable patch, whimpering.

'It's that beast's fault,' Stephen said, slinging his gun over his shoulder and picking Jack up. 'What do you think you're doing?' He shot a look at Bella. 'You know he's allergic.'

'I didn't think—' Bella said, tears springing to her eyes.

'Come in. I'll see if I can find something.' Stephen bundled Jack into the house and Bella and Sean followed.

In the kitchen, he lifted Jack on to the counter and supported him as he rummaged in what Bella realised was her mother's bag. 'Thank God,' he said, finding Jack's Ventolin and popping off the lid. 'We can rely on our Lara to be prepared.'

He held the inhaler to Jack's mouth and with five blasts his breathing began to return to normal.

'Thank you, thank you,' Bella said over and over again.

'Are his tablets in there?' Stephen pointed to Lara's bag.

Bella found the blister pack of antihistamines. She handed them to Stephen, who, with one arm still around Jack, took a glass from the draining board, filled it with water and fed two pills to the gasping little boy.

Finally, when the emergency was over, Stephen carried Jack through to the living room and laid him on the sofa, motioning to Sean and Bella to sit either side of him.

'Wow,' he said, raising his eyebrows.

'Thank you,' Bella said, stroking her little brother's head as he curled up in her lap.

'Let's start again,' Stephen said, after a moment. 'Welcome, Bella, Jack and Sean, to my home.'

He stood and looked at them, smiling, expectant.

'Where's Mum?' Bella said at last.

'Oh. She's fast asleep at the moment. But, Bella, I think your mother and I owe you an explanation.'

Bella stared at her feet, cowed by Stephen's presence, embarrassed by the whole situation.

'You all look completely worn out. Can I get you a drink? Or something to eat . . .'

Bella ran her tongue over her parched upper lip and tasted salt. She hadn't realised how sweaty and grimy she was. Her legs stung where brambles had ripped them.

'Lemonade please, Stephen,' Jack said, sitting up, his face returned to its normal colour, save for the dirt and the sunburn.

'Good boy.' Stephen ruffled his hair.

'Just water'll do me fine,' Sean said.

'Me too, please,' Bella added.

As they sat awkwardly waiting for Stephen to fix their drinks – he was going to great pains with ice and lemon and straws – a loud thump came from upstairs.

'What's that?' Bella asked Stephen.

'What?' he said, smiling broadly as he carried a tray with three tinkling glasses on it over to the sofa.

'That noise. Listen. There it is again.'

Stephen put his head to one side. Again the noise came, a distinct banging – something lifting and dropping, lifting and dropping. Bella saw a tiny flicker in Stephen's jaw.

Jack drained his lemonade, slurping on the straw.

'It's that damn porcupine again,' Stephen said. 'Remember, Bella, from the other night? It gets up on the roof now – don't ask me how – then it thumps and rubs itself against the house. First time I heard it,' he said with a laugh, 'I thought I had a madman stamping about upstairs.'

'I thought porcupines were nocturnal,' Sean said.

'Not this one.' Stephen turned, smiling, but not with his eyes.

Bella and Sean each took a sip from their glasses. The fan turning overhead and the thumping from upstairs were the only sounds in the room.

'So,' Stephen said eventually. 'Tell me how and why you come to be up here.'

'I'd rather talk to you privately,' Bella said. 'Not in front of J.A.C.K.'

Jack, knowing full well how to spell his own name, looked up and beamed.

'Sure,' Stephen said. 'We'll go into my study. Sean, are you OK to stay here? There's a load of DVDs on those shelves. You might as well start getting young Jack here acquainted with my oeuvre. The back door's on the latch, too, in case he wants to get out to the snakes. But keep him away from that mutt, yes?'

Bella was worried about the door being unlocked, but Sean managed to appear entirely neutral as he got up and led the little boy over to choose a DVD from the many hundreds that lined the floor-to-ceiling shelves. Perhaps, now that Stephen was so close, he felt he had nothing to fear from Olly.

'Well then?' Stephen said, as he sat in his office chair and turned to face the egg-shaped seat he had put Bella in. The thumping was much closer to them in here. It seemed to come from right above Bella's head.

She told him about the photographs. When she had finished – she couldn't bear to relate the detail about his hand on her mother's breast – he put his elbows on his knees and his hands together.

'You know what this means?' he said.

'It means you and Mum are having an affair,' Bella said.

'Affair? I'd hardly call it that. I think "affair" implies a bit of a sideshow, don't you?'

'What do you mean?'

Stephen held up his hand and silenced her.

'The point is, Bella, who do you think might be taking these photographs?'

'Yes, we—'

'Did you wonder, perhaps, why I came to the door with a gun? Yes? Well,' he went on, gesturing to the green of the forest that could just be picked out behind the gauze of the insect screens, 'out there is a demented woman who is hell-bent on getting at Lara because she believes I belong to her and not to your mother.'

'I don't want to hear this,' Bella said, curling up and clapping her hands over her ears.

'Don't you? Then why did you come up here?'

'I want to talk to Mum.'

'Oh, and you will, Bella,' Stephen said. He leaned forward and put his hands on her knees and stared at her, forcing her gaze up to meet his. 'My Bella.'

'What?' She tried to break away from him, but he had a firm grip on her legs.

'You are so like your mother, you know? When I first fell in love with her she was only three years older than you are now.'

'She was nineteen? But she was married to my dad then.'

Stephen leaned back, slapped his knee and laughed.

'What's so funny?' Bella said.

He continued laughing until tears formed in the corners of his eyes.

'What is it?' Bella demanded, closing in right up against his face.

'My,' Stephen said. 'You're a fiery girl, aren't you? I like that. No, my darling, what is so amusing is that your mother wasn't married to your dad when she was nineteen. She never married your dad.'

'She did. I saw the pictures. They've got this scrapbook.'

'You still don't get it, do you?' He took her chin between his thumb and forefinger, pinching her hard.

'Your mother hasn't married your father – yet – because

your father is . . .' He jumped up, opened his arms wide and presented himself like a Royal Shakespeare Company lead taking a bow. 'Me!'

If he had plunged her into an icy pool, Bella wouldn't have felt such a physical shock. She fought to get the air back into her lungs, shaking her head, her hands over her ears.

'S'true,' he said, beaming at her, his arms still out.

'I don't believe you.' She continued to shake her head so violently her skull clicked.

'But look,' he said, handing her a piece of paper from a tray on his desk. Then he sat down and observed her as she read, resting his chin in his hands.

Bella studied the report. Then slowly she looked up at him as she let the paper flutter to the floor, undisguised horror scrawled over her face.

'It's going to take a while for you to get used to it, then?' he said, smiling. 'Of course. But, my love, my girl, it's true. It is a fact. And the sooner you come to realise it, the better for everyone concerned.'

'What about Marcus?'

'What *about* Marcus?' Stephen said, picking up the report.

'Does he know?'

'Not yet.'

'Does Mum know?'

Stephen started laughing again. 'What do you think? She's here, isn't she? Look—' He took her hands, holding them tightly between his own. 'I gave you a stable childhood; I stayed out of the picture. But I always knew this day would come.'

The thumping continued, right above Bella's head. She glanced up.

'I need to see Mum.'

'She'll wake up soon.'

'I want to see her now.' Bella pulled away and stood up to go. As he lunged to stop her, she sidestepped him and kicked him in the shins. Then she swung away, breaking out of the study and towards the stairs.

Outside, Dog barked and barked.

'Bella,' Sean said from beside the living-room window, where he had flattened himself against the wall. 'Olly's here.'

'Make sure Jack stays down here,' Bella said. She darted up the stairs and ran down the corridor to the room that was above the study. She turned the lock in the handle and flung open the door.

It was like she'd reached the edge of a precipice; she teetered, stalled completely by what met her. Spread-eagled on the bed, her left leg at an unnatural angle, her naked body covered in cuts and bruises, her eyes wild, was a woman. It took a beat to register that this was her mother.

'Help me, Bella,' she said hoarsely, thumping her body up and down on the surface of the bed. 'Help me.'

Without a thought or word, Bella rushed to the side of the bed, to see if she could work out how the chains were attached. But she was stopped by her mother's cry of terror. Stephen filled the doorway, tears pouring down his face, his gun in his hands.

'It wasn't meant to be like this,' he sobbed.

Bella put herself between him and her mother as he fell to his knees.

'Please forgive me,' he said. 'I didn't mean it to end like this.' He bent his head forward, on to his fist, as if in prayer. Then he reared up and grabbed Bella's arm. 'Please say we can move on from here, rewind a bit, do a bit of an edit?' He smiled up at her through his tears. 'My daughter?' He reached out and gripped on to Lara's leg, making her scream in agony. 'My wife?'

'Jack, come here!' Sean shouted from the hallway.

'Mummy?'

Jack stopped, open-mouthed, in the doorway. Sean, who had just caught up with him, quickly read the scene in front of them and dived on to Stephen, pushing him away from the women.

'Get him out of here!' Lara screamed. 'Get Jack out of here, Bella!'

Dodging round the men, Bella scooped up her little brother and hurtled, almost fell, down the stairs.

'You come back here!' Stephen, who had broken free, roared from the landing. Sean launched at him again, but Stephen managed to sidestep the tackle and Sean plunged down the stairs.

'Sean!' Bella cried.

'I'm OK,' he said, picking himself up. 'You go. I'll keep him off your mom.'

Stephen started down the stairs, with his gun, but his eyes were on Bella, not Sean.

'Quick,' Bella said to Jack, who was clinging to her, whimpering. She flung the side door open and they spilled out into the dusky evening air, still and warm after the cold interior of the house. Half carrying, half dragging the little boy, she stumbled across the grass for the shelter of the forest. Dog ran from side to side on the edge of the lawn, barking up into the trees, as if he were providing cover for her.

A great clattering noise erupted behind them, a noise of struggle. Bella glanced around. Stephen had reached the porch, and was pulling free from Sean, his rifle held up, aiming at her and Jack. She continued to run, praying she would reach the trees in time.

'STOP!' Stephen yelled, and Bella felt herself pushed to the ground as a gunshot rang out into the air.

Sean rolled away from where he had landed on top of her and Bella looked back to see what she had to do to get herself and Jack out of the line of Stephen's next shot.

But she saw, with relief, that Stephen had dropped the gun. She saw the look of outrage on his face. Then she saw the bloom of blood as it spread across his white linen shirt. He looked up at her as he dropped to his knees.

'I love you, Bella,' he said.

Another shot rang out, from somewhere in the forest, and he jolted as part of his skull flew away from the back of his head. He wavered for a second. Then, almost comically, he fell forward to land face first in the dirt at the base of his porch.

'Bella!' Lara screamed from inside the house.

At the sound of her voice, Dog flew indoors, jumping over Stephen's body.

'We're all right, Mum,' Bella called. 'It's all right.'

There was a rustle in the undergrowth and Olly emerged, holding a rifle out in front of him, followed by his three unarmed friends. He walked over to Sean, who was still on the ground, and spat at him.

'And as for you,' he said, bracing himself as he aimed the rifle, his jaw working nineteen to the dozen, his eyes as red as the mess around Stephen's head.

'Don't do it, man,' Kyle said, trying to put a hand on Olly's shoulder. 'You've gone way too far already, man.'

'Lolly, NO!' Jack scrambled to his feet and put himself between his big brother and his sister's boyfriend. 'Get Mummy.' He pointed to the back door. 'She's poorly.'

Olly looked at his brother, then his sister, then his friends. At last, he slung the gun over his shoulder and signalled for

Aaron, Brandon and Kyle to follow as he disappeared into the house, stepping over Stephen's body as he went.

The three boys stayed where they were.

'I'm outta here,' Kyle said.

'Me too,' Aaron agreed. They turned and raised their eyebrows at Brandon, who slowly nodded. Then, as one, they stepped back into the forest and disappeared.

Bella and Sean stood up and brushed the dust from their fronts.

'You OK?' she said.

'I'll live,' he said.

'Snakes!' Jack said, trying to drag his sister to the woodpile.

The Known

'I GOT IN!' BELLA SAID, SWINGING HER BIG PORTFOLIO along the Tribeca street outside the New York Academy of Art. The spring sunshine warmed her after a morning spent indoors, showing her work to a string of professors.

'I knew it!' Lara's voice echoed in the hallway of the newly refurbished Trout Island house. 'Have you told Sean yet?'

'He's not free till seven. Juilliard have this no-phones-in-rehearsal rule. But I'm going to go home and rustle us up a beautiful celebration meal.'

'Lovely.'

Bella moved out along Franklin towards Broadway, heading for Dean and DeLuca. Not being a cook, she planned to buy the entire meal there. Then she'd carry it back to heat up in the sleek kitchen of the large house on West Tenth and Seventh she and Sean had to themselves while Lara stayed upstate for the run-up to Olly's trial.

It had been a strange eight months for everyone, not made any less surreal by the sudden wealth Stephen's will – he had left absolutely everything to Lara – had conferred on the family.

But, as well as providing material comfort, the money had helped them out in many other ways. The major item of expenditure so far, after hospital and legal bills, had been counselling for all of them, Sean included. Bella felt she was making good progress, although there were parts of it she still wouldn't discuss with anyone, shrink or no shrink.

'You'll call Marcus and let him and Selina know, won't you?' Lara said.

'Of course I'll call Dad,' Bella said. Her father – she couldn't think of him in any other way – had moved back to England when everything fell apart. He had, of course, been furious at her mum when he found out the truth, and, for a while, had refused to have anything to do with Lara or her children, poor Jack included. But Selina, who he planned to marry as soon as the divorce was finalised, had proved to be a fantastic stepmother-in-waiting, bringing him round to such an extent that Bella, Sean and Jack had flown over to visit at Easter. It hadn't been as difficult as she had feared. Marcus was doing well, with a large part in a new TV series that, he said, promised to be the next big thing for Channel Four.

'I had a great meeting with Mickelberg today,' Lara went on as Bella swapped portfolio and phone around to ease her aching shoulder.

'Yes?' Bella tried to sound non-committal. Mickelberg was Olly's attorney. One of the best in the country.

'He's convinced the case will be thrown out at court. It's clear Olly believed Stephen intended to shoot you and Jack, and in New York, that's justification enough. The crystal meth and the gun possession will mean two years, worst-case scenario, and, with the six months he's already done, we'll have our Oll back in less than eighteen months.'

'That's great,' Bella said, trying to hide her disappointment.

She didn't want to hear this. Particularly not on this day, when her NYAA success had promised, for the first time through the morass of the past eight months, a brighter, clearer future for herself.

The whole Olly mess was something she had hoped she wasn't going to have to deal with for years.

She stood on the corner of West Fourth waiting for the interminable crossing light to change. Perhaps, shrink or no shrink, she needed to face it sooner rather than later.

'Mum, I—' she began to say, but down the phone she heard a knocking on the Trout Island door and Dog's wild barking.

'Oh. That'll be Gina,' Lara said. 'I've got to dash. But well done, darling. I'm a million times proud of you.'

'But—'

'What?'

'Oh, never mind.'

Bella put her phone in her pocket and, surprised at how slight her frustration was in comparison with her relief at being interrupted, made her way up Broadway to fetch food for her man.

Lara put the phone down and grabbed her crutches. Even after months of having her leg penetrated and encircled by pieces of metal, and further weeks with it encased in a rigid foam walker, she still couldn't put her burgeoning weight on it.

Nearly tripping over Dog, she hauled herself to the front door and undid the high-security bolts. Lots of locks had been part of the brief she had given the architects in charge of the speedy refurbishment of the Trout Island house.

She opened the door. Seeing friends, Dog wove amongst the visitors, winning pats and paw shakes.

'We had a great time!' Gina said as Dog licked her hand. She had taken Jack, Bert and the girls to the library show, the first of the summer programme.

'It was actually not too substandard,' Ethel said.

Jack bowled into the hallway and flung his arms around his mother's legs, nearly knocking her over.

'Steady there, Jacko,' Lara said. He had, understandably, been rather clingy since all the business. 'Do you have time for a coffee?' she asked Gina. 'We could stick this lot in front of a DVD up in Jack's room.'

'I'll come in on the condition you put your feet up and let me get it,' Gina said. 'You should be taking it easy.'

As they went through to the kitchen, Lara told Gina about Bella's success and Mickelberg's confidence about Olly's chances. She eased herself into a chair and Gina busied herself making coffee in the airy kitchen, where the sunlit breeze stirred through the new porch with its gatefold doors.

'Just green tea for me,' Lara said. 'I can't do coffee at the moment.'

'It's so cool Bella's got that house and she can walk to college,' Gina said.

'Isn't it? And it is such a beautiful home. Whatever else you can say about him, Stephen had admirable taste. Come what may, we're going to hold on to that house. And here, of course.'

'Any interest on the forest property yet?'

'Not a peep. Hardly surprising given the history, though. I'm half minded just to let it return to nature, let the trees and the creepers and the snakes reclaim it.'

'I don't blame you.' Gina shuddered.

'That poor woman,' Lara said, pouring the coffee.

'Poor Trudi Staines?' Gina said. 'Reserve your sympathy,

sister. She pulled the wool right over Betty's eyes, and she took his money to do scary things to you.'

'But no one deserves to be buried alive.' Lara shuddered. 'She tried to warn me, you know? But I didn't listen. More fool me.'

'Well whatever, you'll be well rid of that place.'

'And I don't even want to visit his LA palace . . .' Even mentioning it reminded her of the pictures Stephen showed her on his iPad, and the mad plans he had cooked up for her there. And that of course led her back to what he had done to her after he had shown her the pictures . . .

'So many houses for one guy!' Gina said, practised at drawing Lara away from the horrors that still lurked in her memory.

'And Manchester and London, too.' Lara counted them off on her fingers.

'I know. Jeez.'

'But I need to know what's happening with Olly before I can make any other decisions.'

'Not long now.'

'Nope. I hope our attorney's right.'

'From what you say, he's practically a free man.' Gina flapped her hand down as if there were no problem whatsoever.

Lara closed her eyes and prayed she was right.

As soon as she knew the score with Olly, Lara planned to take stock of her wealth. All she knew was it was vast, and she proposed to give a large chunk of it away.

The first thing she aimed to do was set up a fund for Trout Island Theatre. She felt partly responsible for its demise after the abrupt cancellation of *Macbeth*, and James and Betty's exodus to LA amid all the publicly unfolding scandal around Stephen's death. She thought of how the theatre had nurtured people like Sean, and provided a focal point for the community. The idea of it going dark because of her actions was the one thing she still felt guilty about. She even thought she might find some sort of role for herself, perhaps in the administration side of things. Although of course she would pretty soon have other demands on her time.

The phone rang, breaking into her daydream.

'Sorry. Do you mind if I take this – it could be Mickelberg again,' Lara said, levering herself up and hobbling over to the study area she had carved out of the massive living room. 'Help yourself to more coffee, G.' She picked up the phone.

'Hey, Lara.'

She was right. Mickelberg always started phone calls assuming that the person picking up was the person he wanted to talk to.

'I've got some awesome news for you,' he went on.

'They've thrown Olly's trial out?'

'It's not *that* awesome,' he said. 'But as good as. I've been talking to one Detective O'Halloran of the San Bernardino County Sheriff's Department over in California. They dug up a Jane Doe in Joshua Tree Park a year back and have only now come up with an identification.'

Lara sat down and passed her hand in front of her eyes. A dull pain nagged at the base of her spine. She had a feeling she knew what was going to happen next.

'The unfortunate one – she had, too, it appears, been buried alive – was called Elaine Montez, but she also went by the name of—'

'Elizabeth Sanders,' Lara said, her cheeks flushing. Buried alive.

'Correct! My dear, you must be psychic. And, best of all, Molloy's DNA is all over her. Your son saved his brother and

sister from a double murderer, honey. Far from being a delin-
quent, he is a hero. With this news, he'll be out by yesterday.'

Stunned, Lara put the phone down. She didn't know
whether to feel relieved or appalled. But she was spared from
having to make a decision by the warm pain that spread from
within her, pulling round and into the distended muscles of her
womb. It was Stephen's parting gift, beyond all the money and
the houses. They had offered to get rid of it for her in the
hospital, because, they said, it was the product of rape. But she
knew otherwise. She knew it had been conceived the first time
she and Stephen had made love, when she had wanted him –
no, *needed* him – inside her. She had to hang on to that thought.

'Gina,' she called through to the kitchen, as the contraction
declared itself fully. 'I think it's coming.'

A baby, at long bloody last.

A baby.

Note on the setting:

While every single character in this book is fictional, the physical landscape of Trout Island is loosely based on Franklin, a lovely village in upstate New York, where I have spent many summers. The major difference is that, whereas the fictional Trout Island Theatre Co. struggles artistically, the real Franklin Stage Company (www.franklinstagecompany.org), with which I am closely associated, is EXCELLENT. If you are ever up that way during the summer months, I urge you to pay a visit.

Wallywoodshop is real, however, and you can buy his wonderful boards at www.wallywoodshop.com. Pretty Fly Pie . . . is based on Pie in the Sky (http://tinyurl.com/6gz5s6x), as unsurpassable as it sounds in this book, and the library (building *not* people) is based on Franklin Free Library (www.franklinfreelibrary.org) – a magical place that has been a cool and brilliantly resourced retreat for me and my children during several long, hot summers. Thank you, Linda Burkhart, library director, and all the volunteers who help run the place.

Cuckoo

Julia Crouch

Polly is Rose's oldest friend. So when her husband dies, Rose doesn't think twice about inviting her to stay. She'd do anything for Polly.

From the moment Polly and her two small boys arrive on Rose's doorstep, it's obvious she is not the typical grieving widow. But the longer Polly stays, the more Rose wonders how well she really knows her. Could Polly's presence have anything to do with Rose's growing sense that she's losing her hold on her own family and home?

As Rose's world is picked apart at the seams, one thing becomes clear: once Polly's in, it's very hard to get her out again.

'Very enjoyable; expertly paced and cleverly ambiguous' *Daily Telegraph*

'A tale of slow-burning suspense . . . Crouch deftly avoids the obvious and builds up a very convincing air of menace' *Daily Express*

'A brilliant debut novel . . . leaves you feeling shaken and out of sorts' *Heat*

978 0 7553 7799 2

headline